THE HUNGER

www.**penguin**.co.uk

THE HUNGER

ALMA KATSU

BANTAM PRESS

LONDON • TORONTO • SYDNEY • AUCKLAND • JOHANNESBURG

TRANSWORLD PUBLISHERS
61–63 Uxbridge Road, London W5 5SA
www.penguin.co.uk

Transworld is part of the Penguin Random House group of companies
whose addresses can be found at global.penguinrandomhouse.com

First published in Great Britain in 2018 by Bantam Press,
an imprint of Transworld Publishers

Published by arrangement with G.P. Putnam's Sons,
an imprint of Penguin Publishing Group,
a division of Penguin Random House LLC

A CIP catalogue record for this book
is available from the British Library.

ISBNs 9780593078327 (hb)
9780593078334 (tpb)

Typeset in Dante
Printed and bound by Clays Ltd, Bungay, Suffolk.

Penguin Random House is committed to a sustainable
future for our business, our readers and our planet. This book
is made from Forest Stewardship Council® certified paper.

1 3 5 7 9 10 8 6 4 2

For my husband, Bruce

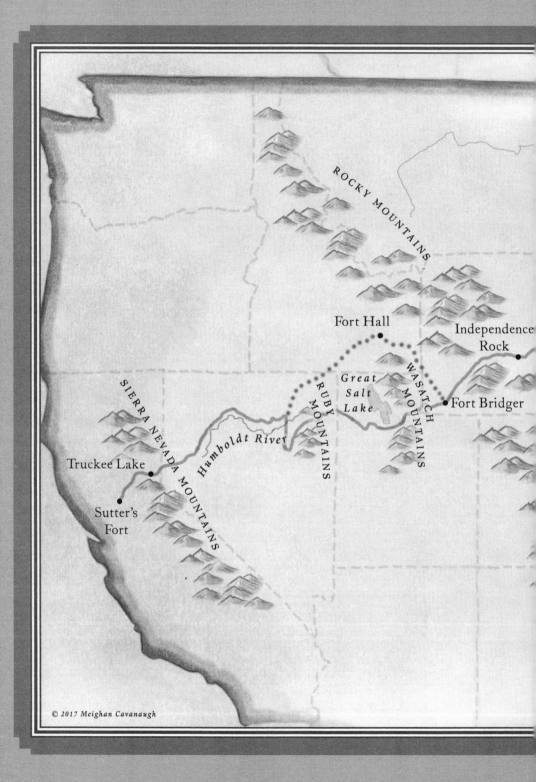

© 2017 Meighan Cavanaugh

The Donner Party Route
(1846~47)

Missouri River

Fort Laramie

Platte River

Kansas River

Independence

Springfield

KEY

———— Donner Party Route

••••• California Trail

PROLOGUE

━━━━

April 1847

Everyone agreed it had been a bad winter, one of the worst in recollection. Bad enough to force some of the Indian tribes, Paiute and Miwok, down from the mountain. There was no game to be had, and a restless hunger rippled through their movements, left barren camps full of black, scentless fire marks behind them like dark eyes in the earth.

A couple of Paiutes even said they'd seen a crazy white man who had managed to survive through this god-awful winter, skimming over the frozen lake like a ghost.

That had to be their man: a fellow named Lewis Keseberg. The last known survivor of the Donner Party tragedy. The salvage group had been sent out to find Keseberg and bring him back alive, if at all possible.

Mid-April and the snow was chest-deep on the horses; the team had to abandon them at a local ranch and go the rest of the way on foot.

It was three days down to the lake after they reached the summit—cold and airy and desolate. Spring meant mud and lots of it, but at the higher elevations, it was still winter and the ground was a blanket of thick white. It was untrustworthy, that snow: It hid crevices, steep drop-offs. Snow kept secrets. You'd think you were on solid ground, but it was just a matter of time before the ledge beneath you crumbled.

The descent was much tougher even than expected, the snow giving underfoot, sodden and slippery, full of some unearthly desire to pull the whole team under.

The closer the team got to the lake, the darker it became, the trees so tall that they obscured the mountaintops and blocked out the sun. You could tell it had snowed an ungodly amount by the damage to the trees: branches broken and bark scraped going up thirty, forty feet. It was eerily quiet by the lake, too. There were no sounds at all, no birdsong, no splash of waterfowl landing on the lake. Nothing but the tramp of their feet and labored breathing, the occasional crackle of melting snow.

The first thing they noticed when mist from the lake rose into their sights was the stink; the entire site smelled of carrion. The rich stench of decaying flesh mingled with the piney air, making it heavy as the group approached the shore. The smell of blood, with its tang of iron, seemed to spring from everywhere, from the ground and the water and the sky.

They'd been told that the survivors had been living in an abandoned cabin and two lean-tos, one built against a large boulder. They found the cabin quickly enough, skirting the banks of the lake, which rippled under a lazy fog. The cabin stood by itself in a small clearing. It was unmistakably deserted and yet they couldn't shake the feeling that they weren't alone, that someone was waiting for them inside, like something from a fairy story.

The bad feeling seemed to have wormed its way through the whole team, that unnatural scent in the air causing everyone to fidget with nerves. They approached the cabin slowly, rifles raised.

Several unexpected items lay discarded in the snow: a pocket prayer book, a ribbon bookmark fluttering in the breeze.

A scattering of teeth.

What looked like a human vertebra, cleaned of skin.

Now the bad feeling was in their throats and at the backs of their eyes. A few of them refused to go any farther. The door to the cabin was directly in front of them now, an ax leaning against the outer wall beside it.

The door opened on its own.

JUNE 1846

CHAPTER ONE

To Charles Stanton, there was nothing like a good, close shave.

He stood that morning in front of the big mirror strapped to the side of James Reed's wagon. In every direction, the prairie unfurled like a blanket, occasionally rippled by wind: mile after uninterrupted mile of buffalo grass, disrupted only by the red spire of Chimney Rock, standing like a sentry in the distance. If he squinted, the wagon train looked like children's toys scattered in the vast, unending brush—flimsy, meaningless, inconsequential.

He turned to the mirror and steadied the blade under his jaw, remembering one of his grandfather's favorite expressions: *A wicked man hides behind a beard, like Lucifer.* Stanton knew plenty of men who were happy enough with a well-honed knife, even some who used a hatchet, but for him nothing would do but a straight razor. He didn't shrink from the feel of cold metal against his throat. In fact, he kind of liked it.

"I didn't think you were a vain man, Charles Stanton"—a voice came from behind him—"but if I didn't know any better, I might wonder if you weren't admiring yourself." Edwin Bryant came toward him with a tin cup of coffee in his hand. The smile faded quickly. "You're bleeding."

Stanton looked down at the razor. It was streaked with red. In the mirror he saw a line of crimson at his throat, a gaping three-inch slash where the tip of his blade had been. The razor was so sharp that he hadn't felt a thing. Stanton jerked the towel from his shoulder and pressed it to the wound. "My hand must have slipped," he said.

"Sit down," Bryant said. "Let me take a look at it. I have a little medical training, you know."

Stanton sidestepped Bryant's outstretched hand. "I'm fine. It's nothing. A mishap." That was this damnable journey, in a nutshell. One unexpected "mishap" after another.

Bryant shrugged. "If you say so. Wolves can smell blood from two miles away."

"What can I do for you?" Stanton asked. He knew that Bryant hadn't come down the wagon train just to talk, not when they were supposed to be yoking up. Around them, the regular morning chaos whirled. Teamsters herded the oxen, the ground rumbling beneath the animals' weight. Men dismantled their tents and loaded them into their wagons, or smothered out fires beneath sand. The air was filled with the sound of children shouting as they carried buckets of water for the day's drinking and washing.

Stanton and Bryant hadn't known each other long but had quickly developed a friendship. The party Stanton had been traveling with prior—a small wagon train out of Illinois, consisting mostly of the Donner and Reed families—had recently joined up with a much larger group led by a retired military man, William Russell, outside Independence, Missouri. Edwin Bryant had been one of the first members from the Russell party to introduce himself and seemed to gravitate to Stanton, perhaps because they were both single men in a wagon train full of families.

In appearance, Edwin Bryant was Stanton's opposite. Stanton was tall, strong without trying to be. He had been complimented on his good looks his entire life. It had all come from his mother, as far as he could tell. He had her thick, wavy dark brown hair and soulful eyes.

Thy looks are a gift from the devil, boy, so you might tempt others to sin. Another of his grandfather's pronouncements. Once he'd smashed Stanton's face with a belt buckle, maybe hoping to chase out the devil he saw there. It hadn't worked. Stanton had kept all his teeth, and his nose had healed. The scar on his forehead had faded. The devil, as far as he knew, had stayed.

Bryant was probably a decade older. Years as a newspaperman had left him softer than most of the men on the journey, who were farmers or carpenters or blacksmiths, men who made a living through hard physical labor. He had weak eyes and needed a pair of spectacles almost constantly. He had a perpetually disheveled air, as though his thoughts were always elsewhere. There was no denying that he was sharp, though, probably the smartest man in the party. He'd admitted to having spent a few years as a doctor's apprentice when he was very young, though he didn't want to be pressed into service as the camp physician.

"Take a look at this." Bryant kicked a tuft of vegetation at their feet, sending up a puff of dust. "Have you noticed? The grass is dry for this time of year."

They had been traveling on a flat plain for days now, the horizon a long stretch of tall prairie grass and scrub. Flanking the trail on either side in the distance, sand hills of gold and coral rose and fell, some craggy as fingers, pointing directly to heaven. Stanton crouched low and pulled a few strands of grass. The blades were short, no more than nine or ten inches long, and were already faded to a dull brownish-green. "Looks like there was a drought not too long ago," Stanton said. He stood, smacking the dirt off his palms, looking toward the far-off hazy purple scrim. The land seemed to stretch on forever.

"And we're just entering the plain," Bryant pointed out.

His meaning was clear: There might not be enough grass for their oxen and livestock to eat. Grass, water, wood: the three things a wagon train needed. "Conditions are worse than we thought they'd be, and we've got a long way to go. See that mountain range off in the distance? That's just the *beginning*, Charles. There are more mountains behind those—and desert and prairie, and rivers wider and deeper than any we've crossed so far. All between us and the Pacific Ocean."

Stanton had heard this litany before. Bryant had said little else ever since they had come across the trapper's shack at Ash Hollow two days ago. The empty shack had been turned into a frontier outpost of sorts for the pioneers crossing the plains, who had taken to leaving letters behind for the next eastbound traveler to carry to a real post office for delivery onward. Many of these letters were simply folded pieces of paper left under a rock in the hope that they would eventually reach the intended recipient back home.

Stanton had been strangely comforted by the sight of all those letters. They had seemed a testament to the travelers' love of freedom and desire for greater opportunity, no matter the risk. But Bryant had gotten agitated. *Look at all these letters. Must be dozens of them, maybe a hundred. The settlers who wrote them are ahead of us on the trail. We're among the last to head out this season and you know what that means, don't you?* he'd asked Stanton. *We might be too late. The mountain passes will be closed off by snow come winter, and winter comes early in higher elevations.*

"Patience, Edwin," Stanton said now. "We've barely put Independence behind us—"

"Yet here it is the middle of June. We're moving too slowly."

Slinging the towel back over his shoulder, Stanton looked around him: The sun had been up for hours and yet they hadn't broken camp. All around him, families were still finishing their breakfasts over the remains of their campfires. Mothers stood dandling babies in their arms as they swapped gossip. A boy was out playing with a dog instead of herding the family's oxen in from the field.

"Can you blame them on such a fine morning?" he asked lightly. After weeks on the trail, no one was anxious to face another day. Half the men were only in a hurry when it came time to break out the jug of mash. Bryant only frowned. Stanton rubbed the back of his neck. "Anyway, Russell is the man to talk to."

Bryant grimaced as he stooped to retrieve his coffee cup. "I've talked to Russell about it and he agrees, and yet does nothing about it. The man can't say no to anyone. Earlier in the week—you remember—he let those men go off on a buffalo hunt, and the train sat idle for two days to smoke and dry the meat."

"We might be happy for that meat farther down the trail."

"I guarantee you that we'll see more buffalo. But we'll never get those days back."

Stanton saw the sense in what Bryant said, and didn't want to argue. "Look. I'll go with you tonight and we'll speak to Russell together. We'll make him see that we're serious."

Bryant shook his head. "I'm tired of waiting. That's what I've come to tell you: I'm leaving the wagon train. A few of us men are going ahead on horseback. It's too slow by wagon. The family men, I understand why they need their wagons. They have young children, the old and sick to carry. They have their goods to worry about. I don't begrudge them, but I won't be held hostage by them, either."

Stanton thought of his own wagon, his pair of oxen. The outfit had cost nearly all the money he made from the sale of his store. "I see."

Bryant's eyes were bright behind his glasses. "That rider who joined up with us last night, he told me that the Washoe were still south of their usual grazing territory, about two weeks down the trail. I can't risk missing them." Bryant fancied himself to be a bit of an amateur anthropologist and was supposedly writing a book about the various tribes' spiritual beliefs. He could talk for hours about Indian legends—talking animals, trickster gods, spirits that seemed to live in the earth and wind and water—and was so passionate that some of the settlers had become suspicious of him. As much as Stanton enjoyed Bryant's stories, he knew they could be terrifying to Christians raised solely on Bible stories, who couldn't understand that a white man could be deeply fascinated by native beliefs.

"I know these people are your friends. But for God's sake," Bryant continued. When he was excited about a subject, it was hard to get him to drop it. "What made them think they could bring their entire households with them to California?"

Stanton couldn't help but smile. He knew, of course, what Bryant was referring to: George Donner's great, customized prairie schooner. It had been the talk of Springfield when it was built and had become the talk of the entire wagon train. The wagon bed had been built up an extra few feet so there was room for a bench and a covered storage area. It even had a small stove with its chimney vented through the cloth canopy.

Bryant nodded toward the Donners' campsite. "I mean, how do they expect to cross the mountains with something like that? It's a behemoth. Even four yoke of oxen won't be enough to haul it up the steep grades. And for what? To carry the queen of Sheba in comfort." In the short time since the Springfield contingent had joined up with the larger Russell party, Edwin Bryant had developed a healthy dislike for Tamsen Donner, that was plain enough. "Have you seen inside that thing? Like Cleopatra's pleasure barge, with its feather mattress and silks." Stanton smirked. It wasn't as though the Donners were sleeping inside; their wagon was packed with household goods—including bedding—like every other wagon. Bryant was a little prone to righteous exaggeration. "I'd thought George Donner was a smart fellow. Apparently not."

"Can you blame him for wanting to make his wife happy?" Stanton asked. He wanted to think of George Donner as a friend, but he couldn't. Not knowing of Donner's connections.

And now, to make matters worse, he was having a hard time keeping his eyes off Donner's wife. Tamsen Donner was a good twenty years younger than her husband and bewitchingly beautiful, possibly the most beautiful woman Stanton had ever met. She was like one of those porcelain dolls you saw in a dressmaker's shop, modeling the latest French fashions in miniature. She had a cunning look in her eyes he found himself drawn to, and the tiniest waist, so small that a man could circle it with his two hands. Several times, he'd had to stop himself from thinking about how that waist would feel in *his* hands. It was a mystery to Stanton how George Donner had won a woman like that in the first place. He assumed Donner's money had something to do with it.

"A group of us are heading out tomorrow," Bryant said, more quietly. "Why don't you join us? You're your own man, no family to worry about. That way, you could get to . . . wherever you're going that much quicker."

Bryant was obviously fishing again, trying to learn the reason why

Stanton was making the trip west. Most people were only too eager to talk about it. Bryant knew Stanton had owned a dry-goods business and a home back in Springfield, but Stanton hadn't shared with him— hadn't shared with anybody—why he'd decided to walk away from it all. His partner, the one with the business sense, had died unexpectedly, leaving Stanton to manage the store on his own. He had the head for that kind of thing but not the spirit for it—waiting on the endless stream of customers, haggling with the ones who didn't like his prices, trying to stock the shelves with products that would appeal to the citizens of Springfield, neighbors he barely knew and certainly didn't understand (exotic toilet waters? bright satin ribbon?). It had been a lonely time and was certainly one of the reasons he'd left Springfield.

But not the only reason.

Stanton decided to hedge. "What would I do with my wagon and oxen? I can't just abandon them on the trail."

"You wouldn't need to. I'm sure you can find someone in the group to buy them. Or you can hire one of the drivers to see to your wagon and make sure it gets to California."

"I don't know," Stanton said. Unlike Bryant, he didn't mind traveling with families, the noise of the children, the high-pitched chatter of the women on the trail. But it was more than that.

"Give me time to think about it," he said.

At that moment, a man on horseback came galloping up, his arrival announced by a swirl of dust. George Donner. One of his jobs was to get the wagon train started on its way in the morning. Normally, he went about it cheerfully, urging the families to pack their campsites and get their oxen hitched up so the great caravan could get under way again. But this morning his expression was dark.

Stanton hailed Donner briefly. It was time to go, then, at last. "I was just about to chain up—" he began, but Donner cut him off.

"We're not moving just yet," he said gravely. "There's been a mishap up the line."

A tremor of misgiving moved through Stanton, but he swallowed it back.

Bryant squinted up at him. "Should I fetch my medical kit?"

George Donner shifted in his saddle. "Not that kind of mishap. A young boy is missing. Wasn't in his tent this morning when his parents went to wake him."

Stanton felt immediately relieved. "Children have been known to wander—"

"When we're on the move, yes. But not at night. The parents are remaining here to search for their son. Some of the others are staying to help them, too."

"Are they looking for more volunteers?" Stanton asked.

Donner shook his head again. "They've got more than enough. Once they pull their wagons off the trail we'll get the rest of the train moving. Keep your eyes peeled for any sign of the boy. God willing, he'll turn up before too long."

Donner rode off again and a finger of dust lifted behind him. If the child had wandered off in the dark, it was unlikely his parents would ever see him again. A young boy might be swallowed up in all this vastness, in the unrelenting space that stretched in all directions, in the horizons that yoked even the sun down to heel.

Stanton hesitated—maybe he should go after them. A little extra help wouldn't hurt. He put a hand to his neck, considering mounting his horse. His fingers came away red. He was bleeding again.

CHAPTER TWO

The wagons stretched across the plain in front of Tamsen Donner for as far as she could see. Whoever had first thought to call the pioneers' wagons "prairie schooners" was quite clever; the canopies did look like the sails of ships, blazing white under the brilliant morning sun. And the thick clouds of dust kicked up by wagon wheels could almost be mistaken for the swell of waves carrying their miniature ships across a desert sea.

Most of the pioneers walked rather than rode to spare the oxen the added weight, taking to the fields on either side of the trail to avoid the worst of the dust. The stock animals—dairy and beef cattle, goats and sheep—were kept on the grassland, too, herded along by switch-wielding boys and girls, the family dog keeping any stragglers in line.

Tamsen liked to walk. It gave her time to look for herbs and plants she needed for her remedies; yarrow for fever, willow bark for headache. She was keeping track of flora she found in a journal, tucking in snippets of the unfamiliar ones for study or experimentation.

Besides, walking gave the men an opportunity to admire her figure. What was the point of looking the way she did and having it go to waste?

And there was something else, too. When she was confined in a wagon all day she began to feel that clawing, discontented restlessness rise up inside her like a trapped animal, the way it used to back home. At least outside, the beast—the *unhappiness*—could roam and give her space to breathe and think.

That morning, however, she soon regretted her decision. Betsy Donner, who had married George's younger brother, was barreling toward her. She didn't *dislike* Betsy, exactly, but she certainly didn't like her, either. Betsy was as unsophisticated as a fourteen-year-old girl, not at all like the friends Tamsen had known in Carolina before marrying George: the other schoolteachers, especially Isabel Topp; Isabel's housemaid Hattie, who taught her which plants to use for healing; the minister's wife, who could read Latin. Tamsen missed them all.

That was the biggest problem. They'd been on the trail for a month and a half and Tamsen was agitated. She'd imagined the farther they moved west, the freer she would feel—she hadn't anticipated this trapped sensation. There'd been distractions for the first few weeks: The novelty of living out of a wagon and camping under the stars at night. Keeping the children engaged day after day on the endless trail, inventing games, turning games into lessons. It had started out as an adventure, but now all she could think about was how tiresome it had become, and how much they'd left behind.

How much *she'd* left behind.

How the dark nag of want only grew with distance, instead of subsiding.

Tamsen had been against the move west from the start. But George had made it clear that he would make all the decisions about the family's livelihood. He'd come to her the owner of a large farming concern, hundreds of acres under cultivation and a herd of cattle. *I was born to be prosperous. You leave it to me to manage our family business and you'll never know want*, he'd promised. His confidence was appealing; she'd been alone and tired of fending for herself after her first husband died of smallpox. She told herself that she'd come to love him in time. She had to.

It was the only way to blot out the wrongness in her heart, the brokenness.

And besides, whatever else she felt, she knew she could always trust Jory. Her brother had thought George was right for her; she'd been inclined to believe it. Had willed herself to.

Then George came to her with the idea to move to California. *It's the land of opportunity*, he'd said after reading books written by settlers who'd made the journey. *We'll be rich beyond our wildest dreams. We can acquire thousands of acres there, far more than we'd ever be able to buy in Illinois. We'll start our own empire and pass it on to our children.* He talked his brother Jacob into going in with him on a huge spread. When she asked about the rumors she'd heard about trouble in California—weren't there already Mexicans living there? They weren't going to just hand over their land. And what about this talk of a coming war with Mexico, the way it had been in Texas?—he dismissed her questions. *Americans are moving to California in droves*, he'd argued. *The government wouldn't let them go there if it were dangerous.* He had even pulled out his favorite book, *The Emigrants' Guide to Oregon and California*, written by Lansford Warren Hastings, a lawyer who had made the journey, to prove it. And though she'd still had many more questions, part of her wanted to feel the same hope he did . . . that maybe things *would* be better in California.

But so far she was just stuck on an endless journey surrounded only by the people she cared for least. Her husband's family.

"Good morning, Betsy," she said as her sister-in-law approached, forcing a smile. Women were always forced to smile. Tamsen had mastered it so well it sometimes frightened her.

"Good morning, Tamsen." Betsy was a square woman, broad in the shoulders and hips with a doughy middle that a corset couldn't control. "Did you hear the news? A boy farther up the line went missing."

Tamsen was not surprised. The wagon train had already suffered misfortune after misfortune: signs, all of them, if you knew how to interpret them. Just last week, she opened a barrel of flour to find it infested with weevils. It had to be thrown out, of course, an expensive loss. The following night, a woman—Philippine Keseberg, young wife to one of the less savory men on the wagon train—had delivered stillborn. Tamsen grimaced, remembering how the darkness of the prairie seemed to enfold the woman's wailing, trapping it in the air around them.

Then there were the wolves following them; one family lost its entire supply of dried meat to them, and the wolves had even carried off a squealing newborn calf.

And now, a boy was missing.

"The wolves," Tamsen said. She hadn't meant to connect the two incidents, but she couldn't help it.

Betsy's hand went to her mouth, one of her many affected habits. "But there were other children asleep in the tent," she said. "Wouldn't they have woken up . . . ?"

"Who knows?"

Betsy shook her head. "It might have been Indians, of course. I've heard stories of Indians taking white children after they've attacked settlements . . ."

"Goodness, Betsy, have you even seen an Indian these last twenty miles?"

"Then what happened to that boy?"

Tamsen just shook her head. Terrible things happened to children—and women—all the time, in their own homes, by people you knew, people you thought you could trust. If that wasn't bad enough, here they were living in close quarters with hundreds of strangers. Odds were that at least one of them was guilty of terrible sin.

But she herself would not fall victim to tragedy, not if she could help it. She had means, limited though they were: charms, talismans, ways to persuade evil to pass by your door.

Unfortunately, however, these were not capable of easing the evil *within*.

Nearby, a man Tamsen recognized as Charles Stanton was herding cattle with a switch. Younger than George, Stanton had the look of a man who spent his days working hard in the field, not in a shop somewhere. He glanced up and caught Tamsen staring. She looked quickly away.

"The truth is apt to be far worse than we could imagine," Tamsen said, somewhat enjoying the way Betsy looked at her in shock.

"Where are your girls this morning? I only see three," Betsy said. Her voice was filled with sudden agitation.

Usually Tamsen had her daughters walk the first half of the day, hoping it would keep them fit and slender. Beauty could be a problem for a girl, but it was one of the few weapons a grown woman had, and she wanted them to preserve theirs if they could. The older girls, Elitha and Leanne, George's daughters by his second wife, would watch after the younger ones: Frances, Georgia, and Eliza. Today, however, only the teenagers walked ahead, with Frances weaving around them like a frisky calf, full of energy and happy to have both girls' attention to herself. Betsy's seven boys and girls were a distance in front of them, heads down, trudging together as mindlessly as oxen.

"There's nothing to worry about. Georgia and Eliza are in the wagon," Tamsen said. "They woke with fevers this morning and were fussy. I thought it best to let them rest."

"Just so, yes. Little ones tire out so easily."

Sometimes Tamsen was amazed to think that she was a mother. It didn't feel possible that she and George had been married long enough to produce three children together. Their babies were lovely, the spitting image of herself as a child, thank heavens. Elitha and Leanne, on the other hand, took after their father: big-boned and a little horse-faced.

But she didn't regret motherhood. Maybe it was one of the only things she didn't regret. She was proud of her girls, in fact: had placed honey on their tongues when they were babies, as the Indian servant in Tamsen's childhood home had taught her, so they would grow up sweet; had braided ropes of balsam fir and tucked it in their blankets so they would grow up strong.

They would always have options; they'd never be yoked into marriage, as she had been not once, but twice.

But Tamsen had her way of getting even, as some might call it.

Stanton met Tamsen's eyes again. Betsy had gone ahead to catch up with her children, and so this time Tamsen didn't look away, not until he did.

She reached out and let her fingertips dance over the wildflower blossoms. For a moment, she thought of the yellow coneflowers that dotted her brother Jory's vast wheat fields, untamable and abundant.

She knew home was ahead of her and not behind, that she should banish memories of Jory's farm—and all thoughts of her life before—from her mind, but she couldn't just now.

The blossoms bent and swayed at her touch, so delicate they almost tickled.

CHAPTER THREE

Mary Graves knelt in the grass and set down her metal tub beside the river. It was a peaceable stretch of the North Platte, slow and gentle, but maybe that was because summer had taken a bite out of it already. The land had all the earmarks of a coming drought.

Doing the washing for the large Graves family was one of Mary's many responsibilities. Twelve people—her mother and father, five sisters and three brothers, not to mention her older sister Sarah's husband—meant a lot of dirty clothes and linens, and Mary preferred to do a little every night rather than let it pile up. It was one of the few times she could be by herself. Her entire day, it seemed, was spent in the company of her family: minding her younger siblings, preparing meals alongside her mother, sitting with her sister by the fire in the evenings to mend clothes. From the minute she rose in the morning until she took to her bedroll, she was surrounded by a clutter of other people, assailed by voices and needs, stories and complaints.

Sometimes it made her feel as if she were constantly standing in the middle of a hard wind, blown in every direction. Even from this distance the sound of raucous laughter and shouting carried to her from the encampment.

Normally she escaped just for the sheer pleasure of standing in silence, listening to nothing but the soft rustling of tall weeds in the breeze. Tonight, however, the reminder of the wagon line nearby didn't bother her so much. The missing boy had left everyone spooked, even her. Poor Willem Nystrom. His family was part of the original wagon party and because there was little mixing with the newcomers, Mary had only ever seen him from a distance. But he seemed like a sweet boy, always playing and laughing, six years old and hair so blond it was almost white. Her brothers Jonathan and Franklin Junior were right around that age, and her heart jumped up in her throat at the thought of one of them simply vanishing from the middle of the camp. It was like one of those old fairy tales, of children suddenly whisked away into a netherworld, taken by angry spirits.

She took comfort in the campfires visible in the distance. The men were driving the cattle out to the taller grass to graze for the evening, hobbling horses so they wouldn't wander off. They inspected axles and wheels for signs of wear and checked over the harnesses so all would be ready for the next day's march. Children were returning to camp with armloads of firewood and kindling. She'd left her little brothers drawing the figure of a wheel in the dirt for a game of Fox and Geese. As much as possible, everyone was keeping to routine.

Mary had just started scrubbing the first item of clothing—her brother William's shirt, stiff with dried sweat—when she saw two young women, Harriet Pike and Elitha Donner, coming toward her through the high grass, carrying washtubs. With a sense of relief that surprised her, Mary waved to them.

"Good evening, Mary," Harriet said stiffly. She and Harriet were close in age but barely knew each other. Mary thought Harriet acted far older than her twenty years, which she attributed to the fact that Harriet was already married with children. It was strange to see her with Elitha Donner, who was not only seven or eight years her junior but, most people said, acted even younger.

"You came just in time," Mary said, trying to sound cheerful. "The light's going fast."

Harriet gave Elitha a long sideways look as she sorted through clothing. "Well, it's not of my choosing. I wasn't planning to do my washing tonight, but Elitha begged me to come with her. She was too afraid to come down by herself."

Elitha said nothing as she worked in the shallow water, but her shoulders were hunched high about her ears. Elitha Donner was fidgety and nervous, like a spooky horse. "Is that so, Elitha?" Mary asked. "Is it because of that boy? There's no shame in that. I think it's put everyone on edge."

The girl only shook her head, so Mary tried again. "Is it the Indians, then?" Mary was actually excited by the idea of finally getting to meet an Indian. They'd seen a few in the distance the first day they'd entered Indian Territory, a group of Pawnee coolly watching from horseback as the wagon train meandered through a valley. But they hadn't come any closer.

Most of the people in the party were scared of Indians, always telling stories of raids on livestock and white children being taken captive, but Mary wasn't. One of the settlers on the Little Blue River had told her that among the Pawnee, the women were in charge. The men did the hunting and went to war, but it was the women who made the decisions.

The idea had amazed her.

"It isn't the Indians I'm afraid of," Elitha said. She was working quickly and kept her eyes trained on her hands, refusing to look up. She obviously didn't intend to be there a second longer than she had to.

"She's afraid of ghosts," Harriet said with a sigh. "She thinks this place is haunted."

"I never said that," Elitha shot back. "I never said they were ghosts." She hesitated, looking from Harriet to Mary. "Mr. Bryant says—"

Harriet snorted. "Is that what's bothering you? One of Mr. Bryant's stories? Honestly, you should know better than to listen to the man."

"That's not fair," Elitha said. "He's smart. You said so yourself. He came out here to write a book about the Indians. Says they told him there are spirits out here, spirits of the forests and the hills and the rivers."

"Oh, Elitha, don't mind Mr. Bryant and his talk," Mary said. She wasn't sure how she felt about Mr. Bryant. He was very knowledge-able. That was obvious. And he'd proven himself capable enough when he set Billy Murphy's leg after he broke it getting bucked off his horse. But there was something disconcerting about the way he seemed to wander around with his attention fixated elsewhere, as though he were always listening to a voice only he could hear.

"But I've heard them." Elitha's brow furrowed. "At night, I've heard them calling to me. Haven't you?"

"Calling you?" Mary asked.

"She's highly suggestible. Her stepmother lets her read *novels*. All those stories have left her giddy," Harriet said to Mary over Elitha's head.

Mary felt a twinge of irritation. She'd known plenty of women like Harriet over the years, women who looked as if their faces had been slowly compressed between the pages of a Bible, all pinched and narrow.

Mary reached over to pat Elitha's hand. "I'm sure it was nothing. Perhaps you overheard people talking in the next tent over."

"It didn't sound like two people talking. It didn't sound like that at all." Elitha bit her lower lip. "It sounded like . . . someone was whispering in a high voice, only it was very weak, like the wind was carrying it in from far away. It was strange, and sad. It was the scariest thing I ever heard."

A shiver went down Mary's spine. She, too, had heard strange things at night since they'd started following the North Platte, but each time she'd told herself that it was her imagination. The cry of some animal she'd never seen before or wind whistling down a hollow canyon. Sounds carried differently over wide-open spaces.

"Now you're just letting your imagination run away with you," Harriet said. "I think you should be careful going around talking about spirits and the Indians and such. People might start thinking that you have heathen inclinations, like Mr. Bryant."

"Oh, Harriet, really," Mary said.

Harriet was undeterred. "Why, there might be a man in this wagon train with his eye on you already—but he won't want to marry you if he thinks that you're a silly, scared girl."

Mary gave her last item an extra-hard twist, imagining instead that it was Harriet's neck, then dropped it in her washtub to carry back to the wagon. "She's only thirteen," she said, trying to keep her voice light. "That's a bit young to be worrying about marriage, don't you think?"

Harriet looked insulted. "I do not. I was fourteen when I got married." Then she turned a cold smile on Mary. "And what about you? Have you ever had a sweetheart? It seems strange to me that you're not married yet."

"I was engaged not too long ago," Mary said shortly, rinsing her hands in the water. "But he died unexpectedly before we could be wed."

"How sad for you," Elitha murmured.

"Fate can be fickle," Mary said, as cheerfully as she could. "You never know what life has in store for you."

Harriet drew herself up again, looking down her long nose at them. "I'm surprised at you, Mary. You're a good Christian. God decides what happens in our lives, all in accordance with his plan. He must've had a reason for taking this man away from you."

The words didn't bother Mary, but Elitha gasped. "You can't mean that, Harriet. God wouldn't be so cruel to Mary."

"I'm not saying it's Mary's fault," Harriet said, though her tone seemed to disagree. "I'm saying that these things aren't random. God was telling Mary that the marriage simply wasn't meant to be."

Mary bit her tongue. Harriet was enjoying being cruel, but she was correct in one respect. Mary would never admit it to anyone, certainly not her parents, but she'd known in her heart that she wasn't ready to be married. Her sister Sarah had been happy to wed Jay Fosdick at nineteen—but Mary wasn't like her older sister, a fact that became more apparent every passing day. When her father announced that they would be moving to California, she'd secretly been elated. She was tired of the small town she'd lived in since birth, where everyone knew about her family's humble beginnings, that the family burned cow dung for warmth so that they could sell their firewood for money, until the plantings took hold and the harvests got better. People would always expect her to be exactly as they thought she was and would never let her be anything more. It was like trying to walk forward and finding that your head had been yoked in place.

When her fiancé was killed, her greatest sense was of relief—though she was mightily ashamed for it. She knew her father had pinned everything on her planned marriage and the better circumstances it would have allowed all of them.

Her sister's marriage had been practical, but it had also been one of love. For Mary, Franklin Graves had always had other plans, she knew. He'd always imagined she'd be the one to make the kind of advantageous match that would save them all. She could hardly count the many times he'd told her she was his only hope.

She could hardly count, either, the many times she'd wished that Sarah had been born the prettier one and not her, the one on whose shoulders others' happiness rested.

Harriet stood, cradling her washtub on her hip. "God has a special plan for each of us and it's not for us to question the wisdom of his ways, only to listen and obey. I'm going to head back to camp. Are you coming with me, Elitha?"

Elitha shook her head. "I'm not done yet."

Mary placed a hand on Elitha's arm. "Don't worry. I'll wait with you and we can go back together."

"Very well," Harriet called over her shoulder as she started back. "Dinner won't make itself."

Elitha waited until Harriet was out of earshot before speaking. "You don't mind me talking to you about this, do you, Mary?" Her eyes were suddenly huge and round. "Because I just *have* to tell someone. It wasn't the voices that scared me, not like I said." She glanced furtively over her shoulder again. "It's always been like that with me. Tamsen says that I'm sensitive—to the spirit world, she means. She's interested in all that. She had her palm read by this woman back in Springfield. Had her fortune told with the cards, too. This woman told Tamsen that the spirits liked me. That they found it easy to talk to me."

Mary hesitated, then took Elitha's hand, cold from the water. "It's okay. You can tell me. Did something happen?"

Elitha nodded slowly. "Two days ago, when we came across that abandoned trapper's cabin . . ."

"Ash Hollow?" Mary asked. She could still picture the tiny make-shift shack, boards bleached bone-white by the relentless prairie sun. A sad, lonely place, like the abandoned farmhouse she used to pass every Sunday on her way to service. Stripped nearly bare by the elements, dark empty windows like the hollow eye sockets of a skull, a stark reminder of another family's failure. *Let that be a lesson*, her father had said to her once as they slowly rolled by it in the wagon, not too many years after they, too, had been on the verge of losing everything. *But for the grace of God, that might have been us.*

The world was fragile. One day, growth; the next day, kindling.

Elitha squeezed her eyes shut. "Yes. Ash Hollow. Did you go inside?"

Mary shook her head.

"It was filled with letters. Hundreds of them. Stacked on a table, held down with rocks. Mr. Bryant told me that pioneers leave them so that the next traveler heading east can take them to the first post office he sees." Elitha looked at Mary uncertainly. "Would you think I was bad if I told you I read some?"

"But, Elitha. They weren't meant for you."

Elitha blushed. "I figured it wouldn't harm anyone. It would be like reading stories. Most of the letters weren't sealed, only folded up and left on the table, so the writer had to know that *anybody* could read them. Only it turned out they weren't letters."

Mary blinked, uncomprehending. She looked at Elitha crouched before her, pale as the rising moon. "What do you mean?"

"They weren't addressed to anyone," Elitha said. Her voice had dropped to a whisper. "And there wasn't any news in them . . . I opened letter after letter, and they all said the same thing, over and over."

"I still don't understand." Mary felt as if a spider were tracking up and down her spine. "If they weren't letters, what were they?"

Elitha thrust a hand awkwardly in her apron pocket. She drew out a small folded square of paper and handed it to Mary. "I kept one of them. I thought I should show it to someone, but I haven't yet. I didn't know who to show it to. Nobody would believe me. Maybe they'd think I wrote it myself, to get attention. But I didn't, Mary. I didn't."

Mary took the paper. It was brittle and fragile from many days in the heat. She unfolded it carefully, afraid it might disintegrate in her hands. The ink was faded, as though it had been written a long time ago, but she didn't have any problem making out the words.

Turn back, it said in a thin, spidery hand. *Turn back or you will all die.*

CHAPTER FOUR

T hey found the Nystrom boy, or what was left of him, later that same night.

A knot of dread clogged Stanton's throat as he followed George Donner through the circle of wagons and headed into the dark, empty plain.

Two of the teamsters had made the discovery just minutes before, as they were driving the cattle out to graze for the evening. Through the fading light, they'd seen a depression in the tall grass and went to investigate. Both were hardy men, but nonetheless what they found had made one of them heave.

Dots of light floated ahead in the darkness and at first Stanton thought they were an illusion of some kind, but as he got closer the pinpricks became flame, and then torches. A dozen men were already assembled in a circle, the torches like a halo of flame over their heads. Stanton knew most of them—William Eddy, Lewis Keseberg, and Jacob Wolfinger, as well as Edwin Bryant—but there were a few from the original wagon party, friends of the boy's family, he'd seen only in passing. A strange noise, halfway between a cry and a howl, rose off in the distance, rolling toward them from across the empty plain like a wave.

"Damn wolves," someone muttered.

As Stanton shoved his way inside the circle, the first thing he saw was Edwin Bryant on his knees. What looked like a red, wet smear in the grass turned out to be a body. He shut his eyes momentarily. He'd faced ugly things before but was hard-pressed to recall ever seeing something as monstrous as this. He opened his eyes again.

The head was intact. In fact, if you only looked at the face you wouldn't think anything was wrong. The boy's eyes were closed, long brown lashes stark against chalk-white cheeks. His fine blond hair was plastered against his skull, his tiny mouth closed. He looked peaceful, as though he were sleeping.

But from the neck down . . .

Next to him, George Donner let out a whimper.

"What happened to him?" Lewis Keseberg asked, prodding the ground by the body with the butt of his rifle, as if it might yield answers. Keseberg and Donner were friends, though Stanton couldn't imagine why. Keseberg was all black temper and violence, hard lines: *your side, my side.* Hard to believe he had the patience to be a father but he had a little daughter, Stanton had heard.

"It's got to be wolves, body torn up like that." William Eddy rubbed his beard, a nervous habit. Eddy was a carpenter, good at repairing broken axles and busted wheels. For this reason, he was popular among the families on the wagon train. But he was jumpy, too, high-strung. Stanton wasn't sure he trusted him.

"What do you think, Doc?" Jacob Wolfinger asked, in his mild German accent.

Bryant sat back on his heels. "I'm no doctor," he reminded them. "And I couldn't say. But for what it's worth, I don't think it was wolves. It seems too neat."

Stanton shuddered involuntarily. There wasn't even a body, not really. There was almost nothing left but the skeleton. Tatters of flesh and scattered bones in a flattened, blood-soaked circle in the grass, intestines lying in a heap and already dark with flies. And another thing troubled him: They were six miles up the trail from where the boy had first gone missing. Wolves wouldn't drag a carcass before devouring it.

"Whatever it was, it was hungry," Donner commented—his face was leached of color. "We should bury the remains. We don't want any of the women or children to see this."

Eddy spat. "What about the parents? Somebody's got to say whether this is the right boy or not—"

"We're in the middle of nowhere. The next white settlement is days away," Wolfinger said. "Who else could it be?" Wolfinger had emerged as the leader of the German emigrants in the party, translating for the ones who knew no English. They kept mostly to themselves, and often huddled around their campfires at night, speaking rapid-fire German—though Stanton hadn't failed to miss Wolfinger's pretty, young wife, Doris, whose hands looked like they were made for playing a piano, not carrying firewood or tugging on reins.

In the end, a couple of men went for shovels. Others wandered back to check on their families, to wake their sleeping children or simply to look at them, be reassured by their presence.

Stanton rolled up his sleeves and took a turn digging.

They didn't need a large hole to accommodate the remains—there was so little of the boy—but they wanted it deep so that no animal would go after the bones. Besides, the physical exertion felt good. Stanton wanted to be tired tonight when he went to bed.

Too tired to dream.

Predictably, although George Donner stayed, he did nothing more than heap a few shovelfuls of dirt onto the grave. When at last they were done, Donner said a brief halting prayer over the fresh dirt. The old words sounded thin in the night air.

Donner and Stanton walked back to the wagons together, along with James Reed and Bryant. Stanton didn't know Reed well and wasn't sure he wanted to. He'd been well known among business leaders back in Springfield, but not well liked.

Reed held a dying torch overhead, but the flame could do little against the darkness that surrounded them. He and Donner floated in and out of the light, their pale faces bobbing on the periphery like ghosts. The ground was uneven and treacherous underfoot, broken up by prairie dog tunnels and clumps of tall grass. The hot summer air, so oppressive during the day, had cooled but was still dry and dusty.

"I've never seen anything like that," Reed said at length, breaking the silence. "I agree with your earlier assessment, Mr. Bryant. If it were an animal that attacked, it would have been messier. The answer is obvious. Indians—it had to be Indians." He raised a hand to stop Bryant from interrupting. "I know you claim to be some kind of expert on Indians, Mr. Bryant. You go live with them and talk to them and take all manner of notes for this book of yours. But you've never *fought* them, never faced them in anger as *I* have. I know what they're capable of." Reed told anyone who would listen that he'd fought in the Black Hawk War, probably so the tough old trail hands would stop treating him like a tenderfoot.

Bryant's voice was mild. "That's right, Mr. Reed. Everything I know about Indians I've learned from talking to them as opposed to shooting at them from across a field. But arguing won't resolve anything. Even you must agree that if we let people think the Indians are responsible, things will go bad pretty fast. We're traveling through Indian territory. The last thing we need is for people to panic. Besides," he said, as Reed opened his mouth to object, "I've never heard of an Indian custom where they slaughter and dress a body like that."

Donner jerked around to look at him. "Slaughtered and dressed? You make it sound like the boy was butchered."

Bryant said nothing. He didn't have to.

"Butchering implies that this was deliberate," Stanton said. Even the words had a foul taste. "But if not Indians, then who?"

The set of Bryant's mouth was grim. "We can't ignore the possibility that whoever killed the boy is *part* of the wagon train. Someone already among us."

The silence was tense. "Nonsense," Reed muttered. The handkerchief came out, as it always seemed to when Reed was nervous. A tell.

"Surely a man like that would stand out, wouldn't he?" Donner fidgeted with his coat buttons. "His behavior would give him away."

Stanton knew that wasn't necessarily true. Seeing the dead boy reminded him of an earlier time in his hometown in Massachusetts, when he'd seen the woman he loved pulled from the ice-capped water and laid out on the snow. Lydia. Fifteen years had passed and he could still barely stand to remember. She'd looked as though she'd just gone to sleep, her expression as peaceful as that boy's: a lie. He remembered her dark lashes fanned against skin that had turned pale blue from being in the water so long, her lips purple as a bruise. Something terrible had compelled her across the thin frozen ice of the river that winter day, an evil that lived among them that he had failed to see. In this, at least, his grandfather had been correct. Evil was invisible, and it was everywhere.

"Sometimes a crazy man can act normal when he has to," Bryant said. "He might be able to hide for a while longer. He might be able to hide his true nature *indefinitely*."

Reed swiped his forehead. "All I know is, it's a good thing Colonel Russell quit when he did. It's time for a new captain."

Stanton glanced over at Donner, whose usual swagger looked a little off-kilter in the bobbing light of Reed's torch. Donner was one of Russell's lieutenants, and he had obviously loved his appointment and all the little duties that came with it. He liked having a say in the way things were run; he certainly liked being looked up to and seemed to crave the admiration of others. Stanton respected him less for it.

"You're not going to try to blame this on Russell, are you?" Bryant asked.

"He never should have been made captain in the first place. This wouldn't have happened under a stronger man," Reed said, clearing his throat. Stanton thought he knew what was coming next. "My reputation, I believe, speaks for itself."

"I'd be careful not to overestimate your position," Donner said, his big wide face shiny as he turned toward the light. "You may be a good businessman, but I don't know that it counts for much out here on the trail."

"I'm already one of the leaders of this party, in fact, if not in title. You can't deny it," Reed said stiffly. Stanton had to agree; whenever an important decision needed to be made, people almost instinctively turned to James Reed.

"You'd have us kill the first Indian we see," Donner spluttered. "You'd have us go to war, when we have no evidence *whatsoever* of what or who killed that boy."

"I see. And I suppose you think that you would make a better party captain than I would?" Reed's voice was cutting.

Even in the scant light of the dying torch, Stanton saw Donner red-den. "As a matter of fact, I do. I have experience leading the wagon train. People know me—and like me. It's important to be liked, James—you shouldn't underestimate that."

Reed scowled at Donner. "I'd rather be respected than liked."

Donner gave him a thin, insincere smile. "That's why you won't be elected captain. You can't expect to just step in and boss people around. You have to earn people's respect—and you haven't earned it, not yet."

Reed stopped dead. His head seemed to swell so full with rage that it might burst. "And do you think people respect you? Everyone knows you can't even stand up to your own *wife*."

At this, the rest of the group halted, too. Stanton shifted uncom-fortably in the dusty air as he watched George Donner's face go pale in the darkness until he seemed almost bloodless. He was standing per-fectly still, his clublike hands hanging at his sides, towering over James Reed. But Reed stood his ground and, in that moment, seemed the stronger.

Bryant broke the silence and stepped between them. "Gentlemen. It's late. We've all had a shock tonight."

Stanton realized he'd been holding his breath, though it didn't seem all that likely Reed and Donner would have come to blows. James Reed had a temper, true, but he was prideful and wouldn't stoop to brawling. Stanton had noticed the care he took with his appearance, his obsessive cleaning of his fingernails and trimming of his beard, the way he end-lessly brushed his coat of dust, despite the fact that within minutes it would be dirty again. And Donner was a blusterer but at his core, too soft, almost spongelike, too dependent on others for his opinions and shape. He was the type to get others to do his dirty work for him.

Still, Stanton didn't like the tension that lingered in the air, even as Reed stalked off without another word.

Donner shook his head. "Madness," he murmured. Then he bid them good night and turned off toward the camp.

For a second, as Stanton watched him recede into the darkness, he envied Donner his waiting family, the company of a beautiful woman, sleeping children exhaling their sweet night-breath into the summer air.

Bryant exhaled. "I hope to God someone else steps forward to lead us."

Stanton nodded toward the departed figures, now lost in the darkness. "Would you choose either one, if you had to?"

"I'd go with Reed before I'd go with Donner. The man's more of a leader. Though if you really want to know the truth, you'd be my first choice."

"Me?" Stanton almost laughed. "I don't think you'll find anyone to second my nomination. The family men don't trust me, with no wife or children. Besides, I don't need the headaches—and I like to mind my own business. If you're so keen on a leader, why don't you volunteer yourself?"

Bryant smiled wryly. "You're not going to talk me out of leaving that easily."

"You still mean to head out, then?" Stanton asked. "Traveling in a small group with whatever got the boy still at large—it could be dangerous."

"True." Bryant tilted his head to one side, as if listening to something in the distance. "You know, it all reminds me of something. An old story I heard a long time ago."

"Something the Indians told you?"

"No." Bryant's smile looked more like a squint. "Something odd that happened to me in my doctoring days. Nearly as wild as a fairy story. If I ever make sense of it, I'll tell you about it," he said, turning away already and raising a hand in farewell. "Take care, Stanton. I'll send word when I can."

As wild as a fairy story. For some reason, Stanton couldn't shake the words from his mind.

STANTON ALWAYS SET UP his campsite apart from its neighbors; he liked the nighttime solitude. He could see their wagons through a scrim of trees, tents set up for sleeping, fires still smoldering against the night; could smell the remains of their suppers lingering on the air. But every site he passed was deserted. Fathers had driven their families inside the tents. It was like this when things got bad: Circles got smaller. People wanted to protect their own.

He knew the mangled body of that young boy should be bothering him . . . and it was. But something else was bothering him, too, persisting like the stench of blood in the air. It was the nagging feeling that something vitally important—some invisible thread—was about to unravel. He'd never liked conflict, but what Donner had said tonight sank in with an uncomfortable clarity. *Don't underestimate the value of being liked*, he'd said. Stanton hadn't gone out of his way to make himself liked; Bryant was his only real ally, and he was leaving.

And the implication that the boy's murderer could be among them had put Stanton on edge. There were plenty of men in the party who might count violence, even perversion, among their qualities. He thought back to what Bryant had said about how dangerous tendencies could be hidden. Keseberg was rumored to beat that young wife of his when he thought no one was looking, and Stanton believed it. The man was a self-taught shark with cards and forgot nothing—the exact type to hold a grudge, and to act on one.

Then there was the Graves family's hired hand John Snyder; he bullied the younger teamsters mercilessly, would often get them to hand over their evening's ration of beer or take his shift as sentry. Unsavory men all, but all brutal in a common, regular way. Hundreds of men just like them had made their way west; thousands, even. Stanton had a hard time picturing any of them as the kind of monster who would mutilate a small boy. That took a special kind of savagery all its own, and it left a tremor in him, a question with no answer.

He knew he wouldn't sleep.

All that was left of his neglected campfire were a few dying embers. Too late to cook supper but he wasn't hungry, not after what he'd seen in the field. He'd rather crawl into his bedroll with the last of his whiskey and try to wipe out the vision that wouldn't go away. He tried to remember where he had hidden the bottle. As he approached his wagon, however, he heard the sound of movement in the shadows. He wasn't alone.

His hand went to the revolver on his hip just as a figure stepped out of the shadows. Tamsen Donner lowered a shawl from over her head. The sight of her drove through him like a knife. Tamsen Donner was too pretty for her own good.

For *anyone's* good.

He pulled his hand back from his holster. "Is there something I can do for you, Mrs. Donner?" He said her name carefully, with purpose.

Her hair was falling out of its upsweep. When was the last time he'd touched a woman's hair? Back in Springfield, there had been a young widow who worked at the milliner's on the same street as his shop, a quiet woman who, twice a week, crept up the back stairs to his room over the dry-goods store. The widow's hair had been a tangle of curls and she'd kept it carefully pinned as though she'd been ashamed of its coarseness, its wildness. Tamsen Donner's hair was dark and fell like water.

She looked up at his face. "The news is all over camp. My husband was gone and I didn't know where he'd disappeared to . . . I suppose I wasn't thinking straight. But all I could think was that I needed someone—and I thought of you."

The Donners had other men in their party, he knew: George's own brother Jacob and a few hired drovers for the oxen. Enough to protect the women and children. But she had come here, leaving her daughters behind to seek comfort from a man who was practically a stranger.

She came closer to him, her shawl shifting so he could see her collarbone and then the tops of her breasts, flawless and white, pressed tight against the neckline of her dress. "I hope you don't mind my coming to see you."

His throat went dry. He had to force himself to look away from her. "Your husband will be back any minute."

Her mouth quirked to one side. "My husband?" Her voice was easy, like watching a rock bouncing down a hill. "You know George. He's good at comforting the others. They need him more than I do right now."

She said it like it was some sort of sacrifice on her part, coming here. Her fingers were cool on his cheek and smelled of a wild perfume he couldn't name, like crushed flower petals and the wind through the prairie. She collected herbs and, it was said, concocted potions, and people whispered that she was a witch who could make herself irresistible to men. Maybe she was.

He kissed her.

He wasn't a saint, wasn't even a good man. He was strong physically but had always suspected that deep down, he was weak. The soft curve of her lips. Weakness. The light touch of her hair grazing against his jaw. Weakness. The smell of her. Weakness.

He felt her cool hands slide under his jacket and seek out his chest, and the heat of realization rose in him. Tamsen Donner had come here with a serious purpose; he saw that now. She knew what she was doing.

Somehow he managed to turn his head away. "You should know better than to tease a man like this, Mrs. Donner."

She brought her mouth to his ear. "You're right. I wouldn't want to cause trouble." The words tickled his neck.

The invisible thread was unspooling.

They were in his wagon before he knew how they'd gotten there, had somehow climbed over the backboard, slipped under the canopy and hidden in its dim recesses. There was no room in the fully packed wagon, and in the end he pushed her up against a chest of drawers that had been lashed in place, the floor beneath their feet swaying like the deck of a ship as he took her, grasping and gripping, nearly blind in the darkness of the unlit room.

When he finished she let out a sharp cry—practically the only sound she made—and he found in that second not a sense of freedom and release but a sense of falling backward. He had to put his hand through his hair and breathe deeply to steady himself, even as he watched her immediately put herself back together, tuck her breasts into the confines of stays and bodice, smooth her skirts, sweep back stray curls. She was beautiful. Beautiful and remote—she seemed even more a stranger than she had before.

He shook his head. "We shouldn't have done this." The weight of it was beginning to sink in. Donner's wife.

For a second, something flickered across Tamsen's face, and the closest word he had for it was *fear*. But the expression was gone so quickly he thought it might have been a trick of the light. She blinked. "There are many things one shouldn't do, Mr. Stanton."

He felt stung, struck by the memory of his grandfather telling him, *Don't tempt the devil, boy,* as though he could still feel the crack of the old man's belt buckle in his face after he was caught kissing a neighbor's daughter out in the churchyard when he was nine years old. How miserable he'd been growing up in his grandfather's house. And angry at his father, too, for leaving him and his mother there.

He realized now that his head was clearing, that his back was stinging with a high, sharp pain. He reached to the side of his neck and felt blood. "You scratched me?"

She looked at him with eyes so dark they were almost expressionless. Unreadable. She brought a hand to his face almost casually. "I hope there won't be any trouble." This time when she said it, it carried a different tone.

"Is that a threat?"

But she didn't answer him. Instead, she swung gracefully over the backboard. He listened as her light footstep faded away. Too late, he saw that she was one of those temptations better left untried, like a whiskey so potent that it left you blind.

He should try to reason with her. He swung out of the wagon and dropped to the ground, shocked when a teenaged girl startled backward out of the underbrush, looking frightened and lost. Panic seized him. How long had she been standing there?

Before she could bolt, he called out to her. "Wait there. You, girl—who are you? Are you one of the Breens?" There were so many children in the wagon train, it was impossible to keep track.

She stiffened, frozen to the spot as though she'd forgotten how to run away. "No, sir. I'm Elitha Donner."

Worse and worse. "What are you doing here?" he demanded.

"I—I was sent out to collect firewood. I was just on my way back to my family, I swear it." Her face was bright red and shiny and the angle of her lip made her look mulish. More telling, however: There was no wood in her arms.

"Tell me what you saw, Elitha," he said, and took a step toward her. "Go on. No lies."

He hadn't meant to frighten her. But Elitha turned and sprinted back into the woods like a spooked deer. His first urge was to run after her, but he checked himself. It wasn't right for a grown man to chase a child through the woods, especially not after what they'd found out there tonight.

He turned back to the wagon, intent on finding that bottle of whiskey. He knew what was waiting for him tonight: a visit from Lydia. Between the boy and Tamsen, he now knew it was inevitable. Poor Lydia would appear in his dreams, clothes clinging to her blue-tinged body, asking him to save her. *I need you, Charles*—words she had never said to him in life but were reflected in her eyes every time she appeared in his dreams. How could he have known her so well and not known the terrible truth?

Help me, Lydia. He turned back to his campsite, to the fire leaching smoke. *Help me see the monsters this time.*

CHAPTER FIVE

Fort Laramie, Indian Territory

My dear Margie,

At last, we have reached Fort Laramie, deep in the Indian Territory. After living out of my saddlebags for six weeks, I was more excited than I thought possible, both because of the promise of a shave and hot bath in an honest-to-goodness tub and because of the possibility that there might be a letter from you waiting for me.

You may be gratified to learn that I spent the entire first week after leaving Independence wondering if I'd just made the biggest mistake of my life. After waiting forty-two years to marry, how could I willingly ride away from the woman with whom I'd decided to spend the rest of my life? Once the shock had worn off, however, I made it a point to get acquainted with a party that joined the wagon train outside Independence. The newcomers, about six families in all, several of them quite well off (to judge by their wagonloads of furniture, servants, and even rumors of fortunes in silver and gold coin) came

*from Springfield, Illinois. We were also joined by a handful of single
men looking to make their fortune in the West.*

*The most prominent member of the party is, undoubtedly, George
Donner. He heads the entire Donner clan, which is composed of not
only his family but also that of his younger brother Jacob. They appear
to be simple men but they must be shrewder than they look, for people
say they had owned a considerable amount of property in Illinois. The
elder Donner is fond of quoting from the Bible but routinely mixes up
the passages. I question whether he's wise enough to lead, but then
again, he is roundly trusted by all, precisely because he knows how to
offend none. The most notable thing about him, besides his size
(portly), is his wife, Tamsen. Most of the men in the party have fallen
in love with her; nonetheless, I have observed in her a certain hardness
that edges close to cruelty. I have seen her make servants cry, and act
coldly to children other than her own. She shuns women who are not
as pretty as she, and has a reputation for dabbling in witchcraft—
likely a rumor born of the other women's jealousy.*

*Then we have James Reed, the owner of a large furniture business
in Springfield. Physically, he is the opposite of George Donner: shorter
and slight with a narrow, drawn face. He frequently worries at his
hands with his handkerchief, which cannot help but make me think
of Lady Macbeth (Out, out, damned spot). But, disagreeable and
argumentative as he can be, he seems a model citizen, as he himself
never misses the opportunity to point out. He is married to an older
woman, a widow with a number of children by her late husband.
Those from Springfield say that the marriage was the salvation of
Margaret Reed, who is thin and sickly and honestly could be taken
for Reed's mother. The Reed party resembles nothing so much as a
traveling circus, with their three large wagons loaded up with fancy
furniture (his company's handiwork, one imagines) and all manner of*

creature comforts. There are servants, including a young woman to do the cooking and wash, and even ponies for the children.

I've saved my favorite new acquaintance from the Springfield contingent for last. Charles Stanton, a bachelor traveling alone in his own Conestoga wagon, is unlike most all the other single men in the party—either hired hands or near-penniless drifters—and I think for this reason we quickly became friends. We were both raised by ministers (though unlike my county preacher father, his grandfather is a prominent Anglican minister, so famous that even I've heard of him) and bear similar scars to prove it. I was flattered when he told me that he'd read the articles I wrote for the Washington Globe *on that revivalist fraud Uriah Putney.*

For a quiet man he has lived a life of extreme color: He was born in Massachusetts and apprenticed to a lawyer in Virginia before running off to fight under General Sam Houston in the battle of San Jacinto. Seeing that he fought in the war for Texas independence even though he has no ties to that territory, he might be either a romantic or idealist. From what I saw of him, I'd say he's a little of both—which means he's doomed to an unhappy life, I'm afraid. He has hinted at some terrible event that drove him from Massachusetts but refuses to speak of it. He isn't sure what he would do once he reaches California, another sign of the restless spirit that keeps him on the move.

A strange mix of souls and, despite the sometimes politicking and intrigues, I will be reluctant to leave them all when I separate from the wagon train tomorrow morning. I decided to commit to that scheme I wrote to you about, joining a small party of men without families on mule and horseback to make better time. I could not convince Stanton to leave with me and I suspect it's because he feels he can be helpful to the larger party, which can be fractious. I am in some ways relieved— at least they'll have one sensible man in the group—and in other ways

*anxious to leave the group before they have successfully decided on
a leader.*

*Fort Laramie is an honest-to-goodness frontier fort, just as the
newspapers describe them. You get the sense of being at the very edge
of civilization, that beyond the fort's adobe walls is a land nearly
untouched by the white man, where nature reigns. I've been told
that this year alone, several thousand wagons rolled through this
checkpoint, and by all estimates that number will soar next year,
barring war with Mexico or hostilities with the Indians. The fort
shows all the signs of prosperity: In addition to the small garrison
stationed here, there is a good-sized trading post, blacksmith's shop,
livery stable, and a bakery. There are several two-story houses inside
the adobe walls, presumably for the fort's owners, families, and staff.*

*Even though this wagon party is among the last of the season, on
our arrival the fort was bustling. A knot of trappers unloaded their
packhorses in front of the trading post, the men dirty and unkempt
in their old buckskins and coonskin caps. Children ran through the
street, shrieking with laughter. A half-dozen Indians mounted on
fantastically colorful Appaloosa and paint horses rode slowly through
the dusty streets, men dressed in Western garb accented with the
feathers and beads of their people lounged in the sun outside the
stables.*

*Unsurprisingly, word spread quickly of a bar at the trading post.
But I was most interested in a hot meal. I am already so tired of my
own cooking. I had barely settled at one of the scarred tables in the
dining hall with a tin plate awash with runny stew when I noticed
a man dressed like a trapper or mountain man in the characteristic
well-worn buckskins, his hair long and white and his wrinkled face as
tanned as leather. His name was Lionel Farnsworth. Unlike everyone
else, he was headed east, not west. What's more, he was traveling*

alone, a dangerous proposition in such sparsely populated territory. He told me he'd already journeyed once to Oregon and twice to California and knew the trails better than nearly anyone.

Farnsworth's opinion of the Hastings Cutoff—the route Donner plans to lead the party through—was quite dismal. In Farnsworth's opinion, the terrain was too rough for wagons and inhospitable to livestock. Donner happened to be with me and he was not pleased to hear that Farnsworth thought the route a waste of time. He proceeded to try to persuade Farnsworth of the error of his thinking, explaining that Hastings himself was going to meet them at Fort Bridger and had promised to guide them all the way to California, but the old man was not swayed. He told Donner in no uncertain terms they should keep to the old route. But he would have had better luck trying to talk a teapot into singing an aria.

In fact, when Farnsworth found out that I planned to take the same route (albeit without wagons and a much smaller party) he tried to talk me out of it, too. After much prodding, it came out that the harsh terrain wasn't the only, or even the main, reason for his hatred of the route. He admitted that he'd seen one other group of Indians, the Anawai, in his travels near Truckee Lake, but he warned me not to meet with them. When I told him I'd never heard of the Anawai, he said that wasn't surprising as the tribe was small and thought to be quite isolated. He claimed that they were particularly savage, and in fact engaged in a terrible tradition, which he had seen with his own eyes: human sacrifice.

I was stunned. Human sacrifice is extremely rare among the plains tribes. Ancient cultures to the south, the Mayans and Aztecs, are known to have practiced ritual human sacrifice, but from what I've read it's virtually unheard of north of the Rio Grande. I asked him to

*describe what he'd witnessed exactly. For obvious reasons, I assumed
he had simply misinterpreted what he'd seen.*

*He told me he'd seen about a dozen Anawai warriors take one of
their braves into the woods. The brave fought to get away, but they
held him tight. They took him far from their camp and tied him to a
tree, binding him hand and foot, and then left him to his fate even
though he had screamed out after them. Farnsworth thought that he
had been begging them to let him go.*

*A profoundly disturbing scene, no doubt. I could understand why
Farnsworth had been spooked. Still, it didn't sound like a sacrifice
ritual to me. From my readings on the topic, I knew that those
chosen to be sacrificed often consider it an honor and go willingly to
the altar.*

*I told Farnsworth that what he'd seen sounded more like
punishment. It was extremely likely this brave had done something
to get himself banished from the tribe. But Farnsworth insisted that
that was not the case. He claimed to know why they did it, too:
The Anawai were afraid of "the demon that lives out by Truckee
Lake" and were making a sacrifice so that it would leave the rest
of them alone.*

*Farnsworth knew nothing more about the folklore but had heard
stories this past year of Indians disappearing from villages not far
from where the Anawai lived, usually the sick and the old and
children, plucked from their beds or gone out for firewood or berries,
never to return. Of course such folktales recur in almost every culture,
but I was strangely moved, perhaps because of the poor Nystrom boy—
he, too, plucked from his bed, never to return.*

*Farnsworth had been reluctant to tell me his story, afraid I'd think
he was insane. He only relented after I assured him that I did want to*

know, that this was the very reason I was headed into Indian Territory, to investigate their strange and mythic beliefs and try to correlate them to some observable reality. He could tell that I was set on heading to Truckee Lake, but he begged me to convince Donner and the others not to go that way, too.

I fear, however, that I have had little sway over Donner thus far, and will not in this. As for myself, I can only admit that Farnsworth's warnings have had the opposite of their intended effect. I can think of nothing now but of the chance to meet this singular tribe and of his tale of the spirit—the demon—of Truckee Lake.

That and of you, my dear. And so I will end my letter here, before you rethink your rash decision to marry such a garrulous old windbag. I sometimes doubt my good fortune, that a woman such as you—so intelligent and wise and beautiful—could have agreed to marry this strange, stubborn fool. For as much as I love you and miss you and wish to be with you, I also know that, now that I have heard about this rumored beast of Truckee Lake, I will not rest until I go there and find out what is going on to my satisfaction. No doubt you are not pleased to read of my intention, but you know this story will plague me to the end of my days if I do not attempt to resolve it. Do not worry for me, my dear Margie, and know that I intend to return to you as soon as it is possible.

Your loving Edwin

JULY 1846

CHAPTER SIX

G ood-bye, good-bye.

The words still rang in Stanton's ears even though the rest of the wagon party, those bound for Oregon, had rolled away hours earlier, leaving the smaller group on the banks of the Little Sandy River. The wagons, over a hundred total, had raised a choking cloud of dust as they departed. Had Stanton imagined how eager they were to leave? Eager to put bad luck and the memory of the butchered Nystrom boy behind them? Eager to separate themselves from the fractious Donner party, as the California-bound group had come to be known? They'd said good-bye to Edwin Bryant and the small party of men who had elected to go with him a few days earlier, back at Fort Laramie, and already, Stanton missed his only friend.

Clouds floated in the sky, fluffy as cotton still on the stalk and so low that you would swear you could reach up and touch them. The plain stretched to the horizon, great patches of green and gold, and

Little Sandy snaking through it. A gentle river, and, true to its name, not wide at all. It was hard to imagine anything bad happening here.

The rest of the wagon train was getting ready to have a feast, a kind of communal picnic. It had been Donner's suggestion—of course—to celebrate the last leg of their trip. He'd plumped their egos good, told them their bravery in electing to take the Hastings Cutoff would be rewarded. They were intrepid pioneers, about to blaze a new trail through the wilderness; their names would go down in history. Stanton suspected the picnic was nothing more than a distraction to keep the others from questioning the decision. There was a rumor circulating up and down the line of aggressive wolves troubling the Indian populations in the territory ahead. The source was a prospector of questionable reliability, but given that there were still no answers in the Nystrom boy's death, the story had everyone on edge.

"Shouldn't we head straight out, like the main party?" Stanton had asked Donner when he'd heard about the plans for a picnic.

"It's the Sabbath, a day of rest," Donner had said, in a patronizing tone. "God will take care of us."

"We can reach Fort Bridger inside a week if we push," Stanton said. "We can't count that we won't be delayed down the road."

"The teamsters say we need to rest the oxen," William Eddy said, giving him a one-eyed squint. Stanton knew it for a lie. They'd barely covered six miles yesterday.

"You know what your trouble is, Stanton? You're too cautious." Lewis Keseberg was smirking, too, fingering his belt. One hand a couple of inches away from his revolver.

Eddy had laughed. "Cautious like an old schoolmarm." He wouldn't normally laugh at him, Stanton knew, but with Bryant gone, and Donner self-appointed captain, the power was shifting. Eddy and Keseberg, part of a pack of men Donner had made a point of befriending, were now acting like Donner's unofficial deputies. And Stanton wasn't one for taking on men who were looking for a fight, especially when the odds were so uneven.

Now, Luke Halloran's fiddle started up in the distance. To Stanton it sounded plaintive, like a child's voice calling out in need. It all seemed wrong: separating from the larger part of the wagon train, heading down this unknown trail, stopping for a picnic as if this were a church event when they should be moving as quickly as possible.

And of course, even though it was long-since buried by now, he still couldn't shake the nauseating image of the dead boy's mangled body, flesh picked down to bone, from his mind. It made the idea of a picnic feast all the more grotesque.

But still he forced himself across the encampment. He dreaded seeing Tamsen and wanted to see her, too; from a distance she seemed even more beautiful to him now, but also frightening, like a newly sharpened knife. In the darkness she softened beneath his fingers; she came to him like a kind of smoke that clung to your hair, your clothes, the inside of your lungs. Two nights ago he'd asked her if she *was* a witch, to have bewitched him so, but she only laughed.

Backboards set on trunks covered with gingham cloth made impromptu tables. Families dipped into their larders to make pies and carved up extra ham. Later, there would be dancing, storytelling. He accepted a bowl of Lavinah Murphy's chicken stew—he didn't think he could stomach any ham, he was so sick of it—and used bits of biscuit to sop up the gravy.

"You eat like you haven't had a meal in a week," Lavinah Murphy teased him. The Mormon widow was leading her brood—which included married daughters and sons-in-law all the way down to her own children as young as eight—west in search of a new homestead among those of her faith. "But perhaps you haven't, with no woman to cook for you. Aren't you tired of being a bachelor, Mr. Stanton?"

"I haven't had much of a chance to find the right woman," he said, forcing himself to swallow his impatience. There was no other way to win friends—and he had no hope of standing up to Donner if he could get no one on his side.

His answer only made the women laugh. "I find that hard to believe, Mr. Stanton." It was Peggy Breen, a hand shielding her eyes against the sun. Doris Wolfinger stood behind her, like a pretty duckling shadowing its mother. Peggy was a big woman, sturdy as a draft horse, who had given birth to a half-dozen sons. Doris, on the other hand, was barely out of her teenage years, spoke almost no English, and smiled uncomprehendingly whenever someone spoke to her. He had to wonder what she was *really* thinking.

"You know what they say about men who remain single too long, Mr. Stanton," Peggy Breen said, mischief in her eyes. "They start acting strangely."

"Are you saying I'm unsociable, Mrs. Breen?" he asked, mock offended. "And here I thought I was being right friendly."

"I'm saying you're *in danger* of becoming one of those sour old bachelors," Breen said, as the other women laughed. "It's better to be neighborly, don't you think? To get along?" Stanton thought he detected a certain shift in Peggy Breen's tone: not an observation, but a warning.

Lavinah Murphy jumped back in, seemingly oblivious to the point Breen was trying to make. "I've been married three times. Where's the fun in being alone, I always say? Better to have someone to share the journey with you. Peggy's right, Mr. Stanton. It would be a shame to waste a man as fine as you."

More laughter. He even caught Doris Wolfinger eyeing him shyly.

"I don't imagine many women would put up with a man like me," he said, to make the women laugh, although he knew, deep down, that it was true. He didn't deserve a good woman, not after what he'd done, or rather failed to do.

"I would bet there are women—even in our little caravan—who think otherwise, Mr. Stanton, and would prove it to you, if you gave them half a chance," Lavinah Murphy said. "Spent less time off by yourself and more time with the rest of us."

He didn't like the subtle implications in her words, in the way Lavinah squinted at him, appeared to study him beneath long lashes. The women had their own kind of power, he knew. All it would take was one accusation and they would be at him. It was the same as it had been before. No one had doubted what Lydia's father had said about him back home, even though he was the grandson of one of the most prominent ministers on the East Coast. It had happened over a dozen years ago, yet it still made his heart seize with a kind of panic.

"I try to steer clear of women I can never have." He stood up, all too aware of how hypocritical the words were and was just grateful Tamsen wasn't there to hear them.

"Then perhaps you'll find a sweetheart on the trail," Lavinah Murphy said. "The good Lord wants us all paired up."

"Soon all the best girls will be taken," one of the younger women chimed in. Sarah Fosdick. She was only recently married herself, and obviously a little drunk. "You'll be left with an old sow." She laughed.

"You'll have to forgive my sister, Mr. Stanton," a voice behind him said. "I think she's had a touch too much spirits."

He turned and saw a girl he recognized vaguely as Mary Graves.

She was sharp-featured and very tall for a woman. He'd never seen her up close before. Her eyes were extraordinary, the gray of an early dawn.

"You're Franklin Graves's daughter, then?" he said, although he knew it. He had noticed her before but it seemed she was always with her family, surrounded by her parents or a horde of little children clamoring for her attention.

"I am," she said. "One of them, at least."

The women's chatter died off as the two began walking together almost unconsciously, simply drifting away from the others to head toward a stand of pines on the edge of the encampment.

"I hope you don't think me presumptuous giving you advice, Mr. Stanton, but you should just ignore them." Her skirts fluttered with every step, grazing the wild prairie grass. She walked with a long, loping stride that reminded him of a young mare, fine and athletic. "They're only teasing you. Married women don't like to see a man by himself. I think it makes them nervous."

"Why should a single man make them nervous?"

She laughed. "It is one of the mysteries of the world, I suppose."

"Edwin Bryant—did you meet Edwin?—had a theory about this. He thought it appeared to be a kind of rebuke, choosing not to marry." As they walked, the picnic shrank to a miniature circus in the distance, a blur of movement and color, until all that was left was the faint drone of Halloran's fiddle carried on the wind and the occasional shriek of a child's laughter. People would talk, of course, if they walked too far together. But Stanton didn't care, and anyway, he wanted to get away from the other women before he said something he regretted.

It appeared that Mary Graves wasn't concerned about gossip, either.

She frowned in concentration. "Rebuking women, or the institution of marriage?"

He hesitated, thinking it over. He liked the quick, easy way she spoke. So many women seemed to turn their words over in their mouths like sugar cubes, until you could never be sure of the shape of the original thought. "Both, I think."

"Some women might find it insulting, but I don't. Not everyone is meant to marry," she said. "Did you know that Lavinah Murphy married her fourteen-year-old daughter to a man she'd only known for four days? My stepsister was right about one thing. There aren't many eligible women left in the party."

He shook his head. "Does this mean you're spoken for, Miss Graves?" He had meant it mostly as a joke, but when her face clouded, the words took on a sudden, hollow seriousness.

"My fiancé died recently. That's why my family is headed west," she said.

"I'm sorry," he said. He felt as if she had been swept suddenly beyond a veil. "Leaving bad memories behind, then?"

"Something like that." She was still speaking casually, but for a moment he saw beyond the carefully arranged look of unconcern, and knew she was truly unhappy. "That could probably be said of nearly everyone in the wagon train."

"You're right about that—still, I'm sorry," he repeated. He had the wild and inappropriate desire to take her hand.

"It's all right. I didn't know him very well." So if she was unhappy, it was for some other reason. Mary Graves brought a hand quickly to her mouth. "That sounds even worse, doesn't it? I'm always saying the wrong thing."

Stanton smiled. "That makes two of us. You'll have to tell me the whole story now."

She ducked her head to pass under the low branch of a small pine. "It's not a very good story, I'm afraid. As a matter of fact, it's terribly common. I'm sure you've heard it before: dutiful daughter agrees to an arranged marriage to a rich man to pay off her father's debts."

"Maybe you're lucky things turned out the way they did, then," Stanton said, and then, realizing how that sounded, hurried on, "I hope they picked a nice man for you to marry, at least."

"He was sweet enough to me. Everyone says we would've had a good life together. Still, who knows?"

Her voice had a low, musical quality that made him wish she would never stop talking. "What happened?" he asked. When she hesitated, he added, "If you don't want to tell me . . ."

"No, that's all right." She snapped a twig off the nearest branch and crushed the pine needles absently between her fingers, releasing the smell of resin. "Two weeks before the wedding, he went out deer hunting with his friends and was accidentally shot. The friends carried him back but there was nothing anyone could do for him. He died the next day."

"That's terrible."

She turned. Stanton knew the expression on her face; it was guilt. "Do you know something even worse? The friend who was responsible, he was torn up with grief. Practically went insane with it. I was shocked, yes, but I barely cried. Do you want to know the God's honest truth, Mr. Stanton? I was relieved. *Relieved*." She mustered a tiny, bitter smile. "That makes me a perfect monster, don't you think? I should have been upset—for my father, if not for poor Randolph or his family. Without the money that would have come from the marriage, my father was ruined. We had to sell everything. Father couldn't stand the thought of starting over in the same place, proving himself to the same people all over again. I put the idea of moving to California in his head. So whatever happens to us, whatever waits for my family in California, riches or ruin, I'll be responsible."

"You, a monster? Nonsense. I think you're a remarkably honest person," he said, and she smiled again.

"Perhaps. Or maybe I feel the need to confess my sins to someone." She turned and continued walking.

"Are you always so forthcoming with strangers?" Stanton asked, as he followed her. The camp was far behind them now, the voices and music faded away to almost nothing.

"I'm still in mourning. When you're in mourning, people will let you say just about anything—haven't you noticed?" She turned briefly, raising one eyebrow. Her profile was long and sharp, like something that might have been formed with a scalpel. "Now it's your turn. There's a reason you're not married already, Mr. Stanton. Are you going to tell me why?"

He fell into step beside her. "Like you said, it's a common tale. Barely merits repeating."

"I told you my story. It only seems fair."

He wasn't sure he could manage as well as she had. "I've been in love once."

"Were you engaged to be married?"

Even after all this time, thinking of Lydia still brought an ache to his chest, like the first deep breath of cold air. "Her father didn't like me. Nor could he bear to lose her, as it so happened."

She stared at him with those wide, gray eyes. Like the sky heavy with clouds, or the flint-gray of a Boston ocean. "Did he want her to end up an old maid?"

"I don't know what he wanted for her," Stanton said shortly, realizing too late that they were on dangerous ground, edging too close to the truth. "He never got the chance to find out, in any case. She died at nineteen, far too young."

Mary drew in a breath. "I'm sorry."

His conscience would let him go no further. He'd made a promise when he was young that he would never tell anyone Lydia's secret. As pointless as the promise seemed from a distance of fifteen years—to a dead girl, no less—he couldn't bring himself to break it. Besides, there were things he had done that he regretted, a long and twisted chain of deceit dragging behind him all these years, impossible to explain to anyone else without seeming like a monster. His heart seemed to be beating five times its normal rate. "It was terrible," he said. "I'm afraid I still can't talk about it."

Mary looked troubled. "I didn't mean to cause you pain," she said. Her hand skimmed his arm, like the touch of a passing bird.

"It's all right," he said, but it wasn't. His throat was closing, the memory choking him.

Mary was looking at him very closely. "What's this?" she asked at the same time her hand passed from his arm to his neck. Her fingers landed briefly on his neck, on the scratches he knew were there: Tamsen's newest marks. "You've been wounded. It looks as though you've been attacked—"

This time her touch wasn't pleasant. It burned. Without thinking, he pushed her hand away.

"It's nothing," he said. "Please don't."

She took a quick step backward, as if a wall had come up suddenly between them. Before he could speak, before he could say a word, her name rang out on the air, clear and clean as a bell.

She spun toward the sound and, with one last look over her shoulder at Stanton, darted back toward camp. She moved with surprising quickness, flashing between the trees like a shaft of sunlight, and then gone.

CHAPTER SEVEN

F our barrels of flour.

James Reed pried the lid off the barrel with dusty handprints and peered inside. Half full. A knock on the side of the next three barrels confirmed that they hadn't been touched yet. Five hundred pounds of flour, then, give or take. An anxious knot formed in his gut. They'd started out two months ago with nearly eight hundred pounds.

He made a mark on the scrap of paper in his hand.

He looked into the next barrel. Sugar, nearly half empty. Eliza Williams, the hired girl, was making too many pies and cakes for the children.

When he finished taking inventory, he climbed over the backboard and dropped to the ground. He took out his handkerchief and wiped the dust off his palms, then after a second's hesitation scrubbed both hands hard. Gave the handkerchief a sniff before putting it away.

Only then did he squint at the full list of figures, forcing his hands to be still and firm. He'd been checking on his family's stores every few days since they'd set out from Springfield. They were going through their supplies at an alarming rate. But no good ever came of worrying, unless there was an action to be taken.

So. First thing, he'd have a talk with Eliza. No second helpings for anyone, not even the children and certainly not the teamsters, who didn't think twice about wasting food. He skimmed the numbers a second time. Had he miscalculated how much they'd need for a family of seven? It was the six servants who threw off his math: the men were gluttons, eating for the pleasure of it without a care to how much it cost their employer.

Still, he knew they were better off—far better off—than many of the families on the trail. Publicly, everyone acted as though there was no problem, but he suspected that secretly some people were beginning to panic. Even those who had taken on more provisions at Fort Laramie had counted on there being more game along the trail. After Fort Laramie, everything seemed to have disappeared, from rabbits to prairie dogs. They were at the end of the traveling season and perhaps earlier pioneers had picked the surrounding area clean.

More likely they figured they could depend on the kindness of their trailmates if they ran out of supplies. Well, they'd be disappointed if they came to James Frazer Reed for a handout. Christian charity could only go so far.

He'd tried to talk Donner into putting him in charge of provisions for the entire party last night. But of course no one listened. No one understood how much danger they'd be in if food ran out higher up in the mountain passes. The signs were all there, if anyone would bother to see.

"Give you authority over my supplies?" William Eddy had only laughed, spitting tobacco a few inches from Reed's boot. "I don't think so. If we let you tell us what we can eat and how much and when, we'll all end up skinny as skeletons. Skinny as *you*."

Reed had ignored Eddy but he'd been tempted to pull out his piece of paper and shake it in Donner's face. "We're down twenty-five beef cattle since Fort Laramie and that was less than three weeks ago. If we didn't eat all of them, somebody is stealing them. At this rate we won't have two dozen head among us by the time we get to California."

Foolishness and pleasure, that was what the members of the wagon train wanted. Look at the Donners' big barge of a wagon, stuffed with feather mattresses and all manner of unnecessary comforts. The hired men gambled their wages away every night around the campfires, losing their pay before it was even earned. People danced around the roasting carcasses while Luke Halloran played the fiddle. And a *picnic*, what was the reason for that? An excuse for George Donner to stand on a tree stump and make a speech to get elected new party captain. Two cattle slaughtered just for that, to reassure them there was nothing to worry about: Look at how much there is to eat, plenty for everyone.

It was meant for a diversion, too, Reed suspected: It was whispered up and down the wagon train that Tamsen Donner had been seen wandering at night, caught in places she shouldn't have been. She was a witch, some of the other women said, could vanish and then re-appear in a different place, could fly on currents of air like the fluff of old dandelions, could charm a man just by breathing on him. Reed didn't believe in that nonsense, but one thing was clear: She was step-ping out on her husband, and making George look foolish just when he needed the wagon train behind him.

Reed straightened up, sore from crouching in the wagon among the barrels and big burlap sacks filled with bran and dried beans, hogs-heads of vinegar and molasses. As he stretched, Donner trotted by on his horse, waving his hat in the air.

"Chain up!" he shouted. His big face was pink from exertion. "Time to move out!"

How he hated the sound of Donner's voice.

But just as Reed turned to say something, he saw two of the Breen boys crawling on hands and knees from under one of the wagons. They were pale and unsteady on their feet, moaning as though they'd been beaten.

Reed's heart jumped in his chest. The boy killed a month ago came to mind, that pale face frozen as though in sleep, the terrible image of a torn-up body. Were the Breen boys sick? Suddenly one and then the other threw their heads down and began to heave violently. The smell was medicinal, overpowering, and unmistakable.

"Hey. You." Reed crossed the distance between them before they could run away. "You've been drinking, haven't you? Don't try to deny it. I can smell it on you."

Both boys—they couldn't have been older than ten—turned sullen faces toward him. "It's none of yer business," said one.

The smell of vomit and whiskey was so foul that Reed resisted the urge to hold his handkerchief over his nose. He doubted the boys had gotten the liquor from their father: Patrick Breen would whip them to within an inch of their lives. "You stole the whiskey you drank away, didn't you? Who did you steal it from? Out with it."

They glowered at Reed. "We ain't telling," the scrawnier, dirtier one said.

Reed was tempted to give them the back of his hand but thought the better of it. People had started to stare.

"Why you bothering them kids?" Milt Elliott, a teamster for the Donners, shook his head.

"It's none of your nevermind," Reed said.

"You ain't the boys' father." This from another of the Donners' men, Samuel Shoemaker.

"Their *father's* probably lying facedown in a ditch himself." The words came out before Reed could stop himself. He cursed his sharp tongue. He could imagine how he must sound to this crowd, many of them hungover themselves from dancing half the night away. His palms started to tingle. He could feel dirt gathering in his eardrums, in his nostrils, beneath his fingernails. He needed to bathe. "Look, I'm only trying to find out where the boys got the alcohol."

"Are you saying it's our fault the boys got themselves drunk?" Elliott said, raising an eyebrow.

"No. I'm just saying that we must do a better job keeping track of all our supplies." He shook his head. He would try again. "We might want to lock up our spirits, for example—"

Tall and angular, always hovering like an ominous scarecrow, Lewis Keseberg pushed his way through the crowd. Reed could've predicted it; Keseberg always seemed to be spoiling for a fight. "You'd like to take our liquor away, wouldn't you? You'd probably chuck it in the Little Sandy when nobody was looking, every drop of it." He jabbed a finger into Reed's chest. "If you try to lay so much as *one finger* on any of my bottles, so help me God—"

Sweat began to collect on Reed's upper lip. He glanced around but didn't see Keseberg's wife or child anywhere. Seemed Keseberg kept anything humane about him behind closed doors, and there'd be no plying him with reminders of family and decency. Still, Reed couldn't let Keseberg push him around in front of all these other people; they'd decide he was a coward. But Keseberg was notoriously unforgiving. No one gambled with him anymore, because he never forgot who cheated, who liked to bluff, and who always held pat. Remembered which cards in the deck had already been played, calculated which were likely to come up. He apparently had a memory as sharp as a blade. He was also a half foot taller and thirty pounds heavier.

He was standing so close that Reed was sure Keseberg would notice that he was *not right*.

Reed imagined that his own secret—the badness in him—was so strong that it could be seen or smelt if you got close enough. It was like the fine trail dust he could never quite be rid of, traces of his sins on his hands or his face, seeping up from under his clothes, no matter how hard he tried to wipe it away.

He reached for his handkerchief again.

"Keep your hands off me," he said, hoping his voice wouldn't shake. "Or—"

"Or what?" Keseberg only leaned closer. *Sharp as a blade.*

Before Reed could answer, a huge slab of a man stepped between them: John Snyder, Franklin Graves's hired driver. Probably the last person any reasonable man would want to tangle with.

Snyder narrowed his eyes but there was a playfulness in his smirk. "What's going on here? This little man trying to tell everyone what to do—again?" Snyder liked to call him *little man*, a reminder that he could push Reed around whenever he felt like it. "I thought they told you last night that you're not going to boss us around."

Snyder turned back to him and Reed thought he had a knowing sort of look in his eye. Reed's blood ran cold. Had anyone else seen Snyder's face?

But the others carried on; no one had seen. No one could know. "That's right. George Donner's captain, not you," Keseberg said.

"I'm only speaking common sense," Reed insisted. This was important. Despite his discomfort, he would try one more time to make them listen. "Fort Laramie was the last outpost before California.

From here out there are no more general stores, no grain depots, no settlers willing to sell a sack of cornmeal. Whoever lost their whiskey to these boys"—Reed pointed a finger at the pair, still flat on their backs in the dirt—"will wish they had been more careful a couple weeks down the road when there's not a drop to be had."

The crowd quieted. Reed sensed a small victory.

"Friends," he continued, "by all accounts, the easy part of the journey is behind us. At Fort Laramie I spoke to men who have been down this cutoff. They say that the road ahead is more daunting than anything we've imagined. I urge you to take this time to make some difficult choices." They were hushed now, waiting restlessly for him to speak. Even Snyder was watching him, his eyes nearly golden in the sun. "Many of us are burdened with possessions, hauling things from home that we thought we couldn't bear to part with. I urge you to shed them *now*. Leave them here in this meadow, otherwise you will *kill* your oxen on the mountains ahead."

The crowd was silent. He saw too late that he'd overplayed his hand, even though they knew—they must know—that he spoke the truth. For miles, they'd been passing the possessions of other pioneers abandoned trailside. Furniture, trunks of clothing, children's toys, even a piano sitting in an open field as though waiting for someone to step up and play a tune on it. He had watched young Doris Wolfinger, the German girl, finger the stiff white keys wistfully, and the sight had brought a deep ache into his chest, one he couldn't quite name.

But like many truths, no one wanted to hear it.

"Look who's talking," Keseberg said. "You and that special wagon you got. Takes four oxen to pull it and that's over even terrain."

"You sure don't practice what you preach, do you?" Snyder asked, almost casually, picking over his filthy fingernails, not even looking at Reed. Still, Reed couldn't help but notice how large and powerful

Snyder's hands were. Couldn't help but wonder how they might feel tightened around Reed's own throat. "We don't need some *hypocrite* to tell us how to behave."

Before Reed could speak, George Donner came through the crowd, leading his horse by the reins.

"We're burning daylight, neighbors. Let's get on with our business, chain up and move out. I want those wagons rolling in a quarter of an hour."

The crowd dispersed as Donner swung into the saddle. He looked pleased with himself, Reed thought. He supposed he should be grateful to Donner for his intercession but he couldn't bring himself to feel anything but resentment, even as the dark thoughts of John Snyder—that hard-looking jaw, those powerful, terrifying hands—began to subside.

As the crowd broke up, Reed spotted his wife, Margaret. She was wrapped in a woven shawl, long tassels made of embroidery thread lifted by the breeze. Seeing her unexpectedly like this, he was struck by how old she looked.

She turned away, but not so quickly that he missed the look on her face. It was pity—or maybe disgust. Reed hurried through the crowd to catch up to her, seizing her by the elbow. "What is it, Margaret? Do you have something to say to me?"

She just shook her head and continued hobbling toward their campsite, moving slowly, as though in great pain. She seemed to be suffering more than she had in Springfield, if that was possible, as though her health was worsening. He was fairly sure, however, that she was doing this for show, to make him feel guilty.

"Go on, Margaret. Tell me what's bothering you now. Get it off your chest, whatever it is I've done to disappoint you so."

She trembled, and it hit him how hard she was trying to control her emotions. Her *anger*. Reed remembered what Margaret had been like when they were first married. A widow, she was experienced in marriage and understood the roles of husband and wife, their separate domains. She had struck him as dignified, diligent, and orderly. She always let him make the decisions in the family, always supported him in front of the children, servants, and the neighbors.

"I don't understand you, James. Why must you seek out these arguments with our neighbors?"

"I didn't go looking for an argument. Those boys came crawling out from under the wagon—they practically *vomited* all over my boots—"

"Why do you do it?" She cut him off, clearly exasperated. "Act so superior, make everyone think you're so much better? You make me a laughingstock in front of—" She stopped abruptly, squeezing her eyes shut tightly. "For the life of me, I don't understand. Why you insisted we leave Springfield in the first place, sell a good business, a beautiful home?" She caught her breath. It was as if she were drowning in midair. "If I had known this, James, I don't know that I would've married you—"

"Don't say that, Margaret," he said mechanically. His wife didn't even look up from the ground. Neither held any illusions about their union; they hadn't married for love. Theirs was a common marriage of convenience, in many ways like brother and sister rather than man and wife. But how many of the people out here could say differently?

"And what about the children? Did you even give a thought to what this is doing to them, taking them away from their friends, their neighbors, all the people they've ever known? You told me when you proposed that you would take *care* of us."

"And I am. That's what the point of all of this is." The kerchief was out and he was scrubbing again; he hadn't even realized what he was doing. He shoved it back in his pocket.

The truth, however, was more complicated.

The truth was that he *hadn't* done everything in his power to protect her and the children. He had made mistakes.

One mistake in particular.

His wife had met Edward McGee once, when she had paid an unexpected visit to see Reed at the warehouse one day. He'd thought then that she'd heard rumors and had come downtown to see for herself. But she had never spoken a word about it to Reed, had never voiced a single suspicion. She had even shaken hands with Edward. Reed could see it still, that strange, half-mocking smile on Edward's lips as he took Margaret's hand in his.

But that was done. He had to put the past behind him. He had to put his fears and his guilt behind him. Had to push the idea of that teamster Snyder's hands around his throat—or around his wrists—out of his head for good. He had to do better. Though it was irrational, impossible, some small part of him believed it was his own sin that caused the Nystrom boy to be killed—that attracted the devil to their camp in the first place.

But no. He had to keep his head about him. Everything would be different once they reached California. Reed squinted up at the sky. The sun was inching higher. Soon they would be off again.

He pulled out the list of inventory and began recounting everything. But no matter how many times he did, the truth kept coming back up. There just wasn't enough.

Something would have to be done.

CHAPTER EIGHT

Indian Territory

Dear Charles,

*I write this letter lost in the wilderness beyond Fort Bridger—
perhaps from the Wasatch Mountains? I am not sure—and with no
idea whether you will ever see this. After the ordeals of the past few
weeks, all I know is that I must make a record of what I've learned. If
this letter finds you, Charles, do not try to follow me. What I do, I do
in the interest of science and the truth.*

*Right as I was leaving Fort Laramie I hired a guide, a young
Paiute seventeen years of age, named Thomas. He was converted by
missionaries (who gave him his Christian name) six years ago, and
has been living among whites ever since. He told me that he knew
of the Washoe living near Truckee Lake that I am seeking and that,
because there had been a Washoe orphan living with the missionaries
who'd raised him, he could communicate with them. He had heard of
the Anawai, too, though he didn't seem to like to talk about them.*

You can imagine how delighted I was to secure a guide who knew the area and this tribe, and even spoke their language. Not five days out of Fort Laramie, Thomas got his first test as our small band came across a Paiute hunting party. The braves were friendly and shared a meal with us that evening around a campfire. They answered my questions about the Anawai. In fact, my interest made them quite animated. They tried to convince me not to meet with them, claiming this particular group was exceptionally dangerous.

As best I could tell from Thomas's interpretation, the Anawai had turned away from their traditional gods and now worshipped a wolf spirit indigenous to the valley in which they lived. The Paiute claimed that the Anawai could suddenly turn quite ferocious and be filled with an unquenchable bloodlust. They ascribed all sorts of atrocities to the group, but from here the story became difficult to follow and exceeded Thomas's ability to translate.

The fact that this strange information seemed oddly similar to Farnsworth's story of human sacrifice made me all the more determined to press on. The rest of the group, unsurprisingly, was reluctant to proceed. You know these fellows—Newell, Anderson, the Manning brothers—big, strong men whom you'd never accuse of cowardice. I managed to convince them to continue on to Fort Bridger with me, pointing out that the wagon train would pass through there and they could always rejoin your group at that time.

After I'd calmed the others, Thomas took me aside. I could tell that he was spooked as well. He told me that he wanted to turn back. I reminded him that I was paying him for his service and that it was an all-or-nothing deal; if he wanted to see one penny from me he would need to stay until the end. He wasn't happy, as you can imagine, and said that given the danger he wanted to be given a gun. But he'd been so skittish, I wasn't convinced he could be trusted not to fire off at any old target—myself included. Besides, I confess I had heard too many stories of Indian guides turning on their employers, even if Thomas appeared to be a good kid, and so I refused. I pointed out that he was surrounded by men with firearms and that we'd see to his safety. Still, he was skittish until we reached Fort Bridger.

I was never so happy to see a broken-down little hole-in-the-wall like Fort Bridger in my life. As you will see, it is nothing like Fort Laramie. Jim Bridger, one of the owners, candidly told me that their fortunes had suffered when the Greenwood Cutoff became popular last year. Now, wagons bound for Oregon bypassed his fort completely. The outpost is like a ghost town.

I learned just how desperate things were the next evening as we sat around a bottle of rotgut in Bridger's office. In a moment of drunkenness, he told us of an incident that happened six years earlier, of a group of prospectors who became lost while traveling through the area now known as the Hastings Cutoff. Some said they had starved, others said they'd been massacred by the unpredictable Anawai. Bridger had gotten to know the prospectors when they'd passed through the fort and so he set out to find them. The situation seemed hopeless; the territory was vast and their resources too few. They were just about to give up when one of the prospectors stumbled into the search party's camp. Unfortunately, the poor soul had lost his mind after living like an animal in the woods and was unable to tell anyone what had happened to the others.

The story sat uneasily with me. It reminded me of an aside Lewis Keseberg had shared with me, that his own uncle had disappeared in this same territory a number of years back.

I was forming a bad opinion of Bridger, in any case. His prices are outrageous, his stock poor quality (mealy flour, rotten meat, watered alcohol). The garrison was redeployed to the busier Fort Hall months *ago, so Bridger and his partner, Luis Vasquez, are on their own. They are desperate men, I think.*

Between the experience with the Paiute hunting party and Bridger's stories, I left the next morning uneasily, taking only Thomas with me. We quickly learned that the way is very bad. Bridger told me that Lansford Hastings had indeed been at the fort, but he left to escort a wagon party through the cutoff. They were about a week ahead of us, so we tried to follow signs of their passage, but the way was thick with forest and undergrowth. We occasionally stumbled across an old Indian trail only to find that it ended abruptly at a canyon or edge of a cliff. It was difficult going on horseback and would be nearly impossible with a wagon. It is imperative that you stop the wagon party from taking this route. You will find only hardship and disaster here.

It took a week, but Thomas and I managed to get through the mountains. We had lost all signs of Hastings's wagon party and spent every minute on edge, hoping to see signs that they'd been by or to hear a human voice—anything to know we were not alone. But the deeper we plunged into the forest, the more isolated we felt. Paradoxically, I had the strangest and strongest impression of being watched.

At this point, Thomas was jumpier than a cat and I began to worry for the boy's mental state. When I pressed him about it the last night we sat together by the campfire, he confessed that when he'd translated for the Paiute, he hadn't told me the entire story. The Paiute had warned us to stay away from the Anawai tribe at Truckee Lake, that much was true, but there was a reason for their violence. The Anawai were kidnapping outsiders to sacrifice them to this wolf spirit.

Thomas told me that he was sorry he hadn't told me earlier, but he had been afraid I would insist on going to see for myself and we would end up being killed. Thomas plainly thought me crazy and impossible to reason with. He was so upset that I began to feel bad for having put him in this position. He is only a seventeen-year-old boy, frightened for his life.

I was just about to dig into my pouch for his wages and release him from his contract when we heard a noise in the brush. We both snapped around. I reached for my rifle and Thomas pulled one of the burning branches from the fire.

The brush crackled all around. Thomas held the branch overhead like a torch. There was a loud snap right in front of us, the sound of weight coming down on a branch and breaking it right in two. I raised my rifle squarely in that direction.

"Show yourself!" I shouted into the void.

Footsteps rushed toward me in the dark. I was about to fire but at that same moment, Thomas turned on his heel and ran into the forest. He was unarmed (he had even thrown the torch to the ground in a panic) and so I felt I had to go after him to protect him. I followed the sound of Thomas crashing through the woods ahead of me, and all the while heard someone following behind me. Within minutes I lost Thomas in the inky darkness. But the noise behind me was getting louder and closer and finally, out of self-preservation, I turned around and fired blindly into the blackness. The flash from my rifle illuminated something in the trees, and I fired again. This time I heard a yelp of pain, distinctly animal, and—my eyes having adjusted to the darkness—I saw the glimmer of yellow eyes and teeth, and then whatever they were, they were gone. I focused every bit of my attention on sound, trying to tell if they were circling around to attack me from another angle, but all the noises died away suddenly.

There was no trace of them—or of Thomas, either. He did not make his way back to the campfire that night. I do not know what has happened to him.

You know what a stubborn cuss I am, Charles, and so will not be surprised to learn that I am continuing to Truckee Lake. I've come too far to turn back now. You may think what I'm doing is rash and dangerous, and of course, it is. But I have been in similar situations in the past and survived. I go to search for Thomas but also to search for truths.

God bless you and Godspeed,
your friend, Edwin

CHAPTER NINE

I t had to be the driest, hottest part of the summer when the wagon train at last rolled through South Pass into the area just north of Fort Bridger. The land was harsher than Stanton had expected. The green pastures abruptly gave way to burnt browns, the grass brittle and dirt like powder, and the Big Sandy River so dried up that it was hardly wider than a creek. The livestock nosed the sparse grass disinterestedly. The party would have to move quickly through this area and hope there were better pastures nearby. They couldn't survive for long in conditions like these. But the plain stretched flat before them for what seemed like a hundred miles: a tortured place.

Stanton's muscles strained. Sweat gathered at his brow and ran down his back. His head hammered with feverish exhaustion. The past few nights, he had volunteered to stand watch over the livestock. It was his way of making sure he wouldn't be in his tent if Tamsen came looking for him. A temporary solution—he would have to confront her eventually—and one that left him blindly fatigued during the day. Still, facing the temptation of her, and the consequences of her wrath, seemed worse.

He was still reeling from the events of three nights ago, when Donner had confessed to Stanton that he knew Tamsen was up to something. It wouldn't be the first time, he'd admitted; Tamsen was a fragile woman, and certain past "occurrences" were part of the reason for the move west. Her latest affair had been on the verge of going public, a scandal that would've made a laughingstock of him—and her. As they staggered home, Donner so drunk that he had to lean on Stanton for support, he swore that he would kill whoever Tamsen was seeing this time. Stanton was surprised by the ferocity with which Donner seemed to defend his wife, despite it all. Though he generally seemed like a harmless enough man, Stanton had no doubt Donner would do what he said.

And so he kept the night watch, even though it meant barely being able to keep his eyes open during the long, hot, dusty days.

When he first caught sight of Fort Bridger, he imagined it might be a mirage. There were the roofs of a few log cabins, and buildings on the verge of collapse. Stanton hadn't realized how eager he'd been to get here—to find a little relief from his own thoughts—until their party approached the fort. Now he was surprised by the weight of his disappointment. This place could almost be mistaken for deserted.

Unease grew and spread: Stanton could feel it like a wind touching down, rippling through the group. This *couldn't* be Fort Bridger, they told each other. Where was the stockade fence, the stout gate, the cannon? In the distance, a handful of smaller outbuildings cowered together. Two Indians chopping wood in a muddy courtyard looked up as the wagon train rolled past but quickly returned to their work.

They found Jim Bridger, the proprietor, inside one of the dilapidated log cabins. It was dim and so smoky that you could barely see. The cabins were low and long, with few openings for windows, though chinks between the logs let in plenty of drafts. The floors were packed dirt, covered here and there with ragged hides. Two Indian women sat in the corner, hunched over baskets and seemingly oblivious to the smoke from the fireplace. A child played at their feet, scrubbing a thumb in the dirt.

Stanton had heard about Bridger at Fort Laramie, stories of his temper and impatience, all blamed on the many years he spent alone in the wilderness. He had been a mountain man roaming the area for a decade before setting up the fort with his partner, a restless Mexican named Luis Vasquez. Paranoid, prone to take the law into his own hands, was how he'd been described by one of the men at Fort Laramie.

Bridger might once have been strong, even intimidating, but now he was wizened, hollow-cheeked, diminished, as if something had sucked out a good part of his insides. He was dressed in tattered and filthy buckskins. His hair was long, thin, and gray. When he looked up, there was no mistaking the strange brightness in his eyes; the man was crazy.

Donner was so tall compared to Bridger that when he thrust out his hand, he nearly struck the man in the face. "I need to speak to the proprietor of this establishment," he said in that expansive, confident tone that Stanton had come to know as completely false.

"You found 'im," Bridger said, without glancing up. Next to him behind the counter was a short, younger man with skin the color of caramel and a dirty apron tied about his waist. They appeared to be taking inventory.

"We'll be staying here for a couple days to rest the animals," Donner explained after they'd exchanged names.

"That's fine. Let us know if you need anything. We got pretty good stocks of supplies," Vasquez said, wiping his palms on the greasy apron, streaked rust-red and brown as though he had been butchering. "Which way you planning to go? North or west?" Both men seemed keenly interested in the response.

"West, of course," Donner said. "We've come to meet up with Lansford Hastings. He said he'd be waiting here to guide settlers down the cutoff."

Bridger and Vasquez exchanged a look that Stanton couldn't decipher. "Hastings *was* here, but he moved on," Vasquez said. "A wagon train come through two weeks ago and he set off with them."

"Two weeks ago!" Donner repeated. "But he promised to wait."

Stanton resisted the urge to point out to Donner that he'd been warned. Donner had convinced the party to make the journey down Hastings Cutoff, said that Hastings would wait for them. Now everyone would see that they'd taken a gamble—and possibly lost.

"No need to fret," Bridger said, squinting in a way Stanton assumed was meant to suggest a smile. "Hastings left instructions. Said any wagons that came through should follow their trail. They're marking it. You won't be able to miss it."

Donner frowned. "And what's your opinion of this trail? Is it any good? We have ninety people in our party, most of them women and children."

Stanton wasn't sure why he bothered to ask. Fort Bridger's fortunes depended on the success of this trail. He hoped Christian decency would keep these men from lying to them outright, but he'd been disappointed by Christian goodness in the past. Few men valued the lives of strangers over profit.

Both Bridger and Vasquez hesitated. "Well, that route is pretty new," Vasquez said finally.

"That it is," Bridger interrupted, his tone brighter than Vasquez's.

"But Hastings is keen on it. He's been down it with Bill Clyman, you heard of him? Clyman is probably the most famous mountain man in this territory, and old Bill give it his stamp of approval."

Donner beamed stupidly. Undoubtedly he would repeat this endorsement to everyone in the party. "That's good enough for me."

"Tell you what, I'll saddle up myself and take you to the start of the pass," Bridger said. "But you'll want to take a few days to rest up, make sure your animals are well fed and in good shape. We got oats, a little feed corn, too. Nothing between here and John Sutter's fort in California. This here's your last chance to fatten 'em up before you head into the mountains."

"And we'll make the best use of it, too, sir, you can count on that," Donner said, beaming at each man in turn as he departed.

Stanton let Donner go alone. He turned to Vasquez. "Do you have a letter for me from Edwin Bryant? He should've passed through here a week or so ago."

He thought he saw a flicker in Vasquez's dark eyes before Bridger spoke up. "What was that name again?"

"Bryant. A few years older than me, wears spectacles most of the time. A newspaperman."

Bridger shook his head. "Don't recall anyone by that name came through this way. There's nothing here for you, anyway."

Stanton felt a quick seize of dread. "He was just ahead of us on the trail," he said. When Bridger said nothing, he went on, "He intended to stop here. He told me so himself." He didn't want to think about what could have waylaid him: Bryant injured, dead, or dying.

"No, no, you're right. He was here, I remember him now," Vasquez said slowly.

Stanton was relieved to hear that Bryant had come through the fort after all. But there was something that rang false about the way the two men were acting. "Bryant was going to leave a letter for me. Are you sure there's nothing?"

"Nothing, sir," Vasquez said. Stanton knew that he was lying.

"Well—you heard Donner. We'll be here for a few more days. I'll check back just in case something turns up," he said as he turned to leave. But Bridger only gave him a stony smile, showing all his teeth.

A GRAY RAIN SETTLED OVER them for the next two days. It would help with the drought so no one complained, but it was just heavy enough to make life miserable. Fires sputtered and smoked; families hunkered down in their tents, shivering out their evenings in mud-spattered clothing and boots, scratching at lice and other vermin that seemed to have infested half the wagon party's bedding and clothes. It was hardest on the older members of the party like Mathis Hardkoop, an elderly Belgian traveling on his own. Hardkoop, no judge of character, had (inexplicably, as far as Stanton could see) come to depend on Keseberg for help, but Keseberg had tired of the old man and—against his quiet wife Philippine's wishes—thrown him out of his wagon. Weakened by the demands of the trail, Hardkoop quickly developed a bad cough and could be found slinking around the fort with his near-empty satchel and bedroll, looking for a dry place to sleep.

A couple of families escaped the wet and mud by renting rooms from Bridger and Vasquez. James Reed moved his large brood into a bunkhouse that had stood unused since the garrison had moved on the year before. George and Jacob Donner went one better by offering Vasquez enough money to move his family out of their log cabin. The two Donner clans would escape the drizzle, be able to enjoy hot meals and boil water in Vasquez's big copper cauldron for hot baths. Stanton was still too much of a Yankee to spend good money when he had a sturdy tent at hand.

Finally, on the third morning of their stay, the rain cleared. Stanton knelt by the river, stripped to the waist, his clothing piled nearby. The water was so cold it took his breath away. Punishingly cold, but again something he had a perverse liking for, no doubt thanks to his grandfather. He washed quickly, only the exposed parts. Donner had promised that it was to be their final day at the fort and everyone was hurrying to get through the last of their chores. He had a long list: inspect the axle and wheels for signs of wear or weakness; clean the harnesses, which had become stiff with sweat; check on the oxen's and his saddle horse's hooves. A beast of burden was only as good as its hooves, and no one could afford to lose one of their animals.

He felt the scream as much as he heard it. He knew her voice, felt her cry in his body, as if it were a message meant for him. He reached for the pistol lying on top of his clothing but didn't stop for anything else. He sprinted in the direction of her voice.

Mary Graves.

She was on her back in the dirt, scrabbling backward. The shock of seeing her that way was nothing compared to the surprise of seeing a man standing over her. He was filthy, his skin nearly leprous from neglect, his eyes red and wet. The stink coming off him was overpowering and nearly made Stanton choke.

These thoughts passed through Stanton's mind in an instant. Later he would remember nothing but a vision of two scabrous hands gripping Mary's shoulders, before he drew a bead and squeezed off two shots automatically.

The bullets caught the man—if he could be called that—in the back. He released his grip on Mary, then toppled forward. Mary had to shove him hard to keep him from rolling on top of her. She tried to stand but sank down in the dirt again. She was very pale, and Stanton could see she was doing everything not to cry.

Stanton was surprised that the man was still alive; he was pretty sure that he'd put both bullets in him. He crouched next to him to see if there was anything he could do. "Don't thrash, you'll only bleed more," he ordered, but when he held a hand out to get the man to lie still, the stranger lunged toward him, nearly taking off Stanton's fingers with rust-colored teeth. Stanton struck him hard in the face; his bones felt spongy, almost rotten.

The man fell backward in the dirt and Stanton resisted the urge to shoot him again. Instead, he turned to Mary, who was still on the ground. "Are you okay? You weren't hurt, were you?"

She shook her head. She was so pale he could see the tracery of veins in her cheeks. "I'll be all right."

There was a bright slash of red on her shoulder. "What's that?" Stanton asked.

She touched the spot with a trembling hand. "It's nothing. A scratch." She lifted her chin in the man's direction. "I was going to see what was keeping my brothers—we'd sent them for a bucket of water—when he came rushing out of the woods. The next thing I knew he had grabbed me and—" She stopped, drawing in a deep breath, and once again Stanton could see that she was trying not to cry.

"He can't hurt you. I'll put a bullet between his eyes if he so much as tries to get up off the ground." Already, the man was twitching again. Not unconscious, then.

But she didn't seem to be paying attention to him. She tried to get to her feet again. "My brothers—have you seen my brothers?"

"Take it easy. I'll look for them just as soon as I get you back to camp." He started to help Mary off the ground when he heard shout-ing. Just then, several men from the party crashed out of the woods.

"What's going on here?" George Donner was the first to arrive, a hand clamped to his hat to keep it from blowing off his head. William Eddy and Jim Bridger were steps behind him. Bridger had leashed up a fierce-looking dog. It snarled at the blood in the dirt. "Who fired a gun?" He stopped short when he saw the man on the ground. "Dear God, what in the name of heaven . . . ?"

Bridger held the dog back with difficulty when it lunged for the stranger. Funny, Stanton thought; the old man didn't seem surprised at the scene.

"I heard Mary scream," Stanton said. Mary leaned heavily against him, and Stanton was all too aware of Eddy scowling. "I found this man attacking her."

Donner looked repulsed. "His face . . ." Donner shook his head. "What's wrong with him?"

"Take it easy now, everybody." Bridger kept his tone friendly. He handed the dog's lead to Eddy and crouched next to the man, binding his hands with a piece of rope. Stanton noticed that the man's wrists were chafed nearly raw. He had sat up but didn't resist; Stanton could tell he was frightened of Bridger's dog, but Bridger handled him care-fully nonetheless. "This here man is that prisoner I was telling you about. Must've got out."

"Prisoner?" Donner obviously knew nothing of the stories Bridger had been telling his new visitors over the last couple of rainy nights. Stanton himself had only caught whispers of it. "What did he do?"

"He didn't do anything," Bridger said with a shrug. "Leastways not like you're thinking. Was one of 'em prospectors got lost out in the woods a few years back now. He got a fever in his brain and went off his nut. You see the way he's acting. We've been holding him for his own good, so he won't hurt hisself." Bridger gave Stanton a contemptuous look. "I'm doing this out of the kindness of my heart. I coulda left him to wander in the woods forever, y'know."

"I'm sure your Christian charity is an inspiration to us all," Stanton said, not bothering to keep the sarcasm from his voice. Whatever had chafed the man's wrists nearly raw, it wasn't the kindness of Jim Bridger's heart. Why would he insist on keeping a dangerous man locked up when there were women and children around? And not for weeks or even months but for *years*? Stanton got a chill thinking about it—as though this monstrous prisoner had been some sort of a pet to Bridger.

Donner and Eddy offered to help Mary Graves up to the wagons. While Bridger forced his prisoner to his feet, Stanton stood, troubled for reasons he couldn't explain, watching Mary moving clumsily between her two escorts, still troubled by the memory of her scream. When she was nearly out of sight, she looked back over her shoulder at him. Her pale gray eyes were the same color as the sky.

NEAR NIGHTFALL, Stanton packed his things. He was ready to leave Fort Bridger and its madmen and its secrets behind. Chaining up couldn't come a moment too soon.

Without warning, Lewis Keseberg stuck his head inside Stanton's tent. "Donner wants you to come with me."

Not so long ago, Donner would have come directly had he wanted to talk. Maybe even brought a bottle of whiskey to share. Stanton wasn't sure when things changed between them, and why.

Stanton looked up from the knife he was sharpening, whetstone in his lap. "Can it wait until tomorrow?"

"You're going to want to come. He's questioning an Indian boy who crawled out of the woods." Keseberg's rotted teeth gleamed wetly in the dark. "Said he was traveling with Edwin Bryant."

Stanton was on his feet and outside within seconds. At the barn, a handful of men stood in a circle around a skinny dark boy, sitting on a bale of hay and draped with a dirty horse blanket. Only his head was visible, his black hair hanging in filthy tangles. This had to be the Indian guide Bryant had hired before departing from Fort Laramie. Stanton had heard of him, a Paiute orphan converted by missionaries, but hadn't met him. He seemed far too young to be leading men through uncharted territory.

"Where's Edwin?" The words were out before Stanton knew he'd spoken. He just managed to keep from lunging at the boy when the boy did nothing but shake his head.

"He told us that Bryant decided to go ahead on his own and dismissed him from service," Donner said. Hands buried in his pockets, he paced restlessly, and Stanton could tell that he, too, found that story unlikely.

Reed stepped closer to the boy, screwing up his face. "Bryant wouldn't let you go unless you'd done something to make him. Did you try to steal from him? What was it, boy?"

The Indian pushed hair out of his eyes. "I didn't steal nothing, I swear."

"But he didn't dismiss you. You lied about that, didn't you? You ran away. You're a coward," Reed said. The boy hung his head again and muttered something indecipherable. Reed looked back at the others. "The only question that remains is what to do with him."

"We leave him here, of course," Donner said, and stopped pacing to stare at Reed. "What else is there to do? We can't take him with us."

Stanton thought of the wild man in Bridger's makeshift stockade, the raw wounds on his wrists. Could they just hand the boy over to Jim Bridger?

"Why not take him with us?" Keseberg asked. "Coward or not, he knows the area and we need a guide. He can lead us to Hastings. That can be his punishment for deserting a white man in the wilderness." It was one of the more reasonable thoughts Stanton had ever heard out of Keseberg's mouth.

"You cannot *make* me work for you," the boy said.

"We won't cheat you," Reed said. Although he and Keseberg despised each other, it was obvious he agreed with the suggestion. "But you heard these men: You can't stay here. You have nowhere else to go. You'll come with us or you can walk all the way to Fort Laramie."

The boy looked from one of his captors to the next. Stanton thought for a moment that he might jump up and try to run away. "You cannot make me go with you. That way—that way is bad. There are bad spirits waiting for you ahead. You cannot pass. It is not safe."

Bad spirits. Stanton thought of messages sent through dreams, of the little talismans of bundled sticks and lace he'd seen Tamsen carrying around with her when she thought no one was watching. When he shouldn't have been watching.

He'd found a satchel of dried herbs beneath his pillow a week ago, after the last time they'd been together. When he burned it, it released a choking smoke, sweet and dizzying.

Stanton crouched so he could look the boy in the face. "Listen to me. What's your name?"

There was a wary look in his eye. "Thomas."

"Thomas." That sounded familiar; perhaps he'd heard the boy's name at Fort Laramie. "First thing in the morning, you'll take me to where you left Edwin Bryant."

The boy stiffened, terrified. "I cannot do that, sir. It was days and days from here. I don't even know where he is." He wasn't going to let wild horses drag him back into the wilderness. That much was obvious.

Donner put a hand on Stanton's shoulder. "Don't waste your time worrying about Bryant. He'll be all right. He knows about Indians and their ways. He stands the best chance of surviving out in those mountains, better than the rest of us."

Stanton stood, twisting away from Donner's hand. "Edwin is out there by himself, most likely lost. We can't just desert him."

"He left *us*, don't you remember, when he headed out on horseback?" Donner said. "It seems to me he made his choice already. I have more than one lone man to worry about, Stanton. There are eighty-eight people in this wagon party, all of them depending on me. You can head out to look for Bryant if you want, Stanton, but the Indian is staying with us."

Stanton knew, deep down, that Donner was right. Even if he managed to round up a search party, the wagon train couldn't afford to wait. They'd lost too many days already.

And there'd been no letter from Bryant. Nothing at all.

He thought of Mary Graves scrambling backward in the dirt, the buck of his revolver as he shot her attacker, what would've happened if he hadn't been there.

He thought of Tamsen—the fine line of her mouth.

He thought of loud Peggy Breen, too, teasing him along the trail, and of petite Doris Wolfinger, with her pale, delicate hands.

He thought of the countless children whose names he still didn't have straight in his head, even after all this time.

He couldn't head after Bryant, he saw that now. He couldn't risk what might happen to the others if he didn't return.

CHAPTER TEN

Springfield, Illinois
March 1846

V*ertraust du mir?"*—do you trust me?—Jacob Wolfinger asked his new wife, Doris, as they lay side by side in their narrow bed on the night before their journey.

Doris had been nervous to come all the way from Germany for a husband she'd never met, with whom she had only communicated by letter. But she'd been relieved to find that, though older than her by many years, Jacob Wolfinger was good-looking enough, and even though he was only the steward of a wealthy man in town, helping to run his many businesses, Jacob was richer than he'd even let on—and most exciting of all, he had a dream.

And though California seemed so far away from the American cities Doris had heard of—Boston, New York, and Philadelphia—it also seemed impossibly exotic. Doris was not afraid of a journey. She was only nineteen. Her whole life lay ahead of her.

"*Ja,*" she answered, taking Jacob's hand in hers. Slowly, she placed it beneath the hem of her nightgown, so that his fingers trailed lightly against her knee. She felt herself flush at the boldness of it.

Though she had been timid when they'd first wed, she had by now come to enjoy her husband's affection. It made her feel as though the matchmakers back home had been right all along, that they'd known far more about love than she did. Shivers tickled up and down her legs and torso as he touched her. Her stomach fluttered with anticipation. She had given herself up to the unknown, had trusted in the future, had allowed the ocean waves to carry her west, and into this man's life. And that trust had been rewarded.

But that night, after he had lost his hands in the tangle of her hair and gasped quietly in her ear, neither of them could sleep.

He rolled toward her. *"Du solltest dies über mich wissen."* You should know this about me.

Doris stiffened at the words. She disliked moments like this one, when she was reminded suddenly of how little she really knew about him. But especially now, when they were just on the brink of heading off into the wilderness together.

He had already used their savings to commission a wagon complete with a big canvas canopy, two pair of oxen, two sets of complicated harnesses. He'd already given the general store a list of the provisions they would need. The money had been spent. There'd be no going back.

But Jacob insisted that he could not bring her along with him until he had confessed all his sins. He sat up, pulled out a bottle of local-brewed *obstwasser* from a drawer by the bed, and began to tell her the story of Reiner, the confession tumbling out of him haltingly.

"Reiner?" She had never even heard him mention the name before.

It had happened six years earlier, almost to the day, Jacob said. He met a fellow German immigrant passing through town. The man, called Reiner, had come to Springfield to visit his nephew, whom he had not seen in a long time. Reiner knew how to make folk remedies from the old country, he'd told Jacob. He was a bit of a snake oil peddler, Jacob supposed, but he'd seen an opportunity. All Reiner needed were the ingredients . . . If Jacob helped him, Reiner promised to give him a generous cut of the profits.

It was easy, Jacob explained to her now, since his employer had trusted him with keys to all his establishments, including the apothecary.

"You stole from him," Doris said. The truth sank in her gut. This was her husband's sin—and perhaps an explanation for his unexpected wealth.

"We took very little," he assured her. "A few packets of powders and a few dozen glass bottles. Nothing that would even be missed."

"So what was the sin, then?" Doris asked.

Jacob paused and would not meet her eye. "Reiner sold the tonics to people in Springfield," he explained, "and then he disappeared. Some say he went prospecting out west. But the people who took the tonic started to get sick. One of them died. A young woman."

"Well," Doris said with a tremulous voice, "the woman had been sick to begin with, right? Maybe the illness was responsible for her death, and not the medicine."

Perhaps, Jacob agreed. Perhaps. "The woman who died . . . Her family was furious. They tried to find the peddler who'd sold her the fatal tonic, but with no luck. No one knew of my involvement, of course."

"And no one ever shall," she said, taking his hand again and squeezing it.

"Except," he said quietly. "Except that I believe—I believe there may be a connection between the woman who died and one of the families traveling west with us. I live in fear of being discovered on our journey."

"A connection?"

"George Donner may not have known the woman who died, but I am fairly certain his wife, Tamsen, did."

Doris considered the man next to her. She was disappointed, suddenly and cruelly. And the fact that they would be traveling with a family he had wronged—that seemed a bad omen, a very bad omen.

"Don't worry, Jacob," she said, though it was as much to ease herself as him. "Try to put it out of your head." But Doris herself could not do so. She had always been taught that the punishments for one's sins worked in mysterious ways. That sometimes even small misdeeds could have great, unforeseen consequences. A lie—and a person's life—hung over her husband's head like a dark, spreading shadow. It was a very bad omen indeed.

But complete faith had rewarded her so far in her short life. So she lay awake that night, looked at the stars through their little apartment window for one last time, and resolved to have faith still.

After all, what other choice was there?

AUGUST 1846

CHAPTER ELEVEN

iscuits. He was sure to want biscuits. Everybody liked biscuits.

Elitha Donner paused, her hand poised above the cold Dutch oven. How many could she take before someone would notice the missing leftovers? Two, three? Father was always blaming missing food on the hired hands—nothing but stomachs on two legs, he called them—so there was probably no need to worry. She settled on two and placed them in the center of her calico square. Next to them she put a hard-boiled egg from breakfast and ham trimmings. The ham was a bit moldy but still edible if you were hungry enough, and poor Thomas was surely hungry.

She tied the fabric into a little bundle, nice and neat. She'd have liked to give him something good to drink, too, but they'd run out of cider weeks ago. Her eye fell on the hogshead of beer. She wondered if she could carry a cup all the way to the shed where he was being kept.

Then: a burble of voices outside the door. The words were masked but she could make out the speakers by tone: Father was talking to Tamsen, Aunt Betsy trying to be the peacemaker the way she always did.

She slipped past the door to the parlor. It was funny living in someone else's house. Everyone acted as though it was normal to be sitting on the Vasquezes' furniture, using their linens and blankets, eating off their tin plates and cups. Treating everything as though it belonged to you, while the real owners were just on the other side of the fort. Elitha heard Mr. Vasquez had moved his family to one of the empty sheds. All those little kids sleeping in a chicken coop, and here they were pretending to be so grand.

It felt like they'd been at Fort Bridger for decades, though in truth it had been only a few days, not even a week. But in that time it had gone from July to August and the nights were hotter than ever. Both Donner families were packed under one roof. You were always running into someone, squeezing through doorways, sleeping four to a bed, and woke drenched in sweat. There was barely room to breathe. It was even worse than it was on the trail. At least living out of the tents you could move about as you pleased and let the dry air cool your skin in the evenings.

And then of course, there were the voices. She'd always heard them, but they had taken on more urgency in the past month, first at Fort Laramie, and now here. Not the voices of the other members of the wagon train laughing and arguing at all hours. The voices *no one else heard*. The ones that had told her to read those letters at Ash Hollow in the first place. The same ones that told her to avoid the wild man in the chicken coop, chained up like a dog—the one who'd attacked Mary Graves.

But even from afar, she heard him, too. He had a voice, just like the other invisible voices, that reached her in moments of stillness and shook her to her core.

Tender thing, the man's voice whispered in her mind, from afar. *Come here*, his voice whispered.

Though she was curious, she kept away. The others may have thought Elitha was a dummy, but she was not.

No one noticed Elitha slip out. No one ever cared what the step-daughters did—that's what she and Leanne were called, even by Father. As long as they didn't embarrass Father and Tamsen and their chores were finished, they were free to do what they pleased. They were supposed to be invisible. And Elitha had gotten very good at it.

So good she was able to slip unnoticed between wagons, in and out of the woods, even walk among the livestock left to graze at night, petting their wet noses and their sleek hides. She reckoned that she probably knew more about the other people in the wagon train than anyone else. She knew that Patrick Breen got drunk and fought with his wife nearly every night, and the widow Lavinah Murphy paid an awful lot of attention to her sons-in-law, in a way that made Elitha uncomfortable. She knew which hired hands lost the most money at cards and which went off to the woods by themselves to pray for their safety before the wagons started off in the morning.

She'd seen her stepmother clamber out of Stanton's wagon all by herself, with Father nowhere in sight.

She hadn't told Father yet about what she'd seen. He might choose not to believe her, after all, and she couldn't help but be scared of her stepmother. Besides, it didn't matter. Any half-wit could see that Mr. Stanton was in love with Mary Graves.

It was a clear night. The moonlight bathed the courtyard in blue-gray light. A crisscross of whispers tickled at her mind, and she knew they were not really whispers but *voices*. She tried to clear her mind and focus. From the buildings she heard the sound of muffled voices—real ones—the occasional stab of a voice raised in anger. Another argument, perhaps between the Eddys and the Reeds.

Quickly, she made her way to the barns, where most of the men had decamped to get out of the rain. She saw the glow of lanterns through the gaps in the boards, heard hoots of laughter. Put any two young men together and before long they'd be questioning each other's smarts, whether they'd ever been with a girl, the size of their peckers.

This, too, she had noticed and observed.

Thomas the Indian was being kept in the next building, little more than a shed, dark and lonely looking. He'd been banished there by Jim Bridger, the man who owned the fort. You'd think Mr. Bridger would be impressed after what the Indian boy had suffered, making his way back all by himself, but no, Mr. Bridger had been as mad as if he'd caught Thomas trying to burn the place down. Cuffed Thomas hard on the head a couple of times until Mr. Stanton stepped between them. The boy had looked lean, almost fragile, his long dark hair falling over his glittering eyes. But when he'd glanced up and caught her gaze, she saw that he was anything but frail. The intensity in his eyes, in the way he held his jaw firm, in the tautness of his muscles, stopped her totally, as if she were the one who'd been hit.

He made her think of a storm in summer, and though others might say it was a fool-headed thing to do, she wanted to run out into that storm, to feel its raindrops that, she somehow sensed, would fall gently against her skin.

She peeked around the corner. William and George, two of Uncle Jacob's boys, were guarding the shed. The boys were only meant to call the alarm if Thomas tried to escape, but William, twelve, and George, eight, took their jobs seriously and carried sticks and switches.

Elitha knew they'd be easy enough to get rid of: William had started to show interest in girls—even his own cousins—and George could be counted on to go wherever his brother went.

So she walked straight for them, not even bothering to conceal the calico square in her hand. "Hello," she said. "Mary Graves is taking a bath at the water trough. She's stripped down to her bloomers."

That was all it took. They were off with hardly a backward glance.

She was alone now with the boy, and her pulse thudded in her ears. She pushed the narrow barn door open and stood in the doorway while her eyes adjusted to the dark. It smelled of old hay and chicken feathers. "Hello?" The blackness remained still as the surface of a pond. "I— I brought you something to eat."

Something stirred. Slowly, she blinked, and Thomas emerged from the shadows, though he kept half hidden, staring at her in a way that was both curious and aloof. Something in Elitha's chest fluttered.

"My name is Elitha Donner." She held out the package she'd brought. "I thought you might be hungry."

He didn't move. She put the bundle down on a bale of hay and backed away. After a long frozen minute, he approached. But he didn't leap out or creep forward like some wild thing, the way she imagined he might. Instead he stepped politely toward the bundle and opened it with careful, practiced fingers. His posture was as straight as a governess's.

"I made those biscuits myself. I would've brought some honey to go with them but I couldn't think how . . ."

He had already started to eat, studiously, though his hands shook, betraying how starving he must have been. His politeness made Elitha want to squirm. Maybe one day, she thought, she'd invite him to join the family for a meal. Neither Father nor Uncle Jacob liked to skimp on food (though for the servants it was another story). Sunday dinners back at the farmhouse meant chicken stew and dumplings, buttered green beans and corn bread, fresh cold milk and cream over berries for dessert.

But she knew it was a fantasy. Tamsen had called Thomas a filthy heathen. He would never be one of them.

But looking at him now, she thought the opposite. He stopped eating and glanced up at her, his eyes two dark pools. Something flickered across them, and she felt suddenly embarrassed by the way she'd been staring at him. She was so used to watching people, to being ignored. It was unsettling now to be seen back.

Unsettling and wonderful.

She blushed at him and smiled. He gave her a slight nod. She took the tankard when he'd drained the beer—she tried not to look at the way his throat bobbed as he drank. She was pretty sure Thomas smiled, just a little, when he handed the jug to her. That was her reward.

It was enough.

That and her realization that, for a moment or two, the voices in her head had gone silent.

CHAPTER TWELVE

T hey found the note pinned beneath a small rock on the top of a boulder, fluttering like a white flag of surrender. Stanton felt something in his own chest rise and then gutter in response.

Donner read it out loud: "Way ahead rougher than expected. Do not follow us into Weber Canyon.—Lansford Hastings, Esq." The wind tugged at the paper in Donner's hand, as though a ghost were trying to snatch it away.

"What the devil does *that* mean? I thought this man knew the trail." Keseberg spat. "He named it after hisself, for crissake."

A strange mood had infected the party since Fort Bridger. It was understandable, given the bizarre incident with Bridger's prisoner and the stories told by the Paiute boy, Thomas, but still, it left Stanton uneasy. They were teetering on a knife's edge: He feared that without Hastings's help, they would soon turn on each other. Impatience crackled in the air. Everyone knew they were racing time now.

The weather would turn soon enough, even if the heat was so oppressive at the moment that they could hardly imagine it ever letting up.

Stanton's gaze skipped over the ground. "Their tracks are plain enough. Despite what he says, it should be easy enough to follow them." They led to a pass completely obscured by forest, dark and impenetrable, the trail swallowed up behind a wall of growth. Above the ranging forest was a wall of imposing white-capped mountains. The majority of the wagon party came from the plains and had never seen mountains like these. "California must lie right behind," Patrick Breen had said breathlessly, unable to imagine that the country could go on for much longer. Stanton knew that the few existent maps, sketchy as they were, said Breen was wrong. But he wasn't going to be the one to say so.

"Is that smart?" Franklin Graves asked. Everyone turned instinctively in his direction; people seemed to listen to Graves. It might've been because of his imposing size; Graves was a large man, made broad of back by long hours in the fields, building up his farm. "Not if Hastings says it's not safe. He must've had a reason for warning us off."

"We can't just sit here on our asses waiting for his permission." That was Snyder, the Graves family's teamster. Stanton noticed that Reed flinched at the sound of his voice. Odd.

Donner's eyes moved nervously from Keseberg to Eddy, to the wheel tracks in the dirt. "We have an Indian boy who knows these parts. We could keep going," he said, testing the idea before the crowd. Stanton didn't care for the look on Donner's face, like a man who had swallowed a pebble but would rather choke than cough it up and reveal his mistake. Donner had fought hard to make himself party captain, seemingly without thinking about the difficult choices that came with the position.

"I been having trouble with the axle on one of my wagons like it is," Graves said. "Can't risk it."

"We should send a couple men ahead to find Hastings and bring him back," Reed said. "He got us into this mess, he can damn well get us out of it." Reed squared his shoulders. He was sweating in the sun. Stanton didn't know why he always suited up like he was going to a courthouse. "I'd like to volunteer."

"You? What makes you think he's gonna listen to you?" Keseberg called out. "Hell, *nobody* listens to you." This got some easy laughs. Keseberg reminded Stanton of the schoolroom bullies who'd made games of plucking wings off dragonflies or crushing ants beneath their feet.

"I'll make him listen." Reed tried his best to sound confident. "Though I'd like another man to ride with me. Safety in numbers." No one needed to be reminded why.

A wind turned over dry leaves in the silence. Last night there had been poker games, drinking, storytelling, and who knew what had gone on inside the tents. Few men would want to leave such comforts to ride blind through unknown territory.

The cowards. They were only too happy to let Reed shoulder all the risk. He couldn't let Reed head out on his own with no one to watch his back. Stanton stepped forward. "I'll go." He deliberately avoided Keseberg's eyes; he knew well enough what Keseberg thought about him. "I'll ride with Reed."

LATER THAT EVENING, Stanton tethered his saddle horse at his campsite and built a fire. Then he unhitched his oxen and drove them to the meadow to graze with the other livestock, nodding to the men who had taken up watch for the night. In the distance, Franklin Graves and one of his boys drove their oxen through the meadow, and when Franklin turned and caught sight of him, the look on his face reminded Stanton of the rumors he'd caught wind of back in Fort Bridger, the unpleasant speculations whirling about him. Keseberg had given him the truth—you could count on Keseberg for the truth if it was unpleasant—that there were some in the wagon party wondering whether Stanton might not be just a little *off*, a little lonely, a little crazy, a potential danger to the others. When Bryant had warned that the Nystrom boy's murderer might be some twisted individual living among them, little did Stanton imagine that he'd be a suspect. No one had gone so far as to accuse him—no one was willing to take it that far, it seemed. But still, Stanton knew the human mind was susceptible to insidious influence, especially when people were hungry, tired, and afraid. He remembered how his neighbors had been only too willing to believe the worst about him when Lydia died . . . Had these people, the ones who knew him from Springfield, finally discovered the story of Lydia? And if they had, how long would it be before they began to turn on him?

Edwin Bryant had given him good advice and he'd ignored it. He should've made more allies when he had the chance. The other single men had made themselves useful to one household or another, finding a place at family campfires or a seat in their wagons, like sickly Luke Halloran or the old Belgian, Hardkoop. Out here, you couldn't afford to be on your own.

And then, of course, there was still the problem of Tamsen, whose thin smile cut into him with a chill whenever they passed, the unspoken power she held over him lingering in her wake long after she'd gone.

A stand of cottonwood striplings bordered the meadow, the farthest outcropping of the dark woods into which the previous wagon party had disappeared. Stanton imagined their wagons simply swallowed up, like sunlight absorbed by so many leaves. He pushed into the ragged little grove to search for enough dry wood to keep his fire going through the night.

But he had only gone a few steps when he startled: Mary Graves was moving among the trees, having clearly had the same idea, and he was so pleased and surprised to see her he almost doubted she was real. But she turned when a twig cracked under his boots. In the half dark, he couldn't read the expression on her face. But she nearly dropped the sticks in her arms.

"Miss Graves." He drew in a deep breath. "What a pleasure to run into you. I hope I didn't startle you." In truth, he was alarmed to find how often he thought about Mary Graves lately, as if all of his other thoughts were fallen leaves easily scattered.

Mary still hadn't spoken to him since her attack at Fort Bridger. But he was sure he'd caught her looking in his direction more than once.

"Only a little," she admitted now. "I'm afraid, after what happened . . ."

"I'm so glad to see you looking well," Stanton said quickly. She'd gone pale, and he hated to think he'd reminded her of the monstrous man at Fort Bridger. "I'm sorry I haven't been able to call on you." Her father had been tailing her day and night.

Her smile was tight but seemed sincere. "No need to apologize. I understand."

"Are you feeling better?" He wondered about the wound on her shoulder. It had been slight, but the man who'd attacked her had been filthy; it would be so easy for the wound to become infected and to fester.

"Yes, thank you. It was nothing, a graze. Once my mother saw that horrible man's condition, she made me bathe in vinegar and soda ash! I feel as though I've been scrubbed raw." She laughed, running her hands over her arms self-consciously. "Actually, I'm glad to see you, Mr. Stanton. I'm the one who should be apologizing. I would've come earlier, but my father . . ." She stopped, blinking, and a sour taste rose in Stanton's throat. So it was as he suspected. "Thank you for what you did that day, rushing to my rescue like that. It was very brave of you."

"It was nothing." He had spent days thinking about her eyes and now he could barely meet them. "I felt almost sorry for him. There was something about the way Bridger handled him, the way he talked about him, that made me think of an animal in a zoo. It made me think . . ." His blood pulsed a little faster. He remembered the night Lydia's father, drunk on whiskey, had joked about looking through the keyhole of his daughter's bedroom to watch her undress. Stanton didn't know why the association had come to him now. Maybe only that he sensed Bridger liked the power he had over his prisoner, liked to watch him chained up in that dark room, going slowly insane.

The thought was so vile and so strong that he was momentarily afraid that he could transmit them to her, like a kind of contagion.

"What is it?" Mary asked. "What's wrong?"

Before he could make up an excuse, he heard a shout. They turned to see Franklin Graves crashing through the brush. He looked first at Stanton but then turned to his daughter. "I told you I didn't want you talking to him."

Although her father towered over her, Mary didn't flinch. "And I told you he's done nothing wrong," she said evenly. "Besides, I meant to thank him for saving me. He did save me, as you recall."

Graves's face was dark with anger. "Believe me, Mary, this man is no one's savior. Now take that firewood to your mother, she's waiting on you. Go on," he added, and raised a hand as if he might hit her. Instead he pulled her roughly in the direction of the wagon train. "Get."

Stanton felt his anger rushing down to some deep, sharp point, as if it were flowing down the blade of a knife. Another father who hated him, resented him—and maybe even envied him. "I don't know what I've done to give you cause to dislike me—"

Graves didn't let him finish. "I don't ever want to catch you talking to my daughter, do you hear me? I know all about you. I know what you did in Massachusetts."

Massachusetts. A word like the first hiss of flame, ready to flare up and consume him at any moment.

At least Mary was too far off now to hear it.

Graves smiled narrowly. "I see you know what I'm talking about. You can't lie your way out of it, not with me. George Donner knew that girl's father, you see. That girl you got pregnant and deserted. He told me you ran off in shame after she killed herself."

Stanton felt as though he'd been hit. This was the moment he'd been dreading and, perhaps, waiting for since they all left Springfield. Sometimes he wondered if the rumors would follow him to the ends of the world. Maybe he would always have to carry them along, like a shadow. A horrible twisted lie that was his burden to bear to the end of his days.

It was his fault, after all. He'd known that Donner and Knox were associates. It was how he'd ended up here in the first place, caught in an endless spiral that seemed determined to keep his past alive. It was just that he hadn't expected George Donner to tell anyone about Lydia. And, of course, Donner didn't know the whole story; he only knew what Knox had told him, which was, of course, the whole problem.

Emboldened by Stanton's silence, Graves took a step closer. Stanton could smell his breath: close and wet and rotten. "How old was that girl, anyway, when you got her that way?"

He wanted to throw a punch at Graves but somehow managed to stop himself. He couldn't speak. The words swelled in his throat to close it, until he felt as if he might choke—long ago, when he made his promise to Lydia, he had gotten into the habit of swallowing the truth. He hadn't said anything when it had happened, hadn't let himself be moved by the vicious things his Massachusetts neighbors said about him.

"So you won't even try to deny it?" For a split second, Graves looked almost disappointed, as if he'd been angling for a fight. "I don't want you near Mary. She's not going to throw herself away on a no-account like you. If I ever see you talking to her again, I'll tell her what I know about you."

So he hadn't told Mary already. One small mercy.

And in this world, Stanton thought, that was increasingly the only kind of mercy to be found.

THE TRAIL HASTINGS HAD BLAZED was ugly, barely wide enough for a single wagon. As he and Reed followed it past a landscape of felled trees and jagged stumps, Stanton fell into the rhythmic sway of his horse's back and tried to keep his mind from swinging back to Mary, to the fight with Franklin Graves, and to the memories he'd resurrected of Lydia. Maybe, after all, Graves was right about him. He was hardly an ideal suitor. He doubted he knew the first thing about pleasing a young woman. After Lydia, it seemed he couldn't keep away from new widows and unhappy wives. He wasn't sure if he'd ever be able to stop himself, as if the need to bury his misery in them over and over again was the only way for him to survive.

And besides, he certainly couldn't provide Mary with the kind of wealth and prospects her father was apparently seeking.

He recalled Lavinah Murphy teasing him at the picnic about taking a wife. *Don't you get tired of being alone, Mr. Stanton?*

She had no idea. The aloneness ate a hole through him. Sometimes he worried that the loneliness had taken everything, that there was nothing left of him at all on the inside.

They stopped the first night to make camp as the sun was sinking behind the hills. Stanton was surprised when Reed came back with a rabbit. It was scrawny and small but it was meat. "Where'd you find that?" he asked, impressed that Reed was able to catch anything, let alone manage to do it so quickly, when they'd seen so little game since Fort Laramie. Even in the thick cover of the woods, there was little birdsong. It was as if the lush growth were a painted setpiece, a convincing impression of life built out of sawdust and paint.

Reed smiled faintly as he flayed it, jerking the skin off the carcass in a couple of tugs. "Lucky, I guess. Found a spring down by those boulders, too. I'll get water for the horses once I get this rabbit over the fire."

Stanton had been wary of heading out with Reed, whom he suspected of having his own reasons for wanting to take a break from the party: Stanton knew a man with a secret when he saw one. But now that they were away from the fray, Stanton relaxed a bit.

The two men caught up with Hastings's wagon party the next day, following their meandering trail through the trees. It looked to have been charted by a drunk, spur after spur ending abruptly at a cliff. Standing at the edge, Stanton could see the canyon far below them, which promised a way through the mountains. But there was no apparent path down to reach it.

They rode up on the wagon party halted dead in the woods. The scene was of frenetic work, the men either swinging axes to clear a path or using the oxen to haul the felled trees out of the way. The wagons remained in a line backed down the trail, bottled up in place. Oddly, there were few women and no children about: no campfires burning, no cooking or clothes washing taking place. A couple of men stood lookout, too, perched high on rock outcroppings, rifles nestled in the crook of their arms. Maybe, Stanton thought, they'd had trouble with Indians along the way.

A big, red-faced man, stripped to the waist, lowered his ax in midswing when Stanton and Reed rode into the clearing. Stanton didn't like the way the men on lookout notched their rifles into their shoulders.

"We're looking for Lansford Hastings," Stanton called out, when they were still far enough away to make for a difficult target. "Is he with you?"

The men exchanged wary looks and didn't answer.

Reed spoke to fill the silence. "Our wagon party is a couple days back. We took the cutoff, just like you, but all we found was a note from Hastings, warning us not to follow."

One of the men laughed darkly. "Then he done you a courtesy, friend. Count yourself lucky and turn around."

"We have nearly a hundred people waiting back at the trailhead," Stanton said. "We need him to guide us."

"Look." The red-faced man hefted his ax. "He ain't good for much, but we need him to get us out of this goddamned forest. We ain't about to let you have him."

It was a strange thing to say. Stanton and Reed exchanged a look.

"We only want to talk to him, that's all," Reed said. Finally, the men gestured for them to come forward, and the sentries lowered their rifles. They walked single file between the long string of wagons. Stanton peered through gaps in the canvas and saw small fright-

ened faces, children huddled together, silently eyeing him in return.
Something had happened. That was clear.

"So, why the sentry?" Reed asked, his voice friendly. "Have you had
trouble with Indians?"

The red-faced man wiped his brow with a bandana. "We got trouble, but it ain't been Indians. We got an animal tracking us, maybe
more than one. Been on our tail ever since we left Fort Bridger."

"Surely you don't have to worry they'll attack in broad daylight?"
Stanton asked. But almost immediately he realized that the tree canopy was so thick it could've been dusk.

"Mostly they been picking off our livestock at night, and we can't
afford to lose any," the man said. "But now some of the dogs have gone
missing, too. Maybe they run off, hard to know."

Stanton was uneasy. He scanned the trees pressing close on either
side of them.

Reed cleared his throat. "You said Hastings wasn't worth much—
what did you mean by that?"

"He's lost his nerve, is all," said the man with the ax. "You'll see for
yourself." He jerked his chin toward a wagon set a way back from
the others. The canvas opening had been laced together with leather
strips. It looked as if Hastings had sewn himself inside. Stanton had
never seen anything like it. He gave Reed a questioning look, but Reed
just shrugged. It was clear their escorts didn't intend to go any farther.
The man planted the ax between his feet and leaned on the handle,
looking faintly amused.

Stanton went forward, wishing he could shake the feeling that they
were being watched—not just by the other men, but by the forest itself.

"Lansford Hastings?" Stanton climbed over the toe board. A scuf-
fling noise came from inside the wagon. "Don't shoot. My friend and
I have come to speak with you. We just want a few minutes of your

time." There was no reply, but no further noises, either, which Stanton decided to take as a sign of acquiescence. He had to unlace the leather strips to climb under the opening in the canopy. Reed followed him.

The first thing Stanton noticed was that it smelled smoky but not of wood smoke. It was as though Hastings had been burning herbs or flowers, and the smell recalled Tamsen sharply to him, the smell of her hair on his fingers, the way her skin tasted. Hanging from wooden pegs were dozens of Indian charms made of feathers, twigs, and string. The wagon looked as though it had been ransacked, the floor a hodge-podge of barrels and chests and hogsheads. As his eyes got used to the dark, Stanton saw a bulky figure cowering at their approach, crouched behind a leather-strapped trunk. A rifle barrel glinted in the dim light.

Under different circumstances, at a different time, Lansford Hastings might have been handsome; he had a square jaw, a strong brow, and dark, sharp eyes. Now his face was powdered with trail dust. His hair was roped in dirty strands.

Stanton came forward cautiously, all too aware of the rifle pointed at him. "Lansford Hastings? We represent another wagon party. We saw your handbill and expected you would be at Fort Bridger to lead us down the cutoff. But when we reached the trailhead we found your note."

At this, Hastings's eyes came to life and settled on Stanton. "Why didn't you listen? You shouldn't have come."

"Look here, Hastings, we came all this way after reading your book," Reed spoke up suddenly, ignoring the look Stanton gave him. "I don't mind telling you that it was quite a shock to get to Fort Bridger only to find you'd gone. And that note. I suspect you're nothing but a charlatan," Reed said. "How could you write those things in your book if the route—"

"It isn't the route that's the problem," Hastings said shortly. "The cutoff is a difficult passage, but it can be done. I've done it." He shook his head. "It's something else entirely. There's something following us."

The charms tacked to the walls stirred faintly, as if a phantom hand had passed along them.

Stanton frowned. "We know. The men told us. Animals—"

"They *don't* know." Now that Hastings was standing, Stanton could smell him; he smelled like something sick and terrified, a wounded animal. "It's not an animal, at least, not any kind of animal I've ever seen." His voice kept skipping into a higher register. "There's no game in these woods—have you noticed? That's because there's nothing left. Nothing. Something's out there eating every living thing."

"A pack of wolves," Reed said. But he sounded uneasy. "That's what we've heard, as far back as Fort Laramie."

"No," Hastings insisted. "I know wolves. I know how they hunt. This is different. The Indians know it, too." Hastings let out a laugh that sounded as if he were choking. "They took a boy, no more than twelve, I swear, and left him tied to a tree out in the woods back over the ridge. They just rode off and left him there. Left him for whatever's out there, feeding. I can still hear him screaming."

Stanton had heard of men unhinged by the wilderness, by too many years fighting the dark encroachment of the natural world. He wondered whether Hastings had simply come undone. But despite his filth and the way his hands trembled, Hastings didn't seem crazy.

Terrified, yes. Crazy, no.

"Right after we left Fort Bridger, a little girl went missing," Hastings said. Now his voice had dropped again, to almost a whisper. "Every man in the party went out to search for her to no avail. And then a couple miles into the woods, we found her body, ripped to pieces, nothing left but the skeleton."

Stanton thought of the Nystrom boy, and the horrible mess of his body. The face turned sideways, as though he'd just lain in the dirt to rest. This girl had been found miles *ahead* of the wagon train, the same way they'd found Nystrom. The hairs on the back of Stanton's neck lifted. The charms stirred again in the stillness. He was sweating. Being surrounded by Hastings's trinkets agitated him, reminding him of Tamsen. *This junk can't protect you; nothing could protect them.* He didn't know where the thought had come from. But it was true.

"You need to tell your wagon party to turn around. Head for Fort Hall and the northern route as fast as you can. These men won't let me go or I'd beg you to take me with you. Save yourselves."

Reed didn't speak until he and Stanton were well away from the stranded wagon party. "The devil take Lansford Hastings. I'll never trust another lawyer for as long as I live." Reed spit on the ground. "Has the man lost his mind, do you think?"

"No," Stanton said slowly. "No, I don't think so."

Reed stared at him. "So you believe this story of monsters in the woods?"

"I don't believe in monsters," Stanton said. "Only men who behave like them."

CHAPTER THIRTEEN

hree days after the conversation with Hastings, they came across the remains of the boy he'd told them about—the twelve-year-old Indian, tied to a tree.

Reed's hands were raw and so was his patience. It had been a bad passage. He and Stanton had returned to the group and, despite the warnings they conveyed, the group had decided nevertheless to continue on the trail. Patrick Breen and Franklin Graves didn't like the trail from the start and complained to anyone who would listen, and soon enough Wolfinger and Spitzer and then the rest of the Germans took up the refrain. Reed suspected it was in part because they simply didn't like the idea of him as captain.

But he'd had little choice but to step up. The news about Lansford Hastings blew all the bluster straight out of George Donner. He had simply looked blankly from Reed to Stanton when they told him, as if he hadn't understood.

"We've made a terrible mistake," Reed had said bluntly. "We were depending on that man and he's deserted us. He lied to us. We'll die out here . . ."

But Donner only shook his head. "I don't know the way to the Humboldt River from here, none of us does. Perhaps we should turn around. We could take the northern route . . ."

"There's no time for that," Reed said. "If we try to take the northern route at this late date, we'd need to winter over at Fort Hall." It would be ruinous for most families. Few had the money to sustain them over the season, not with the high prices the trading posts commanded. A dollar fifty for a pound of flour, and a family could easily eat a pound of flour in a day. Half the families would starve before spring.

Donner had turned away from them, sweating and trembling, refusing to decide. And since then, Donner hadn't spoken a word to anyone outside his family. Reed was convinced that Donner's breakdown was only temporary and got Stanton to agree to keep mum. Jacob Donner, his brother, had agreed to keep him out of sight, and the story going through the wagon train was that he'd fallen ill.

So Reed took charge of the route. Within a day, the forest choked up around them the same as it had done to Hastings's group, and then the ground broke uphill sharply. On the morning of his second day as captain, one of Reed's oxen had come up lame, setting his temper on edge. He ended up being a little too terse with Keseberg, the wrong man to provoke, and they fell into a shouting match that ended when Keseberg drew a knife and had to be pulled away by the arm.

The atmosphere up and down the line quickly turned tense and jumpy. Reed sent brothers-in-law William Foster and William Pike ahead to scout the way and got everyone else started chopping down trees, terrified in his heart that they would end up trapped in the forest like the other party. Reed suggested that everyone start pooling and rationing their food stocks, but he was quickly shouted down, and some men threatened to string him up if he ever raised the idea again.

A small hunting party went out after the wagon train had halted for the night, making the best of the last hour of light left before it would be too dangerous to hunt. Fresh meat was in short supply and no one was willing to slaughter any livestock, so every able-bodied man in the party with a rifle—and even some less-than-able-bodied ones, such as Luke Halloran—ventured out to look for game.

Reed trailed a small group, behind Milt Elliott and John Snyder in the lead. His rifle weighed heavily, his arms aching from swinging an ax all day. He was still puzzling over what Snyder had told him last night—what he'd followed Reed into the woods to tell him.

You know what your trouble is, Reed? You don't understand them people at all.

Only sheep will follow you meek like. The rest of them don't think they need your help.

They're not going to listen to you unless you make them.

Snyder was a twenty-five-year-old drifter who'd never done anything more difficult than bully and whip livestock. Reed had built a furniture business from nothing, led a company of men against Sauk and Kickapoo Indians in the Black Hawk War.

And yet Snyder was right—Reed didn't understand people. The light was nearly gone and the whole time they'd seen nothing, not so much as a prairie squirrel or a single quail, but no one dared say anything out loud for fear it might further jinx them. Reed listened apprehensively to the idle chitchat of the men ahead, worried that Snyder's exchange with Elliott was getting increasingly risky. Snyder knew Reed could hear what was being said and liked to bait him; it was the bully in him. Had he been trying to warn Reed last night?

There's two kinds of men. Sheep and the men that bleed 'em. Don't forget which one I am.

If there was one thing Snyder knew, it was how to make people do what he wanted. All it took was a look from those hooded eyes, a flex of one of his hands.

If Reed could go back in time, he never would've started up with him. He'd been reckless. But he'd been unable to get the feeling of Snyder's hands out of his mind, and the thought of them—big and rough and powerful—had gone somehow from one of dread to one of intense need.

It was stupid. Worse than stupid—deadly.

Say the wrong word to the wrong man and you could find yourself in a jail cell waiting for the circuit judge. Reed had heard such a tale from Edward McGee. You had to be ready to act on offers when they occurred.

Snyder's voice suddenly broke out angrily. "For crissakes," he shouted, then let loose a string of cusswords. Halloran's little dog yipped. Reed picked up his pace. Maybe they'd found game.

What Reed saw as he rounded the turn made his stomach lurch. Hanging between two trees were the remains of a corpse: wrists caught tight with rope, shoulders stretched spread-eagle, head lolling on the neck, but below that—nearly nothing. The spinal column ended abruptly in midair, its vertebrae suspended like beads on a string. Nearly all the flesh had been stripped away from the bone. On the ground: long leg bones, cracked pieces of rib. The spot beneath the body was churned into a frenzy and black with old blood.

"What in the blue blazes is this?" Milt Elliott asked, and nearly tripped over Halloran's little terrier as it sniffed at the bones.

Reed couldn't stop looking at the head, worried to a bloody mess by insects. Something—birds?—had gotten to the eyes. It had to have been a monstrous death, though whether it was worse than starving or dying of thirst high in the mountains, he couldn't guess. He had to speak up before Snyder and Elliott and Halloran brought the news back to the wagon train and all hell broke loose. "We heard about this from Hastings," he said. "The Indians did it. A ceremony of some kind."

"A ceremony?" Snyder growled. He took out his big hunting knife and sawed at one of the ropes until it gave. The corpse swung to the left, so that one hand trailed on the ground. "What kind of fucked-up ceremony is this?"

Reed said nothing. He and Stanton had agreed they wouldn't tell the rest of the party of Hastings's fears. *Something's stalking the wagon train.* It would only spook them worse. Snyder didn't seem to expect an answer, however; like many, he feared the Indians and didn't try and make sense of anything they did.

"Don't it look kinda like that kid we found on the plain, before we got to Fort Laramie?" Snyder asked. He kicked at Halloran's terrier when the dog began to chew at a wrist bone. "Quit that! That ain't right. You can't have a dog eating human flesh. He'll develop a taste for it."

"Quincy, come here." Halloran looked green. Consumption had whittled him down to his bones. It would be a miracle if he made it another month.

Snyder reached down to pull the bone away from Halloran's dog. Suddenly, the dog leapt up and bit him. Red welled to the spot immediately.

"Stupid dog." Snyder brought the wound reflexively to his mouth. He swung a boot at the dog but missed and the terrier lunged for his boot again. Without warning, Snyder leveled his rifle at the dog and squeezed off a bullet, catching the dog in the stomach. The sound the dog made when it was struck was the eeriest thing Reed had ever heard, a high twisted note of surprise and pain that was almost human.

Halloran was a timid man—a sheep, in Snyder's terms—and wasted by illness, but anger propelled him toward Snyder. His hands found the big man's shirt front, but Snyder pushed him back easily. "What the hell? What the hell did you do that for?" He looked to the others for support, but Reed averted his eyes. No one was going to challenge Snyder, least of all Reed. He knew how Snyder could get, knew the power in those hands, and had the bruises to show for it.

"That mutt bit me," Snyder said. "I got my rights. If a dog bites me, I shoot him."

"He barely broke the skin," Halloran said. Blood dribbled down his chin from the last bout of coughing. "Maybe I should shoot *you*."

Snyder's open-handed slap caught Halloran on the side of his face and sent him sprawling in the dirt. Reed flinched. Snyder only laughed.

"Quit crying," he said. "It'll only land you in trouble."

What else had Snyder said to him last night? *You think you know how the world works, but you don't know shit. Men like you make me angry. You're so fucking stupid that you don't even know how stupid you are.*

Halloran rolled off his back onto his hands and knees, his whole body buckling under the force of his coughing fit. Ribbons of bloody phlegm hung from his mouth. Reed was disgusted, and sick with himself, too; he should have stood up for Halloran, but he was too afraid.

Snyder and Elliott started back the way they'd come. Reed stood there, watching Halloran pawing through the dirt to his dog's side. "Come on, Luke. Leave him." It was almost dark, and Reed had no desire to fall too far behind the others.

Halloran didn't even lift his head. "We got to bury him. I can't just leave him here. Would you help me? Will you at least do that?"

Reed's disgust twisted into anger. The ground was hard as rock and they had no shovel. Did Halloran expect they would dig with their hands? And there was tomorrow to think about, another day of backbreaking work clearing a trail, and who knew how many such days they had in front of them?

"Leave the damn dog." Reed shouldered his rifle. "Or you can stay out here by yourself in the dark, see whether there really is something following us." He was relieved when Halloran got to his feet, and felt a heady rush of guilt, too, which brought the taste of sick to the back of his mouth.

All the way back to camp, he pretended not to hear Halloran crying.

CHAPTER FOURTEEN

veryone said it was a miracle. It was God's grace, and proof that they had not been abandoned.

Tamsen didn't blame them; grace was in short supply, like everything was. And how else could you explain, really, what had happened to Halloran? If she had really been a witch, as everyone said, she might have had an answer. Signs, augurs, charms to keep away the devil, ways of reading the future in the drift of the clouds: There was no power in what she practiced, only attention—increasingly, of the unwanted variety.

But some power had touched Halloran, and healed him.

For a week, ever since his little dog got shot, he had barely been able to lift his head. It was a shame about the dog, but Halloran had let himself get too attached to it. He'd even let the dog nip and bite him for fun, like a parent that doesn't know how to discipline his children.

Halloran was coughing up blood regularly now, though he tried to hide it, and would struggle for breath for hours at a time.

Tamsen had tended to him, even taking him into their wagon since he was too weak even to stay on a horse. She didn't know why she felt sorry for him; maybe only because he was an outsider, and lonely, and despised, as she was. She'd spoon-fed him broth brewed from mushrooms scavenged by her girls, the only thing he could keep down. She'd made sure from the time the girls were little they knew the difference between a lacy yellow chanterelle and the deadly parasol, and they knew to try nothing before bringing it back first for her approval. (She gathered the poisonous mushrooms herself, when she needed them; she had a good handful of the deadly parasols, carefully cleaned and dried, waiting to be mixed with her homemade laudanum—all of her supplies hidden and stashed away, kept secret from the wagon party.)

Why Halloran had tried to make the trip west, Tamsen couldn't guess. Halloran hadn't let on how sick he'd been at the outset, knowing that he wouldn't be allowed to join, especially as a man with no wagon or oxen, traveling alone, no family members to take care of him. Then again, no one had imagined the journey would be this difficult. Tamsen didn't know if they were suffering bad luck especially or if everyone who'd made the trip before them had lied: lied in the newspapers, lied in their books like Lansford Hastings (vile, vile man, and mad, too, as it turned out; another reason to resent her husband, who had believed every word Hastings had written). Lured out west to die in the wilderness.

But then: Halloran's breathing eased, the sweats dried up. By the end of the first day of his recovery, he could walk around without help, though not for too long. His coughing went away. The next night he fiddled for over an hour after supper. Previously, on his good days, everyone loved to hear him fiddle. People would crowd around and for a few moments, everyone would forget their grudges and disagreements. No one fought, no one bickered. Most people preferred lively tunes, jigs and reels, something they could dance to, but Tamsen liked the sad songs; melancholy was better suited to the land around them.

But that night he played a reel so fast that his bow was a blur and dancers dropped to the ground, exhausted trying to keep up.

"If this goes on, I'll be able to move my things out of your wagon and go back to my mule," Halloran said. "I won't have to be a burden on your family no more."

"But don't rush things," Tamsen said. She was happy for his health—of course she was. But frightened, too, for reasons she couldn't say. It was as if he had not just gotten his life back but a new life altogether; he was more talkative, feverishly happy, newly optimistic. "You want to make sure that you're good and strong first."

The truth was, too, she'd gotten used to having Halloran around, either in the wagon, tucked in behind the backboard, or propped up with quilts near the campfire at night, keeping an eye on the cooking. George had thought she'd lost her mind when she had insisted they make a place for him in their wagon, but Halloran turned out to be uncommonly easy to care for. He was effusively grateful for every kindness, played with the little ones for as long as his strength would allow, and, when his energy was spent, would listen to Tamsen talk about her early days as a schoolteacher in the Carolinas. Those hadn't been her happiest days—she had been a young childless widow, trying to make her own way—but so different from her life with George that she sometimes marveled that it had happened at all.

At twenty-five, he reminded her, a little, of her Jory. He'd always been a kind of compass for her. She hadn't seen her brother in years now, though, and sometimes she thought her mind made any sort of excuse to look for him in others.

There were even times when Halloran felt like the most courteous of lovers, with a shy smile and gentle ways, though she supposed she was imagining this, too.

His hands were beautiful and graceful—fiddling to thank for that, she supposed. Sometimes, sometimes, she imagined what it would feel like to have those hands on her body.

Did she seek them out or did they find her, these dark brooding men with their secrets? They never stayed, but their effect on her remained, leaving a need for more, like certain addictive herbs that can cause trembling and dizziness when a dose is removed too quickly.

And Halloran's sweetness only seemed to stir up that addiction, served to rejuvenate her hatred of George, the way the gaze of her own husband left her feeling itchy and stuck. She had the familiar urge to do something rash, to lash out, to free herself.

Almost as soon as he was better, however, Halloran removed his things from the Donners' wagon. Of course there was talk about his miraculous recovery. She should have known there would be. That Tamsen had witched him, that she had cast a spell on him. Betsy Donner reported it all, pretending to be shy about it, while obviously relishing the opportunity to lord it over Tamsen.

Tamsen, however, had been called far worse before.

Few people survived consumption when it had gotten as bad as it had with Halloran. Yet he was often the first to step out at the call to chain up and the last to bed down in the evening. He fetched water and firewood for his neighbors after he'd taken care of his own needs, as though he had energy to burn.

Tamsen should have been happy, but she was afraid.

Halloran was different. She couldn't say how, but she knew that he was.

One morning, he started bundling his things for the pack mule, intent of being back to his own, and when she advised him to wait another day or two, he told her brusquely that he knew what he was doing. Halloran had never snapped at her before, no matter how badly he'd felt. She was so surprised that she said nothing to him the rest of the day, only watched as he buzzed about madly, like an insect caught in glass, hitting hard for an exit.

Since then, it had only gotten worse. Halloran argued with one of the Reeds' teamsters when he took his mule through a narrow pass before the Reeds' big wagon, insisting that the oversized vehicle was going to get stuck in the soft ground (he was right, however; they had double-teamed the oxen and managed to pull it out).

Worst of all, the next evening, he had smashed his fiddle against a rock when someone asked if he wouldn't give them a tune after supper. He was sick to death, he said, of being pestered to play for them.

Everyone was shocked into a long silence, but Tamsen had, unaccountably, felt tears burn her eyes. Luke Halloran loved that fiddle like a child. Again the idea came to her that this was not Halloran, that Halloran had died and this was somebody else.

But that was insane, obviously. Far more likely that the weeks of illness had changed him in some way. Or perhaps he'd always been this way, and the illness had obscured it.

When she had imagined the journey, she had imagined hardship, and hunger, and dirt that clung everywhere, like another skin, and could never be sloughed off. But she hadn't imagined this—the people, that she would be surrounded by so many other people, unable to escape their strange, inexplicable prejudices and their sudden, violent changes of mood.

They'd been walking in the shadow of the Wasatch Mountain range for a week and it was hot, even after dark. Tamsen wanted a bath; she wanted to feel clean, even if she knew that by morning she would be crusty with dirt again.

She waited until the rest of the family had settled by the tents so she might have a bit of privacy. Jacob read aloud for the children; George puffed on his pipe, eyes closed, as he had sat in his favorite chair so many nights at home. But now, sitting in the dirt beneath a bowl of unfriendly sky, the ritual seemed incongruous, almost desperate. As if he might, with his eyes closed, be trying to think himself back home, or all the way to California.

With one of the wagons between her and the rest of the family, she filled their largest pot with water and set it to heat over the dying embers. Sounds from the rest of the wagon party carried lightly on the wind, but they were far away. The Donners were not pariahs, exactly, but they had fallen from their rank as the most prominent and influential of the families in the party. And whatever the others thought of her, Tamsen knew only one thing would make her feel better: a bath. She laid aside her blouse and skirt and stockings, stripping down to corset and petticoat.

Using a washcloth dipped in the warm water, she wiped herself with long wet strokes. Around her throat, the back of her neck. Lifting the petticoat to address each of her long legs in turn. It was a miracle what a wet rag could do. She nearly cried with relief as the breeze touched her thighs and calves. She had just started to loosen her corset when she froze. Something had changed.

Something had *moved*.

The hairs on the back of her neck stood up. She couldn't have said whether it was a sound that alerted her, or a shift in the darkness, but she knew: Someone was watching her.

Her eyes went to the bushes, to the dark ragged shadow of the trees. Nothing.

She relaxed. The stories of prowling monsters, of wolves the size of horses, were infecting her as well. She went for her corset again, her fingers slick and clumsy with the laces. It was so quiet. Surely Jacob hadn't stopped reading already. Surely the others hadn't gone to bed.

Surely she was not alone. The sun had only set an hour ago and people were up and about, driving their livestock out to the meadow, cleaning up after dinner.

She got the laces unknotted. She opened her corset to expose her breasts, but this time the wind carried a bite, and she shivered. And then she saw it—a silhouette moving through the shadow of the trees, moving quickly, moving *upright*.

With one hand she reached instinctively for her blouse, anything to cover herself. But with the other hand she snatched the lantern and lifted it high, so the light bounced off the trees and made a lattice of the leaves above them. He ran off almost at once but not before the light seized him, his face pale and narrow and *hungry*.

Halloran. Watching her.

Before she could shout, he was gone.

She dressed with shaking hands. That look—it wasn't desire, but something deeper, something raw and animal. She tried to think where she had last seen her girls, her innocent trusting girls who had come to love and trust Luke Halloran. Leanne had been sitting with the little ones, sucking on rock candy while listening to Jacob. Had Elitha been among them?

She hurried back to the campfire, startling the others from Jacob's reading. George blinked at her as if he couldn't imagine where she'd come from.

"Have a nice bath?" he asked.

She didn't answer. Elitha wasn't with the others.

She knew it was silliness. Paranoia. Elitha had probably lost track of time. She was probably wandering in her usual dreamy way, looking for tadpoles in the creek or climbing trees to find abandoned birds' nests. One time, not long ago, Tamsen had caught her whispering to herself, and when Tamsen had asked what she was playing at, Elitha had gone white-faced and angry. *It's not playing*, she'd said. The girl would have to be broken of these habits, for her own good.

Still, she didn't want Elitha wandering tonight.

Tamsen plunged into a thicket by the creek first. It was just the kind of place Elitha would like, a wild tangle of cattails and sedge, the air sweet with birdsong. "Elitha Donner! Are you out here?" There was no reply. It was quiet as church. Too quiet, everyone said, and Tamsen agreed. It was as if everything living had fled, even the birds. "Elitha, you answer me this minute."

Something rustled in the rushes. Tamsen's heart knocked hard against her ribs.

"Elitha?" This time, she couldn't keep the fear from her voice.

"Just me, I'm afraid." It was only Mary Graves, loping into view on her stalklike legs. "Has Elitha gone missing?"

"Not missing," Tamsen said sharply. Though she had been thinking in just those terms, she resented Mary for using the words. "Just out for a walk, I'm sure."

The two women stared at each other. It was the first time that Tamsen had ever really gotten a look at Mary. She might have been attractive, but her jaw seemed a bit too square, and her eyes were certainly too large for her face. Though only a few years younger than Tamsen, she was probably a virgin.

Maybe that was what appealed to Stanton; Tamsen hadn't missed the way his attentions had moved on. Maybe he wanted an inexperienced woman who'd be easy to impress. It was funny how men would have a fling with an experienced woman—a whore, in their eyes— but settle down with someone who would submit to them, like calves under a yoke.

"I didn't mean to startle you," Mary said. "I saw you headed this way. I've—I've been meaning to speak to you in private."

"I don't have the time right now." She offered no explanation. Mary Graves didn't deserve one.

When she tried to pass, however, Mary stepped in front of her. "Please. It will only take a minute," she said. She looked as if she might put a hand on Tamsen's arm and then thought better of it. "I only wanted to know why you've taken a dislike to me."

For a moment, Tamsen was speechless. She almost—almost—felt sorry for the girl. Mary looked baffled, like a child who has watched an apple fall up instead of down. At the same time, she felt a rush of hard anger: Mary believed that Tamsen owed her an answer. An answer that a less naïve girl would've figured out in an instant.

If Tamsen had been in a different mood, she might have laughed. She might even have explained the way things were. Charles Stanton had chosen Mary, but that did not mean everyone else had to love her, too. Mary had stolen Stanton away from her without even trying. It wasn't even clear that she wanted him.

Tamsen had every right to hate her.

Of course, she could say none of it. She lifted the hem of her skirt and clambered over the high tufts of grass, cutting around Mary Graves. "I don't know what you mean," she said lightly. "And I'm sure we both have more important things to worry about."

Mary didn't let up. She started after her and immediately caught Tamsen, easily matching her stride. "You don't like me," she insisted. "I can tell from the way you avoid me. I only want to know why." She bit her lip. "Does it—does it have to do with Mr. Stanton?"

Tamsen couldn't help but flinch at the sound of his name in Mary's mouth. "What does Mr. Stanton have to do with it?" she asked, and heard her voice sound cold and thin, as if filtered through a layer of thick ice.

Mary hesitated. For a second, Tamsen thought she wouldn't be brave enough to say it. But finally she cleared her throat. "I heard stories," she said simply.

Stories. Another word for wrongheaded lies, like the ones told about her in North Carolina, before she moved to Springfield.

If you're so sure that I'm a witch, Tamsen had responded to the preacher's wife who had hectored her so mercilessly all those years ago, *do you think it wise to taunt me?* It had given her a stupid, momentary pleasure to see the fear curdle on the woman's face. That was the problem with women like Peggy Breen and Eleanor Eddy: They were afraid, always afraid, always of the wrong things.

Now, the temptation to tell Mary the truth was almost overwhelming. She could tell her things about Stanton that she wouldn't expect, set her straight. He was strong and smart, yes, but careless with feelings, his own and other people's. He was made to be a loner; he was made to let people in only halfway.

You don't want to lose your heart to that kind of man, virgin.

But Tamsen knew that Mary's unhappiness would come to her,

whether Tamsen told her how to see it or not. There was a small, mean part of her that was even glad.

"You shouldn't listen to stories," she said only.

Before Mary Graves could respond, someone shouted Tamsen's name.

Tamsen turned, mistaking the voice at first for George's. But it was Halloran. He stumbled through the brush holding his stomach. Hunched, he looked like he had been shot.

All his new strength, energy, and health had vanished; she was shocked by the sight of him, shocked and horrified. He was obviously dying. His eyes bulged in his head. His lips, pulled back in a grimace, exposed inflamed gums and rotting teeth. Tendons stood out on his neck, hands, and arms.

"Mrs. Donner," he said again, reaching out for her. Unconsciously, she stepped back, though they were still separated by a narrow creek. He stumbled on the uneven ground and landed on his knees in the water. But rather than stand, he began to crawl. "Help. Please help."

She forgot in that instant the man she'd seen watching her from the trees, and responded instead to the man she had nursed by her own campfire. She splashed into the creek, ashamed of her first impulse to get away from him, scooping water in her two hands, bringing it to his mouth.

"Go find help," she told Mary. "We need someone to carry him." To Mary's credit, she didn't shriek or argue or faint. She turned and ran in the direction of the wagon train.

He refused to drink. He moaned in agony and seemed not to hear her when she begged him to open his eyes. This close to him, she nearly gagged; the smell of him was already that of a corpse.

As soon as Mary was out of view, however, Halloran opened his eyes. He grabbed Tamsen's wrist with unexpected strength. "Mrs.

Donner—Tamsen," he said, pulling her close to his face, so close that she felt his breath on her cheek. "You're still my friend, aren't you? You were so kind to me, the only one to help me when I got sick . . ."

"Shhh. Easy, now. Of course I'm your friend," she said.

His eyes were huge and bright. Even in the dark, they seemed to glow. She thought again of possession, of someone else inhabiting his body, making him act like a stranger.

She tried to ease his hand off her arm, but his grip was too strong. Not like a dying man's strength at all. A pulse of fear traveled her spine.

"The rest of them, they'd let a man starve even when they got food enough to get by. They're only out for themselves. If it were up to them, I'd be dead already."

"Please, Mr. Halloran." The pulse transformed to a single, unifying rhythm. She was afraid. She could hardly breathe for the smell of rotting. What had happened to him? She had known disease to come back but not like this, not so quickly it would hollow a man in an hour. "You're not well. Be calm, now. I'm going to get you help."

"No one else can help me." His smile ended in a grimace of pain. "I'm dying, Tamsen. That's why I come to you. You were my savior before—will you be my savior again?" He seemed to have difficulty breathing. She had to wait for him to gasp more air. "Will you do something for me?"

"Of course I will," she said. Her voice sounded thin. Why had she left her lantern up on the bank? The darkness was so thick it felt like the pressure of a hand.

His eyes were closed again. His fingers relaxed against her wrist. Yet he was still trying to speak—he whispered something too quiet for her to make out, and whispered it again. She could see the effort it required; he was forcing out these broken words with the very last of his strength.

His beautiful hands, his soft brown eyes, his quiet humor—all of it gone, ravaged by whatever sickness was devouring him. She was surprised to realize she was on the verge of tears.

He was still trying to speak. "I can't hear you," Tamsen said softly. Then, "Be still, Luke." But she watched him struggle to be heard.

She leaned closer—so close that his lips, when they moved again, moved against her cheek. Finally she could make out what he was saying.

"I'm hungry." Again and again: a whispered note of agony. "I'm hungry, Tamsen."

He opened his eyes again, and she saw nothing but a deep pit, and she saw, too, that he was smiling.

He knocked her backward. He leapt, or sprang, pinning her easily, and she knew in a wild way that the rest of it had been a trap, a lure to get her close and unguarded. He was on top of her, holding a knife. Where had it come from? "I won't ask much."

"Please," she said. Her voice broke. She was no longer thinking straight. It was a dream, it had to be, a nightmare that would wake her up with a scream lodged in her throat. This madman was not Halloran. "Please, let me up."

But he only gripped her harder. "You don't know what it's like, to be starving. The pain of it. It hollows you. It's all I can think about. Even my *blood* is starving." He bent to put his face against her neck—he inhaled, he breathed in the smell of her body, he moved his tongue across her sweat, as a dog would. This broke her; it was as if some invisible barrier had been irrevocably breached, as if with a single movement he had undone God's work, and turned her from a woman to a sludge of flesh.

"I could take it if I had to, from you or one of the others. You see, don't you, how easy it would be for me to take it?" He was everywhere and all over her. There was no end to him, to his weight and his stink and his hunger. "But I don't want to do that. I'd rather you gave it to me freely, like a friend would."

The pain in her wrists where he held her helped her focus. Mary had gone for help. She must have gone for help. She simply had to humor him, to play along until someone arrived. "Of course," she said. "Of course. Like a friend would." She wasn't even sure if he heard her. "I've always taken care of you, haven't I?"

She could gasp out the words—he was heavier, stronger than he should be. Madmen, she knew, were said to possess incredible strength. She was nearly blind with terror. If she got free, could she outrun him? It was a risk. And if he chased her down? He still had her pinned beneath him, though he was no longer leaning on her neck with one arm.

"You promise to help," he said finally. "You promise you won't let me go hungry?"

She could only nod. And after a moment, he eased his weight off her—and she managed to grab the knife out of his hand.

Just as her fingers closed around the handle, there was a commotion behind her, the rustle of reeds and the snap of dry wood and voices. She heard Mary Graves shout, "*This* way. Over here."

Tamsen almost cried out with relief. She was saved.

But in that second, Halloran *changed*. At least she thought he did; she saw his whole being twist, contort, as if it had been winched around some broken internal dial, tethered down to hell. Broken apart and changed into something else. He wasn't himself; he wasn't even a man. His eyes were full black, as blank and featureless as the bottom of a well. His face seemed to have narrowed. She smelled blood on his breath. It was as though an animal inside him had erupted at that very moment, breaking through his human shell.

He bared his teeth. *Give me what I want or I'll take it . . . I'm starving.*

The face she looked into wasn't human anymore.

And just as Mary hurtled into the clearing, just as he drew back, showing his teeth, and she knew, in a single instant of calm, that she would die, Tamsen drove the tip of the blade into his throat and yanked it sideways, feeling the resistance of the tendons and the windpipe, snapping them, her hand quickly drenched in a gush of warm blood.

CHAPTER FIFTEEN

Cambridge, Massachusetts

My dear Edwin,

I am sending this letter to Sutter's Fort as you suggested in the hope that it reaches you at the other end of the great Oregon Trail. I am not surprised that you are partaking in this grand American adventure, my friend, as it is surely in keeping with your bold and inquisitive nature. I am envious and wish I could join you, but I am a realist and too accustomed to the comforts of civilization to undertake such a challenge. Besides, I find that my new post here at Harvard University is enough of an adventure in its own right and so I will be content with that.

We arrived in Cambridge from Kentucky two months ago. Tilly found us furnished rooms in a lovely house on Prince Street and has already fallen in with a group of professors' wives and does not think she will miss the Kentucky wilderness too much. We were pleased to read in your last letter that you are engaged. I am of the firm opinion that a man is better off wed than alone in the world.

But let me get to the real reason I am writing, an experience that you may find very interesting and in keeping with the theories you have formed and are so intent on pursuing. I recently had the opportunity to meet an English physician visiting Harvard as part of a professional exchange. His name is John Snow, a quiet man with an impressive high, broad dome of a forehead and piercing eyes radiating intelligence. We met at a departmental tea and after discussing a recent smallpox outbreak far west of Boston, he confessed to me that he was not convinced that conventional thinking that bad air is responsible for the spread of disease is correct. He is investigating other possible causes. He feels there are too many inconsistencies in the miasmic theory and that another, yet-unknown culprit is to blame. He has come to question the very nature of disease and how very specific, very different diseases can pass among us silently before springing suddenly to life and—in the case of some diseases, such as cholera and typhoid—erupt into epidemics. He even spoke of the way in which disease might travel invisibly, carried by people or creatures who show no signs of having it at all.

It was wild, interesting talk, to be sure. And he was so full of new ideas—and yet seemingly not so far from some of the things you proposed during our time together—that I began to think that if I could ever speak to anyone about our experience in Smithboro, it would be him. It was a risk, of course: I questioned the political wisdom of such an act but I, for one, had been haunted by Smithboro for too long and it was burning up within me, desperate for release.

And so I sought private conference with Snow and told every detail of our singular experience, withholding no detail no matter how bizarre. At the conclusion of my story, he sat stunned. I asked him whether he had ever heard of a case similar to this and he mumbled that he had not. Then I asked him by what means would it be possible for us to have witnessed what we did, and he beheld me gravely. "What you are describing is nothing but pagan superstition. Don't you realize that?" he said in his thick, strange accent. "Let me remind you that we are men of science. I advise ye to look to the natural world for your explanations, not to the unnatural one."

I fear I have made a grievous mistake; if he tells the rest of the faculty, they might think me horribly superstitious, and it will surely damage my reputation.

But his repudiation has made me see the light. Edwin, I advise you to abandon this quest you are on, seeking out tales of Indian deities who transform from one form to another—man by day and animal by night. Whether the answer to the mystery can be found in the natural world, as Snow insists it must, I cannot say. The beauty and frustration of nature, Edwin, is that it is infinite in its variations. You should not hold out false hope; it is entirely possible that we will never have answers.

I have gone on long enough. If you will not heed my advice—and I know what a long shot that is—for God's sake do not take any unnecessary risks. Please take the advice of an old friend who wishes to see you again: Buy the soundest horse you can afford, do not travel alone into unknown territory, keep your doctoring kit well stocked, and carry a loaded firearm with you at all times.

Your dear friend,
Walton Gow

CHAPTER SIXTEEN

t wasn't me, Elitha. Tell your stepmother it wasn't my fault.

Halloran's body hadn't yet been returned to camp before she began to hear him—faintly at first, carried to her in snatches, as though on bits of phantom wind. Then louder, more insistent.

Please. Tell her. Tell her I'm sorry.

Elitha put her hands over her ears and she didn't care who saw. She tried bargaining with Halloran when she was alone, but he didn't seem able to hear.

She couldn't speak to the voices. She could only listen.

Please. That monster that wrestled Tamsen to the ground wasn't me. I couldn't stop it, but it wasn't me.

The voices had only gotten worse since Fort Bridger. The only one she knew clearly was the voice of Luke Halloran, who for a week had moldered in the wagon, hovering between life and death. She knew now that the others were dead, and they mostly spoke gibberish. Only once in a while could she make out a word. Sometimes it was like coming in on the middle of a conversation, as if she were the trespasser in her own head and not the other way around.

She had tried to confide in Tamsen. She knew her stepmother believed in strange things, things beyond nature. She had seen Tamsen carefully braiding together stems of rosemary for protective charms, and muddling wolfsbane and lavender to daub behind her children's ears, to keep demons from preying on them.

But when she said Halloran's name, Tamsen's face hardened. She seized Elitha by the shoulders.

"You must tell no one of this," she said. "I never want to hear a word of it again. Swear it."

Elitha had sworn, because she was frightened; Tamsen had gripped her so hard, she left bruises. Tamsen was frightened, too: because of what had happened with Halloran in the woods, and because of what people said about her now. Before Halloran's death there had been whispers, hisses that followed Tamsen and even Elitha. But now the whispers, like the ones inside her head, had grown into a clamor. That she had bewitched him with her potions, turned him into a demon, made him her lover, turned him mad. She had killed him so she could collect his blood and drink it.

No one would speak to Tamsen now. Even Elitha felt the weight of everyone's hatred. People drifted away when they saw her coming. None of the other girls, except for Mary Graves, would do their washing when Tamsen went down to the river, and when Elitha went in her place, she had to endure snickering and muttered insults.

Every bad thing that happened to the wagon train was laid at Tamsen's feet, it seemed. Tamsen was good at pretending that it didn't bother her, but at night, Elitha sometimes heard her weeping.

Elitha couldn't pretend. She burned with shame. And still the voices crowded her head, whispering terrible things and leaving a deep tunnel of loneliness, as if their words were sharp and physical things hollowing out her center. She was desperate for quiet, for peace, for silence.

But Halloran's voice was relentless—a low and nearly constant rhythm submerging her in a place of terror and guilt. He told her in detail things she did not want to hear. He told her of hunger that lodged not in his stomach, but his blood, an excavating hunger that festered like an unclean wound. He told her of the sweet smell of human skin, the deep flinty richness of human blood, the need for it that pulled at his whole being. He claimed to be ashamed but spoke of Tamsen's body with longing, and in his darkest, angriest moments he whispered per-verse, gross things to her that she couldn't afterward forget.

I wonder what you taste like.

I wonder what it would be like to eat you.

I would start very small, a toe, or one of your soft, soft ears.

She began to think, increasingly, of wading into the river to drown herself. She began to dream of the cool dark silence of the water fold-ing over her head.

AND THEN, SHE DID IT.

Tamsen had sent her to the river to do laundry when everyone in the family was busy unchaining the oxen and setting camp for the night. She had not planned to kill herself that night, but standing in the shade of the bank, watching the late sun play over the river, trying to ignore the continued abuse of phantom voices, she realized sud-denly that there was only one solution, and it lay before her. The river looked to her like a bed made with clean linens. It looked like home.

She thought briefly about leaving her boots on the bank; footwear was expensive and there was no sense ruining them when her sisters might get some use out of them. But she was afraid that if she paused she would change her mind. She stepped off the rocks into the gently rushing water. It was colder than she expected but she kept walking. She kept going, to her waist now. She wondered whether she should have filled her pockets with rocks, but already her skirts were so heavy even walking was difficult. The current tugged at her. Farther out there were whitecaps; that was where the current was stronger. With any luck it would sweep her off her feet and carry her downstream.

It would not, then, be her fault. It would not be her choice. Her death would be in God's hands, and she could still receive his mercy. She asked God to make it happen quickly.

The water reached her breasts and made her gasp. It was harder to keep her balance; the current kept snatching at her skirts and her ankles. Suddenly all of the voices in her head went silent, and in their place she felt a rush of panic. She thought of her little sister's face, and Thomas. But it was too late for regrets; she was too deep, and could not make it back to the bank of the river, not in her sodden skirts, and the bodice that squeezed the air from her lungs. She thought of turning to call out for help but slipped on a rock. Her feet went out, and a rush of ice-cold water filled her nose and mouth and blinded her.

She could not kick out from the tangle of her skirts. She didn't know which way the surface was. She was tossed in the currents and couldn't breathe. It wasn't at all like she imagined; it wasn't peaceful, or like sleep. Her lungs cried out for air. Her throat closed around breaths full of nothing but water. Her whole body screamed in protest. She was in pain everywhere.

And the voices came back now, more furious than ever, an angry rush of them, until she knew *they* were the ones pulling her legs, drawing her under, turning her under the whitecaps.

Under the water, the voices were all that was left.

You're mine now, girl. A stranger's voice.

Join me, Elitha. Halloran, almost weeping. *Tender sweet Elitha.*

Then, suddenly, hands seized her. She came up gasping to the surface in Thomas's arms. She had been carried downstream a hundred yards; he had edged out along a fallen tree to intercept her and now pulled her up beside him, grunting with the effort, as she cried and spit up water and the taste of vomit.

He didn't say a word to her, not until they had inched along together back to the riverbank, not until she had finished shivering and coughing. He didn't touch her, either, and didn't look at her while she cried. But finally she was finished, and when she needed a handkerchief, he gave her a rag—wet, but clean—from his vest.

"Why?" he said simply.

She was exhausted, and her throat was raw. He had bundled her in his coat and she felt like going to sleep in his arms, but she didn't see any way to answer him except with the truth. "I can hear the dead speaking to me," she said. "They say awful things. I wanted quiet."

When he lifted his head, a sweep of black hair fell across his face. He needed to have his hair cut; Elitha couldn't help but think this, even in the middle of this chaos.

"When I was a boy"—Thomas always said that when he talked about his days with his tribe, never *before I was made to live with whites*—"they told me spirits could talk to us. Through the wind, water, even the trees."

She shook her head. "That's not what I mean." She took a breath. "I mean . . . actual dead people." She took a long breath; it seemed to cut her lungs open. "You probably think I'm crazy."

He was quiet for a moment. "When my parents were killed, I thought I saw them sometimes, watching me. But they never spoke."

Elitha remembered that her real mother came to her once and only once, the day her father remarried and Tamsen moved into their house. She was only a shadow hovering at the foot of the bed, but Elitha knew it was her. *Don't be sad*, her mother had said. *Your father needs her.*

"The priest said I only saw them because I wanted to." Thomas shrugged. "He said it was all in my head. After that, I never saw them again."

"So you think it's all in *my* head?" That meant she *was* going crazy.

Thomas shook his head. "No," he said simply. "I think the priest was wrong. I think my parents stopped visiting me because they knew I was okay. They knew I had to go on by myself."

Elitha had felt sorry for herself when her father married Tamsen, thinking her whole world had been turned upside down, thinking he had betrayed their mother. What must it have been like for Thomas to lose his family, his tribe, everything he knew? She couldn't fathom it. She couldn't see how he would have the strength for it.

"So, you believe in spirits, and dark things like that?" she asked.

He didn't seem embarrassed or afraid of what she thought. "Yes."

"I do, too."

He moved a little closer to her, and she shivered when their knees touched. "I am going to tell you something that I haven't told anyone else." He was quiet for a bit. She waited, holding her breath. "When I was with Mr. Bryant in the woods, we met a tribe of Washoe. He couldn't understand them, but I could." His voice was hoarse. He was very close to her, and when they accidentally touched, Elitha could feel how cold his skin was. As if he, too, was afraid. "They told me about a demon—a spirit that is very restless, very hungry. It has become many. They have taken on the skins of the men they have consumed."

Spirits prowling the woods, dressed as men. *My name is Legion, for we are many.* Mark 5:9.

Thomas shook his head. "I think you are right. I think the dead

151

speak when they are angry, or restless. I think there are spirits. I think there is reason to be afraid. Maybe the dead are trying to warn you." He nodded toward the darkness. "Something's waiting for us out there."

She thought, then, of the Nystrom boy. She hadn't been allowed to see the boy—hadn't wanted to—but she'd heard the rumors. She thought of the hunger Luke Halloran's voice had described. But Halloran couldn't have been the evil spirit of the Washoe tribe. It didn't make any sense.

"Is that why you ran?" she asked.

Thomas hesitated. Then he nodded. "I was frightened," he said.

She took a deep breath, then reached out and placed a hand on his arm, letting the blanket fall away from her. Now he didn't feel cold. He felt hot, burning hot. "I don't blame you," she said.

He turned to her. They were very close in the dark. "Are you frightened?" he whispered. He placed one finger on the inside of her wrist, and she shivered now for a different reason. His breath brushed her cheek. His eyelashes were long and soft-looking, like the feathers of a bird.

His lips felt funny against hers—not bad, just unexpected. A little wet, a little cool, and soft. Her first kiss. Her heart jumped in her chest at the thought. It seemed harmless; why did preachers and parents get in such a tizzy about it? He kissed her again, as though he knew she wanted another. This time, he was more assured, and something lifted inside her. She pictured her soul like a bird, a soft-breasted robin trying to take flight.

They remained in each other's arms for another minute, Elitha basking in a secret happiness that she wanted to last forever even as she knew it wouldn't, and then she slipped away from him.

If she was gone too long, her father or stepmother would come looking for her.

. . .

HER SKIRTS WERE STILL WET from the river and slapped against her ankles as she pushed back through the woods, but she didn't care. She didn't even care if Tamsen yelled at her for mucking them up.

As she came into a clearing, she nearly ran into John Snyder and Lewis Keseberg, two of her least favorite people in the entire wagon party. Just as quickly as it had come, her good feeling was snuffed out, like a flame extinguished by a hard wind.

Both men were carrying shovels. Before she could pivot, they'd spotted her. Snyder got directly in her way. He was as solid as a buffalo and he had the same wild eye, rolling it so you saw a lot of the white. "Well, if it ain't Donner's girl running wild around the camp."

Keseberg looked her up and down in a way that made Elitha uneasy. "What you doing out by yourself, girl?"

Watch out. Halloran's voice occurred suddenly and strongly in her head, and for the first time it felt not like an intrusion, but a friend. She remembered what Thomas had said. *Maybe the dead are trying to warn you.*

She decided to sidestep Keseberg's question. They wanted to think she was just a dumb girl, so she'd act like one. "What are you two doing with them shovels?" she asked.

"We just finished burying Halloran," Snyder said. "Can't leave him around to stink up the place."

Keseberg took off his hat. There was something wrong with his face, though she couldn't say what, exactly. It was like a sculpture of a face, made all of hard stone. But in certain lights, you could see the cracks.

"Oh, I was just coming to say a prayer for him," she said.

"Trying to make up for what your mama did?" Something ugly showed beneath Keseberg's smile. "You're too late, anyway."

"It's never too late for prayer," Elitha said, trying to pass around them. But Keseberg grabbed her by the forearm.

"You'll do no such thing. Your mama wouldn't want me to let you go off by yourself at this hour," he said. His grip was strong, and damp and too warm.

"Let go of me." She tried to pull away but he held on a minute longer, twisting it just enough so that she let out a little yelp. Snyder liked that. He laughed. Keseberg, too.

"You ain't a child, you know. You're as good as a woman. That means you shouldn't be out by yourself. There are men might take it a certain way, might think your blood is running hot."

She was just about to call out for help—maybe Keseberg's wife was in shouting distance, though of course it wouldn't matter if she had been, the woman seemed helpless—when Keseberg let Elitha go. He gave her a little push so she stumbled before regaining her feet. "If you ever want a nighttime stroll, you just let me know and I'll come and take care of you," he said.

That made Snyder hoot again, and the sound of their laughter burned in her ears as she ran.

CHAPTER SEVENTEEN

Springfield, Illinois
April 1846

The bite of cherry pie leaked its scarlet juices down Lavinah Murphy's chin, and she quickly reached for a napkin. Undercooked, it was—too thin and too red. She'd have done better but wasn't about to tell Mabelle Franklin that. They were throwing this going-away picnic for *her*, after all.

She'd only hauled her whole clan up to Springfield a year and one month ago—just after her husband's death—but in that year, she'd grown restless.

The Franklins understood. They felt it, too. The fear in the eyes of people in the market, sometimes, even here in Springfield, where people were said to be more tolerant. She heard the whispers. Though people pretended this country could be home to anyone willing to make their own way, it wasn't true. They treated you differently if you didn't share their beliefs. Same God, but a different book. They looked at you funny; they didn't trust you.

Well, Lavinah didn't trust them, either.

"Another piece, Mrs. Murphy?"

She shook her head and looked down to see that the pie had stained her hands. A coldness gripped her momentarily. For when she'd looked at her hands she'd seen not the cherry filling, but blood. Her husband's.

"You must be mighty nervous for the journey?" Mabelle went on. "I don't know how you do it. You're so brave."

She didn't just mean the preparations for the trip, Lavinah knew. She meant all of it.

A woman raising a large family on her own was a curiosity in a town like this. But she couldn't very well have stayed in Nauvoo. Not after what happened. Menfolk killed, family driven out of their homes. And Joseph Smith's assassination. These days it seemed wherever Mormons lived together, somebody was trying to drive them out.

"It just seems a shame," Mabelle said. "Not to be among your own people."

Didn't she understand? It was safer that way. Other Mormons meant more trouble.

"I'll have my family," she replied. "And that will be enough for me."

As soon as it was seemly, Lavinah slipped away. She wasn't upset with these people, but she knew what some of them thought. That she was choosing her own safety over God.

As she strolled the pasture, she looked back at the Franklins' yard. Smiled to see all her friends gathered there—what she saw made her heart full to bursting. The golden fields, the pale blue sky. Women's skirts billowing in the afternoon breeze, full like the sails of ships on the horizon. Children—including five of her own, and three her grandchildren—playing hide-and-go-seek in the corn field. Springfield was a lovely town, a peaceful town—and in just a short time, it had come to feel like home. But who knew how long the peace here would last?

Urgency moved her to the far side of the hayfield, away from the merriment and noise. She spied a farmhouse just beyond a rise, weathered gray and sagging. The family that lived there was also leaving with the wagon party on Wednesday. Lavinah had met the husband once or twice. A disagreeable man, only recently married. Funny name, what was it—Kleinberg? No, Keseberg, that was it. She shivered beneath her shawl, remembering the perpetually angry scowl, eyes that could make your blood stand in your veins.

She'd heard stories of an older man, too, the man's uncle, who years earlier had stayed for a while with his nephew. People in town had been afraid of him. They made him seem like a monster in their stories, saying he'd been involved in some kind of mysterious tragedy at sea, and had even suspected he had some role in the death of a poor consumptive woman who'd been taken in by a tonic-selling con. They said the older man had always smelled faintly of blood, like the way it lingered in the shed after you'd done your butchering.

Lavinah tucked her head down and headed home to resume preparations for Wednesday. A long journey was waiting. And freedom, like the kind the founding fathers had written and dreamed of, freedom from fear, lay on the other side.

SEPTEMBER 1846

CHAPTER EIGHTEEN

J ames Reed could almost think that the worst was behind them.

They emerged from the Wasatch Mountain range at last, trudging out of the cottonwood-choked canyons with bloodied, blistered hands and aching backs. The descent was their reward, gentle and long, an easy stroll for exhausted animals and men alike. Relief among the travelers was palpable; people spoke optimistically of the worst being behind them.

Until they came upon the first patch of dry, white land.

It began as a glare in the distance, so pale, so singed of growth, that it looked as if a mantle of snow had covered the land horizon to horizon. It stank. Puddles of stagnant white water lay like open wounds across the otherwise parched landscape. The water was unpotable—they learned that after a cow tried to drink it and took ill.

There had been a fluke hot spell during Reed's first year in America. He had been ten years old at the time but he still remembered it vividly. He had been living on a tobacco plantation in Virginia where his mother worked as a laundress. He earned money working in the fields with the slaves, topping the tobacco plants in the spring, picking mature leaves in the summer.

It was backbreaking work, and that summer it was unbearable. Having grown up in the cold, wet Irish countryside, James had never known heat like that. The fields shimmered. Rows of green undulated in phantom vapor. At least one slave died before the weather broke. Because Reed's mother had asked the field boss to keep an eye on her son, he was sent home every day after the noon meal. He felt guilty resting in the cool of the servants' quarters in the big house while the slaves, he knew, would work until the sun went down.

Now, decades later, he dreamed of the cool tiles of those shaded hallways. Of water poured from clay pitchers. Of shadows and porcelain and ice.

Here, there was nowhere to escape.

THEY HAD CALCULATED, from reports and accounts they had heard from the few travelers who'd taken the Truckee route before, that they would cross the desert in a day.

But a second day came and went. Then a third. The Murphys' cattle, starved and mad with thirst, wandered off in the middle of the night. The party did not have the strength to go after them. They moved in silence, like a long parade of the dead. No one had the spit even to argue.

On the fourth day, the wind picked up, creating small dancing funnels of dirt and salt crystals. The children, roused for the first time in days, clapped. But the wind kept blowing and the little funnels swelled and grew and became whipping, snakelike things, pegging them with stones that split their canopies, blinding them and roughing their skin, and they began to cry.

Most of the wagons had just enough water for the humans. The cattle panicked. They bellowed as they went insane, and the sound was like nothing Reed had ever heard.

It was on the fifth day that Noah James, one of Reed's teamsters, came to tell him his own oxen were dying. They doubled back, heading into the blowing wind. Half a mile later, they came on the Reed family wagons. Two of the three teams were floundering, thrashing in the sand. At least one of them was already dead. The rest danced spookily in the confines of the harness.

"Do we have water?" Reed asked, though he already knew the answer.

James shook his head. "Not enough to make a difference."

"Unhitch that animal, then. And that one as well." Reed pointed with his whip at another dying animal, and, when he saw that his whip was trembling, quickly dropped it. "We'll just have to pull with the animals we've got left."

"With respect, Mr. Reed, you'll wear the others out faster if you do that," James said. "They won't make it another day."

"What do you propose we do, then?" Reed's mouth was full of dirt. His eyes were full of dirt. He knew James was right, but he couldn't stand it, couldn't bear the idea of leaving their wagon. If he did, he would no longer be able to pretend.

It wasn't about California anymore. It wasn't about where they were going at all. It was simply about survival.

George Donner's wagon pulled up. Donner had been a shadow of himself ever since Hastings's betrayal, and Reed had been glad of it— the party had become more efficient without his blustering tendency to make light of Reed's concerns.

Donner looked at Reed and then away. "You can store some of your things with me," he said. "You don't have to thank me," he added, and Reed felt his chest hollow with sudden gratitude; he would not have been able to bear to say thank you, and he felt that Donner knew it. Anyway, both men understood that Donner owed Reed for taking over after the Hastings incident.

Margaret wept when they unloaded their wagons and sorted through their things for the valuables to keep. The children were silent and un-complaining, and dutifully piled their toys on the ground to be abandoned. At the very bottom of the pile was a saddle he'd had made special for Virginia when she got her first pony. The buttery leather was tooled with flowers and vines on the skirts. It had nickel conchos on the latigos like a fine adult's saddle. It had once made him proud. It proved that he'd been a good father, capable of bringing his children joy.

Now, staring at it, he could hardly make sense of its shape or the life it had belonged to.

"Even Addie?" Patty Reed asked, holding her doll up for her father to see. It was a rag doll with a bisque head, dressed in fabric scraps and a bit of lace tied around its waist as a sash. The doll might only weigh ounces, but ounces added up. Eight ounces of cornmeal versus eight ounces of calico snippets and bisque. Ounces, grains of sand, seconds falling through an hourglass: Life was all accounting, and at the end of it, the same tab for all.

"I'm afraid so," Reed told her. He was surprised to feel a sudden tightness in his chest, watching his child place her doll in the dirt, carefully, as if it were a true burial.

The transfer was done in an hour. Already the wagons to be abandoned were no more than ghosts. Reed shot the remaining oxen in the head so they wouldn't suffer any further, and he imagined, though he was not fanciful, that he saw in their eyes a final flicker of relief.

CHAPTER NINETEEN

The sandstorm started innocently enough. White flakes swirled on the air, and Stanton thought they were almost pretty in their delicacy. But by dusk on the sixth day in the desert, the wagon party was forced to stop. Traversing this great emptiness was bad enough under clear skies. Trudging through a blizzard of hard sand was suicide.

The cloud of sand and salt had shaken the wagons like the swells of an angry sea. No one bothered to try to pitch a tent or set up a campsite; everyone bunkered in the wagons. Stanton wrapped a blanket over his shoulders and wedged himself between barrels inside his wagon, where he would have to sleep upright in the tightly packed space, full of household belongings. He hadn't bothered with a lantern. There was nothing he wanted to see. Outside, bullwhips of sand hissed where they scraped over the canopy. The day had covered him in a fine crust of salt. It was on his skin, his lips, even in his eyelashes.

Salt lined the inside of his nose and roughed his throat so that it hurt, even, to swallow.

Suddenly, Stanton heard the crack of a gunshot at the same time the board behind him shuddered. The wood exploded into splinters inches to the left of his head. He dropped to his stomach as best he could in the cramped space, trying to figure out which direction the shot had come from, the front or back of his wagon. From the back, surely. He picked out the sound of rustling, now that he knew to listen for it. Whoever had shot at him was still out there in the dark, cowering by the left rear wheel.

Stanton moved carefully toward the front of the wagon, hoping the sandstorm would conceal the noise of his footsteps. He slipped over the side and dropped, landing in the tangle of empty harness on the ground.

The sandstorm absorbed the moonlight. All Stanton could see was the silhouette of a man headed toward him. He hadn't made many friends in the party, but this was more than hatred, Stanton knew. This was hunger. He was an easy target, with a wagon of his own and no children. Whoever it was wanted to raid his remaining supplies and didn't care if he left Stanton for dead in the process. The storm provided the perfect cover.

Before Stanton could pull his gun from its holster, the man tackled him, knocking him to the ground. The whirling sand obscured details and made Stanton feel as though he were wrestling a faceless phantasm—one, however, who reeked of whiskey. Stanton managed to jerk aside when the man plunged a fist toward his face, and heard a knife blade strike loose sand beside him.

They rolled over and over in the sand, scrabbling for advantage, fighting not just each other but the wind, a giant hand hurling them through the dark. The man was insanely strong but slowed by alcohol, and Stanton got two punches in for every one he took. But his sides ached and he felt like he'd swallowed a pound of grit. He caught the man good in the ribs, though, and heard him cry out, and then Stanton was sure he recognized the voice. Lewis Keseberg.

Maybe he knew he was caught, or maybe he'd just had enough. He stumbled backward, reeling, and staggered off into the storm.

Stanton, exhausted, went down on his knees when another gust buffeted him off balance, and his hand hit something hard in the sand. It was a palm-sized gun, too small for a man as big as Keseberg. He struggled to his feet and managed to claw himself back inside the wagon, feeling his way on his animals' leads.

Once inside, Stanton lit a lantern. He loaded his rifle first in case Keseberg came back and only then looked at the pistol. It had a singular mother-of-pearl inlay he recognized immediately. There was probably not another like it west of the Mississippi.

He felt a stab of disbelief and also disappointment. It was Tamsen Donner's gun.

IN THE MORNING, Stanton rode up to James Reed. Reed looked as if he hadn't slept. His clothes were streaked with salt and his fair Irish skin was so red that he looked burnt.

Reed gave him an appraising nod. "Looks like you came through the sandstorm all right."

"By a hair," Stanton said, and tried to keep his voice even. "Someone tried to kill me last night."

He led Reed over to his wagon and showed him the hole made by the bullet.

Reed crouched low to get a clean look. "Did you see who did it?"

Stanton hesitated. He couldn't see a reason to reveal Tamsen's and

Keseberg's involvement. Better to keep the particulars secret until he had a better sense of where their scheme was headed. "No. Too dark."

"It's gotten that bad, has it, that we're trying to kill each other?" Reed took off his hat and smoothed his sweat-drenched hair. Stanton remembered how Reed had first looked when they set off, like a big-city boss, still starching his shirt collars and shining his shoes. "What are you going to do?"

"I'd like to volunteer to ride ahead. To Johnson's Ranch. We need the food, and most of the families are in a bad way. Some are near the end of their supplies. The ones that aren't won't share with those in need."

Reed squinted at the wagons in the lead, far down the flats. They were as small as beetles. "We could take a day or two once we're out of the desert and slaughter some of the livestock, dry the meat. That would tide us over for a while."

"No one who still has cattle will part with it, not for love or money," Stanton pointed out. "A good number of the cattle died in the crossing or ran off. The people close to starving are the ones who started with almost nothing—the Eddys, the McCutcheons, Wolfinger and Keseberg. And don't forget all the single men. Single men with rifles. Things will get ugly soon."

Reed nodded and glanced again at the tear in Stanton's wagon cover. "They already have." He sighed. "I suppose it might give whoever took a shot at you some time to cool off."

That or he'd risk isolating himself further.

But it was still safer than the alternative, for now. He had to get away.

"So it's settled, then."

Reed nodded.

Not for the first time, Stanton wondered where Bryant was now and tried not to read the worst into the lack of promised letters. Hopefully, Bryant was nearly to Yerba Buena, enjoying that fabled sunshine.

"I want to take another man with me," he said slowly, watching Reed's reaction. He didn't expect to find many eager men for the job. There were plenty of things that could kill a man between where they stood and Johnson's Ranch.

"Will McCutcheon," Reed said. "I think he's the right man to accompany you."

Stanton nodded, understanding: Everything the McCutcheons had was strapped to the back of their family mule.

"I can ask Baylis to handle the oxen while you're gone. Mrs. McCutcheon can look after your wagon."

Stanton only nodded again.

"We are much obliged to you, Mr. Stanton. Much obliged." Reed dusted his hands before extending one to shake.

HE FOUND TAMSEN TRUDGING in the shadow cast by the tall canopies of the Donners' wagons. She had draped a white shawl over her head to protect her from the sun. He dismounted and began to walk beside her.

"Mr. Stanton." She didn't seem surprised to see him. He admired her control. "What are you doing here?"

He reached into his saddlebag. "I believe this is yours."

She froze at the sight of her own revolver. She seemed altered to him suddenly, no less beautiful but smaller somehow, like a flame narrowed by lack of oxygen.

"You might as well take it," he said. "I know it belongs to you."

She did, but with a look of distaste, as if it were a snake or a large insect that might bite her. He stared at her hands, wondered briefly if she might aim the weapon at him, and something in him leapt at the uncertainty of it. Then he hated himself, for it was this kind of attraction—to wrong things, to danger, to *her*—that led to ruin, and he knew it, and the knowing somehow only made it stronger. Her lips were taut and pink. He looked away, suddenly furious with her, with the pinkness of her mouth. She didn't even have the grace to look guilty.

"Don't you want to know where I found it?" he asked, pressing.

She looked at him blankly.

"I took it away from Lewis Keseberg," he said.

"Lewis Keseberg?" She shrugged coolly, pushing the weapon back to him. "Whatever he did, it wasn't me who told him to do it. I didn't give him the gun, either. He must have taken it."

"And when would he have had the opportunity to do that? You like to keep busy, don't you, Mrs. Donner? I must say that I'm happy you've found another plaything." It was wrong of him to imply such a thing, but the beast, chained inside him, held down for these last few months, had reared its head. Stanton was losing control of himself—or he already had, long ago.

Her whole expression curdled around a look of hatred. "You have no right to speak to me like that. Not after what's been between us."

"Don't think I've forgotten," he said, hating the growl in his voice, hating her power over him, yet *drawn* to that power. "I'm reminded every day, when half the train whispers as I pass, and the other half shuns me and rumors spread like a sickness. I'm reminded when Franklin Graves threatens me with hanging if—" He broke off. He hadn't meant to mention Mary.

But Tamsen just shook her head. "I never told anyone."

"Forgive me if I don't take your word for it." He gathered up the reins, ready to swing into the saddle, but Tamsen touched his arm for his attention, as quickly as though she were touching a hot iron.

"I'm sorry, Charles," she said, in a low voice. "Listen to me, won't you? I am not as bad as you may think."

He squinted and turned away. The mountains that had looked like distant hieroglyphs, ragged tears in the sleek shell of blue sky, now seemed far closer. He could make out snow-capped peaks, valleys already frozen over with ice that never melted. He had to hurry.

"No," he said finally, though he still wouldn't look at her. He thought of Lewis Keseberg's hot, whiskey-laden breath, and the reckless way he'd dived after Stanton, almost like an animal. There was no way Tamsen would allow a man like him into her bed, or even, he hoped, conspire with him at all. He let out a sigh. "I suppose you are not." He knew Tamsen was much like the revolver itself—powerful, deadly even, but only when put in the wrong hands.

He glanced down at his own, then gripped the reins, mounted, and spurred his horse into a gallop.

CHAPTER TWENTY

Indian Territory

My dearest Margie,

I am lost. For how many days, I can no longer say with confidence. I write to you as a diversion, to lift my spirits. I don't know if I will come across another human being, someone who will send this letter on its way to you. If I don't, I'll leave it by a river or other place where it stands a chance of being found.

My food is gone. There is no game to be had. I'm only able to survive because of what I learned from Miwok Indians I met years ago, "diggers" forced to forage for their survival. I have been experimenting with anything that looked edible, even bitter acorns and weeds, but because of the drought even these are in short supply. I might've killed and eaten my horse if I thought I could get out of the wilderness on foot. I may still be forced to, if things don't get better soon, though the thought fills me with revulsion.

In this near-delirious state, I recently stumbled on the remains of what looked to be a camp. There was a clearing with a ring of stones laid around an old fire pit. Due to time and weather a single rough lean-to of unstripped logs was falling apart, its roof collapsed. I shifted through the dirt around the fire pit and found things that made me think white men had been here, a group of prospectors, most likely: a tin coffee cup, a half-decayed book of psalms with many of the pages torn out (no doubt for kindling), a few silver coins, two empty bottles that could only have contained whiskey. Among these few items, however, there were many, many fragments of bone. There must have been game here not long ago, I thought, though there was none now.

The bones were curious, however: too big to be rabbit, the wrong shape to be deer. I blame my confusion on a delirium brought on by starvation, or maybe it was just that I somehow anticipated the truth, a truth too horrible to contemplate outright.

It wasn't until I went into the lean-to that I realized something gruesome had happened here. There were human skulls scattered about the floor of the hut. They'd been cracked open, each one of them, as though bashed in with rocks. The long bones I found there were unmistakably human, with their thinner cortical walls. The heads of the major bones—the ones found at the joints, hips and shoulder and so on—were not intact, which they would be if the body had been torn or fallen apart, but showed distinct signs of cleaving. Indeed, there was a rusty hatchet nearby; there could be no question of how these people had met their end.

I staggered outside, dizzy from horror. Whose camp was this? Bridger and Vasquez had told me of vanished prospectors several years back, and this had to be it. I found prospecting tools, pickaxes and shovels, moldering under some bushes.

I struggled to recall how many men Bridger had said were in that party. What could have happened to them? Who had killed them?

Was it the Anawai? None of the evidence pointed to them, though none pointed away from them, either. The cause was just as likely to have been a disagreement among the group that got out of control. An insane stranger stumbling out of the woods. A pack of outlaws, torturing them to give up a cache of gold they were sure the men were hiding. There are, I suppose, any number of reasons a group of men might have turned on one another.

Even though I am not one to spook easily, I knew I could not spend the night there. I rode away as quickly as my horse would take me, eager to leave it far behind.

I have been riding ever since.

Margie, seeing that this might be the end for me, it seems only fair that I should explain why I decided not to remain with you in Independence but continued west. While we had talked about it—and bless you for not trying to stop me—I didn't give you the full truth. You asked me, before I left, why I was so fascinated with Indian folklore and I gave you the answer most people will accept, namely a curiosity about their ways, a desire to contrast their beliefs with those of Christianity and so forth. I didn't mean to deceive you or talk down to you but was afraid that if I spoke with frankness, you might have second thoughts about marrying me and I was afraid to lose you. Here in the wilderness, I've had plenty of time to think about our time together, to think about you, and I see now that I should've told you my true motives. Forgive me for not trusting you with the truth before now.

Funny how dearly we hold on to some truths about ourselves, the power these truths have over us. I told you a little bit about my upbringing. My father was a backwoods preacher in Tennessee. Some would consider him a revivalist, same as the men I exposed in those articles I wrote. But unlike frauds like Uriah Putney, my father made no attempt to deceive. He tried to preach and minister as best he could with his limited education. There was no tolerance in him, no forgiveness. He saw himself as a man of God, but his God was judgmental, fierce-tempered, demanding. And naturally, he modeled himself after his God.

As you can imagine, my childhood was hellish. It was a stifling atmosphere for a curious boy. My father allowed no questioning of faith or his interpretation of that faith. He allowed no questioning, period. I decided at an early age that I would not follow in his mold but would learn to question everything.

I resolved to become a man of science, and there is no greater science of our time than medicine. I apprenticed with a local doctor, Walton Gow. He may have come from the mountains of Tennessee (and would later take me with him to Kentucky), but Dr. Gow was no backwoods sawbones. Walton was highly respected for his skill and thoughtful approach to medicine. His powers of observation were remarkable. He developed a reputation for being able to save the lives of patients in the most dire of situations, but most know him as the man who saved Davy Crockett by removing Crockett's burst appendix when he was in the Tennessee legislature. Walton was a young man at the time and just happened to be one of the few surgeons in the territory.

Being a nurse, dear Margie, you understand that a doctor sees things that make him question what he thought he knew about the world. This happened to me and to Walton Gow one night not long after we'd moved to Kentucky.

I never told you the story, fearing you would think me mad. But in order to understand, you must know the truth.

We were making rounds in a very remote region when we heard of a curious case in Smithboro. We were asked to attend a local man *who had been attacked. The curious thing was that his wounds didn't look* quite *as though they were made by an animal. He told us he wasn't sure what had attacked him, but there was something about his story that rang false. After Dr. Gow insisted we needed the truth in order to help him, the man told us that he had been attacked by a demon that lived in the woods surrounding Smithboro. This demon was known to the locals, but for obvious reasons they were reluctant to discuss it with outsiders. The demon, he explained, had once been a man, but he underwent a strange transformation—no one could say why—and suddenly began living in the woods like an animal. He attacked his neighbors' livestock to survive, killing sheep and goats and dragging their carcasses into the woods.*

We thought the townspeople were suffering from a kind of collective insanity. They were adamant that the story was true. And the man's wounds did look odd, too vicious to attribute to a human!

Gow and I refused to believe their tales, of course. But person after person came forward to tell us of a sighting, an encounter. They told stories of Indians they called skinwalkers who had the power to change into animals, usually for nefarious purposes.

It is commonly accepted that mythologies around the world, in all cultures, often contain narrative elements that derive from a desire to explain unusual natural or medical phenomena, and after a while, Gow and I couldn't help but wonder if such a notion might be at work here. If so, it meant that this disease, if it was one, had affected people in a variety of locations and at different times throughout history, appearing in various waves or epidemics.

I became obsessed with this bizarre case. It was partly the reason I gave up medicine and decided to become a reporter instead. Writing for newspapers, I was free to travel widely and ask questions. Walton didn't understand why I couldn't live with this unsolved mystery, and yet in his most recent letter to me he has finally admitted to feeling haunted by it, too.

Here and there, I came across other stories of people attacked by wolves who appeared to recover but then became strangely violent. There was even one stupefying case where a family in Ireland was suspected of having been transformed into creatures much like the old European tales of werewolves, except for one member, a young girl. The rest of her family had disappeared like the man from Smithboro, but she remained and, mystifyingly, showed no sign of the affliction. Is it possible for certain individuals to be able to resist a particular disease and, if so, how to account for it?

What I have seen and heard seemed to overlap with various Indian beliefs and legends and this was the purpose of my Western journey: to meet with the tribes in question and speak with them directly. Not to learn their mythologies, exactly, but to try to discover whether some of them share common roots in actual medical histories.

But as I write these words, lost in the wilderness, I am forced to question what good will come out of my endeavors. I thought I was chasing the truth and knowledge; I fear now that maybe all I have done is throw my life away.

Dearest Margie, I hope you can find it in your heart to forgive me for the foolish choice I have made. I can only hope that God smiles on my quest and will keep me alive. With his help, I will return to your side.

I remain your loving
Edwin

CHAPTER TWENTY-ONE

Who knew that Eden could be found in the foothills below Pilot Peak? After crossing that godforsaken salt desert, the dry, cracked-brown patch of land looked like the most beautiful place Reed had ever seen.

Hell, it seemed, was behind them.

The livestock tore hungrily at scrub grass and crowded three deep at the tiny watering hole. People tumbled out of their dust-caked wagons into the spring-fed creek, gulping down muddy water, pouring it over their heads. Lavinah Murphy and her family were on their knees, hands joined and eyes closed, thanking God for their deliverance.

Reed watched all this with satisfaction but also with a bruised ego. He'd taken over as leader, had gotten them through the worst trial of the journey, but did anyone think to thank *him*? Of course not. Instead, many found ways to blame him. The group's loyalties, he'd come to realize, had little to do with fact and all to do with feeling. And once again, Reed was forced to accept that he did not inspire people to like him—hadn't and perhaps never would. For many people did not like the truth, it seemed—thought it was a dirty and distasteful thing, impolite and complicated. They didn't have the patience for it—for numbers, liters, rations, portions, reasons. Many simply preferred the sweet, momentary pleasure of hearing whatever they wanted to hear. Which was Donner's skill in spades, or had been, before the once-jovial man had caved in on himself.

But whether the others appreciated him or not, it *had* been Reed's careful eye on rations and his urging to start out earlier each morning than the morning before that had gotten them here mostly intact. Under Donner's waffling supervision, they'd all have been dead long ago.

Now Reed had yet another unpleasant but necessary task in front of him: It was time to ask the families if there had been any deaths and tally their losses. He sighed and took up the reins. Leading the train were the Breen and Graves families, the ones who hated him the most, who irrationally blamed him for the route they'd taken because he was their leader at the time, because they were the kind of people who always needed someone to blame for their misfortunes.

Next came the families whose allegiances were shifting, or who chose not to take a side. This included Keseberg, the crafty German Wolfinger and his ragtag band of German emigrants, plus Lavinah Murphy's sprawling clan. Will Eddy and his family rode with them, as did the McCutcheons.

At the end of the line were the families *everyone* eyed resentfully because they were wealthy, a fact that Reed acknowledged with perverse satisfaction because his family still counted among them. The two Donner families were surrounded by a small army of hired help and nearly a dozen teamsters between them, which made Reed feel a bit more secure. Too often now, he caught Franklin Graves and Patrick

Breen muttering together, eyeing the Reeds' store of food when it was unloaded.

But they would not break him, not the way they'd broken George Donner. Reed didn't hide in his wagon. He stubbornly rode up and down the line, enduring their bitter stares, refusing to give them the satisfaction of letting them know he was afraid. These days he and Tamsen Donner had one thing in common: They were easily the most hated people in the party.

All in all, he tallied that they'd left a third of the wagons behind in the desert. No one had died. However, an awful lot of possessions had been abandoned and livestock lost.

But looking back, he knew, was a trap. They'd come this far. There would be no going back, not now, not ever.

THEY WERE MAKING THEIR WAY from Pilot Peak when they came on the Indian corpses. The two fragile-looking scaffolds were easy to spot given the dearth of trees. Reed and a few others went over for a closer look. The scaffolds stood about the height of an average man. The shrouded bodies were surrounded by objects that must have been left in tribute to them: an old knife with a dull edge and braided leather grip; necklaces made of carved bone and feathers striped black, white, and blue; a buffalo robe, the fur dulled by the sun.

William Eddy swiped his face with a forearm. "What do you think—Paiute?"

Reed shook his head. "Probably Shoshone," he answered. "We're passing through their territory."

John Snyder was deliberately standing too close. Reed felt his presence like a slick of sweat on the skin. "What—you an Indian expert all of a sudden?"

"It was in a book I read about the Indian Territory." Back in Spring-field, after what had happened with Edward McGee, and the shame he'd narrowly avoided, Reed had for a time thought about becoming an Indian agent for the government. But appointments were hard to get. He now felt foolish about it, as though he'd been stubbornly pur-suing some childish dream. Too late, he saw that this escape to Cali-fornia was a childish dream, too. He hadn't learned his lesson with McGee. Snyder might have been big and mean, where McGee was slight and charming, but both were actors in a vision that had come crashing down.

Reed's life was full of broken fantasies.

Keseberg stooped to pick up one of the necklaces. "Seems like a waste, leaving all this stuff for the dead."

Reed tried to picture Keseberg's pale wife wearing such a thing, but his imagination failed him. "It's for the dead man to use in the next world," he said. "Probably best to leave it alone." The bodies both-ered Reed. They seemed exceptionally thin for adults but too tall for children.

"I don't see any Indians here to stop us," Keseberg said.

"You shouldn't mess with Indian graves," Franklin Graves said. "The redskins are touchy about that."

Keseberg ignored him, stepping forward to flip back a corner of the deerskin shroud. Now Reed understood why the bodies were small: They had been burned. All that were left were charred remains. Patches of cooked flesh still clung to blackened bone. The skulls were papered with bits of scorched flesh; empty eye sockets seemed to stare at them reproachfully. Several of the men quickly backed away. Eddy turned, coughing into his sleeve.

"Savages," Keseberg said. "What am I always saying? They're all savages."

Reed had no love for the Indians, per se, but he hated Keseberg and his ignorance more.

Still, at the moment he was most bothered by the corpses, more than he could say. It didn't make any sense. He had heard how the Indians cared for their dead during the Black Hawk War from one of the scouts.

"Something must have happened," he said. Under the blazing sun, the blackened faces appeared to grin horribly. "I never heard of a tribe burning bodies like this."

"Maybe they were sick," Franklin Graves said. "Had some kind of disease and didn't want it to spread."

Disease. The word lingered in the air like a hiss. The group stared at the scaffolds in silence. He knew they were all thinking of Luke Halloran. Had he gotten some kind of disease—the same one that might have struck these two Indians?

"What are these?" It wasn't until Mary Graves spoke up that anyone realized she had arrived behind them. Elitha Donner, too. Reed had heard she was plucky. Reed thought, however, there might have been something wrong with her; he sometimes saw her walking by herself, murmuring, seeming to argue with the air.

Franklin Graves's face darkened with anger. "Go on," he told his daughter. "Get back. This is no sight for a woman."

But she sidestepped him when he looked as if he might grab her. Reed had to credit her: The girl had spirit.

"There are carvings here," she said, and brought her hand to the bark of a nearby tree. There were squares within squares, slashes that looked like lightning bolts. Stick figures of men but with strange, heavy heads. "Perhaps there's a story here as well."

"It isn't a story." Thomas, the boy from Fort Bridger, spoke up. Reed had almost forgotten him. He was always hiding under one of George

Donner's wagons in the evenings, and who knew where he got to during the day. He'd been no help at all during the desert crossing; Reed had half expected that he would run off, as he had done with Bryant.

"These are charms against bad spirits." Thomas spoke as though he were surrendering each word against his will. "Protection from the hungry ones."

"For the dead?" Breen moved a hand almost unconsciously to his rifle. "Hell, why do the dead need protection?"

Reed thought back to what Hastings had said when they'd found him cowering in the wagon. *Something's out there eating every living thing.*

"So is it spirits that been clearing out all the game from the woods, is that the idea?" Snyder asked. Thomas looked away. A muscle twitched in his jaw.

To Reed's shock, it was Elitha Donner who answered. "They don't just eat animals," she said, in a soft singsong. Her eyes were clear and blue and troubled. "They eat men."

Reed felt a current of unease travel across his skin. "You've been filling her head with tall tales," he said to Thomas.

"He's trying to help us," Elitha barked back, spinning away from Reed. "He's been trying to help us all along but you won't listen to him."

Snyder leaned over Elitha, sneering at her. "You don't understand, girl—he's not one of us. He ain't trying to help you, he's just trying to get under your skirts."

"They burned the bodies so the hungry ones wouldn't get them." Thomas's voice was even, but he was obviously struggling to maintain control. He pointed to the basin opening before them and to the mountain in the distance. "We've entered the place where the evil spirits live." He tapped the trunk of one of the trees, pointing to the symbols carved into the bark, then gestured to the bodies. "You may not want to believe me, but the proof is right before your eyes."

"Proof?" Patrick Breen rolled his eyes. "I don't see no proof, just a lot of ignorant heathen nonsense. I trust in the Lord—you hear that, boy, the *Lord*—to guide and protect me."

At that, the young man stepped back from the crowd, arms raised in surrender. He shook his head slowly as he backed away, a sad smile creeping across his face. "Then the Lord must be mightily displeased with you, because he has led you into the valley of death. Make peace with your Lord before it is too late, because the hungry ones are coming for you."

CHAPTER TWENTY-TWO

Tamsen felt herself changing, hardening. They'd left the great white desert only to descend into an endless sagebrush plain of the Great Basin. The sun had eaten away at her beauty, ruined her skin and her hair, melted away her graceful curves, leaving her bony and sinewy. Beauty had been her armor. Without it, she'd grown afraid.

Why hadn't she gotten George to take some of the Nystrom boy's hair, the boy killed at the beginning of their journey? That would've made powerful talismans to protect her children, but she'd been afraid of anyone finding out. She worked secretly because even George didn't like her dabbling in what he called "heathen practices." Now there was nothing she could do to help her children, and she was taken aback by her own dread for their well-being. She'd never thought of herself as maternal, exactly, but maybe she'd been wrong.

Perhaps she'd been wrong about everything.

. . .

LATE SEPTEMBER AND the mountains were closer still, white-fleeced and rutted with shadows. But down on the plains, it was hot. She was more grateful than usual that evening as they made camp. She had walked the entire day to spare the oxen and couldn't wait to take off her boots, though she dreaded it, too, because the first moments of relief were always followed by an ache so deep she might never stand again.

Tamsen felt ill as she sat down on a rock and took a bit of willow bark powder to ease her pain. She knew she wouldn't eat her dinner tonight. Over the past few weeks, she had taken to skipping meals whenever possible so there was more for the children. The two families were top-heavy with men. Nearly as many teamsters as family members, plus Betsy's teenaged sons from her previous marriage. Men had big appetites and Tamsen was afraid the girls would be edged out. It was easier, in a way, to put her girls first. Sometimes she thought her own hunger was too much, that if she were to eat a full meal again it would kill her. The wanting of it was so bad it erased her completely— she no longer knew herself.

Sometimes she forgot to respond to her own name.

And then there was Keseberg. She was doing her best to avoid him after he did a strange thing shortly before Stanton left. He had found her in a rare moment alone, one of the few times she was away from the wagon, where George now spent most of his days, as well as from all of her children. "I know you want him gone," he'd hissed at her, speaking not of Stanton at all but of her own husband. Somehow he had been able to tell she was tired of the tedious discontent of her marriage. "And I can make it so we're both happy."

She had recoiled from him—his reeking breath, his leering smile, and worst of all, the look of *knowing* in his eyes. "You don't know me," she'd replied, as calmly as possible. "You don't know what I want. If you did, you'd know that I don't want *you*."

It was enough to send him slinking away, muttering, "This ain't the end of it," over his shoulder. It seemed she'd made another enemy without meaning to.

She'd been racked with nerves to find her pistol missing the next day, and further confused when Stanton accused her of conspiring against him. It was only later that she figured it out: Keseberg had meant to kill Stanton and pin his death on her, as some sort of petty vindication for her dismissal.

She had been disappointed, yet relieved, to have Stanton gone for a time. He had insinuated, even briefly, that she had made Lewis Keseberg her latest lover, which was outrageous on many counts. Keseberg revolted her, for one thing—physically, morally, in every way imaginable. But what sickened her nearly as much was the readiness with which Stanton had leapt to the conclusion. It only proved to her that Stanton couldn't and never would understand her at all.

No, none of these men could, and it was a fact Tamsen was coming to grasp more clearly by the day; even as hunger ravaged her from within, it seemed to carve out space for her to see things plainly.

She took more of the willow bark, then closed her eyes and took a deep breath, listening to the evening routine: Samuel Shoemaker and Walt Herron unhitching the oxen and driving them to the riverbank; George and Jacob setting up the tents; Betsy getting ready to make dinner. Through it all floated her daughters' high-pitched voices. Frances, Georgia, Eliza, Leanne—she ticked off the names in her head as she heard them speak.

She opened her eyes. Where was Elitha? She jumped up, nearly crying out at the pain in her feet, and rushed over to where the girls were playing beside the cookfire and Betsy was starting to set up the tripod. As always, they'd set up at a distance from the rest of the wagon train, far away enough to pretend the others didn't exist, close enough for safety. The four girls were playing cat's cradle with a bit of string, but there was no Elitha.

"Where's your sister? Why isn't she with you?" Tamsen demanded. She hated the worry that had wormed into her heart.

Their innocent little faces tightened suddenly. "She went to look for something," Leanne said, cowering in anticipation of her mother's wrath.

"You're coming with me. We're going together to look for Elitha, do you hear me? Hurry along now." They had to come with her, there was no alternative. She didn't trust anyone to keep them safe, not even Betsy. No one else understood that evil was only an arm's length away, waiting to swoop down on them, whether animal or spirit—or man.

They swept through the camp. Anyone she asked about Elitha only shrugged or gave her a blank look. They wanted nothing to do with her and, besides, were anxious to put the long dusty day behind them.

Keseberg: She saw him from a distance, swaggering like he always did, and leering at her with a look of narrow dislike. A sudden certainty coiled in the bottom of her stomach: Keseberg knew where Elitha was. Hadn't she caught him staring in her daughter's direction on other occasions? And he wanted to hurt Tamsen, he'd made that clear.

"Go back to the wagons," she told her children. "Quick, now."

"I thought we weren't to leave your side," said Leanne.

"Don't backtalk me. Just do it." She had to push Leanne in the direction of the wagon, but still she merely ducked away under the Breens' baseboard, hanging back with her three sisters.

Keseberg loped casually toward her, hitching up his belt, smiling with long, gray teeth. He had a colorful shawl yoked around his shoulders. She had never seen it before, but dimly it registered some association.

"Mrs. Donner." Keseberg tipped his hat. The name sounded like an insult in his mouth. "What a surprise."

"I'm looking for my daughter Elitha," she said.

"The girl done run off, did she?" Keseberg barely turned his head to spit. "Can't help you, I'm afraid. I ain't seen her. And believe me"—he turned to grin at her again—"I been lookin'."

A black revulsion moved through her, like a serpent uncoiling deep in her blood. Then she realized where she had seen the shawl before. "You stole that," she said. "You stole it from an Indian grave."

He only shrugged. "So what? I take what I want—just like you. You act like we're different, Tamsen. But we're exactly the same. We are two of a kind, you and me."

Without warning, he grabbed her wrists and pulled her to him. Her daughter Leanne shouted and started to run to her. But she yelled at her to stay back.

She had put out of her mind how disgusting he was, but it was impossible to ignore up close. He smelled rancid, as though he never bathed or washed his clothes. The skin under his scraggly beard was inflamed and scabby, his teeth gray from neglect. He might have been thin but he was strong and used his height to his advantage. "You're not thinking, Tamsen. A man like me could be useful. You have enemies. You need someone to be your friend."

"Is that why you went after Charles Stanton? You wanted to make it look like I killed him to punish me?" She tried to push away from him. "Let go of me."

"It don't pay to refuse me. It's better to be my friend. Besides, I know what you did with Stanton." Keseberg spat the words at her. "I heard what you did in Springfield, too, all those men you been with, so don't pretend that you don't like it."

He had to be talking about Dr. Williams. Jeffrey. She thought the story hadn't gotten out, that George had managed to keep it contained. She'd been lonely and Jeffrey Williams, though he was more than twice her age, was intelligent and far more cultured than George. But, like Charles Stanton, Jeffrey Williams had been a mistake. She had been looking for comfort but all she found in these men was a tempo-rary distraction. It wasn't the kind of thing a man like Keseberg would understand, however.

She tried to wrench away from him, but he got a hand around her dress and pulled, ripping the fabric. Without thinking, she brought her knee up hard between his legs. He doubled over backward, gasp-ing. All at once, her children darted out from the shelter of the wagons and eddied around her torn skirts like a current, asking if she was okay. The littlest one, Eliza, was crying.

"Come," was all she could say. There was a tight, airless feeling in her chest, as if he still had his weight against her.

They had turned away from Keseberg when he finally got his breath.

"You're too old for me anyway. All used up," he choked out. "But those stepdaughters of yours will do just fine. That Elitha's been sniff-ing around."

She froze. Her blood felt like a sluice of ice in her veins. "You stay away from her."

He managed to smile, too. A horrible, ragged smile, like something cut by a knife. "I reckon she wants a man to make a woman of her."

Fear crested to panic. Elitha, Elitha, Elitha. Where could she be? Tamsen turned with her children and ran, plunging back through the camp, ignoring the stares they received. Tamsen swept past the Reeds, hoping to find Elitha with her friend Virginia, but all she got was a sour look from Margaret. Through the trampled path that cut across the middle of the encampment (more grumbles, dark looks, mutters). Past the last cluster of wagons, the sun starting to set behind their weather-worn canopies. The children were starting to whimper, frightened to be so far from the rest of the family, and Tamsen was tempted to turn around but then Keseberg's leer would rise up before her eyes and she knew she had to go just a little farther . . . Into the wild sage, the low branches snagging her skirt like a child's hand. A distance from the camp, not far from the river—she could hear the lowing of oxen and cattle just ahead—when she thought she saw movement out of the corner of her eye. Dragging the little ones nearly off their feet, Tamsen swept into a small clearing to find Elitha kneeling in the dirt, with a lantern set beside her. She was using a stick to dig. Tamsen couldn't tell why. The sun had set by now and everything was cast in bare and flickering light.

"Elitha!" she called out, half in anger, half in relief. Elitha started. "What are you doing here? Didn't I tell you"—Tamsen had released her grip on Frances and Eliza and reached down to jerk her stepdaughter to her feet—"you were not to leave my sight, didn't I tell you that?"

Elitha's hands were coated in dirt. Her dress was filthy, too. "But I found lambs' ears. I knew you'd want it. Didn't you say so?"

Lambs' ears. Tamsen used it for one of her remedies. But she was still gripped by a fear that rocked her chest like an inner earthquake. Without thinking, she slapped Elitha hard. Before she knew what had happened, her palm was red and stinging and Elitha was holding her cheek, looking up at her in shock.

But not in pain. In fury. She had never seen Elitha like this before, face knitted together, eyes flashing. She wanted to apologize to her and at the same time, shake her for giving her a fright. For the dizzy fear that still consumed her.

"You—you can't treat me like a child," Elitha said. "I'm nearly a grown woman."

A grown woman—Keseberg's words echoed in her head. Elitha had no idea what a risk it was for a woman to wander away from the wagon train unescorted.

"This is serious, Elitha, and I need you to listen to me and, most importantly, to *obey* me—"

She broke off. Even with the children shifting around her restlessly and the wind rattling the sage, Tamsen heard something moving. She went very still, as if some inner coil inside her had been wound tight. Was she imagining it?

Her first thought was of Keseberg. Perhaps he'd followed her, thought he would scare her good. Maybe it was only that sounds carried strangely over the hollow, making it seem like something far away was right beside her.

No. There was movement all around them, as though they were being surrounded.

"Get behind me," Tamsen ordered. "All of you." She lifted Elitha's lantern and adjusted the wick to increase the flame. "Who's there? Whoever it is, you might as well head back to the wagons. I'll not put up with any nonsense tonight."

But the man who hobbled out from the sagebrush and rocks was not anyone she knew. She lifted the lantern higher, and the figure squinted and moved back slightly into the shadows, crouched. She blinked in the darkness. She could see that he was lean and rangy and crusted brown all over like a skeleton caked in mud or as if he'd grown an outer coating of bark. Like he was part of the wilderness.

She blinked again, as the dizziness returned. Maybe it was the headache from earlier returning, or that she'd taken too much willow bark powder to make it go away. She couldn't be sure of what she was seeing.

"Who are you?" she demanded. The thought of the children behind her amplified her fear; her protective duty rose within her like a fire in the wind. "What do you want?"

No answer. She couldn't quite make out his face but he stared at her with the intensity of a mountain lion, eyes glittering in the lamplight. He was definitely not an Indian. A mountain man, maybe, attracted by the activity of the wagon train. A white man who'd been in the wilderness a long time, maybe lost and on his own. His eyes had an odd, feral quality to them with no glimmer of human intelligence.

"Be calm," she said, in a low voice, when one of the children whimpered. "It's all right." Could they see what she was seeing?

Then there was a second man, and a third, she could swear. The lantern was too dim to show much: only shadows, impressions, movement. A chill lifted on her neck. The way they moved was all wrong. She thought of Luke Halloran, the broken way he'd crawled and lunged. They were like wolves: They circled the way wolves did, they spoke without saying anything out loud.

Wolves separated their prey, isolated them, and picked them off, one by one.

Tamsen turned and saw Elitha, trembling, too far from the others. Isolated.

Before she could shout, one of the shadows lunged in Elitha's direction.

Tamsen's heart sounded a rhythm of panic in her chest, in her head, in the back of her throat. She dove toward Elitha.

Another of the shadow figures scuttled to intercept Tamsen, clawing for her throat. He opened his mouth to reveal a nest of teeth, pointed and inhuman. She swung the lantern with all her might at the man, if that was what he was. The glass chimney shattered as it made contact with his jaw. The fount cracked, throwing oil all over his face.

The children began to bolt. "Stay together!" Tamsen screamed. But it was hopeless. They scattered, children darting through the sage like rabbits, eyes wide with fright.

Within a second, the man's head was engulfed in flames. The sound that came from him was like nothing she'd ever heard, like a renting of the world itself that briefly revealed the pit screams of hell. He clawed at his face, but that only spread the flames to his hands, then his arms. The fire devoured him as though he were made of kindling. The other two men began to scream and retreat from the one that was burning, scattering like dumb animals.

Tamsen got hold of Elitha. "Go after the children, take them to the wagons—now!" Her heart seemed trapped in her throat, choking her.

"The dead . . ." Elitha muttered, looking stunned and confused.

Tamsen shoved Elitha hard in the back. "Don't look back, just run."

The stench from the burning man was overpowering. He flung himself against rocks and scrub as he tried to save himself but only succeeded in setting the whole plain ablaze: sagebrush, reeds, and striplings, all of it caught.

Within seconds the men were lost, as thick billows of smoke funneled toward the sky and made her eyes burn.

She backed away, holding her apron to her mouth, coughing. She wanted to run, but she had no strength left. And she had to try to douse the flames with water from the river, or it would be too late. They would lose everything.

But the fire had taken hold. It raced along the ground, it jumped from bush to bush. Before long, it was a wall of flame in front of her, defying her. Even after dozens of others came sprinting toward her from the camp, the fire spread faster than they could work.

More people came with buckets, and some with shovels, throwing sand onto the fire. Others tried a bucket brigade from the river, tossing bucket after bucket of muddy brown water on the conflagration.

Still, the flames gained.

Samuel Shoemaker wiped his forehead and surveyed the scene. "We're losing ground. We need to hitch up the oxen and move those wagons." The men around him began arguing: Could they round up the oxen in time? The animals had already moved away, frightened by the flames. Maybe they could try to push or drag the heavy wagons to safety—though that seemed like a fool's errand. Some damned the families that had remained back at their campsites, thinking the fire was no threat.

"Let them burn," Baylis Williams said, his face streaked with soot. "If they're too shortsighted to see the danger . . ." Tamsen was shocked; he was normally a gentle soul.

Tamsen cleared her throat. She had to warn them of the danger that was stalking them—something far worse than these rabid flames. "I was attacked," she shouted. "That's how the fire started. Some men came out of nowhere and went after the children."

The others stopped their arguing. "What men?" Graves narrowed his eyes. "White men, or Indians?"

"White men, I think." But not men. Not quite. How could she explain, without playing into the hands of the people who wanted to discredit her?

Keseberg's laugh was like the hollow echo of metal on bone. "There ain't no white men besides us around here," he said.

A murmur rippled through the crowd. Her throat was still raw from smoke, still raw from screaming. She put her hand to her head, trying to think clearly. She hated doubting herself, but suddenly she felt another swerve of dizziness. It wasn't possible this had all been a kind of hallucination brought on by willow bark—was it? Most of the time, Tamsen kept a clear head, but there were times when she wondered if the strange, twisted, tortured part of her had taken over, occluding everything else.

Now, everyone was staring at her, but their looks were not ones of sympathy.

"Funny how you're always in the middle of it whenever things go wrong," Keseberg said loudly. "I think you like the attention, Mrs. Donner."

The wind shifted, blowing the smoke away from them, and as the smoke lifted, the whole camp seemed to disappear before her eyes, dissolving into the darkness.

She broke out in a cold sweat.

But the impression was over just as quickly.

Now, she looked around at the rest of the gathered group and realized: Even if what she thought had happened *had*, there was no way she'd ever get them to listen to her.

And in fact, it didn't matter. Because if what she'd seen *had* been real, then they were all as good as dead anyway. She saw that now, the memory of the feral men's eyes still hovering in her mind, hardening into a certainty.

"We're not going to stop this fire," Eddy said, turning his back on the flames. "We gotta move the wagons. It's our only hope."

Tamsen watched as pandemonium broke out among the group,

spouse arguing with spouse, some throwing down buckets and shovels to sprint for the wagons, others pulling on their neighbors' sleeves, trying to make them stay. "It's every man for hisself," Franklin Graves muttered as he trotted past Tamsen, nearly knocking her off her feet.

With a fresh pulse of terror, Tamsen saw that he was right.

CHAPTER TWENTY-THREE

E
dwin Bryant found the corpse in a cave.

It was the first body he'd come across, man or animal, in the weeks he'd been lost, other than the scattered bones at the prospectors' camp, which had been around for years.

This one was, ironically, a sign of life, of normalcy. You expected to find half-decomposed animals if you walked in the woods long enough. It was the way things were in the wilderness: knots of flies, the sweet-sick smell of decay. But in the days since Fort Bridger, he'd seen nothing at all. Absolutely nothing.

He'd found the cave by accident, during a sudden sweeping rainstorm that had driven him to look for shelter. The cave was small, one of a handful pocking the side of a rocky rise. He was so weak he almost gave up the climb and bunkered where he was. But although myths of wolf-men and diseases that made vampires and corpses of all stripes he could handle, Bryant had never liked storms. So he'd hauled up through the crags, winded by even this limited exertion, and ducked into the first shelter he found.

He'd brought a bundle of sagebrush with him as fuel for a fire, and he was just looking for the best spot for it when he saw it: a male, probably in his midthirties, though it was hard to tell because of the decomposition. Probably an Indian, most likely a Washoe given where he was, or where he thought he was.

The cause of death was apparent enough. The Indian had a wicked gash in the skull, probably not accidental. The impact was too neat, and likely caused not by a fall but by the impact of some heavy weapon, but he couldn't tell for sure—he was no expert in wounds or trauma. He had other injuries, too, deep cuts that could've been made by a wolf or bear, even a mountain cat. That was a funny thing. Bryant had seen no trace of predators in the area—no scores in the bark of the trees, no droppings, no dens.

The man had nothing with him, no bow and arrow, spear or rifle, not even a blanket. He had not been here long before he died. Bryant considered whether whoever—or whatever—had killed him had attacked the man inside the cave but quickly dismissed the idea. There was no evidence of blood except trace amounts on the stone. Bryant had to double over inside the cave to fit; it seemed unlikely that there had been a struggle inside the enclosure.

Which meant that the man had been injured elsewhere and climbed up, or been carried up, ten feet of rock just to die. Running away from something, most likely. Bryant pieced a story together in his head of a man attacked, mortally wounded but able to flee from his assailant. In a delirium, he had run until he saw the small cave; perhaps he mistook it for salvation.

Perhaps he only wanted to die in peace.

Bryant made a pillow of dried sagebrush as far as he could from the body in the narrow space. Every time he struck his flint, he imagined the man might sit up, blinking, irritated at having been awoken. He expected he was going a little mad. He had been alone long enough, without company for weeks now. And without food, except what he could scavenge: a tiny fish, a few eggs stolen from a bird's nest. Mostly, he was getting by on insects and acorns. At one point he'd choked down a handful of roots but they'd given him heaves and he'd thrown up nothing but bile for hours, since there was nothing to throw up.

He drank water but though it filled his stomach, it did nothing for his hunger. After the first three or four days the gnawing had diminished—thank God, it had been like a jaw chewing out from inside him—and he felt clearer-headed, optimistic, certain that starvation had been like a sickness that had slowly passed off. It was another day before he realized he was traveling erratically, circling back over terrain he had passed before. He would wake suddenly in the mud, having lost consciousness without knowing it. He had to rest frequently; he gasped for breath. His heart raced after walking a hundred yards.

He was dying—slowly, at first. Quicker now.

All because he was hungry. All for lack of game, of meat, of food disguised as the flesh of other animals.

The corpse was dark: the color of smoked ham. It was hard to estimate how long he—it, the body—had been dead. Not too long. It smelled of rot but only faintly. The body was barely human anymore, though. His soul was long gone. He was nothing but a shell.

Shipwrecked men survived by eating the bodies of sailors who perished before them, Bryant knew. It was the law of the sea. He'd even heard a story about it once. Something Lavinah Murphy had been saying around a fire back in the early days of their journey, a story about a German shipwreck and the unlucky survivors.

The sagebrush crackled as it burned. The smoke reminded him of Christmas, and Christmas reminded him of goose, and the crackle of sizzling fat, and going to sleep full and happy with the sound of his mother's laughter in his ears. His eyes burned before he realized he was crying.

No one would know.

No one would blame him.

His hands went to the knife in his sheath.

Through the smoke, Bryant thought for a moment that perhaps the man was not a man at all, but an animal in decay. There was no sin in eating animals.

Why couldn't he stop crying?

Not because he would do it, but because, at the last second, he couldn't. He wept because it was no animal, it was a man, and he'd known deep down he would not be able to go through with it. He wept because that meant he would die—probably here, in the cave, to become another rotting corpse warming the air with putrescence.

It was then that he heard noises below the cave: the sound of horses' hooves clipping stone and the murmuring of human voices, even though he couldn't make out the words. He looked over the ledge to see four riders slipping through the sagebrush. They were Indians, probably Washoe, given the location, skinny as scarecrows under their old deerskins. Bryant tried to decide if they seemed dangerous. He could tell it was a hunting party, but what kind of luck had they had? Would they try to kill him for food? He pictured a village of emaciated women and children waiting for the hunters to return.

If he did nothing he would die. If he called out he might very well die, but sooner and quicker, impaled or gutted or shot full of arrows.

Bryant stood and waved, shouting to get their attention.

Custom demanded an exchange of gifts, so Bryant gave the Indians everything he could spare. His navy blue bandana, picked out by his fiancée in the general store in Independence just before the wagon train pulled out. The band on his hat, braided leather studded with tiny silver beads. And finally, his waistcoat, which he'd bought from a haberdasher in Louisville with his first paycheck as a newspaperman. With each item he passed to them, the men smiled, each in turn, until they decided who would accept which gift. These gifts earned him a place at the fire and a share of their evening meal: acorn bread, vegetable root dried like jerky, and a handful of mushrooms.

He forced himself to eat slowly so that he wouldn't get sick. He bowed his head to each man in turn to show his gratitude.

They seemed to know the words he'd learned from the Shoshone, and he augmented this limited vocabulary with gestures and pantomime and drawings in the dirt. They indicated that there was a lake ahead, high up in the mountains, but that he should avoid it. They said the lake was home to a spirit that, they claimed, consumed the flesh of men and turned them into wolves.

"Na'it," one man said to him repeatedly while pointing to the figure he'd drawn in the dirt. Bryant didn't know what they were trying to say.

He led them up to the cave and showed them the corpse, wondering if they might have known the man in life, if he had been of their tribe. Bryant asked as best he could whether they knew what beast or spirit had killed the man in the cave. To his surprise, they had been repulsed by the sight of the corpse, had insisted on setting fire to it immediately without so much as a prayer.

Perhaps because it was so dark and the nuances were lost, or because of the mushrooms he'd eaten, which he was sure were mildly hallucinogenic, he couldn't figure out what the drawings were meant to represent. But it seemed the Indians believed that the man's brutal death was not the work of a man or beast but both, somehow. A man in a wolf's skin, or a beast in a man's skin? It was impossible to tell from their drawings, and they spoke so quickly, and so quietly, Bryant could only make out every third or fourth word.

When he woke, he expected to find the hunting party gone. But they were waiting for him, the horses packed and the fire smothered. The senior man wore Bryant's vest over his buckskin tunic, which made Bryant smile. One of the men offered an arm to Bryant and helped him swing up behind him on horseback, and Bryant gladly accepted. With a grunt, the man in Bryant's vest turned his paint mare west, to follow the trickling stream toward the snow-capped mountains looming in the distance. He would live, it seemed, a few days more.

He was glad to ride out of the clearing, which still lingered with the faint sweet smell of burned flesh.

CHAPTER TWENTY-FOUR

t had to end.

Meet me, James Reed had whispered as he passed by John Snyder. *Eight o'clock, at the cottonwood down by the watering hole.*

Reed wished he could remain with his family after dinner, reading a story to the children by the light of the fire while Margaret mended clothes and Eliza Williams scoured the dishes. Ironic, when you considered how many nights he'd sat at the family dining table in Springfield, wishing he could steal away to meet Edward McGee.

But he had a reckoning coming with Snyder, one he couldn't put off any longer.

He hadn't forgotten the advice Snyder gave him the last time they'd met privately—*don't forget what kind of man I am.* Beneath the veneer of civility, John Snyder was a wild beast, and Reed had foolishly given this man the power to destroy him. Reed could barely stand to be in Snyder's presence any longer, fearing what he might do. If this journey had become a trek through hell, the episodes with Snyder only made it more so, a punishment that, incomprehensibly, Reed seemed to have designed for himself.

At quarter to eight, Reed kissed the children on the head and bade them good night, each in turn. He told his wife that he had to speak to the Breens about some trivial matter; she especially disliked the family, so there was no chance she might ask about the visit later. Once he was out of sight of his wagons, he pulled out his handkerchief and dabbed sweat off his forehead. Once, twice, three times. He stopped himself from overdoing it—lately he noticed his hairline had begun to recede from the habit.

But for good measure, he wiped his mouth three times, too.

He shouldn't have kissed those children, not with his filthy mouth. He was too unclean. They were innocent, those children. The only good, innocent thing in his life. He didn't deserve them.

He arrived at the appointed place well before Snyder and saw him from a distance, lumbering down the slope in his unhurried way. On the horizon, a brilliant band of orange and yellow dissolved into a thick, nighttime black. Snyder came to an abrupt stop in front of Reed.

As Snyder reached for him, however, Reed stepped backward. He'd played the scene in his head a hundred times but had never gotten past this moment.

"No." Improvisation would have to do. "Listen. I came to tell you it's over between us. It has to end."

Snyder reached for him a second time, more aggressively. "What makes you think you get to call the tune? You're done when I say you're done."

Reed managed to avoid him a second time. "Listen to me. I'm serious. I won't do this anymore." Snyder's face twisted into an ugly sneer. He would be angry now. "I was unhappy, looking for a way to escape. But I don't have that luxury anymore. I've got a role to play.

People still look to me—some of them, anyway. If I should fail them, what will become of the wagon train? They need me."

"Don't you have a high opinion of yerself," Snyder said. He took a heavy step toward Reed. "I could tell 'em about you, about what you let me do to you. That you asked for it, you wanted it."

Reed tried to swallow but found he couldn't. "You'd be implicating yourself, too," he finally said. But he no longer knew whether Snyder cared. He felt sick—how could he have let himself fall prey to a man like Snyder? How could he have wanted him so badly?

How was it possible Reed wanted him still? The strong bulk of his shoulders. The moments of hard, rough, frantic forgetting.

"It don't matter what I done," Snyder said. "I'm not the one who's a pervert."

"*Some* of those men won't feel the same way, you can bet on that. They'll never look at you the same."

"What about your *wife*?" Snyder's expression was pure, vicious glee. "How do you think she's gonna look at you after I tell her what you done, on your knees, how you begged for more?" He laughed when Reed's face crumbled.

"You wouldn't dare," Reed said. He was light-headed with fear. This was surreal, a bad fever dream. "You don't have it in you."

Snyder punched him in the face. The blow landed so hard that Reed nearly blacked out. The next he knew, he was lying on the ground. Snyder straddled his chest. The pain was a relief—it brought him out of the sticky, anxious heat of his thoughts and into the present moment. He gasped for air. Another blow ground the back of his skull into the sand. He was being crushed under Snyder's weight. *He's going to kill me*, Reed realized, struggling to comprehend the notion, even as it was happening.

"Fucking faggots," Snyder said. But he sounded calm. "I hate fucking faggots . . ."

He wanted to kill me all along.

But before Snyder could strike him again, they both heard voices, too far off to be distinct but unmistakably raised in argument. Then the sound of a gunshot tore through the air, a violent punch that echoed through the hollow. Snyder backed off Reed's chest, startling like an animal.

"What the hell is going on?" he said.

Reed didn't answer. With effort, he managed to stagger to his feet and lunge for his horse, barely making it up into the saddle. Blood dripped from somewhere on his swollen face. He was having a hard time seeing straight. His thoughts had gone numb, a faint buzz at the back of his head. It took all his concentration to stay on his horse—part of him wanted to fall off, to fall away from himself and vanish. To be wiped clean from this earth.

By the time Reed rode back to the camp, the argument was in full swing. Diminutive William Eddy was chest-to-chest with Patrick Breen, easily twice his size. Eddy, a dead shot, held his rifle firmly, but he wasn't threatening Breen with it, at least not at the moment. The two were red-faced, shouting over each other's words. A small boy, no older than three or four, stood to the side, bawling. A circle had formed around them.

Reed swung wearily out of the saddle, the spot on his face where Snyder had hit him throbbing. He could hardly think through a red haze of pain. "What's going on here?" His voice sounded distant.

Breen did a double take. "What happened to your face?"

"Never mind that," Reed said. His breath came a little easier now. He blinked, trying to clear his vision. Took out his handkerchief and began to wipe down his face, carefully, methodically. "What's the argument about?"

Breen made to grab the crying little boy, but Eddy stepped in front of him. "I'll tell you what happened—this little thief broke into my stores and stole the biscuits we were saving for breakfast."

Biscuits. Reed had had his last biscuit a week ago. Probably nobody in the party had enough flour left for biscuits except the Breens and the Murphys. He thought of the incident with Stanton and the gun. It was a miracle no one had forcibly tried to take food away from the Breens yet, under the circumstances. Not that he could say this to Patrick; he had firearms and he was prepared to use them.

"They're just biscuits, Mr. Breen. What do you propose we do—hang the boy?" He looked down at his handkerchief, which was now drenched in his own blood, and then quickly back at Patrick Breen.

"Nobody's going to lay a hand on Peter," Eddy said. "Not unless they want a bullet in the gut." So the kid was Eddy's son.

"He's a thief. He deserves a good whipping." Breen spat, barely missing Eddy's shoe. "Kids don't come up with these ideas by themselves."

"What are you saying?" Eddy's voice was dangerously low. "Are you saying I put him up to it?"

"The apple doesn't fall far from the tree, is all."

Eddy began to shoulder his rifle and Reed only just managed to push the barrel aside. "Will, you don't want to do that."

"You came around asking for food," Breen said. "Don't deny it."

"You refused to give me a bite," Eddy returned. "Not very Christian of you. My family is starving and you got cattle on the hoof. You won't slaughter your livestock even if it means saving my family's lives."

When Breen frowned he was an ugly man. "It ain't my fault your cattle run off or that you didn't bring enough provisions with you. I might let you *buy* a cow if I had one to spare, but I brought these cattle with me for a reason."

"This is an emergency. None of us knew what we were signing up for."

Reed's head throbbed. He needed a cold compress and willow bark powder. He could still hear Snyder's voice in his head, like the shard of some fractured dream. *Faggot.* "The Eddys are not alone," he said, stuffing the soiled hanky into his pocket and doing his best to draw up his height. Even still, his voice sounded thin above the shouting. "It's no secret that a good number of families are nearly out of provisions."

"That's right," Amanda McCutcheon said. Already, her face looked hollowed out, as if over the course of the journey all her fat had simply burned away in the heat. "If my Will don't get back soon, I'm going to be in desperate straits." Will had gone ahead with Stanton to seek out supplies—with Reed's permission.

Reed held up his hands to quell the murmuring. Panic, barely suppressed, vibrated the air almost constantly now. And who, besides a monster, would be able to stand by and watch a child starve to death? Patrick Breen would. Of that he was sure. This party had its share of monsters.

And sins.

"We have to face the possibility that Charles Stanton and Will Mc-Cutcheon may not return," he said, sternly but calmly, "or may not return . . . *in time*. It's a long, dangerous way to California."

Lavinah Murphy squinted at him. "What do you propose we do about it?"

He was so tired. "You know my thoughts. We must pool our food—"

He was nearly drowned out by an explosion of protest.

"—and begin strict rationing. It's the only way," he persisted.

"Why should my family suffer because someone else was too cheap to bring enough?" Patrick Breen was shouting now. "It's not my fault. It's their tough luck. I'm not going to let my children starve." Some in the crowd murmured in agreement.

Things were turning ugly faster than Reed expected. "Let's not start with blame. Every family in the party has had plenty of bad luck . . ."

"Easy for you to say. You're one of the ones who needs help, not one who'd be making the sacrifice," Lavinah Murphy said.

Faggot. I'm not the one who's a pervert. Was it possible that what had happened in the desert, that all his losses, the cattle roll-eyed and plugged with bullets, or vanished overnight, was punishment for his own wrongdoings? "True, Mrs. Murphy," he said quietly. "True enough. But didn't I sign a voucher promising to pay John Sutter for any charges Stanton incurs on our behalf? I'm not without generosity."

Breen shook his head. His beard and hair were overgrown. They were all starting to neglect themselves, losing the will to keep themselves clean and tidy. To remain civilized. Day by day, they grew wilder, filthier, more animal. "It's easy enough to make promises when it's not food out of your mouth."

There would be no resolution, Reed could see that. But things could get very ugly, very fast. Every man in the party had a rifle and would use it to defend himself. On the other hand, Reed's heart went out to William Eddy, who'd counted on finding game to feed his family. He was a crack shot, the odds had been in his favor; how was he to know the plains had been unaccountably depleted? Today it was the Eddys who were suffering. But tomorrow it would be the McCutcheons and before long, his own family.

He caught sight of his wife, making her way to the gathering. How small she looked, wrapped in her shawl. She was still mourning the loss of their wagon. She blamed him, he knew. He thought not of *her* belongings but of his daughter's doll then, the bisque and calico scraps—frayed, love-worn—buried in the earth miles back, a final bit of hope now covered in dirt and gone.

Reed was just about to speak again when John Snyder pushed his way to the front of the crowd. Reed hadn't seen him approach. He would have thought Snyder was drunk if he didn't know there was almost no alcohol or beer to be had. Besides, there hadn't been any time—he had just been close enough to smell him, to smell the familiar reek of his sweat, the smell of harness leather on his fingers.

"Hang on, everybody," Snyder said. "Before you listen to one more word from that man"—he jerked his head in Reed's direction—"there's something you should know about him. He's not the man you think he is."

The air went out of Reed's lungs. Even after Snyder's attack underneath the cottonwood, even despite the burn of bloodthirst he'd felt in Snyder's muscles, his anger, the blood staining Reed's handkerchief—despite all of it, he'd *still* thought that maybe the teamster wouldn't dare make good on his threats . . .

"What are you talking about?" Breen asked, and Reed could see, on Snyder's face, how much pleasure he was taking in the sudden hush of attention: the same pleasure he always took in crushing and destroying, in leaving open wounds.

Reed never gave Snyder a chance to respond. He couldn't afford to. If he let Snyder speak, he'd be strung up by nightfall.

He launched himself at Snyder, knocking him to the ground. For a moment they were pressed together, cheek against cheek. Snyder's hands on his wrists felt familiar, the breath on his face intimate. Reed couldn't see what the others were doing but he heard their shocked murmurs, the sharp intake of breath. He expected someone to separate them, but no one came. No one stopped him.

The tender spot on his face throbbed; his aching head pulsed like it was set to explode.

The seconds passed like hours. Snyder had a choke hold on him, but Reed would not surrender his grasp on Snyder's collar. Finally, Snyder let go of Reed's throat but only to reach for his belt, for the hunting knife kept there in a sheath. Reed had seen Snyder play with it a dozen times. Snyder meant to kill him; there wasn't a question in Reed's mind.

Faggot. Faggot. What about your wife?

One second, Reed was waiting to feel the knife plunged into his side, cracking his ribs apart. But the next, it was his hand holding the knife.

He thrust it to the hilt in John Snyder's chest.

For a split second, Reed felt relief fly through him, as though this, in the end, were what he'd wanted all along. Sweet air rushed into his lungs even as Snyder went soft, letting out a long dry hiss like the sound of wind escaping the plains. Then Reed stared, with no feeling at all, as John Snyder fell back, lifeless, his eyes rolling open and unseeing to the sky.

CHAPTER TWENTY-FIVE

ary Graves had been just about to turn in for the evening
when she heard the swell of voices and saw people rush
past their campsite. Had something terrible happened? Her
first thought was of another fire, or an Indian attack, or a
raid on the remaining cattle.

Her heart sped up. She followed the crowd to the Donners' campsite. George Donner, sitting by the fire, looked up at the sudden inter-
ruption. Lewis Keseberg and William Eddy held James Reed between
them. Reed looked terrible. The man was shaking uncontrollably. A
huge welt was rising on his forehead, and a dark bruise blackened his
jaw. Then she saw that his hands were wet with blood.

Keseberg shoved Reed to his knees. "We were fools to follow this
man. Dragged us over the mountains and through that desert. I told
you all that he didn't know what he was doing, but you wouldn't listen
to me! And now he's up and killed a man—"

Donner finally stood up. "Who?"

"The teamster John Snyder."

Mary was immediately relieved: She didn't like Snyder. Nor did Donner. No one did. There were some people in the party you could probably kill and there was a chance you'd get away with it; Mary had to admit that her own father might even be one of them. And unaccountably, she found that she felt sorry for Reed, a man her father hated.

"What do you want me to do about it?" Donner asked, with genuine puzzlement. He looked over the assembled crowd as if surprised to see them there.

"You're our fucking leader, aren't you?" Keseberg said. "Or *were*," he spat. Mary was surprised. He had once been one of Donner's staunchest defenders. But a man like Keseberg didn't know loyalty. "He just killed a man in cold blood. Didn't give Snyder a chance to defend himself. What do we do with him?"

"Murder's a capital offense," Samuel Shoemaker said, as though anyone needed reminding.

They might have acted like George Donner was still the party captain, but it was James Reed who had been leading the wagon party for weeks and they knew it. He'd done the brutal, dirty work, found a trail through the desert and listened to their bickering and complaints. He had served them selflessly, kept his calm in the face of panic and loss, and yet now they were talking about stringing him up. *If only Charles Stanton were here.* The thought came to Mary automatically, but once she noticed it, she didn't mind it warming somewhere in her chest. Stanton would talk sense into them. He wouldn't let them hurt Reed.

The longer Stanton was away, the more Mary came to inwardly rebel against her father's admonishments and her own hesitations. Without Stanton's calm presence, she felt even more keenly how he'd been the only truly sensible person among them.

She knew he had terrible secrets that ate at him from within, and that these were things she ought to know about a man before she'd be willing to trust him, but she had begun to realize, too, that only a man with a conscience could be so seriously afflicted by his own past as to show it in his every gesture—the apology in his shoulders, in his voice, in the way he avoided eye contact with her despite the tension, the *good* tension, she knew they both felt.

"That may be true within the sovereign territory of the United States of America," Donner was saying now. "But I remind you all that we are outside that territorial limit. We are no longer governed by U.S. law." His eyes went to Reed. What, she wondered, could he be thinking? Reed had fought him from the start and had displaced him at the head of the wagon train. But Donner only shook his head. "If you kill this man, you will be in essence taking the law into your own hands."

"You're talking a lot of fucking nonsense as far as I'm concerned," Keseberg said, smiling crookedly in a way no one could mistake for friendly. "I'm talking biblical law. He killed John Snyder. He deserves to die."

As hideous a person as Keseberg was, people seemed to listen to him. He had a kind of power over them.

As for Mary, her own voice felt stifled in her throat. She needed to say something, but caution held her back.

She had always been a practical person, to a fault. She wished sometimes she were passionate, that her beliefs came pouring out of her unfiltered and uncensored.

Perhaps it was those qualities Stanton had been drawn to in Tamsen.

Mary kept quiet. She was glad, at least, that some of the others did not agree with Keseberg. "I'm not going to kill a man unless a judge orders it," Milt Elliott finally said. "We don't want to do anything that'll get us in trouble later."

"Banish him." Tamsen spoke up suddenly. Everyone turned to her with a faint rustling of cloth. Despite everything that had happened—despite how much people despised and distrusted her now—she held her head high and was unafraid to make eye contact. To Mary, she looked almost regal.

Something twisted in Mary's stomach at the sight of her. People were still afraid of her, that much was clear. Peggy Breen and Eleanor Eddy told anyone who'd listen that the woman was using her witchcraft to draw the life from George Donner like a succubus. And then there'd been the incident with the fire. Mary didn't buy into the worst of the rumors—still, she saw that Tamsen was taking a serious risk now, in speaking up for Reed.

Taking a risk where Mary had not.

"It's God's place to judge him, not ours," Tamsen said. "For those of you who think this is too lenient a punishment, just remember: A man can't survive out there on his own. Sending him out is as good as a death sentence."

Keseberg glowered at Tamsen. Mary caught the look. "Most of you mighta only thought of John Snyder as a servant. That he was only good for driving the oxen and doing what he was told. But he did his part. We owe it to him."

Donner frowned. "We need the facts. Do we know why Mr. Reed did what he did?" Before Keseberg could answer, Donner raised a hand to shut him up. "James?"

Reed swallowed. His eye was nearly swollen shut. "You all saw what he was doing, and you know the kind of man he was. He was a liar, hoping to ruin lives with his lies. He came at me—I, I had to defend myself."

"Don't speak ill of the dead." Keseberg cuffed him, shoving him down on his hands and knees again.

"He could get a wild hair up his ass and speak out of turn," Walt Herron said. Walt had been the closest thing Snyder had to a friend. "But like Keseberg said, that's no reason to kill him."

A murmur went through the crowd. Mary turned and saw a momentary disturbance in the knot of people before she saw Margaret Reed shove her way into the clearing.

She spoke directly to Donner, as though the others didn't matter. "Don't kill my James, I beg you." She was a small woman, and sick, apparently. But there was still something fierce about her, something hard-edged as a blade. "He's done a terrible thing, I don't disagree. He's killed a man and he deserves to be punished. But I ask you to consider the circumstances, and all the good he's done for the wagon train."

"Good—what good has he done? He nearly got us killed in the desert," Keseberg said.

"We would've had to face that godforsaken miserable desert no matter who was leading us," Lavinah Murphy chimed in, with a determined air about her. She had pushed her way toward the front as well and stood just behind Margaret now and slightly to the right, like a soldier behind a captain. As a mother of thirteen, the lone woman in the wagon train leading a family, Lavinah was well respected in the group, though there were some who whispered about her Mormon beliefs.

Keseberg looked taken aback. Mary wasn't sure she'd ever heard anyone stand up to Keseberg, and perhaps the man himself hadn't, either.

"James got us through, didn't he?" Margaret demanded. "No one died, even though we all thought we might."

No one objected. What she said was true.

"Killing him isn't going to bring the man back," Margaret went on.

"Listen to me, every one of you, before you make your decision. I don't know why James did what he did, but I beg you to consider the *whole* man and see if you can't find it in your heart to be merciful. I was a new widow, sick, with four mouths to feed. James Reed married me when no one else would. He's provided a home for my children, put a roof over their heads and food on the table. He's treated those children as though they were his own. Only a man of remarkable generosity and kindness would do such a thing, don't you think?"

Mary felt tears welling in her eyes as she listened.

"He worked his fingers to the bone for the children of a man he never knew," Margaret said, her body shaking visibly, but her jaw and stance firm. "What kind of man does this? I beg you"—she walked the perimeter, looking each man in the eye—"find some other way to punish him, yes, but don't take his life. Spare my husband."

There was a long silence. Reed had been hanging his head during this speech, perhaps rightly aware that a wrong word would be the end of him, but now Mary saw him wipe his face against the shoulder of his jacket, and she wondered if he was trying to swipe away tears of his own.

Mary could hear the wind hissing in the distance. She could hear her heart drum a beat in her throat, in her head. The sun seemed to glare down on them like a lidless eye.

Donner finally asserted himself. "He goes with nothing—no horse, no food."

It was as if all Margaret's strength deserted her at once. With a small noise of shock, she collapsed beside her husband. It was impossible to tell whether she was relieved or upset, but she cried over him as though something in her had been split open.

Meanwhile, Keseberg gave Tamsen another hard stare before spitting on the ground at her feet. "Get him out of here before I kill him

myself," he said, pushing his way curtly through the crowd and causing Lavinah Murphy to stumble as he did.

Mary rushed toward them then, knowing that if she waited a moment longer, her chance would be gone. As Tamsen lifted Reed to
his feet—miserable, stunned, still bleeding—Mary came around and
wrapped an arm under his weeping wife, helping to lift her to standing. Tamsen caught her eye, and Mary felt something pass between
them, something like understanding. She suspected that Stanton,
should he ever make it back to them, would disapprove of any sort
of bond between her and Tamsen. For some reason, though, this
thought pleased Mary very much. She wasn't sure what she wanted
from Stanton, but it wasn't his approval.

After that night—James Reed folding away into its darkness forever, without a single protest, which unnerved her more than anything else had—Mary moved in with the Reed family to give them
help. She pitied Margaret—now twice a widow—and it felt good to be
of use.

CHAPTER TWENTY-SIX

Springfield, Illinois
May 1840

James Reed had made it all the way to the livery stable to fetch his saddle horse before he realized he'd forgotten his new hat. Walking back to his office, he could picture it hanging from a peg on the wall: broad-brimmed like a Quaker's, made of black brushed felt with a narrow band of plain brown leather. He could wait until tomorrow and ride home bareheaded—having left the old one, rotted from sweat, at the haberdasher's—but the lapse of concentration bothered him. It wasn't like him to be forgetful. It wasn't like him to ride through town hatless, either, and he dabbed his brow with his handkerchief self-consciously at the thought, then twice more.

When he swung open the door to his office, however, he was surprised to see the new junior clerk, Edward McGee, sitting behind his desk, an open ledger in front of him. McGee looked up.

It was he who should have been startled, but instead Reed felt like the one who had been caught where he shouldn't be.

McGee's wavy hair was a light gold, his eyes were dark and uncommonly beautiful. At the time, those eyes had not looked guilty but full of a kind of knowing that made the boy seem older than he was. He had the same long, sharp nose, the sculpted cheeks and jaw of the young Irish lords Reed had seen from a distance as a child.

"McGee, isn't it?" Reed said as he closed the door behind himself. "You're the one who replaced Silas Pennypacker."

McGee ran a hand through his hair.

Reed cleared his throat uncomfortably. "It seems you have mistaken my desk for your own," he went on.

A youthful grin crept across McGee's face, lighting him up. Then he quickly corrected it, once again giving Reed a knowing look, as though the two of them were sharing a secret. "I beg your pardon, sir. It isn't what it looks like—Mr. Fitzwilliams sent me to find this. He told me exactly where it was kept. I disturbed nothing else on your desk, sir."

"And did Fitzwilliams direct you to open it as well?" he asked with a curt nod toward the ledger.

McGee looked Reed steadily in the eye. "I wanted to make sure I had the correct volume. The accounts can be confusing sometimes." The young man was incorrigible—and lying, certainly.

Reed felt a pang of alarm as McGee rose from the chair—taken aback by his tall build, the way his shirt pressed firmly against the muscles in his chest. There was an energy about him, something Reed couldn't quite pinpoint, that made it seem like he was going to reach out and touch Reed.

Reed held still, waiting for it.

But instead, McGee retrieved his jacket and moved toward the door.

For some indefinable reason, Reed couldn't let the clerk leave just yet. He remained where he stood, blocking McGee's way. "Why don't you take a seat, Mr. McGee, and have a glass of whiskey with me? Perhaps I can help explain the ledger to you."

McGee did not retract his bluff, if that was what it had been. He stayed and made himself comfortable as Reed poured two generous shots of whiskey from the bottle he kept in a desk drawer. They sat in chairs by the window, the fading afternoon sun falling across McGee's lap, tracing fingers of light over his jaw. He seemed to be perpetually grinning even when he spoke, and Reed found he often lost the thread of McGee's words as he stared at the younger man's mouth.

McGee told him how grateful he was for this job—the business of real men, he'd said—after a failed apprenticeship with an actor. At first, the story seemed far-fetched to Reed—perhaps even fabricated—but as he learned more about McGee's childhood in New York, the father who had been distant and cruel, and then the loss of both parents to illness, he began to soften toward the young man. There was a darkness in McGee's past, that was certain—something he wasn't telling Reed. But Reed didn't pry. He wasn't interested in the details, only in the way McGee looked at him—like he was a light in all that darkness. It seemed impossible.

"But enough about me," McGee said then, though he didn't seem at all ready to stop talking. "My background is hardly worse than what anyone might read in the news." He laughed, and the sound caused Reed's stomach to flip with anticipation. He crossed and recrossed his legs. "I read every newspaper I can get my hands on," McGee went on. "Do you enjoy the news, Mr. Reed?"

"Me?" Reed frowned into his whiskey; he had no desire to answer questions. He felt once again caught, exposed. "I suppose I follow the news as much as any other businessman."

This prompted McGee to reel off a series of delightfully horrific stories he'd read recently. How bodies were still being found two weeks after a terrible tornado had struck Natchez Trace and that Christian ministers were protesting the opening of some scandalous play in Philadelphia. Then a strange tale about a German ship that became stranded at sea and how, as the weeks without rescue dragged on, passengers and crewmen had to resort to cannibalism to survive. Edward's eyes glowed as he heaped on detail—describing how they gutted a corpse in a lifeboat on the open sea, cracked rib bones apart to suck out the marrow—and Reed wondered once again whether Edward might be making it up. But why would he—merely to prolong the moment? Was he also reluctant for their time together to end?

"I was wondering, Mr. McGee, if you might care to join me for dinner? I was just on my way to the chophouse up the street." Where had this idea come from? He had been on his way home to dine with his family. Margaret and the children were expecting him. Yet it seemed very important that this conversation with his new junior clerk not end. "They do a very fine lamb with mint jelly. You have my permission to crack the bones for the marrow, if that is your wish." Reed had made a kind of joke—something he didn't usually do. He was surprised by that.

He was surprised later, too, when he realized he'd never remembered to bring home his new hat.

The inevitable started that night, because Edward McGee really *had* seen something in Reed with those searching eyes—had discovered, or sensed, the secret that lay deep within James Frazer Reed. He knew what Reed wanted, probably well before Reed had admitted it to himself.

The change occurred over dinner brandy, the liquor relaxing Reed, lowering his reserve. He let his gaze linger on the clerk, who did not look away. At one point they both reached for the bottle of brandy and the young man's hand rested on Reed's. It was only for a moment, but that was enough. Reed would remember that touch for the rest of his life.

The next six months were bliss. Reed turned into a besotted school-girl. To think he had gone so long in life without love.

They passed as business associates, Edward acting as Reed's private clerk. It was only natural, wasn't it, for a man's assistant to accompany him on business trips out of town, to long lunches at the club, to work late in the office? They carried on right under everyone's noses. Reed was amazed that they got away with it.

Edward had even mentioned the possibility of the two of them run-ning away together. Going to California to start a new life. Reed could let go of all his responsibilities: Margaret and her brood, his business, his large house and grounds! Sure, he'd worked hard for these things but did he really want them? Didn't he want freedom instead?

Reed had been a striver all his life, desperate to leave the poverty of his youth behind. And yet he could not choose freedom. It didn't seem real. It seemed an illusion. And he couldn't bring himself to leave his family behind. It was something he simply could not explain to Ed-ward, who had no family to speak of.

You're afraid to be happy, Edward said to him reproachfully. *You don't trust me.*

But Edward was wrong. Reed *did* trust him. Far too much. And that was the root of all the trouble.

REED HADN'T BEEN ABLE to see then what would follow in the years to come. The gradual frustrations that would arise between them. The aching and uncontrollable jealousy, the suspicion that McGee had transferred his affections to other men. Reed didn't know then about the accounts, either. It would still be several years before Fitzwilliams started pointing out the irregularities—insisting there could be no other explanation but one: Edward had been stealing from them, slyly and steadily, for years.

How could Reed have known then that when he would later confront the young man, McGee would threaten to tell the whole world what had been going on between them, would demand hush money—a large sum immediately and a regular annuity on top of it? That McGee's demands would threaten to ruin him, ultimately leaving Reed no other choice than to flee Springfield?

How could Reed have known that the Donners' plan to travel west would ultimately save him?

He couldn't have known, of course. He couldn't have known any of it. And maybe it wouldn't have changed anything if he had. Because the slant in Edward's smile had snagged in his heart like a fishing hook. The loneliness in Edward's dark eyes—*that* had been real, Reed was sure. It had called to him, had echoed his own, had rendered him powerless. The boy's touch had brought him to life. There could be no helping it. What would come, would come.

OCTOBER 1846

CHAPTER TWENTY-SEVEN

t first, when Mary Graves saw the rider in the distance, she mistook it for a long shadow. They had left the arid basin the day before; the last hundred miles of the trek had been a long uphill climb, and they'd come up over the ridge to see a valley of wildflowers and pine grass, sweet-scented and pale green, that nearly startled Mary into crying. There were pine trees to be split for firewood. And a river: shallow but wide, throwing off a dazzle of light.

Mary watched the shadow lengthen and materialize on the horizon: a horse, liver chestnut, the color of Charles Stanton's mare.

Her father, walking beside the oxen with a switch, lifted his head and brought a hand to his eyes. "He's back," was all he said.

Stanton had two young Indian men with him, Salvador and Luis. The Murphys, Graveses, Reeds, and Fosters rushed him; the other families had pulled ahead on the trail. The children came running at the shouts of joy and laughter as he unstrapped his packages, sounds long unfamiliar to the wagon train. Stanton smiled at everyone, and tried to calm them, too, as they grabbed for his supplies.

And yet Mary, who had begun to dream of his return, to think of him less as a man of mystery or some sort of savior and instead as a touchstone of reality—a person, perhaps the only person, whom she could trust—Mary, who had so many times glanced up to see a floating mirage in the distance and felt her heart leap at the sight of him, found that she was too shy to come forward now, and instead hung back.

"Everyone's near to starving," Bill Foster, Lavinah's son-in-law, said bluntly. But it must have been obvious. Mary saw him as Stanton must: a scarecrow in clothes now too big for him, shirt bloused around his waist and skin-thin arms, pants held up with a length of rope.

"I ran into the Breens and Eddys up the trail. They told me how bad things have gotten," Stanton said. "But I'm back with enough to last us a while."

"I hope you brought bacon," Mary's little brother said, running up to him. "We ain't had bacon for weeks." How gaunt his face had gotten. Five years old and Franklin looked like a little old man.

"We should have a big feast to celebrate, like we did at the parting of the ways," Virginia Reed said. Her eyes were feverishly bright. The children were turning into strange, stalky insects, all eyes and spikes and desperate twitches.

Stanton, in comparison, looked like a man in color among a wash of wraiths even after weeks in the saddle. "Now, hold on there," he said easily. But she noticed he stood between the settlers and his mules. "We're not out of the woods yet. Take it easy with these provisions. We're a long way from Sutter's Fort."

Amanda McCutcheon pushed her way through the crowd. "Where's my Will? Isn't he with you?"

Mary's heart hollowed. In her excitement, she hadn't even noticed that McCutcheon was missing. She doubted the others had remarked on it, either. They were too hungry to think of much else.

"He took ill on the trail," Stanton said quietly. "But don't worry; he made it to Sutter's Fort and that's where he's resting. He'll be waiting for you there."

"Ill? He must be powerful sick not to come back for us . . ."

"The doctor says he'll recover. With the weather starting to shift, I didn't want to wait any longer."

The weather *was* starting to shift; funny, Mary hadn't noticed until he mentioned it. It had happened in the past handful of days. Even the hot afternoons had lost their edge and the earlier sunsets brought longer, cooler evenings.

And that meant winter wasn't far behind.

Two nights earlier, she'd sat up late with her brother William. They lay on their backs on the cool ground to look up at the stars, a favorite pastime back in Springfield. The wide black sky, the vastness that usually filled her with optimism, made her feel small and fragile that night. Nature had shown them these past few months how vulnerable they were. Her brother must've felt the same, for he asked Mary if she thought they were going to die.

The question was on everyone's mind so she wasn't surprised, but it filled her with rage. Not at the unfairness of it, for she understood that life was deeply unfair, and, truly, had never expected otherwise. But it angered and astonished her that fear and hopelessness had so easily taken root among them. Mary believed in certain fundamental truths, and one of them was in life's persistence—in the incredible will within each of us to go on, to thrive, to improve, and, when tested, to do good.

As the crowd shifted, she found her way next to Stanton with renewed determination, despite the fact that so far he had yet to look in her direction.

Beneath the burble of the crowd, she was able to speak softly, so no one else could hear. "You came back for us."

"I said that I would, didn't I?" He smiled grimly as he started to loosen the rope rigging on the nearest mule.

Had he come to forget about her these weeks away, or worse, come to believe that she had led the general persecution against Tamsen? After all, it had been Mary who brought the rest to the scene of Halloran's murder. If he believed that about her, she couldn't blame him. But she *could* set him straight. Not because she needed his favor but because she wanted it.

Unfortunately, it didn't seem he was going to give her that chance, which of course made her desire it all the more.

With hardly a glance in her direction, he turned back to address the group. "If everyone is ready, we can distribute the rest of these provisions. No pushing, or arguing. It's all been sorted according to the amount of money you put in. Let's start with the Murphys . . ."

THE PARTY QUIT EARLY for the day. Everyone was anxious to have their first proper meal in weeks, to celebrate their salvation. Mary wasn't ready to celebrate, not until she'd had a chance to say her piece. She kept an eye out for Stanton, hoping for a few minutes alone, but he was constantly surrounded by members of the wagon train intent on hearing about the trail that lay before them or about Sutter's Fort—at this point, a destination as elusive and chimerical as heaven. She wasn't sure if he was really that busy or trying to avoid her.

But she wouldn't give up. It simply went against her nature. Her father had called her stubborn more times than she could count, and perhaps about that he'd been right.

So she waited on the periphery, behind the well-wishers and the curious. She would be patient. Finally, he saw her hovering just out of earshot. He ducked to say something to the two Miwoks before striding out to meet her.

"Will you speak to me, Mr. Stanton?" she asked. Her voice sounded high and nervous to her ears.

He only nodded.

They walked side by side, and Mary felt she might burn away. She was overwhelmed by relief and terror all at once. She had prayed for him to return, prayed that she would be given a chance to set things right between them, and now that he was here, she did not know what to say to him.

"I feared—" She stopped, overwhelmed. "I feared I would never see you again."

"Perhaps that would have been for the best," he said, his voice low and hard.

She reeled as though she'd been slapped in the face. "Can you really hate me so much?"

"Mary." His voice softened.

"I don't see how you can." She pushed on defensively. "You have hardly given me any chance at all to prove myself to you. We haven't even spoken since—"

"You don't need to prove yourself to me, or to anyone. I don't hate you, Mary. Not in the slightest." At this, a broad smile spread over his face, though he attempted to tuck it away.

Now she thought she must be dreaming—perhaps hunger and exhaustion had gotten the better of her, because she couldn't make sense of his words.

"Well, if you don't hate me, then why have you been avoiding me?"

she insisted. "Why did you say it would have been for the best never to see me again? I fear that either I do not understand you, Mr. Stanton, or you do not understand yourself."

"More likely the latter," he said, his smile melting into a rueful half grin. "You see, it's not at all that I hate you but that I fear I quite like you. That's what keeps me away, if you must know. But I can't have you off thinking badly of me."

"*Me* thinking badly of *you*?" Now it was her turn to smile. "I have thought of little else but you, though none of the thoughts were bad." She was shocked by her own boldness and tempted to cover her mouth to keep a surprised laugh from bursting out.

He beat her to it, though, and his laugh was like water running over stones in the creek—fast and free and clear. She wanted to enter that laugh and to swim and bathe and splash in it, to drink it down and be cleansed by it.

"Well, that's a relief, then," he said, though she was the one who felt relief—was nearly dizzy with it.

This feeling amazed her. How neatly the answer came to her, that this man, Charles Stanton, who had, even before she'd realized it, occupied so many of her thoughts—this man was *the* man for her. The person for her. She knew it in this moment, suddenly and definitively, as though it had been preordained, as though her life had been building up to it from the start: She, Mary Graves—the serious, ever-practical, always patient Mary Graves—was giddily, stupidly, happily in love with Charles Stanton.

And because she was so certain of it, she felt the truth would have to be known. She must tell him. Soon. Very soon. But not now. Not yet.

After all, since they met, they'd spent nearly as much time apart as together. She would wait, at least, until the latter outmeasured the former before she would give full voice to her feelings. It seemed only right, and she wanted to do things right, now more than ever.

As they wandered along the creek, the late-afternoon sun comfortable on their shoulders, she started to tell him about the things that had happened while he was away—about Snyder's death and Reed's banishment. That hit Stanton hard—he'd come to trust in Reed, and he admitted that it scared him how quickly the group could turn.

She told him about the rest, too: The old Belgian, Hardkoop, had taken ill and been left behind, and then Jacob Wolfinger had tried to go back for him, never to return. She told of how the sounds of Doris Wolfinger's soft crying seemed to hang in the air for many nights thereafter, as though the realization that her husband was gone for good had come to her only in gradual waves.

"I don't know what to make of everything that's happened to us," Mary said truthfully, feeling more overwhelmed than before as the weight of it all piled back on top of her. "I can't tell who's good or who's bad anymore. It seemed so easy back in Springfield. But not one of those good people lifted a finger to help poor Mr. Hardkoop when Lewis Keseberg threw him out . . . Or went back to look for Mr. Wolfinger when he disappeared. It's like everyone is just out for himself . . . Everyone says Tamsen's a liar, with her tales of shadowy men in the basin. Even those who once trusted her seem to despise her now, but I saw her after they brought her back from the fire. I don't know why she would have made up a story like that."

Stanton shook his head. "Tamsen likes attention, but not the negative kind. You're right, Mary. It is very strange."

"And then there's Mr. Reed," she went on, not eager to linger on the theme of Tamsen and her disconcerting stories. "Reed didn't seem capable of killing a man in cold blood like that . . ."

"You're right about that, too. That doesn't sound like the man I know." Stanton's voice was hard, distant.

"It just makes no sense, no sense at all." She looked toward the horizon, hazy with sun. "That's why I'm so glad you're back, Mr. Stanton. One of the many reasons." She blushed. "You always seem to make sense. I—I feel safer around you."

He appeared to withdraw then—it was subtle but she felt a tiny space had reopened between them. He stepped closer to the river to avoid their elbows brushing, and a coldness rustled through her that had nothing to do with the changing weather.

"I don't know why you have given me your trust—again and again, Mary. I want it, of course, but you must know I don't deserve it." He had stopped walking and was staring quietly at the flowing river.

"Whatever you've done, whatever happened in your past, it can't be as bad as you imagine." She touched his arm gently. "The sin has atoned for itself—I can see that in you, in the way you carry the burden of it. You must forgive yourself." She said these words because she believed them to be true—the Bible teaches forgiveness in others so that God may bestow forgiveness on all.

She thought, fleetingly, that he might cry, but he only let out a heavy breath and pushed a hand through his hair. "I can never forgive myself— it would be like letting her die again. I already fail to save her, over and over again, in my dreams. Every night, I watch her drown again."

Mary's breath caught in her throat. She knew what he was referring to: the story of the girl he had loved—and whom he left when she was with child.

"I planned to marry her, you know," he said. "I had come to tell her so that very day." Mary watched his knuckles turn white as he clenched his hands and flexed them. Then he turned to look at her, as if expecting her to protest.

"Then it wasn't your fault," Mary said, though she could tell the words didn't touch him. Mary's father had told her that the poor girl had killed herself *because* Stanton had abandoned her. But now she could see that perhaps there'd been another reason altogether. The man—the boy—her father described hadn't sounded like Stanton at all. It seemed absurd now that she had doubted Stanton, even for a minute.

The shadow of a lone cloud, high overhead, rippled over the landscape in front of them. It was a sign, like the hand of God touching the valley.

They walked slowly for a few more minutes, listening to the gentle sluice of the creek and the far-off noises from camp. He squeezed her hand and she liked how it felt, the strength in his fingers. Strength she could depend on.

"There is something more than the loss of her, and the horrible manner of her death, that haunts me, Mary."

She waited.

"I had no money, and nowhere to go when all of this happened. My reputation had been destroyed, I couldn't get a lick of work, and I was cast away by my own family, you have to understand. But still it's no excuse for . . ." He trailed off, squinting at the fading sun. It had been setting earlier and earlier, Mary noticed, and she shivered at the knowledge of autumn's descent, and of their limited time.

"No excuse for . . ." she prodded, both dreading to hear it and needing to, needing to understand him, to know him. And, she sensed, Stanton needed to be known *by* her.

"For accepting his help."

"His?"

Stanton sighed. "Lydia's father gave me the sum of money that got my life started. He was paying me off, you see. Paying me to leave, to help make the whole tragic incident go away. His money got me all the way to Virginia. When the law office no longer suited me, I went off to war in Texas. But then I found I still had nothing to return to and nowhere to start. With what remained of his . . . *charity*"—he seemed to choke on the word, but pushed on—"I was able to set up a shop in Springfield. I thought with the last of Knox's money finally spent, the past was good and dead, then. But it wasn't. Knox ran into difficult times of his own, and called on me to repay my debts to him. He was very demanding, and I, well . . . I couldn't say no to him, Mary."

She felt a chill; darkness was descending and she wanted to beg him to stop here. She didn't need to hear more. She knew men could do desperate things for money. Her own family had certainly tried everything to change their own circumstances. It had always been up to Mary to take care of her family, and though she resented it, she understood it, too.

"Don't you want to know why I couldn't refuse him, Mary?" he said, his voice guttural and low.

"You felt guilty. Anyone would have." A bird cawed overhead. She couldn't make out what type in the silvery dusk.

"But I *was* guilty. Don't you see? Not of Lydia's suicide, but of other things. Knox knew . . . he'd discovered the affairs I'd had since."

Affairs. Mary felt heat rise to her face. She slipped her hand out of his. So Lydia's father had, in a word, blackmailed Stanton.

Which meant that whatever his indiscretions had been, they'd been reckless—and there'd been many of them.

Stanton sighed. "I knew Donner was an old friend and business associate of Knox's. He was, in fact, most likely one of Knox's primary informants. But when I heard the Donners were heading west, I sold everything to join them. I hated George Donner, but I hated Knox more. I needed a way out." He ran a hand through his hair. "But I've learned better now, Mary. I see now that there's never a way out from the past."

Mary sucked in a breath. She had no idea what to say to him, what could take away this kind of pain—the grief and shame he had carried for so many years. She'd thought she'd understood what had plagued him but was beginning to see that the secrets of Charles Stanton's past were layered over one another, folded in on themselves, and unfolding still, into the future.

He lifted his gaze to her: sorrowful, but did she see the slightest glimmer of hope? "That's why I've been trying to avoid you, Mary. It's for your own good. I don't deserve your trust. You deserve someone better than me."

Maybe he was right. Maybe she shouldn't trust him. Maybe he didn't deserve her help after all. But then, didn't all men deserve a second chance?

"How can I help you, Charles?" she asked quietly, unable to meet his eyes, but feeling the boldness of his first name on her tongue.

His voice came to her, low and crushing. "You can't. Don't you see, Mary? My heart died long ago, frozen over in that river. There is nothing of me left to save."

But Mary was not one to be so easily swayed by melancholy words. She took his hand again, and even though he wouldn't look at her, she kissed his knuckles. "I don't believe that," she said.

And her words were a promise.

She had thought she wanted to love Stanton, not to save him—but now she saw that the two might be one and the same.

Still, as she walked away from him, she remembered that there was one person who would never be saved. So that night, Mary said a quick and silent prayer for Lydia, the poor beauty frozen forever, and the unborn child within her, who was never to be known.

CHAPTER TWENTY-EIGHT

The early fall heat had finally broken, releasing refreshing winds from the north, blowing clean the sheets and wagon covers, breathing renewed energy into the party. Stanton had found them and supplies had been distributed. Tamsen should have felt better. The others only met her gaze fleetingly these days, with a kind of heat and disgust in their eyes, but she could live with that. She didn't mind being ostracized or hated, so long as she had her children.

The haunting nightmares full of men with caked, chapped, inhuman skin, burning alive—of sweet Halloran turned ugly and foul, grasping at her, hungering for her—should have subsided. They hadn't, though. She didn't know what to believe, whether the threat she had witnessed—the creeping, dancing shadows—had been real or the mad invention of a mind corrupted by a terrible secret, something almost as hideous as the creatures she thought she'd seen.

Certainly she couldn't trust Elitha, who babbled about the voices of the dead to anyone who would listen, or the younger girls, to support her claims. They didn't know what they'd seen, either—it had all been a cloud of movement and panic that ended in an eruption of smoke and flame.

There was a giddiness in the air now, but it unsettled her—it was the high of a drunk gambler down to his last coin. Hope, Tamsen realized, could be a very dangerous thing, especially when dealt to desperate hands.

The Sierra Nevada, already holding open their arms to the first temptations of winter, were yet before them, looming in evergreen and rich purple, topped in white. She was continually shocked by the fact that the others seemed to forget the obvious: that the mountains, like most beautiful things in this world, were deadly.

Tonight she strained to listen for every stray noise. She was tossing fretfully under her wedding quilt, lying on the hard ground, in a tense half sleep when she heard raised voices near the tent. She jostled George's shoulder—how did the man manage to sleep so soundly?—as she reached for her dressing gown. George stumbled on her heels as she exited the tent.

To her surprise, she saw Charlie Burger, the teamster who'd been guarding their tent, on the ground wrestling with William Pike, Lavinah Murphy's son-in-law. Tamsen had been nervous about traveling with Mormons, having read newspaper accounts of the fighting for control of townships in Missouri and even in Nauvoo, Illinois, not that far from Springfield. But Murphy's brood was friendly and well behaved and hadn't tried to convert anyone. William Pike, the riverboat engineer married to one of Lavinah's daughters, was one of the last people Tamsen would suspect of thievery. But how else to explain him being restrained outside their tent in the middle of the night? Did it have to do with supplies? Everyone'd been paranoid about their rations.

When Pike saw Tamsen, however, he ripped free of Burger and lunged for *her*. Burger had just managed to restrain him a second time when a warm gob of Pike's spittle landed on Tamsen's cheek.

"Where is he? What have you done with him?" Pike shouted at her. If Tamsen didn't know better, she would've thought Pike was drunk. His hair was wild and his face tear-streaked and red. This entire scene didn't make sense. The Murphys and Pikes had no reason to steal food, she realized; as far as anyone knew they still had a decent supply, all things considered. And he was shouting at her as though *she* were the one who'd taken something from *him*.

"What in the world is he talking about?" George asked, rubbing fists in his sleepy eyes. George's brother Jacob and Jacob's wife, Betsy, were emerging from their tent, Betsy whispering to an unseen child to go back to bed.

Pike twisted against Burger's grip as he made for Tamsen a second time, his feet struggling for purchase in the sand. "I know you've witched him away, like you've done with the others!"

"Not this nonsense again," Jacob muttered.

"God is punishing us for sheltering you in our midst." Heaving against Burger, Pike managed to free his right arm. He fumbled for his pocket. "'You shall not suffer a witch to live,' that's what it says in the Bible!"

He grabbed his small snub-nosed pistol and aimed it at Tamsen.

The next thing she knew, she had thudded to the ground, dirt in her mouth. *I must be shot*, she thought, though she felt no pain. Her husband stood over her. Slowly, it came to her: George had shoved her out of the way to face Pike, unarmed and in his nightshirt. A thrill of feeling alerted her to what was happening. She was under attack. Her husband had come to her defense without hesitation. All of his usual bluster seemed gone.

Tamsen had been attacked before, of course, but only ever verbally. Only with suspicious eyes and cold shoulders and harsh whispers. Nothing had ever gone this far, and she was shaken.

Pike's gun was still drawn but apparently unfired, Pike confused and blinking at the sudden turn of events. But before anyone could speak, a shot rang out: Charlie Burger put a bullet in William Pike's back.

A look of pure astonishment bloomed over Pike's face as he dropped to his knees. A patch of red spread across his white shirt from where the bullet had come through his chest.

Tamsen gasped, scrambling to sit up. The girls were awake now and crying. "Stay inside!" she screamed as a couple of their faces appeared in the flap of the tent.

"What the devil?" Jacob roared at the same time, as both Donner men rushed to Pike, easing him to his back. The young man's eyes were glassy, staring sightlessly up at the night sky.

Tamsen heard others rushing from their tents in answer to the gunshot. In another moment there would be crowds and angry shouting and more accusations. Meanwhile, William Pike scrabbled spastically with his right hand for the pocket of his trousers. What was he searching for so desperately—another gun? Did he mean to kill her even if it took his last breath?

Tamsen watched, frozen, as he reached into the pocket—and drew out a rosary. Wood beads on string, so well used that the varnish was worn off. So he had remained a Catholic in his heart, even in Lavinah's strict Mormon household. He breathed a sigh of relief when Tamsen placed it in his palm and closed his fist around it. "I hope Lavinah will forgive me," he gasped, bringing the rosary to his heart. Then he was still.

Tamsen sat back on her heels, faint. What had driven the man to come after her? Pike seemed the last man in the party to shoot some-one in their sleep. She wiped the spittle from her cheek and looked up to see Mary Graves standing in the crowd, staring at her in astonishment.

Harriet Pike, William's wife, broke through the cluster of onlook-ers a split second before her mother, Lavinah. Both women dropped to their knees beside the dead man, Harriet shaking him by the front of his shirt, as though that might bring him back to life. "William! What have you done?" she screamed, her voice painfully raw, as though she'd drunk lye.

Lavinah wrapped her arms around Harriet to calm her, but she was still shaking. "Their boy is missing," Lavinah said to George, her hands clutched tight to Harriet's arms. Harriet was wailing so loud it was hard to hear her mother speak. "William woke in the middle of the night to find him gone. He got it in his head that your wife was responsible." She glanced at Tamsen. "We begged him to come to his senses, but he would not be persuaded. When he left, we thought it was to look for the boy. We had no idea he would come here."

"There's a child missing . . ." George repeated, seemingly coming out of a stupor.

"Henry, my grandson. He's only one year old," Lavinah said, fight-ing tears.

"I found this." Harriet withdrew something from her pocket and held it out in her flat palm for all to see. Tamsen recognized it right away; it was one of the charms she'd given her children to carry for protection. A good-luck charm. It seemed ridiculous that a primitive and harmless trinket could cause such fear and suspicion. Besides, its presence didn't prove her guilt; it easily could've fallen out of the pocket of one of her daughters, but Tamsen didn't dare say so, know-ing it could implicate the girls instead.

"Do you deny this is yours?" Harriet thrust the talisman in Tamsen's direction.

Tamsen remained silent. To speak would be just as damning.

To her surprise, though, Mary Graves pushed her way through the crowd that had gathered, an indignant look on her face. "Why, that's ridiculous. How is that proof that Mrs. Donner had anything to do with your child's disappearance? Anyone could've put it there. Someone who didn't like her, for instance." Tamsen saw how Peggy Breen and Eleanor Eddy shrank back at Mary Graves's suggestion.

"That's enough out of you." Franklin Graves was suddenly at his daughter's side, the brute giving her a rough jerk to silence her.

But Charles Stanton, tall and strong and determined, put an arm on Mary to steady her. Tamsen felt a violent pang at the sight of him. He was clearly smitten with Mary. She had lost him entirely to the girl now, and though she'd given up on him for herself, the realization still stung.

"With respect, Mr. Graves," Stanton said, "you shouldn't speak to your daughter like that. She's talking sense—more sense than anyone else I've heard tonight."

Franklin Graves glared at him with real hatred in his eyes. "Why, you've got a nerve talking to me like that. I ought—"

But before the argument could escalate further, Graves was cut off by George, who stepped in front of Tamsen, sheltering her with his broad body. "Now listen to me, everyone . . . You're wrong, Mrs. Pike. My wife has been with me all night in our tent, I can assure you. She couldn't have left that item at your campsite. You have my word on it. We need to turn our focus toward finding the boy."

"Not you," Franklin Graves said. "You'll be doing no such thing. We got rid of Reed when the power had gone too far to his head, and now looks like you're the next. Can't have murderers among us and I don't care the reason."

George swelled like a tom turkey puffing out its chest. Tamsen had seen that look before when he was ready to reprimand a servant or take the foolish preacher back in Springfield to task. "What utter nonsense!" His voice rose over their heads, sounding more confident than he had in months. "I will not waste my breath defending Tamsen—I have already done so on too many occasions. As for William Pike . . ." George paused, standing over the man's body, where his wife still wept. He swallowed hard, then looked around at the gathered crowd. "Pike was a good man. But he was acting out of fear. This is what happens when we give in to our fears. I do repent for it, but I will never apologize for protecting my wife."

Charles Stanton stepped forward. "There is a child missing and we can't go on shouting and deliberating until he is found."

But as if in direct response, everyone began talking at once: Peggy Breen sputtering, Patrick Breen rushing to his wife's defense, Jacob Donner wedging himself between the Breens and his brother, Harriet Pike still wailing over her husband's prone body. Finally, Franklin Graves broke through the cacophony once more. He wagged a finger at George Donner. "Enough! I daresay I speak for everyone when I say I'm done with you . . . you Donners, with your money and your arrogance, and now this! Going around thinking you're better than everyone else—and another man dead! Who'll be next, I ask you?" The crowd had gone quiet, listening to Graves, and a tremor of fear moved through Tamsen. "I've had enough! From now on, you keep to yourselves if you know what's good for you." He cut a line with his arm in the air as though severing all connection with them.

For a moment, George Donner seemed horror-struck, the color drained from his face, as he realized what this meant, what Tamsen had already realized. The Donners would be pariahs to the rest of the wagon train—would be left to fend for themselves just as Reed had—

and it was all Tamsen's fault. But he recovered quickly, gathering his wife protectively under one arm. "As you say—so be it," he said as he turned his back on the crowd.

Don't go—it's a death sentence. The words rang in Tamsen's head but she wasn't sure for whom they were meant, the men about to head into the darkness to look for the missing child, or her own family.

For if the creatures she'd seen before—the men who'd surrounded her in the basin—were real, if they were still out there, they'd be waiting like wolves for the party to do exactly this: divide up into smaller and smaller groups so that it left them *all* more vulnerable. She and her family weren't safe among this hateful crowd, but they were no safer without them.

Still, she kept silent. Because maybe she was wrong. Because even if she was right, no one would ever believe her: a witch, speaking of fantastical illusions. Even to herself it sounded absurd, nightmarishly strange, a trick meant simply to scare and manipulate. And what punishment might they devise for her then?

AND SO THE WAGON TRAIN CONTINUED, the Donners allowing more and more distance to slide between their wagons and the rest, as promised. It was a relief, at least, to move apart from the Murphys, and Harriet Pike's unbearable grief. After a few days, they'd let the gap grow until there was no sign of the rest of the wagon train except tracks in the dirt.

Tamsen tried not to let her worry consume her. After the barrenness of the Great Basin, it should have been a blessing to be traveling through the mountain meadows, even in their smaller group. They were surrounded by signs of life; an abundance of alders and pine grew beside a meandering stream. There was enough grass to feed the oxen.

But for all the land's beauty and serenity, Tamsen couldn't shake the unease that had settled into her chest. She listened hard for a crackle in the underbrush, watched for movement in the trees, became increasingly convinced the creatures she'd seen in the desert *were* out there and that they were watching.

The Donners were alone, of course, following a stream they'd started calling Alder Creek for all the alder trees lining its banks, when the axle on one of their wagons broke. The rest of the party was by now unspooling a fine thread of dust several miles down the road.

"Damn it," George Donner cursed under his breath. He was lying on the ground, looking up at the underside of the wagon.

"It's too much for the both of us," his brother Jacob said, squatting down beside George.

"Nonsense," said George. "We can handle this, you and I, with Burger's help of course."

Tamsen eyed her husband and then his brother. George was being stubborn. There was no way he was capable of fixing the wagon axle on his own. It had only been a week ago that they'd had a problem with the brake—the shoes mysteriously engaging with the rear wheels even when the lever wasn't being applied—and George had been so flummoxed he'd had to have William Eddy effect repairs.

Tamsen knew what her husband's skills were, and what they were not.

"George," she said to him quietly. "This is not a time for pride." She wasn't sure why she'd said it, though. He'd protected her. It was because of this that they were separated from the others in the first place.

"We could send a couple of the men for help," said Jacob. "The rest of the group are bound to stop sometime for the night." He peered up at the darkening sky.

Tamsen knew it was too early for night; the sky meant a storm. It felt like snow, even though it was only the end of October. Once again, panic curled itself inside her gut like a sleeping snake.

"We," George grunted, trying to adjust something Tamsen couldn't see, "don't. Need. Them."

Jacob sighed, before turning to Charles Burger, who'd remained with them. "Let's send for Eddy, at least," he said quietly. "After all our generosity to his family, the man owes us. I think we have to replace that axle and he'll know best."

So against George's wishes, they sent Charlie Burger and Samuel Shoemaker on foot—no saddle horses left—to find Eddy and remind him of the Donners' earlier generosity. Beg, if necessary. Tamsen almost voiced her objection to the plan, sure more than ever that the shadow creatures were out in the woods, and that this was just another invitation for them to close in. But seeing the necessity, she once again remained silent, choking back the warnings like swallowed smoke. They were sending two men, after all, and both would be armed. They would be safe enough. They had to be.

Tamsen thought wildly that perhaps the men would bring Stanton back with them, too. Even after all the hatred between them—she had certainly moved on ages ago from the longing and the craving she had felt around him in the early weeks of the journey—she still felt *something*. Despite the way he'd scolded her, almost jealously, after Keseberg came after him with her gun. Stanton was, quite simply, the kind of man you could trust, in spite of, or perhaps *because* of, the fact that no one did.

In the meantime, Jacob's older boys started pulling the cargo out of the damaged wagon.

While they worked, Tamsen took the younger children into the field. It was swampy where the wagons stood, but beyond a stand of scrubby pines there was a proper meadow. Tamsen sent the girls to pick wildflowers for her mixtures. As she supervised, she looked to the white-capped mountain range visible in the near horizon, looming larger than ever. It was pretty here, not a bad place to remain for a time, but she thought fleetingly of James Reed. He would have insisted they needed to press on for California, and he would have been right. Winter could close off the passes any day.

She looked again at the gathering darkness of the sky. They were, even now, at the mercy of its whims.

She heard her husband cry out in pain, followed by men's voices swelling in panic. She ran back to the wagons, calling the children to follow her. She found George kneeling beside the wagon, his face white with pain and shiny with sweat, his arm disappeared behind one of the wheels. Burger and Shoemaker, the two teamsters, had not yet returned with Eddy. The rest of the men had jammed a long branch under the wagon bed and were leaning on the far end.

"Hang on there, George," Jacob said. He faced the others. "One, two, three—that's it, put all your weight on it."

The pole slipped out of position once, then twice, amid a lot of cursing and groaning, but finally the end of the pole bit and managed to hold up the wagon bed long enough for George to free himself, falling backward onto the mud.

He raised his right hand, his left hand circling the wrist for support. Tamsen nearly fainted; it looked like he was wearing a bloody mitten, his hand was so chewed up. It was a paddle of mashed, pulpy flesh drenched in blood. Her husband's eyes were rolled back in his head, nearly unconscious.

Tamsen dropped to her knees beside him. "Bring me some clean water! Tell Betsy to put some water on to boil! Milt," she called to one of their teamsters, "take the children away, they shouldn't see this.

And have Elitha fetch the satchel with my medicines and Leanne tear fresh bandages."

She worked on him for the better part of an hour. Mercifully, he'd passed out so she didn't need to worry about hurting him further. She cleaned the open flesh with water and then the very last of their alcohol. The hardest part was bandaging it up so that the pieces would heal correctly. She didn't want to leave him crippled. Jacob paced behind her the entire time while the other hired men moved away, spooked. "We were using the pole to hold up the wagon bed and it slipped," Jacob explained as Tamsen tried to make sense of the crushed fingers.

The first fat wet drops fell from the sky as she was finishing up. They were not quite rain, not quite snow. "We'd better set up the tents," Tamsen said to her brother-in-law. "This is as far as we get today." She wondered, but didn't ask aloud, just how far ahead the others had gotten by now.

They hobbled the last remaining oxen to graze and set up the tents under a huge old tree with broad branches that made a natural shelter. They tried to make George as comfortable as possible, propping his hand in place with pillows.

"He'll be wanting some of your laudanum when he comes to," Jacob noted.

Burger and Shoemaker *still* had not returned by the time the sky had completely darkened. Tamsen tried to banish the worst from her mind. They had a rifle; no shots had been heard. Surely if they'd encountered any danger, they would have at least tried to defend themselves.

"How far away could the rest of the wagons be?" Betsy muttered as she wrung her hands.

"I'm sure they didn't want to walk back in the wet," Jacob assured her.

Sure enough, the snow had started to accumulate in a slushy layer.

An hour later the wind shifted, cold and dry, and the snow become lighter, fluffier. It was going to pile up, Tamsen could tell.

The hired men slept on one side of the tree, piled into their tent. Tamsen persuaded her Betsy and Jacob to forgo a separate tent and for all the members of both families to make do with one.

"Are you sure?" Betsy asked as she tried to find space for all the children to lie down.

"It'll be easier to keep warm," Tamsen said, though that wasn't the reason. *Safety in numbers*, she thought.

It had gone quiet around them. The wagon party, at its height, had been over ninety people. Even with deaths, losses, and departures, they'd still been like a moving village. Now, Tamsen glanced around at this diminished group of no more than twenty and felt just how shockingly small they were, facing the mountains, and the winter, and the night. The silence was oppressive—no one even snored. The only thing she heard was the soft hiss of snowfall and the occasional sound of snow slipping off the waxed cotton overhead.

CHAPTER TWENTY-NINE

dwin Bryant had been with the Washoe for close to a month now. Though the great Washoe tribe was scattered throughout the mountains and beyond, he'd been brought to a small and highly organized village, which consisted of two dozen bark-wrapped shelters stretched across the red dirt clearing. Lazy plumes of smoke rose above a few of them, burning off the morning chill. Gray sky hung low over it all.

Bryant was feeling better, but with no horse or food, he stood little chance of survival on his own and he was sure the Washoe knew this.

The leader of the small group was called Tiyeli Taba, which—as best Bryant could tell—meant something like "large bear," because as a young man he had brought down a huge grizzly with a single arrow. Tiyeli Taba let Bryant stay in his *galais dungal* with his family, shared his food with him. Food wasn't particularly plentiful, mostly nuts and roots and toasted wild grasses, but they gave him the same portion as the other men. Not knowing when or how he would leave the village,

Bryant tried not to think about the life he'd abandoned. He wanted to think it was suspended in time with his fiancée, his friends, Walter Gow, and Charles Stanton all waiting expectantly for him. One day, he would return and life would continue exactly as he'd left it. He wanted to believe this even though he knew it wasn't likely. Without his letter-writing, he felt untethered, undefined. Anything might happen, and no one would hear of it. Margie might wait forever, never knowing . . .

Each night as they sat around the campfire, Bryant coaxed the elders into telling him their tribe's folktales. It was laborious as he had to stop the speakers frequently to clarify what was being said and, in the end, he could only guess what they were trying to tell him. Then one day a hunting party returned including a young man, Tanau Mogop, who had scouted for a military regiment and spoke some English. Bryant was overjoyed.

The first evening with Tanau Mogop, Bryant asked him to find out if his tribe knew anything about the prospectors' camp he'd stumbled on earlier. He had not been able to stop thinking about the collection of bones and skulls in the abandoned cabin. If anyone knew the secret of what had happened in that grisly camp, it would be this village, which appeared to be the closest. Tiyeli Taba sat meditatively without saying a word, but two of the men, agitated, began speaking simultaneously to Tanau Mogop.

Tanau Mogop turned to Bryant and explained that the camp he'd stumbled on had indeed been built by prospectors and that they'd lived there for over a year, trying to find gold in the river and rocky caves. The tribe had nothing to do with the prospectors, the elders made clear. They would pass close by from time to time to make sure that nothing bad had happened. Occasionally they would leave a pouch of pine nuts or tubers if the prospectors looked hungry. There was still game then, mostly rabbits, and they did not worry that the

white men would starve. But then one of the prospectors became infected with the *na'it*.

"*Na'it?*" Bryant asked. "What's that?" He recognized the word,
could swear it was the same word one of the other Washoe had used
when they first found him by the cave.

"It is the hunger. A bad spirit that can pass from man to man. A
very old myth among our people, though it had rarely if ever been
upheld with proof. But what had happened to the white man . . . it was
certainly the *na'it*. That's what the elders say."

"How does this happen?" he asked. "How does this . . . *na'it* . . .
work?"

Tanau Mogop listened patiently to the elders before explaining. "In
the ancient tales, the *na'it* will attack a man to eat him, but we think . . .
we believe that sometimes the man survives the attack, only he has
been infected with the bad spirit. Before long, he will be *na'it*, too, and
will want to eat the flesh of men."

Bryant remembered stories he'd read of how the Incas, when first
confronted with Spanish conquistadors over three hundred years ago,
had mistaken the tall, light-skinned Europeans for gods. Then again,
he suspected those stories had been a mere invention of the Spanish.
But could the *na'it*-worshipping Anawai have mistaken a white-skinned
stranger with a ravening hunger as the sufferer of a punishment by an
ancient evil spirit? Perhaps if they truly had no other context to explain
the white man's sickening behavior . . .

He rubbed his lower lip. Of course, if it was a proper *sickness* they'd
experienced, there might be any number of diseases that could be said
to exhibit similar symptoms. Walton Gow had told him of the work
of a British researcher, Thomas Addison, on a strange type of anemia.
Sufferers of Addison's anemia, as it was called, were said to rarely, but
on occasion, exhibit a desire to consume blood. Bloody meats. Organs.

Surely it was conceivable that there were more diseases like this out there that had not yet been studied or fully understood. This *na'it* might be a variation of Addison's anemia.

But the coincidence—the similarity to the incident in Smithboro, the man who seemingly had devolved to an animal state, killing live-stock with his teeth and bare hands—felt uncanny.

Which is to say, it was just what Bryant had, in some form or another, been chasing all along.

"So it is your understanding that one of the prospectors killed the rest after he was infected with the *na'it*?" Bryant wanted to be clear. "Killed them"—he thought of the bones he had found, picked clean—"and ate them?"

Tanau Mogop nodded solemnly. *"Na'it* are never satisfied. *Na'it* want everything. *Kill* everything."

"And you're saying that this condition is contagious? That it can be passed from a person exhibiting the symptoms to someone who is healthy?" Anemia wasn't contagious; that meant this might be a new type of disease, a contagion like rabies. A disease that made men desperate for raw meat. Human flesh. And frightened the Indians enough to kill anyone with the symptoms.

Na'it *kill everything.*

From the *galais dungal* later that night, Edwin stared into the empty distance and wondered if he would ever leave this place and see his friends again. He was starting to think Margie was a figment of his imagination, marvelous and unlikely, an invisible friend he'd dreamed up to hide the fact that he was a lonely old bachelor destined to die alone.

Tanau Mogop saw him and asked if there was something Bryant wanted.

"I must find my way home," Bryant said. "Do you think your people could help?"

Tanau Mogop whittled while he thought. "I will ask Tiyeli Taba," he said at length. It was not a small thing to ask, he explained, because they would have to cross through Anawai territory to get to Johnson's Ranch.

Tanau Mogop shook his head. "The Anawai were not always this way, though. They only began the practice of sacrifice five or six summers ago. Protection against the *na'it*."

Bryant's hands froze around the arrowhead he'd been honing. Something Tanau Mogop had said began twirling through Bryant's head, activating a theory, a suspicion, you might call it, that had been nagging at him these last weeks. "Six years ago . . ."

Tanau Mogop nodded and ran the edge of his knife hard against a whetstone. "They do many shameful things, this group. They will choose a man among them to offer up to the *na'it*, to satiate the evil spirit. But this is wrong. This is what *feeds* the evil spirit, what gives it strength."

Bryant could understand this notion, why certain parts of their tribe might have been moved to sacrifice their own people to cannibals, perhaps to keep other cannibalistic men—or monsters, really—at bay.

Tanau Mogop had said the Anawai had begun *actively* worshiping the *na'it*—had begun making sacrifices to the *na'it*—five or six years ago. It seemed abundantly clear to him that the resurgence in perceived *na'it* activity all began around that time—around the same time that Bridger claimed the lost prospectors had disappeared. He pictured the spooky camp, the disturbing signs of cannibalism.

The vanished white prospectors might not have been victims of the disease at all.

They were its originators.

CHAPTER THIRTY

December 1831

Through the window of his grandfather's Victorian—one of the more prominent homes in the area—Stanton could see the wide white swath of frozen river that cut through the middle of town. School was closed and children, shrieking with delight, skated close to the banks.

But it was farther down, at a bend that opened up into a wider pond abutting the woods, where he'd promised to meet Lydia. For today was the day they had planned to run away.

When he first arrived, at the very spot where they'd spoken yesterday, he was convinced she hadn't come at all, had changed her mind or been delayed or too scared.

He heard the gong of the church bell.

Then he saw her. All by herself, this tiny dark figure inching farther and farther out onto the frozen pond, where the ice thinned.

"Lydia!" he called out. "Lydia!" She paused for a second, but she did not turn.

It took him a moment to understand that she had heard him. A second more to realize she wore no overcoat, no hat or scarf. In fact, she appeared to be dressed in her nightgown even though it was midafternoon. He felt frozen in confusion. The blood began to pump furiously in his veins, and he cleared his throat, calling to her again.

She did turn, at last, but from that distance, he couldn't see the expression in her dark eyes. The only noise she made was when the ice broke underneath her.

In an instant she disappeared.

Stanton snapped out of the trance that had briefly held him—he was dashing through the biting cold before he knew it, the scenery passing in a blur, panic making his ears ring. He must have been screaming, because suddenly there were many footsteps in the snow, shouts echoing off the trees. He ran until two men grabbed hold of him to keep him from following her.

By then, the body had been pulled out of the water. Someone else had gotten there first. Icy water ran off her hair and face in rivulets, the nightgown plastered to her pale blue skin.

For one cruel moment, he thought he saw her eyelids flutter—thought there was still a chance, somehow, that she had lived.

And then, like the surface of the pond itself, the truth finally cracked open, and he plummeted.

THEY'D GROWN UP almost next door to each other. Stanton's father was a surveyor and was away often, so he left Stanton and his mother with his father, a prominent minister. It was a strange childhood. Stanton's grandfather, the Reverend Resolved Elias Stanton, was impossible to please and it seemed he was doubly so with his grandson. Perhaps this was why Stanton became close to Lydia; her house provided an escape. At least, this was his reason in the beginning. As they got older, he fell hard for the girl, who had always struck him as mysterious, even as a child, despite how close they lived.

There was something dark about her soul, something remote and flickering, like a flame in wind, and Stanton, well . . . he was young— too young to understand what had made her that way.

Lydia's mother had died when she was very young and she lived alone with her father in their big house, bustling with servants. She could be high-handed and people blamed this on her father spoiling her. It was true. She expected to have her way and she exasperated adults to no end, though the person she beviled the most was Stanton. It was because she knew he was in love with her—that had to be it.

There had been nothing between them, other than a few frantic kisses stolen in the hallway, or in Lydia's attic, or behind the house, at the place where the boxwoods grew tallest.

The Lord knows Stanton wanted to do much more than that, but he hadn't had the opportunity, and, truth be told, might not have known what to do with it if he had. His grandfather and mother had made sure to keep him sheltered from the realities of what occurred between men and women in the dark.

He'd always imagined he would do everything the right way. He would make a man of himself in the world, and would earn Lydia's love properly. He'd ask her to marry him, and then the fantasies that had begun to bubble within him would become reality. There was a confident ease with which he believed that all of this would come to pass—he trusted his love for Lydia the way his grandfather trusted the firm hand of God.

But when Stanton first told her of this dream, she started acting coldly. It was sheer torture. He became sick with worry, thinking he'd disappointed her or overstepped the bounds of their friendship. Or worse: that she'd found someone else.

The fall of 1831 flew by, and Stanton hadn't seen Lydia for months, other than a curt nod in the market or across the aisle at church. It was approaching the holidays by then and they were having a terribly cold winter, when he finally pulled her away after church one Sunday. Her father had taken ill and she'd come to the service alone. Stanton noticed her hands were icy and pale, and he wondered where her gloves had gone.

She led him back toward the woods, where they fought angrily. She told him to leave her alone, that she'd never wanted his advances. He was crushed, the years of their friendship and the flashes of heated intimacy between them racing through his mind in a confused blur. Where had he misstepped?

He begged her to explain, to help him understand, didn't want to push her or make demands and yet refused to accept her dismissal outright. There was something she wasn't telling him, and he simply had to know it. She owed it to him to give him a reason why she would never be his. Give him one reason, and he would take it, and go away forever.

Finally, she relented, and gave him the reason—one he'd know soon enough, anyway.

She was pregnant.

He stuttered in confusion and embarrassment, the cold suddenly creeping through the threads of his good wool coat—the one he saved for Sundays. "But . . . how?" He felt the burn of his cheeks. He might have been inexperienced, but he was not stupid. He knew where babies came from. He understood: There had been someone else.

His jealousy, his fury and hurt, were tempered by worry. "Who is it? Are you to be married?"

It was then that she began to cry—at first faintly, so that he thought perhaps a light snow had begun to fall again. But then harder. She wouldn't say a word.

He got down on his knees. Her hands were too cold, and he clutched them between his own, rubbing them vigorously even as she wept. Maybe by restoring warmth to her, he would restore the Lydia he knew—or thought he'd known. "Whoever it is, it doesn't matter to me," he said through her tears. "I have always loved you and I always will. Please marry me, Lydia, if you love me back."

She finally stopped crying—the tears left tiny tracks through her wind-chapped skin, and she seemed to him like a painting in danger of blurring until its true form became lost forever.

"Do I know him? Has the cad gone and left you, Lydia?"

She shook her head. "He has not left. He . . . I . . . I cannot ever escape him, Charles."

His concern had reached a peak now. "I will not let a monster ruin your life, Lydia. We will go to your father. He will make whoever it is pay."

At this she cried again, in broken, heaving sobs, and pulled away. She ran toward the woods and he followed, calling out to her, finally grabbing her arm and twirling her around. She fell into him, saying something over and over again and even as his ears finally began to comprehend it, his mind refused to.

ItwashimitwashimitwasHIM. It was Father.

The secret fell like a blanket over the woods. Even the birds were silent as the details, slowly and painfully, emerged: Mr. Knox had been forcing his daughter into his bed for nearly two years.

Sickened, shaken, Stanton held on to her, panic and nausea cours-
ing through him in equal measures. All this time he had stood by, not
seeing, not helping. Could he ever forgive himself? Ever be worthy of
another woman's trust?

"I will make it better," he kept saying, though he had no idea how.

She begged him never to let anyone know of the shame she had
experienced, saying she couldn't live with the notion that anyone
might find out. In some dreadful, twisted way, she wanted to protect
her father. Eventually she pulled herself away, wiped off her face, insisted she had to be home before her absence was noticed.

That was when he made the promise: "Meet me here tomorrow. I
will make it right."

She nodded once, and said, "Please don't tell anyone." Then she
flew from him.

He stalked the woods for hours after their conversation, shivering
as the afternoon dove rapidly toward night. His legs had to keep moving, or the horror would somehow suffocate him.

At last he returned home and went straight to his grandfather's
study. He had a problem, he knew; his grandfather was a good friend
of Knox's. Stern and unforgiving as he was, the chances of him believing Stanton's story seemed slim to none. But that didn't matter. The
truth didn't matter, so long as he could fix it.

And so he wove the tale: He told his grandfather that the baby was
his. He asked to do the honorable thing and marry her immediately.
In his young mind, he thought permission, and means, would follow,
no matter the quantity of stern lectures he might receive.

But that wasn't what happened. Instead of granting them permission to marry, his grandfather threatened to disown Stanton. Lydia's
father had already cast him as the playboy and villain, and Stanton had

no choice but to play along—no one would have believed him. Money was power—he was beginning to see that—and Knox was able to buy his own version of the truth.

Stanton only realized the worst of it later: that Knox never wanted him for a son-in-law—not when he knew the man's terrible secret. Not when he considered him below their station.

Not when he still wanted her for himself.

If permission was not an option, it didn't matter. They would run. There was no plan in place but there didn't have to be. Love, and the truth, would carry them, would set them free.

That was what he believed.

TINY FLECKS OF SNOW swirled around Stanton's head as he entered the Knox house several days later for the funeral. He looked up at the sky, white flannel stretched across the horizon. A storm was coming.

Inside, the parlor room had changed overnight. The furniture had been pulled out to accommodate the coffin, as dainty as its occupant, standing on trestles in front of the fireplace. After a push from behind, Stanton went up and peered inside. There was Lydia, his Lydia. He recognized the dress they had put on her, cream flannel with a tiny rosebud print; she had hated it, thought it made her look like a child. He'd heard Mr. Knox had the female servants prepare the body and they hadn't bothered to curl and fix her hair the way she normally wore it. Instead, they'd left it long and combed it out over her shoulders. She didn't look at all the way he remembered her.

Worst of all was her skin, white and chalky. Her eyes were closed, her face slack and inanimate. She was not Lydia as he'd known her.

That made it slightly easier.

He tried not to hear the muffled sobs of Lydia's father, but they were everywhere, muffled and yet stifling somehow, like a heavy snow. Stanton could hardly breathe, trapped in the weight of that sound.

Afterward, he spent the day fitfully, so preoccupied and moody that his grandfather sent him out to chop wood in what was now a heavy snow. He chopped until he had raised a healthy sweat under his clothes and his mind had finally been able to forget his worries, at least for moments at a time. But no sooner had Stanton stepped inside the house than his grandfather ordered him to take a wheelbarrow of firewood to Knox as a neighborly gesture.

He stacked the firewood outside the kitchen entrance. He was too numb to protest.

The door opened in his face and there stood Herbert Knox looking down at him. His cravat had been loosened and his starched collar unbuttoned. His gray-streaked hair was mussed. He was in his cups, Stanton judged.

He insisted that Stanton come inside. He sat next to Mr. Knox in a dining room chair that had been placed in the parlor for the viewing. He stared ahead at the coffin, not wishing to speak for fear of betraying Lydia.

"Do you know why I've asked you in?" Herbert Knox's voice boomed, echoing off the high ceiling.

Stanton gave one tight shake of his head.

Knox waved his hand. "You can speak freely. I gave the servants the afternoon off. There's no one in the house except you and I." When Stanton still said nothing, Knox leaned toward him and Stanton smelled alcohol on his breath. "There's something I want to talk to you about." He paused, his gaze sweeping over Stanton's face. "You were close to my daughter. I want to know—did she tell you her secrets?"

Don't tell anyone, please, she'd begged.

He began to sweat.

Herbert Knox rose to pace around the room. "Because I know my little girl had secrets, Charles. Secrets even you don't know. Do you believe that? There are things about my daughter you know nothing about."

"I imagine everyone has secrets," Stanton said, finally, though he felt like he was choking on his own saliva.

"My daughter was pregnant, Charles. Did you know that?" Stanton started, but tried to hide his surprise. "Don't think she didn't tell me. I know who the father was."

He once again felt how the air seemed to refuse to come into his lungs. He heaved a breath.

Mr. Knox plunged ahead. "You needn't act so guilty, Charles. Your attraction to my daughter was understandable. It's your behavior that was not." So he was going to persist in his denial. Stanton thought he was going to be sick, though he didn't know which would have been worse—Mr. Knox accusing him of being the father, or confessing to be the one at fault himself. The room seemed to be shrinking. Stanton's head pounded. "Lydia and I were very close," Knox went on, a distant look on his face. As if he were somewhere else. "Much closer than most fathers and daughters. She was all I had after my wife died, all the family left to me in the world. She told me everything."

Stanton jumped to his feet, repulsion like a poison flooding his veins, his mind. He had to flee from the house, flee this abomination.

The sudden movement seemed to snap Herbert Knox out of his strange reverie. His stare was cold and reptilian now. *He knows that I know,* Stanton realized. Inebriated or not.

Please don't tell anyone. Lydia's pleading voice wrapped around his throat like a noose.

Herbert Knox, wrapped in a stink of alcohol and sweat, suddenly had him by the arm in a wild man's grip. He pulled Stanton close so he could search his eyes, to know what he was thinking. "You think you know the truth, but you don't understand. You thought my daughter loved you, but you were a child to her. She pitied you, following her around like a lovesick puppy. You don't know what love is, son . . ."

The next thing Stanton knew, Knox was sprawled on the floor, rubbing his jaw in surprise. Stanton had punched the man so quickly that he had no memory of it except the soreness of his knuckles.

Knox gazed up at Stanton, his glazed look quickly replaced by something steelier. "If you really love Lydia, Charles, you'll protect her memory. She would hate being gossiped about. You know that."

"You think I won't tell anyone . . ."

"No one would believe you if you did." Knox started to rise from the floor, slowly and deliberately, watching him. "You've already made your bed, Charles. You may as well leave Lydia in hers. No one will take your word against mine, son. Not after how you've behaved, dogging my daughter over the years. Not after you already went ahead and took the blame." Stanton nearly blacked out from anger.

He was on him, straddling him, his knuckles becoming as bloody as the old man's face. Over and over again, pummeling that sick, smug grin. Wanting to make those gray eyes glaze over forever. Knox was death itself—he'd destroyed everything good in the world.

Herbert Knox would have met his maker that day, had it not been for the housekeeper, Mrs. Talley, running in and screaming. Her hollering drew the other servants, who pulled Stanton off the bruised and bloody mess Knox had become.

Stanton was heaving, crying, shaking. The servants stared at him in wonder and horror, and he was eventually dragged home to his grandfather in a cloak of fear and shame.

He was left in his bed for hours—maybe days. His grandfather didn't come to him at all. Neither did his mother. No one came. He wondered if maybe he, Stanton, had died, and was caught in a kind of purgatory, a world defined by the edges of his bed and the boundaries of fitful, nightmarish sleep. Outside his window, a blizzard raged.

Finally, morning dawned, and his grandfather called him into his office. Stanton realized his whole body ached—from the struggle, no doubt. There were scabs on the backs of his hands.

Would his grandfather whip him? Beat him within an inch of his own life? Send him out into the streets? He couldn't fathom the many ways in which Mr. Knox might try to ruin his life now, what sort of punishment he might devise.

He heard his mother weeping in her room, the door firmly locked. He didn't blame her. She was powerless to help him.

Gingerly, he pushed open his grandfather's study door with a creak.

His grandfather said nothing but nodded for him to take a seat. The room felt eerily silent—the snow had quieted the whole world.

What happened next floored Stanton.

It seemed, according to his grandfather, that Herbert Knox had "taken pity on the grief-stricken boy." His grandfather produced a letter in a fat envelope. The sum of money inside it caused Stanton to rock backward in his chair.

"This," his grandfather explained, "is to help you start over, to make a new life for yourself. Courtesy of the Knox family." He paused. "On the condition that you never return."

Stanton was frozen. He didn't want Knox's money. He didn't want his so-called charity, the sum of which was so great it seemed clear evidence of Knox's guilt. It was hush money. Stanton wasn't a child; he could see that.

"Take it, boy," his grandfather said. "You are no longer welcome here."

Stanton may not have been a child, but still, he was young. If he had another choice, he didn't know it. If there was a way to make things right, to reveal the truth, he didn't see it.

The wad of money stared up at him. How could he have known that one day Knox would want it back—long after it had been spent?

How could he have foreseen the many ways—and many women—he would seek to drown out the memories of this time? Who could say if there was a specific point at which Stanton's innocence in Lydia's death no longer mattered, became subsumed in all the mistakes, and affairs, that were to follow . . .

Maybe he *was* naïve, then. Maybe he *was* a child.

He couldn't make it right for Lydia, could not bring her justice or peace. And neither could he continue to live in this town, next door to the man who had betrayed her trust and love. He would go mad or one day kill Knox, or both.

There was nothing he could do, it seemed, but take the money and leave.

A real hero would have known what to do, surely—would not have built his whole life on a foundation of rot and guilt and horror.

But Charles Stanton was no hero.

Forgive me, Lydia.

NOVEMBER 1846

CHAPTER THIRTY-ONE

The snow kept falling over Alder Creek: It was dainty, pretty, even. Unrelenting.

Often as her husband slept, fitfully, Tamsen would stare at him in wonder, remembering how she had once longed for his death—prayed it would come as a pleasant and nasty surprise: neat, tidy, over with quickly, as it had been with her first husband. How she fancied she'd find an improved opportunity elsewhere, that her beauty, like a fishing hook, would save her yet, fetching her a better catch than before. Those ideas seemed remarkably naïve to her now, set as they'd been within the larger belief that life would be good to her, despite everything—that she would turn it all around, would carve out a space for happiness. That it was a thing you could get to by clawing at it.

She knew better now, though. And knowing it allowed her to forgive George, at least a little, for the terrible entrapment she felt their marriage had been. He'd given up his own safety for hers, for no good reason at all, except that she was the mother of his children. Except that he, unaccountably, adored her.

In a practical sense, she hardly needed him. George wasn't good for much more than bluster and bright-eyed cajoling. No, what she did need, though, was that very adoration.

For someone to care.

TEMPERATURES DROPPED.

Two days now they'd been hunkered inside the tents. The snow came up to their knees and obscured the way ahead in a thick blanket of white. It had begun to harden in place. Everyone shivered together, fully dressed, under quilts and blankets. George was delirious and feverish. His skin burned but was as pale as the snow. Every time he cried out in pain in his sleep, the girls whimpered, terrified. Tamsen made him drink tea made with ginger, bee balm, and cinnamon, good for infection.

It was late. She slept now only in snatches—an hour, maybe two if she was lucky. Burger and Shoemaker had eventually made it back, during a break in the snowfall, but only with the bitter news that Eddy had refused help. They had no choice but to wait out the weather now. They were as good as stuck.

She was sitting at George's side, sleepless, when she heard a sound outside the tent: a gentle schussing, as though someone was gliding by on runners. A sleigh, that was what they needed, but a sleigh out here in the wilderness? Impossible. She was so desperate to be rescued that she was hallucinating.

Tamsen threw her cloak over her shoulders and picked her way out of the crowded tent. She listened for the crunch of boots on snow, but instead she heard something else: whispers. No matter how hard she strained she couldn't make out what was being said.

Something was out there. If you'd asked her a month ago she'd have said it was wolves, but now she was filled with a worse kind of dread. Once again the visions she'd had in the basin came back to her: the shadow figures with their strange appearance, like something long-dead come back to life; the sickening smell of the one that had caught fire. Pushing through the fear was a current of anger. She'd let everyone dissuade her of what she'd believed to be true. Kept her head down while they mocked and isolated her.

But she'd been right, and she knew it now—could *feel* it.

No, could feel *them*.

They had followed her here. Had been, possibly, tracking their party all this time.

Her mind raced. Should she awaken the others and demand their help? Would they even listen? If they once again ridiculed her, the danger might only get worse. There wasn't much time. The creatures moved fast.

She shuddered, turning toward the mouth of the tent to try to find a rifle, remembering again the way their faces writhed in the fire.

Fire. They had been terrified of the fire in the desert. They had scattered after the broken lantern set the dry plain aflame.

Tamsen paused, listening again. There they were—the distant, hungry whispers, moving through the branches of the trees as drifts of snow blew to the ground.

She couldn't be imagining it, could she?

She thought again about rousing the hired men to help, but they were slow to get out of bed and she would not let a second pass while the creatures could be closing in on her family. She would not allow these men to stop her from doing what was right.

Not this time.

Fire. She had to build a fire, *now*. She focused her mind on that.

Carrying wood slick with frost in her arms, Tamsen made her way through the snow as far as she dared go toward the woods. Her boots filled with frigid slush. Her hem cracked with ice. Her fingers turned numb, bloated from the cold.

She cleared a spot on the wet ground and stacked the wood as quickly as she could, occasionally stopping to look over her shoulders. Crouching, she thought she saw eyes glittering in the dusk, glittering with the reflected light.

"Go away," she said out loud, her voice thin in the cold.

From the old flames, she set a twig alight and carried it to the newly built campfire. Carefully, she lit the tinder at the base. The tinder caught but just barely, sending up a smoky plume. She would build a third one, too. The others would say it was a waste of good logs, but she knew better.

As she was working, Solomon and William, Betsy's teenaged boys by her previous husband, crept out from the tent, shoulders hunched against the cold. "What are you doing, Aunt Tamsen?" Solomon asked.

She straightened up. On the air, their breath seized and turned white. "There's something in the woods—can you hear it, boys?"

"Wild animals?" William asked. He was the younger of the two and was always looking for adventure.

Tamsen hesitated for a second, then nodded.

"We should hunt for it. Father says we could use some wild game."

"These animals . . . aren't the kind for eating. And though you're a very brave boy, William, you shouldn't go out hunting after dark." She had to clench a jaw to keep her teeth from chattering. "Will you help me build some more campfires, though, to keep it away?"

The brothers looked puzzled. But they were good boys and helped her in the end. They built three new fires, making four in total. By this time, the oxen had started lowing, but it was too dark to go searching for them and make sure they were okay. Tamsen's heart felt as if it might splinter in her throat, as if it might shatter like ice and cut her open from the inside out. She remembered how Elitha had screamed when the man got a blackened arm around her. How he'd sniffed at her neck. The cadaverous look of his face and the wet, pulsating motion of his nostrils.

As if he'd found them by smell.

They were still out there. She could hear them. The wood was wet. It wouldn't light fast enough. Why hadn't she thought to bring out her rifle anyway? Maybe the noise would have at least scared them off. Would four fires be enough? No. They must build more. As many as they could. In a circle, all around the tents . . .

A hand came down on her arm and she nearly screamed.

But it was just Jacob. He had given his heavy coat to George, piled it on top of his brother's blankets, though it did nothing to stop the shivering. Now he wore only a filthy shirt. The cold had turned his nose red already.

"What are you doing?" He shook his head, rubbing sleep from his eyes. "It's as bright as daylight out here. Go on," he said, to Solomon and William. "Go get some sleep."

She saw that the boys were pale with cold and exhaustion. She had lost track of how long they'd been outside.

"There's something out there," she said, once they were alone. "Something watching us. You can hear it."

They both stood still, listening. Sure enough, within minutes, a murmuring rose above the lowing of the oxen.

"Do you hear it?" she whispered.

When Jacob nodded, she nearly wept. She had almost begun to wonder whether she *was* going crazy.

"It sounds human," Jacob whispered. "Perhaps some of the others, looking for us?"

Tamsen shook her head. "No."

They stood together in silence, and after a minute they saw dark figures moving between the trees, caught behind the haze of smoke from the fires. They appeared and then vanished, then reappeared again. Circling, pacing, *stalking.*

"There," she whispered.

Jacob was quiet. "Those are mere shadows cast by the flames, Tamsen," he said gently. "And the whispers—it could just be the wind. Or our minds playing tricks on us." But she heard the tremor of doubt in his voice, saw the way he shivered, listening hard.

"Maybe. Or maybe something's been following us. Ever since the basin," she said, emphasizing the last word only slightly.

Jacob turned to her. "Tamsen," he said quietly, placing his big hands on her shoulders. He looked into her eyes. "What is this really about?"

She wanted to cry, or scream, or tear at her brother-in-law's face. How dare he keep questioning her?

"We're isolated from the rest of the party," she reminded him, "and I bet they—the creatures, the monsters—they know we have an injured man in the tent." She paused, even as the truth she'd already known sank in deeper, thudding into her gut. Her voice dropped to a hard whisper. "We're going to die. After everything—after everything. We made it this far. And now they're going to get us." She was shaking so hard she thought she'd fall.

"There's no such thing as monsters." But Jacob lifted his rifle to his shoulder. His eyes watered from the dense wood smoke, but he didn't falter. "Go wake the men. We're going to bring the oxen in, to be on the safe side." So some part of him *did* believe her. "Tell them to bring their rifles."

"The oxen aren't worth dying over, Jacob. Let them have the cattle." *Maybe they'll be satisfied*, she nearly added, but then stopped herself.

"With no oxen, we can't get the wagons out of here even when the snow recedes." Jacob didn't look at her. He didn't take his eyes off the figures moving behind the scrim of smoke. He had to see them, too. See how their forms moved with an animal hunger. Shadows didn't move that way. "If we lose the oxen, we'll be trapped."

She knew she didn't have to remind him.

They already *were* trapped.

CHAPTER THIRTY-TWO

M ary gazed around her at the snow-covered cabin and the makeshift lean-tos nearby, which stood like crumbling sugar cubes, and thought how quaint they looked, almost inviting, if one didn't know better. Instead they were a kind of purgatory.

It was William Eddy who'd spotted the abandoned cabin first, nearly a week ago now, and it had indeed seemed like a vision under the pine trees: a log cabin in the middle of nowhere, undoubtedly built by an earlier family of settlers that had tried to make its way through the mountain wilderness.

The first flakes of snow were already falling by then. The children, tired as they were, ran around trying to catch snowflakes on their tongues.

Except for the Donners, the wagon party had maneuvered successfully into the hollow, past the inky black lake scattered everywhere with boulders. The place was dark and still as a mausoleum.

"We rest here for the night," Patrick Breen had said then, though that had been days ago. They had left the Donners behind, and already Patrick Breen had taken on the role of captain.

The Eddys had dragged their meager possessions into Breen's dwelling, but Breen had pushed them out. "I got more children; we should get the roof," he'd argued.

Meanwhile, the Murphys had claimed a second cabin. Its roof had fallen in and weather had beaten its walls to a state of collapse, but they propped it up as best they could to keep the weather out. It shared no clean line of sight to the Breens, which was fitting; a feud had broken out between the two families and they hadn't spoken a word to each other in a week.

The rest had found shelter where they could. The Graveses had joined the Eddys in a tent pitched under a large pine and invited Margaret Reed and her little ones to join them. As for Charles Stanton, he kept to himself in a tiny tent on the outskirts of the area, with a view of the lake's dark surface.

They sheltered their fires from the snow as much as possible, building them up near the cabin and the lean-to, then gathered to try to warm their hands. And since then, the snow had just kept on coming. Everyone was growing restless, and worried.

Mary still felt the burden of Charles Stanton's confession on her own heart, too. She believed, powerfully, that she was in love with him, but this place seemed inhospitable to love, and she almost couldn't bear the idea of telling him now. There would be another chance, later, she told herself. When they got to California. At least when the pass cleared and they made it over these peaks to the next ranch. It wasn't that far. And love was like forgiveness—deep and patient. It would be waiting for her on the other side.

"WE'LL TRY TO FIND a pass through the mountains tomorrow," Breen said now as they gathered around the fire. But he'd been saying the same thing night after night, and if this storm didn't blow through soon, Mary didn't know *what* they would do. Breen nodded in the direction of mountain peaks they'd been able to see just days ago, but which were now invisible. Mary thought he was delusional; the snow was coming down faster and heavier than she'd ever seen in Illinois. "Everyone try to get some sleep tonight."

But in the morning, they found that one of the oxen had gone mad. At first, Mary thought its pained moaning was just the echo of snow dissolving into the lake.

The animals lowed like this every morning, bellowing their hunger, asking for grain that would never come. They were penned in a haphazard circle of the remaining wagons and had stripped all the grass to be found under the snow. Now, they had nothing left to eat. They bumped restlessly against the wagons, hoping for escape.

But then she saw it: There were gouges—open wounds—in the side of one of the beasts, as though it had been attacked by wolves in the night, yet somehow managed to live. Its eyes were bloodshot and a line of foam coated its lower lip. It lolled its big head menacingly as the men approached it, snorting and pawing the ground.

"Waste not, want not," William Eddy said, and promptly shot it between the eyes.

"Damn it, Eddy," Patrick Breen cursed. "That was *my* cow."

The other cattle grumbled and shuffled away. Eleanor Eddy whimpered.

They harvested the meat and built up big fires, but Mary was one of many who hung back. She'd seen the way the beast's eyes rolled in its sockets, heard its deranged bellowing. She knew stories of dogs and raccoons that could infect humans through a bite. True, she'd never heard of a cow getting sick that way, but she wasn't going to take any chances. They still had rations enough; she refused to touch the animal's flesh.

But many others—too many—were hungry. And the smell of the roasting beef that night drew them out, willing to set aside their caution for a taste of fresh meat.

There were no stories around the campfire, no laughter or songs or shared bottles of whiskey like in the early days on the trail. They'd run dry of all of that long ago. Now it was just the sound of ravenous eating, the smack of lips and teeth tearing flesh off bone.

All around them, the snow came so fast it blurred the world behind a veil, and swallowed the sound of the babies wailing in the cold.

CHAPTER THIRTY-THREE

D awn broke pale gray and carried the taste of ash.

The sky was thick with clouds. Snow fell lightly; the storm wasn't over yet. Sometime in the past hour, the accumulation had put out the bonfires. Thick black tails of smoke now lifted into the sky.

Stanton stamped feeling back into his feet and met the other men around the embers of the last fire, hoping the warmth would drive the numbness from his chest. Rumors reached him quickly; one of Patrick Breen's boys, his namesake, had gone missing in the night. Patrick, his friend Dolan, and his oldest son, John, had set out to look for the younger Patrick at daybreak.

But midmorning, Patrick Breen and the other scouts returned. They had not found any trace of the boy, nothing but a slick of blood in the woods that seeped through the fresh snowfall.

Meanwhile, William Graves hadn't woken since last night's feast. "His forehead's hot to the touch," Elizabeth Graves, his mother, said through tightened lips. James Smith, a teamster who'd also partaken of the meal, sweated like he was in the tropics.

Thirteen-year-old Virginia Reed had run off, too, and no one could account for when she'd gone. They feared the worst.

And then there was teenaged Eleanor Graves: She took to dancing in the snow, claiming she was a fairy princess. Pink-cheeked, delirium in her eyes.

Stanton stood with others in the choppy snow outside the Graveses' shelter, eyes downcast, no one knowing what to say to Franklin and Elizabeth, their family seemingly disproportionately afflicted, and so quickly. Inside the lean-to, Margaret Reed cried into Amanda Mc-Cutcheon's arms for the loss of Virginia.

"It doesn't make sense. How could William and Eleanor get ill so fast?" Elizabeth Graves murmured, her face blank with grief. "They were fine yesterday morning. Just fine."

"What we've been through . . . it was bound to take its toll sooner or later," Eliza Williams, the Reeds' servant, said. She sat huddled on a stump next to her brother, Baylis.

"It's just like when Luke Halloran got so bad so fast, don't you remember?" Lavinah Murphy stood bundled with a shawl over her coat. She looked from face to face as though trying to convince them. "His fever spiked so high and he acted funny, like he had a brain fever."

A wail broke from Elizabeth Graves's throat. "You mean my William and Eleanor got the consumption?"

"No—consumption don't come on real fast like that," Eliza Williams said, shaking her head. "I tended to some consumptives over in Taylorsville. It builds up in a person. It isn't like that at all."

Stanton thought of Halloran those last few days, his fevered glittering eyes, the nonsense he spouted when anyone pressed him, how he'd attacked Tamsen. He'd never known a consumptive but thought of an epidemic he'd witnessed as a boy in Massachusetts, smallpox breaking out all over town as though it had been carried on the wind. The children died first, it seemed, the young and the old and the very weak.

It made sense now. This madness might be contagious, something a body could carry with it, hidden inside. It might take very little to pass along the disease.

Stanton hated to be the one to break this bad news to them. Not only bad news, but the worst possible news under the circumstances. Reluctantly, he stepped into the center of the circle, coughing to get everyone's attention. "I think we have to look to what all the people who got sick have in common. And that's that they ate some of the meat last night."

Talking ceased. They looked at each other, brows lifting in realization as they tried to remember which of them had partaken. Faces paled in recall.

"That's right," Elizabeth Graves said, a hand rising to her mouth in alarm. "Both my William and Eleanor had some of that beef. The teamster, too. I saw him."

"Does that mean we're all going to get sick?" Baylis asked, his voice rising.

"Maybe. Don't panic, now," Stanton said, spreading his hands for their attention. "Let's see what happens. Maybe there's a reason only some of us took ill. Maybe it won't affect everyone."

Mary Graves looked to Stanton, her gray eyes clouded with worry, and he knew why. Her parents had pressed all her siblings to eat last night, to partake of the rich red meat while they could; it might be their last chance for fresh food in a while. They'd given all of the family's share to the children. Stanton had skipped it because Mary had shared her concerns with him. Thank God he'd listened to her.

"Are you saying that cow was diseased?" Lavinah Murphy asked, paling. Her entire family had been at the feast. "It looked perfectly fine—before it was attacked."

Those gruesome wounds. Stanton turned to her. "Maybe that's it—maybe it was the attack. Maybe whatever attacked that cow was diseased—"

"A wolf, it had to be a wolf," Baylis Williams broke in, saying what they were all thinking. "What else could it be?"

"Wolf, or bear," Stanton said. "Maybe whatever's been following us is diseased." He pointed to the dark forest surrounding them; eyes followed.

The part he didn't understand was how this disease could pass so quickly, how a victim could succumb within hours. It seemed somehow faster in the young, as though the disease fed on the able-bodied and strong. Again, he cursed Edwin Bryant's absence; his medical training would come in awfully handy right now. But there was nothing to be done for it except make their best guess.

Stanton paced in front of the group, pointing again to the woods. "If we don't want whatever's waiting for us to come back, night after night, trying to pick off the cattle, bringing that *disease* with them, we've got to do something."

Patrick Breen, withdrawn deep into his worry, looked up. "What are you saying? We may need those cattle to keep us alive through the winter."

Stanton turned back to face the group. "I'm saying we slaughter them. Today. We can store the carcasses in snow. It'll be easier than trying to guard twenty live head of cattle." He looked at Breen. "It's your livestock, Mr. Breen. It's your decision. If we don't do this, we stand the chance of losing those cattle one by one to whatever's out there, and that won't do any of us any good. What do you say?"

ALMA KATSU

All eyes were on Breen, the big man looking even bigger wrapped in his heavy coat, a bear pelt hanging from his shoulders. He glanced at his wife, Peggy, her eyes red from crying, and she gave an almost imperceptible nod. "All right then, we'll do what you say. For the good of the wagon party."

Every grown man in the party gathered by the lake, bringing knives and axes and rope. It was hard, tiring work and within an hour the men were drenched in blood: blood up to their elbows. Their hair was matted with it, and they lost the grip on their weapons. A dozen scrawny flayed carcasses hung from the trees, dripping warm blood that melted the snow underneath. Steam rose from the ground and carried a warm, fecund scent.

They'd have to stack the meat like cordwood in the snow to freeze, close enough for Patrick Breen to keep an eye on it but far away enough so the diseased wolves, if that was what they were, would not be led to their door.

Stanton helped pack the carcasses in ice and snow. It was a huge quantity of meat. But not enough to see sixty people through an entire winter, if it came to that.

He prayed it wouldn't.

He thought of the narrow mountain pass that he'd ridden through just a few weeks back—it would be just two weeks' journey in fine weather from the pass to Johnson's Ranch but one they simply couldn't risk in these conditions. The land was hidden under deceptively deep drifts of snow. It was clear now they couldn't even make it *to* the pass.

The boys were sent to root through snow for more firewood. Stanton, William Eddy, and Jay Fosdick, husband to Mary's sister Sarah, set to work skinning. Behind them floated sounds from the lake, the steady chop of metal on bone . . . and men shouting.

The shouts rose up from the lake, growing louder in pitch.

A scuffle had broken out. Stanton laid down his knife and joined the swarm of men flowing like ants to the water. He pushed his way through the crowd to see Noah James and Landrum Murphy squaring off. Both were young, under seventeen.

"What's going on here?" Stanton said, trying to get between them.

Noah glowered. "Murphy's too careless with his knife. He almost cut my hand off."

"It's his own fault," Landrum Murphy sneered. Landrum was a strapping farm boy with his mother Lavinah's plain, broad face. "He's standing around catching flies. This is men's work we're doing." He was playing to the crowd. "If he can't keep up, Noah should go back to the cabins with the *women*."

It was a low blow. Red-faced, Noah lunged, but Stanton caught him before he could do any harm. Still, Stanton was surprised by the boy's strength. He could barely keep a grip on him.

"You shouldn't be out here anyway. Weren't you both sick this morning? You should be resting." Stanton pushed Noah back a step, but the boy wasn't listening. The murderous look in his eyes gave Stanton a chill.

But it was Landrum Murphy who charged, bloodied knife drawn. Noah, the quicker of the two, leapt out of his way but then stumbled in the choppy snow. The crowd danced back, too, as Landrum threw himself at Noah and knocked him to his back. In a split second, he drove the knife into Noah's chest.

A gasp ran through the circle, and for a second, everyone froze.

Landrum sat on Noah James's chest like a cobbler at his bench. Before anyone could pull him away, Landrum brought his knife to Noah's face—prettier than Landrum's, almost as pretty as a girl—and sliced off an ear. He held it up for a split second, watching it tremble in his fingers like a freshly caught minnow.

And then snatched it up with his teeth, grinning.

Panic. Shouting. Stanton grabbed the boy before he could reach for Noah's other ear. It took two men plus Stanton to tackle the boy and pin him. Everyone was shouting. Stanton took a boot to the head, a ringing shock he felt in his teeth, but didn't let go.

Murder, someone screamed. *Murder. Devil.*

He gripped Landrum Murphy in a bear hug. The boy's chest and shoulders heaved with each breath, his whole body thrumming with excitement. Stanton couldn't help but notice Landrum was hot to the touch. Burning up.

"What the hell has gotten into you?" Stanton shouted at him, frightened beyond sense. And Noah lay with a ribbon of blood unspooling from his ruined face, and his chest sticky with blood, as another dust of snow began to fall. "What the hell is wrong with you?"

Eliza Williams danced backward, away from Noah. "It's madness, that's what it is. After what we've been through, we're all going mad."

He had heard of men going mad in the wilderness, driven to talk gibberish and crawl on all fours. He had heard of men lost for months in the snow forgetting their names, forgetting who they were, or that they were men at all.

But this was something different.

He thought of the Donners, miles back by now, and they hadn't caught up. Surely they'd been forced to camp somewhere just as the rest were camped here. What would become of them? It seemed almost a certainty that they would've been beset by this same madness. He felt a pang of regret that he was powerless to help them, but he was needed here.

He then thought suddenly of Halloran—he'd heard how Halloran had played the fiddle like a madman just days before he died. But that had been far enough back down the trail. "I wouldn't doubt it," he said shortly, "but maybe madness is part of the sickness, too. Maybe it can catch."

THAT NIGHT, Charles Stanton watched the layers of snow gathering on the pass and thought of Mary. Pure as snow. He wanted to love her with a clean heart. How all this snow and all this danger seemed to want to erase his past as badly as he did—to blot out everything. But as it did, it began to blot him out, too. To change him. His grandfather would say even this horrible situation was part of God's plan, but Stanton would be damned if he could see what it was. It made him certain of one thing, however: his love for Mary Graves. She seemed more and more every day like the image of an angel his grandfather used to keep on the wall in their home—perfect, pure, but also untouchable.

The rest, sleepless, watched *each other*. The disease, if it was a disease, might work like any other kind of sickness. They watched for sneezing, for coughing, for signs of fever.

Noah James died before morning.

CHAPTER THIRTY-FOUR

The Donners had been more than a week at Alder Creek, and every day, it snowed. Elitha felt like the whole world had shrunk to the size of the tent, to the sprawling branches of the giant alder tree, to the distance between firepits. The snow melted away near the bonfires they burned every night, at Tamsen's insistence, but beyond this circle the landscape was nothing but a thick blanket of white. Snow halfway up most of the trees. Tamsen and Uncle Jacob decided it was too deep for the wagons. They debated how far they might get on snowshoes, if they had any, but all that talk amounted to nothing, since they didn't.

They were stuck, among an ever-deepening landscape of snow and ice.

But there was one good thing about the snow, about their remote high nesting place in the mountains: It seemed the dead had not been able to follow her there. Even they knew to stay away from this cursed place. For the first time in months, her head didn't echo with disrupted arguments and cussing and nonsensical conversations. Which left room instead to hear the moaning of her father, sick and bundled, still, at the back of their tent, where Tamsen tended to him hour after hour.

For the first time, she wondered if her father would die. Death had been chasing them a long while, she knew, but it had never gotten this close. Now it was at their heels like a begging dog; the smell of it was in their hair and under their fingernails. It was everywhere, and it was waiting.

Thinking of this made her miss Thomas, terribly. She missed the way he smiled at her when no one was looking, missed kissing him when they were able to steal a few moments alone. Now they were separated by who knew how many miles and snow so deep you could disappear in it, sink like a stone. No telling when she would see him again—if ever.

Then there were the things waiting for them in the woods. She knew what they'd seen in the basin was real. She knew whatever those creatures were, they were after them, biding their time.

The grown-ups did not like to talk about it, but sometimes, at night, when she woke to the sound of Tamsen weeping, or heard the crunch of her uncle's boots outside the tents, she knew they were out there. Those times she knew, too, that the reason the ghost voices hadn't followed her was because they were also afraid.

It was getting so hard to find dry firewood. There was talk of burning the wagons, or trying to take down a tree. They were eyeing the oxen, too, as food got low. There was grass under the snow, but the cattle couldn't get enough to keep them alive and they would start dying soon. "Either that or those *things* out there will get them," Uncle Jacob had said bitterly. That was what he called them—because no one could say for sure *what* they were. Shadows. Shapes in the darkness. As though their worst inner fears had taken shape and grown limbs, as though the demons that had often visited Elitha's mind in the form of voices had sprouted into half-living monsters come to haunt them all.

She had overheard Aunt Betsy whispering to her husband one night: "We're going to die here, aren't we?" He had no response.

That was when the bad thing happened. They were huddled together in the tent one evening, listening, always listening now. They were packed tight, sixteen people in a tent that usually held just one family. All the bodies kept them warm, warm enough to stink of sweat and oils and all the rest that came with a body. The air was thick with expelled breath. Outside, two of the teamsters were on guard with rifles, acting as lookouts and keeping the bonfires fed.

Then: an unmistakable scrabbling outside the tent. There was no door, only an old cowhide hanging over the opening, so that bitter cold air slipped past its edges and froze whoever was sitting nearest. Something was standing right outside the tent, separated by only a flimsy bit of hide.

Everyone looked up. Aunt Betsy stopped singing. Fear brought its own kind of cold, freezing the air in Elitha's lungs. Why hadn't the men on watch called out?

They were dead, perhaps. She had a sudden image of the teamsters gutted, and charred creatures with human hands picking at their ribs. They were already steaming out their heartbeats in the snow.

Uncle Jacob grabbed up his rifle and pulled back the hammer. "Who's out there?" He got to his feet, crouching to avoid the low ceiling.

No answer. Then there was the crunch of a foot on snow, then another.

The cowhide started to lift . . .

Aunt Betsy screamed as if someone had grabbed her.

Jacob fired. The flash lit up her uncle's face, alien and terrible in the glare. The tent filled with gun smoke. Elitha's baby sister Eliza screamed and the little ones began to cry.

Outside, someone screamed, too—a high-pitched shriek so unexpected and childish, Uncle Jacob froze. It was Tamsen who pushed the flap aside, to find Virginia Reed—Elitha's friend, though she hadn't seen her since their families separated—on her back in the snow, the right arm of her boiled-wool coat dark with blood.

THEY CARRIED HER INSIDE and Elitha's father was rousted from his pallet to make way for her.

"I'll never be able to explain this to her mother if she dies," Jacob said, as Tamsen eased off Virginia's coat. It was a funny thing to say, Elitha thought; did he really think they'd ever see the rest of the wagon train again? The distance between camps might as well have been an ocean. Then again, Virginia had found her way here, somehow, and on her own, it seemed.

"It looks like the shot just grazed her, thank God," Tamsen said. "She'll pull through if it doesn't get infected."

Jacob was still white-faced. "What is she doing here? By herself, in the middle of the night?"

"Maybe there's trouble, wherever the rest of them are. I hope to God whatever it is, it didn't follow her here," Betsy said, wringing her hands. Jacob was still breathing hard and was pale as a sheet. He was back on his stool with his head in his hands, the rifle out of arm's reach.

Elitha sat next to Virginia, willing her to wake up. She considered Virginia her best friend among the girls of the wagon party, and felt terrible; she had forgotten all about her, and had spent little time with her since meeting Thomas. She hadn't even missed Virginia; all her concern had been for him.

Now she knew that if Virginia died, it would at least in part be her fault.

And then they'd never know why she'd really come.

CHAPTER THIRTY-FIVE

Edwin Bryant recognized the trail to the abandoned prospectors' camp as soon as he saw it.

He'd traveled north by northwest from Tiyeli Taba's village on Tanau Mogop's horse, which he tied to a tree several yards away. The wind riffled through the branches of the surrounding pines, sounding alive. A shiver ran down his back.

He built a fire and carried a burning stick into the tumbledown hovel as a torch, knowing it would be as dark as a cave inside the shack. The items he'd found earlier waited for him: the tin cup, book of psalms, coins, bottles. He inspected them for identifying marks, particularly the psalm book. The flyleaf, the most likely place for an inscription, was gone as were the next thirty or forty thin, onion-skin pages.

He got down on his knees and shifted through the trapped dead leaves and pine needles that had fallen through the collapsed roof. He picked carefully through the loamy dirt, setting aside the edible bugs that he found, insects being his main source of food now.

At the end of an hour, the only thing he'd turned up was a tattered shirt, decayed by long exposure to the elements. He sat back, stretching the fabric between his hands, feeling his spirits sink. Had it been a waste of time to return? What had he expected to find?

Bryant put the shirt next to the other items and went outside, grateful for fresh air free of the musty taint of the cabin. On his last visit, he'd respectfully piled the bones he'd found outside the cabin, a way to mark the horrors that had taken place here. Staring at the skulls now, Bryant wondered if there had been any survivors. Was there a way to know how many men had been at the camp? He counted five skulls. Yet someone had severed the limbs from the bodies. Had it been one of the prospectors or someone else?

He pulled the prospecting tools from under the bushes and sorted through them. There were a dozen shovels, though that proved nothing. He imagined it likely that a man who'd come all this way to prospect might have brought more than one shovel. Nine pickaxes of varying design. A number of dented tin ore buckets and a half-dozen sieve pans. Bryant inspected the tools one by one, looking for identifying marks. Though the heads of most of the implements were covered with rust, he could make out the manufacturers' marks: *Greenlee, Beatty, Stanley.*

It was then he noticed crudely scratched names on some of the wooden hafts. Probably meant to identify the owner when disagreements broke out. He sorted them by name. *Whitely. Gerjets. Appleby. Smith. Stowe. Dunning. Foulkes. Peabody.*

Keseberg.

Bryant's gut twisted. He recalled now with decent clarity a fact that had slipped from his mind these past weeks. Lewis Keseberg had mentioned a relative—an uncle—who had gone prospecting out in these very mountains a handful of years ago. He hadn't thought much of it at the time, though he was sure he did write of it to his fiancée.

But now he realized it was too much to be coincidence. Lewis Keseberg's uncle had been one of *these* prospectors, and had surely died
along with the others. Or had he?

That night as he sat next to the fire, sucking the wet innards of insects from their shells, Bryant wondered what exactly had happened at
this doomed place—how it had all started. Of course, it was still possible there'd been no disease whatsoever, that the prospectors had all
been attacked by an external force—but surely there'd been enough of
them to defend themselves from such an attack, which meant he was
likely right in assuming the threat had come from within.

No, he felt more sure than ever that there *was* a disease to blame, the
same one he'd seen in Smithboro, and that this sickness, this strange
desire for human flesh of which the Indians had spoken—had even
associated with their preexisting myth of the *na'it*—must have started
here. Tanau Mogop had told Bryant they'd suspected the Anawai
brought it on themselves by associating too freely with the mountain
men who trekked through their forests. The Washoe were wary of
outsiders, who were known to pass on sickness. They'd said the outbreak of behavior, and the behavior of sacrificing to the *na'it* had
begun around exactly the same time, in what had been a relatively
peaceful area. What else could explain it but the introduction of white
men carrying the disease? But how?

How did disease spring forth in one place or another, seemingly out
of nowhere? Surely one of these prospectors would have had to catch
it first, then spread it to the others, and beyond.

He thought of one of Gow's last letters to him, in which he'd mentioned the work of Dr. Snow, and his belief that disease could spread in
myriad ways. Snow had told him that in fact humanity's entire understanding of disease, our connection of the disease to its symptoms,
might be erroneous. Namely, that a disease and its symptoms were

not necessarily the same thing. That the disease is something alive but invisible—almost *like* a spirit, in fact—that then takes hold in the body and *causes* symptoms, sometimes different symptoms in different people. Sometimes, even, causing *no symptoms at all.*

He thought, too, then, of the story of the large Irish family he'd heard about, who had apparently all succumbed to a similar sickness, save for a young girl who had remained remarkably symptom-free.

Bryant tossed the shells into the fire and listened to them crackle as he turned the mystery over in his mind. He lay on the bare ground, hoping for sleep. As Bryant watched the flickering orange flames, his mind drifted.

The row of skulls winked at him in the firelight. The flames danced, vibrant gold and blood red.

In his hands, Bryant turned over the haft with Keseberg's name on it, and memories of Keseberg on the wagon trail came back to him. A series of mostly ugly encounters: Lewis shoving his still-pregnant wife back into their tent. Lewis picking a fight with James Reed. Lewis sitting outside his camp, cutting up rabbits he'd caught for dinner, his hands washed in blood, a look of concentration on his face, as Halloran's little dog paced excitedly nearby. Bryant recalled the knife slipping in Keseberg's damp hand, the blade catching the flesh of his palm. Blood swelling, a fat line of red. Halloran's terrier seeing his chance and lunging at Keseberg's hand, lapping up the rabbit meat—and Keseberg's blood—hungrily.

A deep horror stirred within Bryant as he thought of that dog, thought of Keseberg's mean face and presumptuous swagger. How the man had roamed among them like a form of plague himself—something disgusting, something to be feared.

The more he turned the pieces over in his mind, the more he was sure he had something. A hunger that spread from man to man. A disease, perhaps invisible at first—or invisible in *some*, like the girl from the Irish family who'd all gone mad and became something more like wolves than humans. They had celebrated her good fortune, believing she had survived where the others had succumbed—until the day, many years later, that she was found squatting over a neighbor's baby, her mouth and hands smeared with blood.

A disease that turned some men into monsters. But others were able to hide their monstrosity on the inside.

Bryant sat bolt upright, bathed in sweat. The implication stared him in the face.

Keseberg's uncle had carried the disease.

That was how the sickness got here. That was how the prospectors had all died.

Keseberg's uncle, like the Irish girl, must have been carrying the disease in his blood, perhaps even unbeknownst to him. He had been the one to bring it to this territory a half-dozen years ago, causing an outbreak that had not only resulted in the death of the rest of his group but subsequently rocked the local tribes, amplifying some of their ancient belief systems and driving fear throughout the inhabitants of the mountains.

And if this was true, it was even possible that others in his family carried the disease . . . or some sort of trait that allowed them to survive it.

Others like Lewis Keseberg.

It might be a long shot, but if he was right, then everyone in the Donner Party—nay, everyone in the entire territory—was in jeopardy. He had to warn them.

But then he paused. He thought of what lay ahead—not for him personally, but for the future of science.

A new letter began in his head.

CHAPTER THIRTY-SIX

F or two days after she regained consciousness, Virginia refused to say why she had come or what had happened at Truckee Lake. At first Elitha thought she was just being stubborn, until she realized from Virginia's gestures and frantic signals that Virginia did not want the grown-ups to know.

Whatever had happened, she was ashamed. Even at night, alone, she would say very little. She did tell Elitha about the slaughtering of the cattle, the strange behaviors, and that fighting had broken out. How the younger ones, teenagers and children, were succumbing first. "They say it's a sickness," she said. Virginia's extra-wide eyes made her look perpetually surprised. "They say Mary Murphy has got it now, too."

"Is that why you left?" Elitha asked. "Were you afraid you were going to catch it, too?" But Virginia didn't answer, only saying that Mr. Stanton and Mr. Eddy had gone for help but failed and Mr. Keseberg was trying to make himself the leader. But she would say nothing more, and when Elitha tried to get details from her, she only pulled the blanket up to her chin and pretended to go to sleep.

The adults debated what to do with her. "We can't send her back, not until she heals," Jacob said, still worried about Virginia's mother, Margaret. "It's not like we can send her back by herself, and we can't spare the men from standing watch," Betsy said. Even Elitha could see that Betsy was feeling overwhelmed with so many children and so few adults.

"If Virginia made it here by herself, the way must be reasonably passable," Tamsen had said, sizing the girl up shrewdly. But Virginia insisted it had taken her the better part of an entire day and that she'd nearly gotten lost and it was practically a miracle that she got to Alder Creek at all.

"Don't send me back. Please," she begged.

Several days after her arrival, on a surprisingly clear day blowing no snow, Lewis Keseberg arrived at the camp so early that the bonfires hadn't yet burned themselves out.

"I had a feeling she might be here," Keseberg told Jacob and Betsy and Tamsen. They stood together outside in the chilly dawn. The damp wood smoke still hung in the air. "She worried her mama something awful. I come to fetch her back." Mr. Keseberg was being much nicer than normal.

"And Margaret Reed sent you?" Tamsen said. Elitha could see that Tamsen wasn't fooled.

"I come because I'm the one in charge," he said, a little too loudly. "It's not like she has a husband to take care of these things and keep her girl from running wild." Virginia absorbed this blow quietly, without blinking. Everyone knew James Reed had likely frozen to death somewhere in the wilderness. "Now, come on. We need her. We're almost through slaughtering the cattle. Even the girls got to pitch in."

Slaughtering cattle; that meant there would be food. Elitha tried to remember how many cattle the Breens had. A dozen, surely. The idea of all that meat made her stomach twist with longing. Elitha knew the talk of cattle would persuade Tamsen to give Virginia up. There wasn't much food at Alder Creek, just the last scraps from the tough old oxen. They didn't need any extra mouths to feed.

Her boots squelched in the mud as she stepped up to the campfire. "I want to go, Tamsen. I volunteer to go and help Virginia."

Tamsen looked surprised to see her. That always happened—everyone was always surprised to see Elitha. She was the kind of girl that other people forgot all about. Except for Thomas. Thomas always looked like he was expecting her.

"Stop talking nonsense," Tamsen said. "You belong with your family."

She belonged with Thomas—but she couldn't admit that to Tamsen. Besides, Virginia had run away for a reason, and even if she hadn't yet told Elitha what it was, she could hardly stand by and watch her head off alone with Keseberg, back into the danger she had fled. "Virginia will need help getting back. You said it yourself: She's lost blood and she's weak. She'll do better if I'm with her." She didn't mention that Virginia had talked about a disease spreading. She'd be careful. She was afraid, but her desire to see Thomas was stronger than her fear. And no disease could be scarier than the creatures that had been watching them night after night. "C'mon, let me go. I'm not a little girl anymore. I can take care of myself." Then: "Trust me. Please."

Those words, at last, seemed to do it. "Very well. I expect you'd be safer in a larger group," she said quietly. Tamsen helped her pack her few belongings. Before she kissed Elitha good-bye, she gave her one piece of advice: She must never let herself be trapped alone with Lewis Keseberg.

. . .

ELITHA COULDN'T BELIEVE the conditions at Truckee Lake. The shelters were scarcely better than her family's tents. And they were just as crowded; she couldn't believe all the people that came spilling out of the cabin where Virginia's family was staying with the Graveses. At least Thomas was among them—spotting her, he ran up to her and threw his arms around her in front of everyone.

"What are you doing here?" he whispered.

His touch warmed her everywhere all at once. She was blushing; she could see how people stared. "I came to see you."

His expression changed. It shuttered and grew cold. "You shouldn't have come," he said. "It's not safe here."

"It's not safe where I was, either," she replied. She knew if he told her to go back, her heart would break.

But he simply said, "Come on," and slipped his hand in hers.

He was leading Elitha away from the crowd when she spotted Keseberg with Virginia. He'd bent so they were face to face and was saying something to her very quietly. She'd gone all stiff, and her face was white as the snow around her. Elitha got a twist of bad feeling in her stomach. What did he want?

It was two of the Graves girls—Lovina Graves at twelve, Nancy at nine—who later let Virginia's secret spill. Lewis Keseberg had told the girls that they were going to start putting a child out each night as a sacrifice to the wolves. He said their parents knew all about it, so it was no good going to them. They'd agreed to leave the decision up to him so they didn't have to choose which child would have to die. The grown-ups had come together on this so the majority would survive, just like those Indians who strung up one of their boys. Sacrifices had to be made.

But he'd spare you if you went into the woods with him and did what he told you.

"It's not so bad," Lovina Graves said, though her expression told a different story. She smiled funny as she told her story and was as fidgety as a hummingbird. "He just feels under your skirts and stuff."

"He put it in my hand and made me hold it," Nancy Graves said, so low Elitha almost didn't hear her. Nancy was so thin she looked all hollowed out like a ghost.

Elitha felt like she couldn't breathe, like she was being held underwater by an invisible hand. She was a fool for coming here. She realized quickly she couldn't tell Thomas about all this; it would only put him at risk. He was no match for Keseberg.

She had been at Truckee Lake less than twenty-four hours when it was her turn. She had ventured into the woods with Thomas; it was his idea to try to look for fish in the creek.

There were worse things than going hungry, Elitha wanted to tell him, remembering Virginia's white-faced, terrified nod when Keseberg stooped to speak to her.

Lying flat on her stomach on the hard surface of the creek, Elitha pressed her face to the ice, looking for movement. Thomas had gone off to find a rock to smash through the ice. In truth, Elitha knew nothing about fish. She had grown up on a farm and had only tasted fish once or twice in her entire life. Still, it seemed like a good idea; from the things Thomas told her, Indians knew the best ways to get through tough times. Thomas had taken one look at the creek and said they probably wouldn't find any fish suitable for eating, but by then Elitha was so excited he didn't have the heart to call it off. So he went to look for a rock and Elitha brushed snow off the icy surface of the creek and slid out on her knees. She could make out nothing, however, but a dark tangle of frozen branches and rotted leaves, a rush of black water beneath the surface.

Now that she had been with Thomas, she had thought she would feel different, but other than an ache lodged high between her legs, she felt nothing but a deep contentment, as if in becoming a woman she had fallen into a sleep untroubled by dark dreams. It had been her idea; she'd asked Thomas to meet her last night at the wagons. No one went out to the wagons anymore. It was dangerous being out at night, even with the bonfires. There were always at least two men patrolling with shotguns, and in the shadows they might be mistaken for one of *them*.

She had brought a blanket, though she didn't dare bring a candle or a lantern. Thomas appeared, seemingly out of nowhere. He knew how to be practically invisible; they were alike in that way.

When Thomas climbed over the backboard and saw that she had made a makeshift bed for them, he turned to her. "Are you sure this is what you want? Think about it, Elitha. Your family will not let you be with me. Once we are down from this mountain, they will not let us be together."

There was no sense worrying about the future. She would be Thomas's woman, if only for one night. And she would go to her grave without regret.

They would all be going to their graves soon enough.

Kneeling now on the thick frozen surface of the creek, Elitha heard a whisper behind her and paused to listen. The hairs lifted on her neck. The whisper kept going, a susurration like the hiss of wind.

The voices. They were coming back. She couldn't make out the words they said but they were there, clawing at the edge of her consciousness like a sick headache. Some of the voices were new; that meant more people had died. She tried to close her mind against it.

Suddenly, she felt a presence behind her. It was like being visited by a ghost, like a dark shadow stepping across her mind. She spun around and saw Keseberg, coming up the ridge, his breath steaming in front of him. "Well, lookee here," he said. He grabbed Elitha by her shoulders before she could scrabble away and lifted her to her feet, as if she was a doll. "What are you doing out here all by yourself?"

"I'm not by myself," she said quickly.

Keseberg grunted a laugh, as if she'd said something funny. "I know. You got your Indian sweetheart. What a shame, a nice girl like you just gonna throw yourself away like that."

"We love each other," she blurted out. She didn't know why. It seemed important. Where was Thomas? She wanted him to save her, and she wanted him to stay away, all at once.

Keseberg pulled off a glove and put his bare fingers against her cheek. Her blood froze at his touch. "You think them savages even know what love means? They don't love the same way as a white man," he said, as though it were a fact. Elitha pictured Keseberg's wife, Philippine, a slight woman with light brown hair, usually with a bruise somewhere on her face. She'd never heard Philippine speak. Did Keseberg love his wife? Had he ever loved anyone? Elitha was pretty sure she knew the answer to that.

"I'm gonna yell."

He backed her up against a tree. She focused on a bead of mucus hanging from the tip of his red nose because she didn't want to look into his eyes. "If you cause trouble for me, I'll make trouble for your boyfriend. You know I can, too. Ain't nobody gonna help no Indian."

She felt the truth of this in her bones. She pressed her spine into the tree trunk, steeling against the first touch of his hand. Wearing so many layers of clothes, she knew that even if he put his hands on her breasts he wouldn't be touching them, not really. Still, the thought made her shiver. She remembered how Thomas had stepped close, nuzzling her neck, only last night.

But Keseberg wouldn't do anything serious, the girls had said. She tried to calm herself with that thought, even as her stomach seemed to have lodged itself somewhere in her throat and her whole body went rigid in protest. He was just going to touch her. She could stand that and Thomas would be safe. She almost wished he would hurry up and get it over with . . .

Keseberg grabbed the front of her coat and yanked it open, yanked the front of her dress open, too, exposing the bare skin of her throat and sternum. She cried out in surprise. But he got one hand around her mouth. His fingers tasted filthy. She thought about kneeing him but she was worried that wouldn't stop him, it would only make him angrier. He seemed like the kind to hit you if he got angry; his wife, Philippine, was proof of that.

"You ain't as pretty as some of the other girls," he said, in a low voice, as he pushed one knee between her legs, parting them, "but you'll do."

Too late, she realized that he wouldn't just touch her and be done with it. Too late, as he moved his hand to undo his belt, she realized he intended something far, far worse. A voice in her head yelled *run, run, run*. Was it one of the dead? It didn't matter; her legs were rigid with fear.

Then, suddenly, a terrible force struck them both, knocking Keseberg away, driving her into the snow. She tasted blood in her mouth where she'd bitten down on her tongue. A horrible screaming echoed through the woods. At first, she thought it was one of *them*.

But it was Thomas. He and Keseberg were on their knees, grappling in the snow. Thomas had surprised him but Keseberg regained the advantage quickly. She scanned the ground for a rock, for a branch, for something to use as a weapon.

Keseberg finally pushed Thomas off him, sending the boy to the ground. He stood up, heaving, shaking off the snow—like some horrible shadow, doubling and redoubling as the sun set. "You think you can fight me, boy? You think you're going to save her?" He put a boot into Thomas's side, hard. "Well, the joke's on you. She's a whore. She *wants* me. She wants me to make a woman of her."

When Keseberg lifted his foot to give Thomas another kick, Elitha lunged. She threw herself at him, knocking him backward and pinning him in the snow. He thrashed, trying to unseat her.

"Get off me, you stupid bitch." He shoved her to the ground. Snow slid down her skirts and beneath her collar. The cold made her gasp. She was tired. Tired of fighting him.

"Leave us alone, just leave us alone," she shouted. Keseberg came for her again and she closed her eyes, waiting for his fist. A strong hand grabbed her and hauled her up from the snow.

"Come on." It was Thomas. Turning, dizzy, she saw Keseberg hanging back, doubled over as though looking for patterns in the ice. She and Thomas plunged through the snow, floundering, struggling to their feet each time. Thomas looked over his shoulder at her. His face was flushed and his breath ragged, pulling her so strongly that her shoulder burned.

"Run, run," he kept saying. *But why*, she wanted to ask him. They were way out in front of Keseberg, halfway to the cabins. They didn't have to run anymore.

Then she saw what was in his other hand: a small knife, no bigger than what you'd use at the dinner table. A fine, thin line of blood clung to the edge, and a line of blood was visible on the snow behind them, like a fine skein of red thread. Keseberg wasn't following them. He couldn't. He wouldn't let them get away if he could help it.

Thomas, Thomas, she thought. *What have you done?*

CHAPTER THIRTY-SEVEN

Mary Graves watched that next morning as Mary Murphy escaped from her family's cabin with the Eddys' baby in her arms. Eddy and William Foster followed her tracks in the snow, but by the time they caught up to her, the teenage girl had already killed the baby and was devouring her liver. Eddy shot the girl where she stood, Foster unable to do anything to stop him.

After Mary Murphy came Eleanor Graves, Mary's own sister, who had taken to dancing barefoot in the knee-deep snow, her toes going blue and frostbitten. When her mother tried to force her into the tent, she screamed and pulled away, bolting for the woods, her long dark hair streaming wildly behind her like a wave good-bye.

"We're going to leave. We're going to make a run for it," Stanton promised Mary. He had sharpened his hunting knife and was cutting an old deer hide into strips. "We're going to make snowshoes. It'll be easier to get through the snow. I saw a pair in my grandfather's house . . . I never used them but I think I remember how they were made."

"We're going with you. I think we're strong enough not to slow you down," Sarah Fosdick, Mary's sister, said when she saw what they were doing. She sat next to Mary and began stringing strips of hide to wooden frames they'd made from the staves of empty flour barrels.

They sat together through the afternoon working on the snowshoes. Miserly slivers of sunlight fell through the cracks in the walls to illuminate their work. There were little children underfoot everywhere in the cabin since the adults were afraid to let them outdoors. Mary glanced guiltily at the children, knowing she would be leaving soon but they would not.

We'll send help as soon as we're able.

Sarah was sitting next to her on the floor, humming while she laced deer hide strips to a frame, but when they heard the shot, she stiffened and looked at Mary. She asked, "What could that be?"

The few remaining cows started lowing, panicked.

Stanton was the first one out the door. Franklin Graves and Jay Fosdick snatched up their rifles and were right behind him.

There was a second gunshot and a tangle of raised voices. Then a volley of shots, sounding like thunder.

The waiting was unbearable. Mary's mother, Elizabeth, knew what it meant when Mary got restless. "Don't go out there," she warned. "Mr. Stanton can take care of himself."

There was another volley of shots, a few sharp cries. Mary could wait no longer. She leapt to her feet and ran outside.

There was yelling down by the lake, coming from behind a curtain of pines and boulders. Mary started to run in the direction of the voices, slipping in the choppy snow.

Finally, she found Stanton. He had an arm around Thomas, the Indian boy. He'd been wounded—shot; his right shoulder was pinched high and he had a hand pressed to his ribs. Blood showed through his jacket, a dark spreading patch. "What happened? Will he be all right?" she asked, running up to them.

She saw her answer in Stanton's expression. "Tell Mrs. Reed to boil some water and make bandages." Margaret Reed wouldn't lift a finger to help, Mary knew that. The woman hated Indians as much as her husband. She caught herself wishing Tamsen were here; Thomas would stand a better chance with her.

Amanda McCutcheon agreed to tend to Thomas. Elitha Donner had joined them by now, pale with fright. She obviously loved the boy. Amanda had Thomas strip off his clothes from the waist up, then sit on a stool. She sluiced water over the opened flesh, careful not to touch the wound herself. The cuts went deep, gaping so wide that Mary thought she could see to the rib bones. She forced herself to watch everything Amanda did, knowing it could come in handy. Any one of them could be the next to die, especially the ones nursing the sick.

"Hold this," Amanda said, guiding Elitha's hand to clamp the end of a bandage against Thomas's side while she wound the rest around his torso.

People were talking outside the shelter, too low to hear. Mary left Thomas to dress and tiptoed to the entrance.

"I say we wait." William Eddy stood in the middle of the gathering. He'd lost half his weight on the climb up the mountain and looked like a scarecrow. "I ain't seen any signs of the disease in 'im myself."

"But once it begins to show . . ." It was Peggy Breen. "Look what happened with Noah James and Landrum Murphy. It moves fast. We can't wait until this Indian boy up and attacks people. Look around you—we're down to mostly women and children. We got kids to think about."

"It's only an accusation," Stanton pointed out. "There's no proof other than Keseberg's word."

Peggy Breen crossed her arms. "Why would Keseberg shoot at the Indian boy if he hadn't seen what he said he did?"

Mary drew back, her heart pounding. So Keseberg had claimed something about Thomas—claimed he had the disease. She didn't know what Keseberg had said, but her stomach sank as she began to realize it didn't matter. The idea was in everyone's heads now.

They continued to argue but she had no doubt which way it would go. She felt weak, like she was about to drop to the ground. Mary ran up to Elitha and Thomas, who was stiffly buttoning his shirt. "The two of you, listen to me: Thomas has to run now." When he gave her a quizzical look, she said, "They're coming for you."

He stopped doing up the buttons to stare at her. "What are you talking about?"

Amanda McCutcheon, in the corner putting away the spare bandages, glanced over her shoulder at them. Mary didn't care.

"They're afraid you're going to succumb to the sickness." She pushed a trunk against the rickety wall. "Keseberg says it's why he shot at you. Says he saw something he didn't like. You've got to climb up and slip out under the roof"—cowhides and tenting lashed haphazardly to the timber walls—"and run. Don't look back. They'll kill you if you stay, Thomas." She wanted to think otherwise, but she'd seen how the group had become. Quick to target, even quicker to act. Paranoid. Panicked.

Thomas didn't hesitate—it seemed he, too, understood the hopelessness of it. He started to climb onto the trunk but stopped, turning back to Elitha. "Are you coming with me? Or are you staying here?"

Mary's heart went out to Elitha. To go with him was sure death. They would have no food, no weapons, and then there were those wolves, prowling the woods—whatever creature it was who'd started this contagion in the first place. And the snow; there was so much snow they'd never get through. And yet for Thomas, this was his only chance of survival. If he stayed, they would surely kill him.

But it wasn't the same for Elitha.

Elitha ripped a blanket off the nearest pallet and threw it over her shoulders. "I'll be right behind you. Climb."

But the men rushed the shelter before Thomas could get over the wall.

Mary tried to block their way but her own father took her by the arm and dragged her out into the snow, holding her tight.

Red-faced Patrick Breen and his friend Patrick Dolan, Spitzer the German, and Lewis Keseberg grabbed Thomas's legs, pulling him down. They hustled him outside, stepping past Mary and Elitha like they weren't even there.

Mary went to chase after them but her father warned her, "You'll only be hurt if you try to stand in their way."

She managed to break free and pushed past him, Elitha on her heels.

Soon they were marching Thomas into the woods. Elitha caught up to them first, throwing herself at the two men holding Thomas's arms behind his back, but the big German Spitzer brushed her aside like she was a gnat.

"Go back, girl. This ain't for you to see," Breen warned.

Mary struggled through the deep snow behind them. "You don't have to kill him. Just let him go. You don't have to worry about him—he'll leave you alone."

"He'll turn wild like the others and then he'll come for us. Maybe kill one of us, one of the kids. You seen what happened to Landrum. Is that what you want?" Dolan asked, his voice angry.

"You don't know that! I swear we'll go, you won't see either of us again if you just give him a chance," Elitha begged.

The men continued walking as though neither of the women had spoken, eyes fixed straight ahead. They walked until Breen called a halt. It was a still spot, with only a slight breeze riffling the branches of a nearby pine. You could barely hear voices drifting up from the cabins, the only sign of humans in all this wilderness. By now, Franklin Graves had caught up to them and yanked Mary back hard, with a look that said he wouldn't let her have her way, not this time, for her own good and the good of their family. You can't stop angry, unreasonable men.

The men stepped back from Thomas. Dolan lifted his rifle, bracing it against his shoulder.

Thomas was eerily calm. His eyes flicked to Elitha's face. "You shouldn't have followed me. Go back now. Please."

Keseberg nodded in Elitha's direction. "Make it easy on her. Tell her we're right. Tell her you can feel the disease inside you." But Thomas said nothing, choosing to stare over their heads.

Mary looked wildly from man to man, trying to think of a way to make them understand that they didn't have to do this, but the words didn't come to her. They weren't interested in reason, however. They were slaves to their anger and fear.

Elitha was crying wildly now. She pointed at Keseberg. "He put you up to this, didn't he? Whatever he told you is a lie. He's doing this to get back at me and Thomas, because we wouldn't do what he said." They weren't even listening, Mary saw. They didn't so much as raise an eyebrow, and Keseberg only smiled at her, looking pleased.

Dolan pulled back the hammer.

Elitha's scream and the shot rang through the trees at the same time. Thomas remained on his feet for one weightless second—Mary's hope buoyed—maybe Dolan had missed.

Then Thomas toppled backward into the snow.

CHAPTER THIRTY-EIGHT

Springfield, Illinois
July 1840

Reiner had not changed much in fifteen years, Lewis Keseberg thought. His uncle's hair was a little whiter and the skin on his face a little more ragged but otherwise much the same as when Lewis had last seen him, as a boy in Germany. Reiner had the same easy smile, the same wildness twinkling in his eyes. Both made something in Lewis's gut turn over. He'd been content to hope Reiner had died, and seeing him again at his doorstep this evening had spooked Lewis more than he could say. You couldn't trust his uncle's smiles, and, he knew, those eyes held sickening secrets.

Reiner had just appeared on Lewis's doorstep with no forewarning. Not that Reiner was ever one to write letters, but it was unnerving, still; Lewis had only started renting this homestead a few months ago. How had Reiner been able to track him down?

Lewis brought out a bottle of a neighbor's home-brewed whiskey, potent stuff, and two tin cups. *"Warum bist du hier?"*—why are you here?—he asked in rusty German, eyeing his uncle as he set the cups down on his splintered old table.

That easy grin. "The family curse," he laughed as he sat in one of Keseberg's chairs and gulped down his liquor.

So. His uncle had fled the homeland. "What'd they get you for?"

"The usual. Not that they could prove anything. A man goes missing but there's no body to be found—who's to say it's murder?" His uncle huffed out another laugh, then leaned back in his chair and squinted into the corners of the cabin, hidden in shadow. "Where's your father gone off to?"

"He's in jail. Back in Indiana."

Reiner raised an eyebrow. "You left him to rot in jail alone?"

Keseberg's cheeks went hot. "I'm making a fresh start."

His uncle's stare fell heavily on him but Lewis didn't dare meet his eyes. He remembered Reiner's wrath from his childhood; it was epic and unpredictable. A thrashing for spilling a teaspoon's worth of salt on the floor, a tooth knocked clear out of his mouth for rolling his eyes at something Reiner had said.

But Reiner simply laughed again. "No fresh starts for men like us. What you are, it's in your blood. You can never deny it."

Lewis looked around his cabin. The gathering dusk hid its shabby nature. It was a simple cabin, one room with a sleeping loft. This table and the two chairs were about all the furniture he owned. "Not much room here for guests, Uncle," he started to say.

Reiner poured himself another drink. "It will only be for a few weeks. I'm headed west for a spell. Heard about a prospecting gig out in the mountains."

"California?"

His uncle nodded. "I hear it's lawless out there. Men like us can roam free, if you know what I mean. No one watching."

Heading out to make a fortune in gold. The idea flared up in Lewis's mind like a mirage. To leave behind the daily grind of farming, plowing fields, watering and weeding. It was hard to carve out a living for yourself when you had nothing, came from nothing.

But—no. Lewis had plans. He'd get himself a wife, work hard, fit in. He had never known happiness as a child—his father had been abysmal as a parent and his mother disappeared before he'd formed any memories of her—but he'd vowed not to make the same mistakes as his father and uncle and the rest of his family. He'd resolved to be different. He would not be a failure. He would break the family curse.

If he could just hold on and get through these tough times, it would get easier. It had to.

The older man reached into his pocket before dropping a handful of wadded currency onto the table. "I can pay my way. I'm not asking for a handout."

Keseberg's eyes widened at the sight of the money, more than he'd made in an entire year. "Where did you get this?"

Reiner poured a generous amount of whiskey into his cup. "I've been selling patent medicines. My own recipes from the old country. I've been doing well."

"So I see . . . But if the medicines are selling so well, why go all that way to California?"

That was when Keseberg knew his uncle was lying. The older man stretched back in his chair. He fixed his nephew with a stare, watching intently for his reaction. "I got a sickness no tonic can fix. Gold fever, I think they call it." He winked.

Lewis felt ill. *More like blood fever,* he thought.

It wasn't until that evening, as Keseberg made up a spot on the floor for his uncle to sleep—Lewis didn't invite his uncle to share the loft, couldn't quite bear the thought of lying next to him through the long night—that Reiner made the offer.

"Why don't you come with me?" The older man had just peeled off his filthy jacket to ready himself for bed and stood before his nephew in his stained shirt. He fixed those wolf-bright eyes on him. "What's keeping you here, anyway? This lousy farm? Because it looks like another in that string of failures of yours, son."

"Don't call me son," he said, stung. "This is what I want to do. This is my choice."

His uncle shrugged. "Suit yourself, but you're making a mistake, my boy. There's a reason why we Kesebergs are always on the move. If you stay in one place, they will catch onto you."

The family curse.

It's not going to get me. Not that he could say this to his uncle; it would be like waving a red flag before a bull. "I'll be careful."

But the older man wouldn't give up. "I worry about you. You haven't spent enough time with the Keseberg men, your father away in jail, you living in the new world with no uncles, no grandfathers. You don't know what it will be like, how the feeling comes on you so strong that you can't say no to it. When it does, how will you take care of yourself?"

For an instant, Lewis Keseberg was eleven years old again and standing next to his father in the smokehouse. A huge carcass hung from a meat hook, swaying gently. He could still hear the drip, drip, drip of blood hitting the muddy puddle under the body, still smell the iron tang in the air. The shape of the carcass not like an animal at all, but like a human.

The surge of something like desire that moved through him so powerfully he swayed, too.

How that feeling had never fully left him since.

A shiver ran down his spine.

All Lewis wanted was to get away from Uncle Reiner, from the eyes like fire and the carrion stink of him. "I'll be fine, Uncle. My father taught me enough. I can get by." He could hold it down—the lust, the thirst, the hunger.

Reiner rolled on his side to face the fire. "You think you know what's in store for you but you don't. Go on to bed, boy. One day, you'll see."

No, Lewis Keseberg decided as he climbed the ladder to his sleeping loft, putting distance between him and that frightening old man. It was good, in a way, Reiner showing up like he had. There were times Lewis could feel his honorable intentions slipping away from him. There were times, nights especially, when it was hard to resist the hunger that burned in his veins, when he gripped the corners of his bed and bit his knuckles and held in a rage that wanted to devour him, or wanted *him* to devour the world—he wasn't sure which. Sometimes he wanted to give up, give in to the curse. *Keseberg men, we were made like this; it's in our nature, it's in our blood.* But seeing Reiner was as good as getting hit by a bolt of lightning. Lewis didn't want to end up like that, always on the run, untethered, alone.

Though as he lay in the dark, imagining grabbing his uncle's neck between his hands and squeezing so hard the skin turned purple and blood dripped from his lips, Lewis knew the odds were stacked against him. That Reiner was probably right—it was only a matter of time.

DECEMBER 1846

CHAPTER THIRTY-NINE

ary named the snowshoe party Forlorn Hope because that was what they were: the wagon party's last hope. In the end, only eight of them set out: Mary and Stanton; her sister Sarah and her husband, Jay; Franklin Graves, though he seemed too sickly and had lost half his weight; Salvador and Luis, the two Miwoks who had accompanied Stanton from Johnson's Ranch; and William Eddy.

The Murphys and the Breens refused to participate, which Mary found a relief. They ridiculed the idea and predicted the group would be back in a day—if they didn't freeze to death. It was unclear if Salvador and Luis really wanted to go, their loyalty to Stanton at its limit, but they didn't seem to want to stay behind with the men who had just killed the Paiute boy.

The ones leaving were reluctant to take much; there were so many remaining who needed to be fed. Patrick Breen and Dolan said that they should leave with nothing. They were going to die anyway, and whatever they took would go to waste.

They chose their provisions carefully. They were weak, and every ounce would matter if they needed to run. They packed an ax, some rope (tied around Eddy's waist like a belt), and a blanket each, worn over the shoulders like a cape. Stanton and Eddy each took their rifles. Margaret Reed and Elizabeth Graves snuck them a few days' worth of dried beef. At the last minute, Mary saw Stanton slip some extra items in his coat pockets, though she didn't know what they were.

It wasn't snowing the morning they left, a good sign. Elizabeth gave Mary's father a brief kiss, the first sign of intimacy between them that Mary had seen in a long while. The loss of both William and Eleanor had been almost too much for her mother to bear.

Mary found it was harder to say good-bye to her remaining siblings. This was the first time in their entire lives they would be separated. The three younger Graves sisters and two boys hugged Mary and Sarah tightly. "Don't cry. We'll send help and then we'll all be together again," Mary said, hugging them in return. She wasn't sure if she really believed what she was saying.

As the dawn broke over the horizon, bright pink with a fine edge of blue, they started toward the mountains.

CHAPTER FORTY

tanton had grown old in a week. He was dazzled by snow, sunblind and sore—a vast, unending series of heights and valleys, all of it made identical beneath a blanket of white. They walked ten hours a day, by his estimate, but only seemed to make a few miles. They would need over a month to reach help.

They had rations for five days, and so had begun eating only at night.

Mary kept track of the days by knotting a length of string, a long brown thread pulled from the hem of her skirt, and each knot seemed to tie down something fluttering inside Stanton's chest—some tiny part of him that still awoke to the idea of love. He was amazed she could make the knots at all, that her fingers could still bend when his, brittle, blackened by frostbite, were often useless even after he'd warmed them by the fire.

Evenings he gathered wood, compelled through his exhaustion by a stubborn animal force that wanted him to live. They slept sitting up, hunched by an open fire, when they could sleep at all. Charles, Eddy,

Franklin Graves, and Jay Fosdick took turns standing watch at night, though Graves was failing quickly and sometimes could hardly be roused in the morning.

Usually, the fire melted out a hole beneath itself. By morning, the snowshoe party would lie encased at the bottom of a pit six or more feet deep, and the climb to the surface of steep white walls used energy they could little afford to waste. Stanton feared the day when one of them would be too weak to make the climb.

For days they had had no sign of the wolves—or beasts of any kind.

But as they began to weaken, Stanton sensed a change. He began to hear noises in the woods—whispers, the hiss of quick-footed movement through dead trees. He knew how predators tailed injured animals, dying animals, and waited for them to falter. The snowshoe party was dying, slowly but surely, and the diseased wolves had picked up the scent.

Another day of darkness transmuted into a landscape of dazzling white: Stanton welcomed the night, if only because he could rest his eyes. Often he felt as if they were bleeding, or as if someone were tickling them with a knife; when Eddy had lost his vision altogether temporarily, he had had to walk with one hand on Stanton's belt.

Mary collapsed next to him. They huddled together under the same filthy blanket, though it did little good. It seemed he was always wet, always cold, always hungry.

Her face was sunburnt, her nose raw and peeling. She reached into her pocket and brought out a strip of dried beef. "Your dinner." She always said that, *dinner*, though it was his only meal of the day. "Eat slowly."

"How much is left?" It hurt to eat. His stomach recoiled and grasped all at once. His teeth sang with the cold, and the slow decay of too long with too little. "Enough for how many days?"

She shook her head. "Don't think about it, not now. We'll find something."

The sky was darkening fast, but the fire wouldn't catch; the wood was wet. Eddy took his turn with the flint, then Stanton, and then Jay. Stanton stood back and saw the sun pooling behind the mountains, saw daylight pouring, melting away, and his exhaustion turned to a primal kind of fear.

"Take the ax," he told Jay. "Get a tree down. Get branches down, get something down." He went toward the woods at nearly a sprint, despite the clutching pressure of the snow. He had thought an hour ago he could not walk another step, but now he was electric with fear; without fire, they had no chance. They'd freeze in their sleep. And fire seemed to keep the wolves, or whatever was following them, at bay.

The thwack of the ax head rang through the hollow. Slow, though— too slow. Even if Jay could fell a tree they would never split the wood in time. Stanton plunged into the deep shadows of a stand of solemn, stooped evergreens. He ducked beneath the branches to feel for wood dry enough to burn; he found twigs, kindling, nothing they could use for any length of time. He kept going, losing sight of the camp, desperate, half mad—from the snow, the endless climb, the hunger, the pointlessness of a fight they kept fighting.

Beneath a massive pine he found some wood largely protected from the weather by the funnel of branches above them. He collected as much as he could; it would last them an hour, maybe more, long enough for Jay to split some wood from a tree.

He had turned back to camp when, from the corner of his eye, he saw movement. Fast, like a wolf running between the trees.

But they were not wolves.

Another shadow, another dark thing moved fast between the trees.

He dropped the wood in the snow, keeping hold only of a stub of pine. He struck his flint against it. *Catch, damn you.* Sparks flew harmlessly into the snow. His fingers were clumsy, frozen stiff. He almost dropped the flint but managed to grab it at the last second.

He heard the thing behind him only seconds before it would have jawed his neck.

He turned blindly, swinging the branch like a club. Heard it connect, saw the dark and twisted thing, half man and half beast, fall back between the trees.

A kind of demon. A monster.

There was no other word for it.

Stanton ran—or as close to it as he could in the knee-high snow. Sweat poured down his face, instantly freezing in place, pulling at his cheeks, forcing his mouth into a grimace.

Panic surged through him, mingling with disbelief.

Tamsen had been right.

The sudden clarity moved through him with the sharpness of an icicle—seemed to still his heart and uncloud his thinking all at once. The truth was like that, sometimes. Not like being saved, as his grandfather had once told him, but the opposite: cold and terrible and paralyzing.

Now, his mind raced, his blood flowed too fast in his veins. He strove for breath as he fumbled for his rifle on his back. Where was his rifle?

It had never been a pack of diseased wolves preying on them, attacking the cattle, looming in the tree line. Had it?

It had always been . . . these *things.*

No. No. He was coming unhinged. He slowed and looked back at the trees, squinted.

The shadows darted and lunged, morphed into the snowy night.

Where was his rifle?

Then he remembered he had propped it against the trunk of a tree at the edge of the woods. He would have to sprint to reach it. The snow here was over his knees now; the darkness had come.

He threw his weight into each step. *Don't look back, just go.* His blood pounded in his ears. Then he heard it: a wet kind of panting, a ragged excitement, as if whatever was pursuing him had to breathe through thick, damp rot.

Closer. Closing in on him.

Whatever had attacked him, whatever he'd seen, it was real. They were real.

I'm sorry. He didn't know what for—for not believing the tales Tamsen had spread through the party? For not protecting them?

For a life wasted not in sin, not really, but in the strangling belief of sin?

He could see the rifle now, and beyond it a thin trail of smoke, the beginnings of a campfire. Maybe it wasn't too late for him.

He was only feet from the rifle when the *thing* sprang. He felt the swipe of something sharp and painful on his calf; it felt as if someone had pressed a red-hot brand to his flesh. Then burning pain in his right calf, too, and he was wallowing in the snow like a baby. He tried to crawl forward on his hands and knees, but something had his legs and was dragging him backward. Another slash to the back of his head, the pain so intense he saw white flashes.

He could not die this way.

Not now.

Not yet.

His fingers grazed the very end of the rifle stock. Slipped. But the thing had him now, had a mouth around his ankle—Stanton gasped in terror as he saw human eyes, a human nose . . .

Whatever it was, it had been a human once.

And yet it was not human now, this creature. Its teeth weren't human; Stanton felt them hook deep beneath his skin, down into the muscle, and something wet and terrible probing between them that he knew must be a tongue.

He kicked the thing once, hard, in the face. It didn't let go, but for a moment he had a little more room and, twisting, he got a hand around the gun.

He rolled again onto his back and brought the rifle to his chest, firing directly at the eyes.

The monster released him. Stanton didn't wait to see if it was dead. He struggled to his feet, and the pain when he put weight on his right leg blacked his vision. There were more of them, massing in the trees. He fired again, blindly, not sure whether he was aiming at the shadows. He stood there shaking and bleeding into the snow, and saw them regrouping, flowing into a dark fluid mass. He lifted his rifle again when a sudden movement made him turn: One of them had sprung at him from the left, had ambushed him, and before he could aim it was on top of him, driving him backward into the snow and knocking the rifle from his hands.

It smelled like a corpse left too long in the heat. But its fingers were cold, and slimy, and wet—rotten. He choked on the smell. He tried to throw it off but he was pinned and too weak to fight. Its mouth seemed to double, its jaw unhinging like that of a snake. He saw teeth sharpened like iron nails, and too many of them, far too many—a long slick of throat, like a dark tunnel, and that horrible tongue slapping like a blind animal feeling for its prey.

Then an explosion split his forehead in two. The thing recoiled— Stanton tasted vomit—it scuttled backward, half its face hanging like a broken shutter. It *moved*. It was alive.

There was shouting. Mary was at his side, knees down in the snow, tugging him. Crying and screaming. "Why did you leave us? You know it's not safe. What were you thinking? Why did you leave?"

William Eddy was right behind him, holding a smoking rifle. But his eyes were fixed on Stanton's leg, and his expression didn't lie.

"Pretty bad, huh?" Stanton asked. "The monsters got me." It sprang from his mouth before he realized how crazy it sounded.

Was it crazy?

Maybe that was the curse of these mountains—they turned you mad, then reflected your own madness back at you, incarnate.

Like some sort of biblical punishment.

Mary kept hold of his arm, as though he might get up, climb to his feet, and walk away.

Stanton could *feel* the disease as it entered him, the shiver of something dark and slick and alien in his veins, so cold that it burned. How long would it take, he wondered, for him to turn? Several days? A week? He would be dead by then, at least, frozen to death or consumed by the monsters when they returned.

And even if it hadn't been the disease—it didn't matter now. As injured as he was, they'd never get him back to camp, or close enough to the ranch to get help.

"Go," he said to Mary. "Run. There are more. They'll be here any minute."

"I can't leave you," she said.

Did she believe him? Could she possibly understand? It was too cold to cry, but even in the dim light from the distant fire—they had gotten it burning, after all—her pain was visible. There was no part of her face it didn't touch.

"You have to." He looked to Eddy. The urgency and horror still swam inside him, making him dizzy, sick. He had to rest his head . . . "Go. Get as far from here as you can."

Eddy picked up Stanton's rifle. "You want me to reload it?"

"No, take it with you. You'll need it. I'll be fine." To Mary: "Go now. I want you to live, Mary. Without that, there's no point. No point at all."

Still, she wouldn't move from his side. "I won't leave you. I won't." Her voice was like the crack of ice; she was breaking. They were all breaking.

His mouth began to sting and water. His vision began to glaze and sparkle. Mary's pale face loomed so close. He wanted so badly to kiss her.

But he didn't trust himself. Who knew what the taste of her lips might do to him?

Who knew what the sudden hunger singing in his veins might do to *her*?

"Go," he said, one last time, a final surge of certainty moving through him, taking the rest of his strength with it. He was glad that Eddy hooked her under the arms and hauled her to her feet. He wouldn't have had the will to ask her again. He might have pleaded with her to stay with him. He might have begged her to lie down in the snow, her arms wrapped around his chest, until the beasts came to devour them.

He might have kissed her until he'd devoured her himself. He curled his fingers into the snow, trying to cool the rising heat in his veins, making him burn.

For a long time he could still hear her shouting, screaming his name, calling for Eddy to release her. Finally it became as distant as the whistle of wind through the peaks.

He waited until he could not tell the difference before reaching into his pocket. He'd brought two items with him, sentimental indulgences. One was his tobacco pouch; it held his last twist of Virginia gold. He had to blow hard on his hands to put any motion in the joints; then, he carefully took a sliver of paper and placed the last shreds of tobacco in it. Licked the end of the paper and rolled it between thumb and forefinger. Somehow got the flint to strike, caught a lucky spark. Babied the tiny spark into a flame. Took a deep breath and carried the spicy, warm smoke down into his lungs. Good. A last good thing.

The heat inside him was all-consuming now, but he tried to still his mind. Memories passed through him like shadows over water: His grandfather, usually so stern and unforgiving, counseling a parishioner for grief over the death of his wife. The rain running hard on the roof in the attic of Lydia's house, how she pressed against him, her hair tickling his face when she leaned down to kiss him. His life could've stopped at that moment and he'd have been fine with it. He had failed her, and had struggled to make it right ever since; maybe, after all, this was his penance. *The mills of God grind slowly, yet grind exceedingly fine.* He wondered where Edwin Bryant was, and hoped he was alive.

He forced himself not to think about Mary—not yet.

Finally he had smoked the cigarette down to his nail beds and released it to the snow. From his other pocket, he took out a small pistol. Mother-of-pearl inlay, pretty as a piece of jewelry. He'd held on to it, thinking it the perfect reminder of Tamsen Donner. Beautiful but deadly. He checked the chamber for a bullet.

Only now did he close his eyes and imagine Mary's face. He coaxed it up from the darkness of his mind and held it, let it burn there like a star, his final memory.

The gun was small, and fit nicely between his teeth.

The remaining seven members of Forlorn Hope were halfway up the next ridge when they heard the shot ring over the valley.

By then, Mary had stopped screaming. She stumbled only once. Then she kept walking, blinking hard against the sudden onslaught of blinding snow.

G od had abandoned them, Tamsen knew. She only wondered how long they'd been left to the mercy of a godless world— had it been so since the very beginning? Had it happened the night she took Jeffrey Williams, the family doctor, as her first lover, or long before then? Had the devil followed her all this way? Or maybe the devil was in her, and had been since the day she was born.

Maybe it was the devil who was keeping her alive.

THE NIGHT HE WAS BITTEN, Solomon Hook, Betsy's son by her first husband, had been taking a tin cup of hot water to the watch-standers. Until that moment, it had been a peaceful night at Alder Creek. Tamsen and the rest of the family heard his cry from inside the tent and went running out into the cold and wet to find him on the ground, a shadowy figure darting away toward the woods.

Tamsen screamed and when Walt Herron pulled a rifle and shot in the creature's direction, she didn't feel any kind of vindication, only a new depth of terror. There could be no denying that something deadly and inhuman was out there, inching in on them.

Jacob rushed his stepson into the tent and Tamsen looked to the boy's wounds while Betsy stood to the side, crying into her hands. A foul smell clung to the boy from the creature like a miasma, a bad omen. The boy didn't look too bad but there was a tear on the side of his neck that worried Tamsen, and even as she cleaned the wound, she sensed something was wrong.

Solomon revived the next morning and by afternoon, it was as though nothing had happened. He went with Leanne to gather firewood, scooped snow in a bucket to melt for water. He had a good appetite. He seemed indefatigable.

By night, his cheeks were red and hot to the touch. He was damp with sweat.

The next morning, he rushed about, knocking his brothers and sisters over in the cramped tent. When Betsy chided him, he rushed out into the cold without his coat or mittens and wouldn't heed their demands to come back inside. He wouldn't let Tamsen check his wound or put on a fresh dressing.

His eyes were bright and dancing, his mouth crooked in a strange, faraway smile. The memory of Halloran pulsed in her mind. It frightened her but she didn't know how she would explain it to Jacob or the boy's mother. She decided to say nothing and keep an eye on him. He was, after all, a teenaged boy. Children recovered quickly.

But every hour he got worse. More agitated, more aggressive, more manic. Tamsen saw Halloran in everything Solomon did and said, the hostility and impatience. She was tense in his presence, waiting for him to snap. The moment came when he lunged toward little Georgia, one of Tamsen's daughters. Quick as a hawk, she darted between them and shoved Solomon away. Jacob's eyebrows shot up while Betsy rushed to her son's side.

"What do you think you're doing?" she demanded. "You could've hurt him. He's injured, or have you forgotten?" But Tamsen had seen the look of horror flash on Solomon's face. He knew what he had *almost* done. It was his last cogent human thought. He dashed out of the tent before anyone could stop him and disappeared into the night.

It took two men to keep Betsy from running into the darkness after him.

That was the beginning of the end for Betsy. She was mad at everyone at first for keeping her from trying to save her son. "He was beyond saving," Tamsen tried to tell her, but Betsy refused to believe her.

"We got to find him. He can't survive out there on his own," Betsy pleaded with her husband. She was clearheaded enough to know she couldn't go after him alone, at least. "Whatever's out there, they'll kill him. They'll rip him to pieces."

He was seen two nights later. One of the sentries—the luckless Walter Herron again—was attacked when he strayed too far from the bonfires. The creatures scattered into the darkness when John Denton, the second watchman, arrived but not before Denton saw wild-eyed Solomon Hook with them, a clumsy wolf pup at his first hunt. There could be no mistaking it, Denton swore on his life.

Betsy wailed and threw herself at Denton, calling him a liar, but Denton stood firm. "Your boy's . . . changed."

Tamsen swallowed. "He's become one of them."

No one argued with her.

They understood how it worked now.

CHAPTER FORTY-THREE

————◆————

Christmas: Dawn, low on the horizon, was just visible on either side of the smoke blackening the sky from the fire.

Mary wouldn't have known which day it was if her sister Sarah hadn't told her. Mary had lost the knotted thread three days ago; she had left Stanton behind, she had heard a gunshot, and she had simply let the thread fall, and let her thoughts fall with it, her memories and hopes.

She was an animal now. She rose when they told her, followed the person in front of her like a mule on a pack train, sat when they were done for the day. When she was thirsty, she would melt snow in her mouth. The ache of hunger had transformed into a different pain: She couldn't eat, she would never be hungry again. There was something bestial in her stomach, a terrible pain ripping her apart. She couldn't feed it.

Sarah wouldn't stop talking about the Christmases on the farm in

Springfield. "Do you remember the year Mama made matching dresses for us out of that red calico? Didn't we think we were something special in those dresses? I wore mine until it fell apart and she used the skirt panels in a quilt."

Stop, Mary wanted to say. But she didn't want to speak, either. She couldn't stand to hear her own voice, unchanged, carried on the stillness of a world that no longer held Charles Stanton.

Since she'd abandoned Stanton, her sister had taken care of her as though she were an invalid: *Sit here, not too close to the fire, try to sleep. Keep hold of the end of my blanket and follow me.* Sleep was elusive. It was the only thing she looked forward to—oblivion, a silence so complete she didn't have to think about what had happened.

Sometimes during the day she would startle into sudden awareness—When had it started snowing? When had they passed into the peaks?—and she'd realize she'd been dozing as she'd walked.

On and on. They had inched their way over the summit, where winds were so strong the snow blew sideways, and were now working their way down. It was difficult to know how many days had gone by because they were all the same, just mile after mile of snow. Luis had fainted several times in the past three or four days. Most mornings, her father was too weak to make it to his feet and had to be lifted or carried and set upright, staggering on like a corpse compelled by witchcraft to walk.

Now, on Christmas, he could go no farther. He fell to his knees several hours before nightfall, and could not be brought again to his feet.

Through the haze of the campfire smoke, Mary saw her sister and brother-in-law bent over her father. Their voices, too low to hear distinctly, tickled the edges of her consciousness. Luis and Salvador, the

Miwoks, huddled miserably together under the same blanket, like skeletal birds interlinked by a single ruche of feathers. They seemed to be living off of leather scraps they trimmed from their clothing, chewing and chewing to soften it in their mouths and make it last.

Sarah broke away from her husband and came to sit beside Mary. For a long time she was silent.

"Papa's dead," she said at last.

Mary tried to reach down, to pull up some thread of sadness or regret. It was as if the mountain cold had reached into her center and frozen her through the core. "We have to bury him," she said.

Sarah shook her head. "We must keep moving."

But it was as if something had snapped in Mary. She held her ground. "I'm done," she said. "I want to go back to the rest. There are too few of us now. They'll pick us off, all of us. We have no chance."

Sarah gripped her sister's shoulders between icy fingers. "There's no way back now, Mary. We've come too far."

"We put the others at risk," she said, realizing now that it was true. "We wanted to march ahead to seek help, but we've cut the party down in size. The shadows will come for them as they've come for us. Don't you see? We separated ourselves into smaller groups, made ourselves easier targets. We doomed ourselves, and by doing so, we've doomed the others, too."

"Mary," her sister was saying, and she was shaking her, hard.

Or was it the cold causing her to shake?

She could easily picture lying down, letting the snow swallow her up. Surrendering to the cold. Numbness spreading to her fingers and toes, ears and nose, throat, and finally her chest.

But she hadn't imagined it. She *was* lying down.

Sarah had gone somewhere. Maybe she had never been there—maybe none of them had.

Snow fell on Mary's eyelashes, stiffening them, tiny icicles fracturing the firelight. Or was it sunlight? Somehow morning had come. There was no hunger left in her—no feeling at all.

The snow was dazzling, endless.

Sarah appeared before her, lifted her, forced her to her feet, and took her hand.

They trudged on, into the blinding light.

CHAPTER FORTY-FOUR

Springfield, Illinois
September 1840

I t was sudden and overpowering: the smell of burning hair. Acrid, unearthly.

Tamsen screamed . . . and dropped her curler on the floor.

Quickly, she doused it in water and breathed a sigh of relief as steam rose and the iron tong cooled.

She was nervous, distracted. Luckily, she hadn't lost much hair, only singed a few strands.

She had risen early to get ready for the ceremony, but in truth, she hadn't been sleeping anyway. It was as though she could feel the weight of the rest of the house sleeping around her. She'd grown up here, and now it was her brother's home. Every night, he lay in the big four-poster bed just through the far wall. If she listened hard enough, she imagined she could hear him breathing, hear him thinking. Was he having the same thoughts that she was?

For as long as she'd been back, sleeping in this old room, she'd been haunted by memories that seemed to have been burned into her skin since she first left.

Beauty, at least, was her solace. She tried again with the tongs. Back in North Carolina, she could always find someone to help fuss with pomade and tongs, someone who enjoyed fawning over her and receiving her attentions, but here in Illinois she had no women friends, no female admirers who looked up to her, as if hoping her beauty and intelligence would somehow rub off on them. Here, in her brother's home, she was on her own.

Tamsen chose her second-best dress to be married in, a blue wool challis with a pleated bodice and full sleeves. Her best was a sage-colored broadcloth, but green was unlucky for weddings. Ever since she had read of the English queen's wedding in *Godey's Lady's Book* a few years back, she had dreamed of a white dress if she were to remarry. It wasn't the expense that had stopped her—George Donner had offered to send to Chicago for any dress she wanted. But marrying George Donner meant she would be living on a farm and would not have many occasions for a white dress. It would be a highly impractical purchase.

Still, that wasn't the reason, either. She knew that one extraordinary thing was bound to make the ordinariness of her life all the more painful.

Besides, she didn't feel clean enough on the inside for white.

Through the window, the wheat fields of her brother's farm were bowing and rising like the tide of a golden ocean. The sky was a perfectly clear cerulean. Her heart swelled. It was so beautiful, the gold gently reaching up to kiss the blue. It made her want to cry. When she next came to Jory's farm, it would be as a visitor, a stranger. Another man's wife—again.

When Tully died, her brother had begged her to come to Illinois, pretending it was to help him, though really she knew it was his way of helping *her*. He didn't want her to be alone.

But she was. Marrying George wouldn't change that. She would always be alone, in her heart. Her first marriage had proven that.

Being back here, with the brother whom she'd tried to forget, proved it, too. How she ached with everything she could never say.

Jory was suddenly in the doorway, as if conjured by the heat of her thoughts. His broad shoulders looked a bit squeezed-tight in his best suit of brown wool, the one he saved for Sundays. "You're a vision, Tamsen." She noticed a slight strain in his voice, and her breath leapt in her chest.

Of course, it was natural for him to be emotional on a day like today, wasn't it?

"The wagon is ready whenever you are." He cleared his throat. She watched his Adam's apple rise and fall. She thought how funny that word was—Adam's apple. Hadn't it been Eve's?

To avoid his eyes, piercing and bluer even than her own, she stared instead at the stubble along his jaw and nodded.

She stood up and followed him to the door, then took Jory's hand as he helped her into the wagon, and in the warmth of his palm she felt an impenetrable sadness. She didn't want to let go, but forced herself to as she slid next to him on the bench. He placed a cloak across her lap to protect her from the morning chill.

The wedding would be held in the Donner farmhouse since it was nicer and bigger than her brother's. Jory's three children—two girls and a boy, none older than eight—sat in the wagon bed behind them, whispering among themselves as if they sensed their aunt's tension but did not understand what it meant. Jory had asked Tamsen to come west for the children's sake after their mother had died. *I can't raise daughters on my own*, he had written. *They need a woman to bring them up right*. What Jory had not said outright, but she could tell from his letters, was that *he* wanted badly to see her, too. He had been devastated by his dear Melinda's death.

They'd tried everything within their power to save his wife. When the only doctor in the area said nothing more could be done, Jory had given most of their savings to a traveling merchant, a smiling German who claimed his tonics would cure her.

He was nothing but a snake oil peddler, Jory had written bitterly afterward. *We did just as he told us but it was no good*.

Tamsen was ashamed to admit the way she felt when she first got the news of Melinda's death, so near to the timing of her own husband's. Ashamed to admit that it had felt, for a moment, like fate. Ashamed to accept the way it broke her open all over again, the idea of seeing her brother after all these years apart and separately married.

Ashamed that her first thought was that the snake oil peddler, the scam artist from Germany who'd led, however indirectly, to Jory's wife's death, must have been sent by the devil himself to torture Tamsen, to reawaken long-buried thoughts.

Jory had not been wrong to make the request, of course. Tamsen had been at ends after her first husband, Tully Dozier, had died. It was hard to be a young widow in a small town—men assumed things about women who had known a man's attentions and suddenly had to do without. There had been incidents. All of them heady and exciting at first, but then ultimately empty.

Still, when Jory's invitation came, Tamsen was torn. She planned to tell him no, but the bolder part of her heart had agreed—for his children's sake, she told herself.

Now, she watched as Jory's strong hands flicked the reins over the horse's back, nudging her into a trot. He stole a sideways glance at his sister. "You're prettier than a picture today, Tamsen. I hope George Donner knows what a lucky man he is."

"I'm sure he does." She forced a smile.

Jory fidgeted with the reins. "Are you sure this is what you want, though? It's not too late to change your mind."

"Now, where is this coming from?" She tried not to sound upset.

"You don't know this man, not well. It's only been three months."

No, she certainly didn't know George Donner well—but she'd never know *any* man as well as she knew Jory. He ought to realize that.

"I know enough." Tamsen knew that her future husband had means: two large farms that belonged to him and his brother Jacob. Fruit orchards—apples, peaches, pears—and cattle. A nice house on eighty acres.

"He's so much older than you. Do you think he can make you happy?"

She didn't answer. The question felt far too weighted. She wondered if Jory could possibly sense that. But if he didn't—if he didn't understand why it hurt when he protested her marriage—then he couldn't possibly feel the way she did.

And Donner—he would give her security. A roof over her head, a place in a community, money in the bank. With George Donner, her life was set, her worries would be gone. He was handsome, too, in his own way—though she wasn't moved by his looks, hadn't felt excitement rise in her when he'd been bold enough to kiss her.

Nothing like the tingling sensation she felt now, in anticipation of turning this new leaf—and leaving everything else behind.

"I know what's best for me," she said quietly. "George Donner is best for me. It's not like I can just live with *you* forever," she added.

Jory cleared his throat. Something flashed across his eyes, and she wondered what it was. "All I'm saying is you shouldn't be in such a rush. I'm sure you could do better. And I know the children will miss you." He paused. "We all will."

She bit back the anger that wanted to lash out and transform itself into sobs. How could Jory be so thoughtless, so unaware? She needed something to hold on to right now. George Donner would be her anchor.

"I know what I'm doing, Jory. My mind is made up. Now, let's talk no more about it," she said, pulling the cloak tighter around her. She moved along the wagon's bench, so that their legs were no longer touching, and felt the chill where his heat had been.

Jory took her at her word. There was no more discussion the rest of the way to Donner's farm.

THE TIN ROOF on the Donners' farmhouse gleamed silver in the morning sun. George Donner owned a big house, twice as big as Jory's. Unlike Jory's, it was freshly whitewashed, scrubbed, and well-tended. A stoneware jug filled with a great clutch of wild asters stood by the front steps, a welcoming note. This lifted Tamsen's spirits somewhat, as did the way the guests all glanced sideways at her, admiration and envy in their eyes.

Jory helped the children down from the wagon while Tamsen stood to the side, suddenly hesitant. Sounds drifted through the open windows, men's and women's voices, muffled knocks and bangs as chairs were being set up in the front parlor for the ceremony. George's cook would be preparing the wedding breakfast, frying up bacon and eggs, putting a pan of biscuits into the oven to bake. Plump apple pies, George's favorite, would be cooling in the larder.

The door opened suddenly and out stepped George Donner. Such a big man, he looked constrained in some way by his somber black suit. His eyes blinked in surprise or amazement as he looked in her direction. He had a kind face and kind eyes. She reminded herself that she had made the right choice.

"My dear—you are a vision." Donner's words were just like what Jory had said to her earlier, and yet they seemed to fall, lifeless, through the air. His lips trembled as he kissed her hand. "How have I been so blessed, that you have agreed to be my wife?"

His young daughters Elitha and Leanne stood behind him. They had been babies when their mother died and now Tamsen was to be not even their first stepmother but their second. No wonder their eyes were guarded; mothers were transitory creatures. It didn't pay to become too attached.

Elitha, the oldest, stepped forward and held out a clutch of flowers, stems tied together with a broad satin ribbon. "For you, ma'am," she said, her voice as faint as a whisper. It was an odd assortment; flowers, yes, but a bit of everything else, too: herbs, grasses, even weeds. A strange offering for a wedding day.

"They gathered it themselves," George said when he saw the confused look on Tamsen's face. "Because of your interest in botany. Remember, you told me that you wanted to write a book one day about the flora in this area, on medicinal plants? When Elitha and Leanne heard this, they gathered an example of every kind of plant they could find on the property and made this bouquet for you."

Tamsen had forgotten that she'd told him that. He hadn't laughed at the idea of a woman writing a scientific book like some of the men she'd told back in Cullowhee. George had remembered and what's more, he had shared the idea with his daughters. That meant more to her than the offer to buy her a fancy dress.

Suddenly, his kindness made her want to cry. Instead, she bit it back and smiled at him first, then at his daughters. "Thank you, girls. I'm touched by your thoughtfulness." She took the arm George had extended to her. It was solid and strong, and still, she felt like she was floating on air—or becoming air. Disappearing.

She risked a glance toward Jory, but he was looking after the children and did not catch her eye. At that moment, something within her shattered. It was a kind of knowing.

Love was not meant for everyone.

She held on to George's arm to steady herself and took a deep breath. "Shall we go in, Mr. Donner? I believe it's time to start the ceremony."

JANUARY 1847

CHAPTER FORTY-FIVE

They had all gone. She'd agreed to it—safety in numbers, they figured. In daylight, they had packed only what they could carry and made in the direction of Truckee Lake.

George, of course, would not make it.

So Tamsen had stayed behind. It hadn't been a thought, so much as an instinct, a need.

Tamsen laid out the last of the dried beef. Three strips, each the size of her index finger. Was there a way to make it stretch, last a bit longer? Perhaps boil it, make broth with it?

She sat next to her husband and dabbed his forehead with a wet cloth. He was unconscious most of the time now and she was under no illusions that he would recover. She thought of the irony: how his injury and subsequent infection had protected him from having to witness the worst. His foolish, bumbling pride had, in a way, sheltered the softness of his character.

Still, she wouldn't quit. She knew now that this was not a weakness but a form of compassion, and though any hope of affection had long since fled her, Tamsen felt that perhaps, when it came down to it, it had been her life's calling all along to witness his slow decline, and to feel the gradual, resilient loss of a person she had not allowed herself to love, or even to know.

She had the idea that George's death would mean something—that he would hold out for her sake a little longer—and that his last act of kindness, though not at all intentional, had been to give her a purpose, a reason to keep living.

Outside, the bonfires, blazing in broad daylight, deformed the sun behind a veil of smoke. Even now she could hear the whisper of soft footfalls: Walt Herron, one of the teamsters, had died last week and, perhaps sensing her defenselessness, the pack had grown bolder.

She'd used a blanket to drag Herron's body into the woods for them. It would, she hoped, buy her a little time. She envied George his unconsciousness. She had had to listen through the night as they feasted on Herron's body: the crack of bones, the wet smack of their hideous tongues, the animal grunts of their pleasure.

When she woke him to get him to eat, George refused her. "I told you already, you shouldn't waste food on me," he mumbled, his mouth barely moving.

"You need to hang on just a little longer," she'd said, the words floating out of her now by rote.

"I'm not afraid to die." He closed his eyes. "You should take the others to the camp at Truckee Lake."

He didn't know everyone else had already gone ahead, along with the five hundred dollars from their savings that she had tucked into her daughters' hands. She was terrified to give her daughters over—but even more terrified of what would happen if she didn't. At least this way they would have a chance.

But Tamsen had stopped telling George what was happening weeks ago. He certainly didn't know that Herron was dead or that the girls had left—and half the time, he still asked for James Reed or for Charles Stanton, apparently having forgotten they had split from the group weeks ago.

"I'm not going to leave you," was all she said now.

She tried to press him to take some broth, but he refused it.

"Why did you stay? You could have saved yourself." His voice faltered. "It isn't because you love me." He said it calmly, with acceptance. Then he closed his eyes, as if the words had exhausted him. "I haven't given you much to love, perhaps."

For so long she had wanted nothing more than to be rid of him. And yet now, given the chance, she *couldn't* leave him—it felt physically impossible.

"You're my husband, George." It was by no means an explanation, but she knew it would be enough for him. To her surprise, she found she was on the verge of tears. She had thought she was long past crying. "Now drink."

He died later that night, slipping away in his sleep.

Maybe it was her imagination, but as she sat there, next to his cooling, lifeless body, she thought she could hear the rustle of the pack sniffing closer to her tent. Scenting her loneliness.

She held the rifle to her chest all night.

In the morning, she built up the fire again, noting the strange, scrabble-footed tracks at the periphery of camp. She fished a shovel out of the wagon, determined to bury George deep so the monsters wouldn't be able to get his body. But the ground was frozen hard. Her arms shook. She nearly fainted with the effort of it and was forced to give up.

So, using the blanket like a sled, she dragged him out to the bonfire pit instead. She stoked the fire higher, watched the column of smoke thickening to a pillar, then rolled the body of her husband into the flames and turned away from the choking smell.

She had to move quickly.

She would carry nothing but the rifle and ammunition, and a small satchel of herbs. Their remaining savings, thousands of dollars, she would hide in a hollow tree in the woods. If she lived, she'd come back for it later. She cut away strips from the hide hanging in the entrance to make her last meal, choking it down by telling herself there would be food waiting for her at the other camps. Bacon and biscuits and an orange, like Christmas. Huckleberry jam and hot tea with rose hips.

She stayed up for a second night in a row, hugging the rifle to her chest. Dozed off occasionally in her chair. Around midnight she was pretty sure she heard the beasts scratching around the burnt-out funeral pyre, looking for scraps. She fired a few rounds in that direction, hoping to scatter them.

In the morning, she wrapped herself in the best blanket, slung the rifle over her shoulder, and started along the creek.

CHAPTER FORTY-SIX

T he sun had started its descent by the time Tamsen arrived at the far side of the lake. It was a scene of eerie stillness, so quiet that her first thought was maybe everyone had left or died.

The silence gave her a bad feeling.

Even from this distance she could see the huge blackened pits indicating old bonfires, just like at Alder Creek. The remaining wagons looked nearly abandoned; the canopies were torn, destroyed by exposure to the elements. The place had the feel of a ghost town—a hostile ghost town, as if within the silence was an echo of an angry voice. Had she made a mistake?

She could smell the stink of rot; it made her dizzy and sick. She was weak, and had to lean on a thin tree for a bit to fight down the urge to throw up. Where were all the people? If they were dead, where were the bodies?

She reached the first cabin, separated from the other cluster of lean-tos by a patch of trees. Inside, it was a mess, clothing and blankets scattered over the dirt floor, trunks emptied and overturned, filthy clothes alive with flies. She expected to find someone inside, a sick child or two waiting for a parent out fetching wood or water. She picked up a pocket Bible lying in the rubble. *To Eleanor love Aunt Minnie*, it read on the endpaper. *May this be your comfort.*

Then she saw it: Keseberg's rifle. It was unmistakably his—she'd seen it in his hands many times, the way he carried it around casually as if to remind the others to keep their distance. Her heart rate picked up as she scavenged through the other belongings in the cabin. Had Keseberg done something to the others? Was that why it was so quiet? She felt sick again but swallowed her nausea, moving methodically through his things. Maybe she'd at least find something to eat—stolen rations from the others, dried meat, anything. She was shaking and cold and acting out of an instinct to survive. She'd pillage whatever he had, then be gone, search for signs of life in the other lean-tos, search for signs of her daughters.

But she didn't find anything to eat. She found instead, beneath a pile of sticks—as if intentionally hidden—a stack of papers tied together with a thin strip of leather. She knew she should hurry, should leave, but a horrible feeling of suspicion rooted her to the spot. It was dim inside the cabin with the sun setting outside, but she squinted, her hands trembling as she lifted the papers and saw what they were. Letters.

Letter after letter after letter, all of them from Edwin Bryant, addressed to Charles Stanton. How long had they been hidden? Her eyes were bleary in the darkness and she feared that she might be hallucinating all of this, but something compelled her to open them, one by one.

They began as urgent warnings about the hazards of the trail—*turn around, avoid the Hastings Cutoff*—and then became more rambling, describing rumors of spirits and creatures that fed on human flesh.

Tamsen shivered. Bryant knew. He knew about *them*.

The truth sent a shock through her fingertips—it was just as Tamsen herself had suspected, but seeing it written out felt like a new weight had fallen inside her stomach.

She read on. In his later letters, he referred to the creatures as diseased men. He talked about a kind of contagion.

She thought back on everything that had happened. Halloran had been acting funny ever since his dog bit Keseberg. Had even Halloran caught the disease, that early on the trail?

Keseberg.

Lewis Keseberg knew, too.

He'd kept the letters, hidden them from the others.

But why? She'd never liked Keseberg, knew he wasn't trustworthy—but what could he possibly stand to gain from keeping the truth about this disease from the rest of the group?

It was then that she heard the creak in the old wooden door, and swiveled around.

She gasped, dropping the letters, and nearly fell backward against the wall. Keseberg stood in the doorway. She'd thought that after weeks stranded at Alder Creek, she would be overjoyed to see another person, anyone from the wagon party again, even Peggy Breen. Anyone but him.

The last of the evening's light fell on his shoulders, and from where Tamsen was crouched in the corner of the cabin, he seemed even bigger than she had remembered.

In his hand was an ax. He'd been chopping wood somewhere, then—for the fires, maybe. Maybe the others were still alive. Maybe,

maybe . . . Her pulse raced and her mind refused to form a clear thought.

"Well, well, Mrs. Donner. You came back," he said, with a smile.

She scrabbled away until her back was up against the far wall, but she was still only a few feet from him in the small space.

"I suppose you know my secret, then," he said, with a nod toward the letters. "Suppose it was sentimental but I couldn't bring myself to burn 'em. Didn't know how long I'd be able to keep those safe from prying eyes, but attacks from wild, bloodthirsty creatures do tend to distract a crowd."

Her stomach twisted and she fought the urge to retch.

"What—what have you done to the others?" she demanded. "Where are they?"

Keseberg sighed. "Your girls are all right. You know I like the pretty ones."

She was tempted to dive at him, scratch his face, but was too afraid.

"The Breens," he went on, listing methodically. "A few of the kids and both parents. Doris. There're a handful of us yet, near forty."

"But the camp is so quiet."

"They know to keep inside. It's what we agreed. To keep 'em safe."

"To keep them safe," she repeated dumbly. From the creatures, of course. That's what he meant.

Cautious relief began to course through her—they were alive. He'd said they were alive. Keseberg was a liar and a cheat—but why would he lie about that?

They were just around the bend in the lake. So close by. She could holler and they would hear. In a moment, her girls would be in her arms again.

"So you—you've kept away the awful . . . *things*," she said cautiously. "How?"

"Fires," he said. "I was just about to start up tonight's."

She nodded slowly, and began to stand. "I ought to be seeing the girls, then."

She tried to slip past him, pushing back out into the brisk cold, where moonlight now hit the snow and sent up a faint blue glow from every surface.

She was about to use the last of her energy to dash the few hundred yards toward the other huts, when something—she couldn't say what, but it was a kind of knowing, deep in her bones—made her turn around again.

Keseberg was still standing there, watching her. She looked at his face, really looked at him in the moonlight. There was that leering quality that had always unnerved her but something else in his expression, too, that she couldn't quite name. She might have said it was loneliness. That was when she understood what was bothering her: He didn't look hungry. He didn't look as if he'd lost weight, as if he'd suffered much at all.

Then she glanced down again at the ax. Its blade was covered in blood.

"I—I . . ." She backed away.

But his voice came out calmly across the cold air. "Tamsen, wait."

She turned and tried to run, pushed through a low scrub of trees, but then tripped on something and fell to her knees. It was a large, heavy stick strewn in the snow.

No. A human bone.

She gasped and began to cry—hot tears that immediately froze to her cheeks in the cold.

She had seen too much. Had come too far.

"It's not what you think," Keseberg said, a note of warning ringing out in his voice.

She looked around her. She had stumbled not far from a pile of what she thought had been snow, but now saw was something else entirely. It was a pile of corpses, all frozen, swollen, and blue.

At the base of the pile lay a thin woman, mangled, her body in an unnatural position. Dead, like the others. There was a deep gash in her forehead but she wasn't bleeding.

Tamsen forced herself to look at the body. It was Elizabeth Graves, hideous with death, her eyes staring sightlessly at the sky.

The world wobbled underneath her. She willed herself not to faint. Suddenly, Keseberg was kneeling beside her.

He put an arm around her.

"Get away!" she cried out, trying to shove him back.

"Tamsen, Tamsen," he began.

"No!" she shouted, crawling now across the snow.

He was so close, and he smelled disgusting, like he was exuding some foul stink through his pores. He grabbed her ankle and she fell to her stomach in the snow.

"I ain't proud of it, you know," he said then. His voice was strange, oddly high, and rich with emotion. "But it's the only way, y'see."

She tried to kick at him, to wriggle away.

"I'm not going to hurt you, you little bitch. Just like I didn't hurt the others," Keseberg said. "Tamsen, just listen to me." He yanked her, hard.

She was shaking, crying silently, and the skin on her cheeks felt stiff from the frost collecting there.

"Bryant was right about this disease. I should know. It's in me, like a curse, y'see. But not like those things out there in the night. Not like them."

"Let me go," she said hoarsely, trying once again to pull her leg from his grasp.

"Not until you hear me out," he said. "I did it—I did *that*—" His gaze fell on Mrs. Graves's face. "I cut them up, hoarded them, the dead. I had to. We're out of food, Tamsen. There's nothing left. They're all going to die. They would have already if it weren't for me. I saved 'em all, y'see, Mrs. Donner. It's because a' me your daughters are still alive."

"I don't understand."

"They wouldn't do it on their own," he said grittily. "They'd never agree to it. It's unnatural. It ain't right. But it's the only way to live. They gotta eat something. We all do. They just don't want to have to know where it's from. They keep to the inside, so they don't have to see it. Don't have to believe it." His eyes glittered, as though he was thrilled with the arrangement, and his own heroism.

She knew what he was saying. She wished she didn't understand what he meant, that she didn't have to imagine the truth of it.

He was feeding the dead to the living. Human flesh. And they didn't know.

"My daughters. And Elitha, and Leanne . . ."

"They're all alive, like I said. Though Elitha's sick. She might be the next to go." His eyes moved toward the pile of bodies again, and she realized with another wave of disgust and horror that he was already imagining cutting up Elitha's body, feasting on it, feeding it to the others. She was dizzy with it; her stomach clenched in pain.

"I been keeping the creatures at bay," he explained then. "Leaving bits and pieces for 'em. Just enough so they won't come sniffing around too close to camp. I got it all measured and meted out." She recalled with sudden clarity how, even just out of Illinois, the other men had already begun to warn against playing cards with Keseberg. He didn't just cheat, they said—he memorized every hand that was played.

"I know we can make it a month," he went on, "though we still got at least six or eight weeks before the passes clear enough to haul the remainder of us out. We'll have to lose at least one more."

He let go of her and rolled up his sleeve. Even in the darkness, she could see oozing red wounds, claw scratches, bruises, bite marks.

"Whatever them creatures got, it don't harm me. They can't infect me. I'm safe. That's why it's up to me. It's only up to me."

She had stopped crying.

She had started to listen, with an eerie sort of calm, to what he was saying.

"Maybe it takes one demon to keep the others away." He paused. His eyes glistened with tears now. "Lucifer had been an angel first. I always remembered that."

HE'D FIRST TASTED HUMAN FLESH back in Illinois, learned from an uncle who later disappeared while prospecting out west. He'd developed a taste for it. A hunger for it, really, though he'd kept the lust in check, was repelled by it even as the desire bloomed. He found that the taste of human blood never satiated him, but made the need for it even stronger.

Tamsen swam up to his words through a kind of fog. Had he knocked her out? Had she fallen and hit her head? Or had her consciousness slipped away for a time? It didn't matter. She was back at the cabin now, without remembering how she got there. Her rifle was gone. No doubt he had taken it. She was sitting in the snow and listing like a broken doll, and Lewis Keseberg crouched next to her, watching her closely as though he was worried about her health.

"I thought you were like me for a while," he said. "I heard about you back in Springfield. How you lured Doc Williams into your bed, them other fellas, too. I said, there's a woman who knows what she wants and isn't afraid to go after it."

"I'm nothing like you," she said. Her mouth was full of the taste of iron.

"You're more like me than you think. We take what we want, you and I. We do what we have to do." He smiled at her, but he was wrong. No one knew that the thing she had wanted for so long that the wanting had cleaved her in two had made her unable to love, almost unable to feel.

No one knew who had first held her heart, and never let it go.

Not even Jory.

For how could she tell her own brother that it had always been him?

"No," she said now. "I do not take what I want. I am not like you at all. Everything—everything I have ever done has been for others. Has been so my children can be safe. And I'll prove it to you."

"What are you saying?" Keseberg asked.

"I'm going to help you," she said.

SHE REMAINED IN HIS CABIN. If she left, if she saw her daughters one last time, she knew she might lose her resolve. That it might break her. So she made him promise never to tell them that he had seen her. Never to speak of what happened next.

That night, after Keseberg had got the fires going, Tamsen mixed together the last of her sleeping herbs—lavender, chamomile, mint, and a few final drops of laudanum. She stirred them into melted ice from the lake's surface and drank them down, waiting for the sleep to come.

As she began to drift off, Keseberg approached her. "I'll wait until you're asleep, like I promised," he said, and she knew he would keep his word.

"You'll make sure," she repeated again anyway. "You'll make sure it'll go to them first. You'll make sure it'll go to the girls," she said.

He nodded.

He settled across from her on the floor, waiting, cradling the ax in his arms.

Her eyes fluttered closed and open, closed and open. The cabin was gone. She saw instead those wheat fields outside her brother's window. The sweep of late summer sky bending low and wide and blue over the swaying grain—waves and waves of it. A whole sea made of gold. She heard children laughing. She sensed the flicker of a feeling she hadn't known since her own childhood. And at last, she slept.

March 1847

James Reed was halfway across the ridgeline when the big bay gelding buckled suddenly underneath him, floundering in the deep snow. For a moment, Reed was afraid they would both go down.

The footing had been treacherous every inch of the way from John Sutter's fort. If it wasn't heavy wet snow, it was slippery mud higher than the horses' fetlocks. A wet, miserable time of year. But there was no choice. Putting off the rescue operation until it got warmer was out of the question. He was afraid he'd already waited too long.

Reed urged his reluctant horse on. A string of men on horseback and supply mules snaked behind him.

Seven days out from Sutter's, the snow was now chest-deep on the horses. It was clear they could go no farther on horseback; they'd be better off traveling on foot. This meant they could take far fewer of the precious supplies he'd worked so hard to gather, which troubled Reed but couldn't be helped. The rest they strung up in the trees to use for resupply on their return. The bundles, swaying high in the branches, looked like misshapen insects' nests. In that moment, he made himself a promise: When they came back this way, his family would be with him. Margaret, Virginia, Patty, little James, Thomas.

It was the promise of this reunion that had kept him going through his hard months of exile. He wouldn't have lasted a week if his stepdaughter Virginia hadn't snuck out of camp to provide him a horse and supplies for his journey. Clever girl. Only thirteen years old and she knew what to do. A cloth bundle contained food from their diminishing store: dried beef, currants, hard-boiled eggs, and the last of the family's beer in a canteen. He had fought back tears as he thanked her.

"You was always a good daddy to us," she said to him as she handed over the reins.

When Reed had arrived at Sutter's Fort in late October, a cold wind was already blowing from the north. Sutter's Fort was sprawling and strong, with thick adobe walls and cannon—no hole-in-the-wall like Jim Bridger's place. Sutter had a couple dozen Paiute, Miwoks, and Mexicans working for him, and a steady stream of nearby settlers came in every day for supplies, the post, and the latest news.

Reed had been delighted to find Will McCutcheon at the fort, nearly recovered and working for Sutter to earn his keep. Between the two of them, they talked Sutter into lending them two mules and a few supplies, though Sutter warned them they wouldn't make it over the mountain.

He was right. The winter had already arrived at the higher elevations. They made it nearly to the pass before they had to admit defeat and turn back.

"The pass will be snowed over until February," Sutter had told him, and so, when the California Battalion came through the fort signing up men to fight for independence from Mexico, Reed joined them. He had been in the militia during the Black Hawk Wars. He knew how to soldier.

While in Yerba Buena, he spoke at gatherings about the party stranded in the mountains, appealing for donations. It was there he heard that a few survivors had made it to Sutter's Fort. William Eddy was quoted in half a dozen newspapers, telling of the hardships they faced: starvation, hard snows, and a strange disease that ravaged men and turned them into monsters, the way rabies acted on dogs to make them violent and blood-hungry.

Blood-hungry. Reed thought of the Nystrom boy and Hastings's deranged rantings and the corpse of the Indian boy found strung up between the trees.

The newspapers said a rescue party was already gathering. He resolved to lead it.

AS THEY DESCENDED into the pass, however, Reed saw no signs of cabins, or of any life at all. Even the lake was invisible. All Reed could see was a valley of white; a few sparse pines poked through the long sheet of snow. They looked suspiciously like the top portion of much bigger trees.

As they made their way lower, the black surface of a lake became visible between snowy hillocks. Then: irregularities in the uniform white. A square of brown that might be part of a damaged cabin. Wispy smoke plumes lifting to the sky. A camp.

The last stretch was agonizingly slow. He had to keep his eyes nearly closed against the blinding glare. He fought the urge to run toward it. It would only exhaust him. Discipline had gotten him this far. It would get him the rest of the way.

He saw indications of life, evidence all over of activity, of survivors—but no actual life, no humans, no shouting, no cattle, not a single horse in sight. Big fire-blackened pits ringed the cabins. An echoing sort of quiet.

As he moved toward the first cabin, he was touched by a deep and resonating fear—it worked on him like an interior bell, sounding through his whole body. He was suddenly self-conscious in front of the hired men. Afraid he would find his family dead, afraid he would break down. For he loved them—he had to believe that. It was why he was here. It didn't matter that he'd been sent away in disgrace.

Run away with me, Edward McGee had once said. But Reed had told him no. Edward had been full of rage and hurt, a kind of righteousness that came with youth; he accused Reed of not wanting to abandon his family because he was afraid, but Reed wasn't afraid. He wasn't hiding. That was what McGee hadn't understood. Reed *did* love them, in his way. Perhaps he sensed that the love they bore him back was different—more enduring, more forgiving—than the kind he'd find in Edward McGee. And in that, he'd been right, hadn't he?

But Edward McGee didn't matter now. And what had happened with John Snyder didn't change things, either. Reed once thought that love was akin to passion, but he saw now that it was something different entirely; that it was, perhaps, a kind of faith.

Given the stillness in the valley, he fully expected the cabin would be empty, that the newspapers had gotten the story wrong, that Sutter had sent them to the wrong place.

He pushed open the door and almost shouted. A cluster of skulls stared back at him from the reeking gloom.

Not skulls—*near* skulls. People so emaciated they looked like skeletons.

One of them moved and let out a faint groan.

Horror and hope swept through James Reed in a dizzying wave. He'd found them—some of them, anyway. They were alive.

And then a hushed, ragged voice emerged from the darkness. The voice of a girl, young, almost unrecognizable. "Father?"

It was Virginia. His daughter. He could make out her features now, though they'd been ravaged by hunger and transformed—teeth jutting from a drawn face. There was a pause, and he wasn't sure if he'd be able to stand the emotion that took hold of him by the throat. But then it was as if a bright light lit him from within, and he felt certain—more certain than he'd ever been in his life—that he *did* understand what love was.

He fell to his knees and reached out a hand.

HISTORICAL NOTE

The term "historical fiction" can seem like an oxymoron. History is comprised of actual events, after all. Events are made of facts. Fiction, on the other hand, involves the creation of fancies. Fiction is fact's step-sister; it is fabulation, something that looks and sounds like a fact but is wholly imaginary. You can marry fact and fiction, of course, and this generally results in something pleasing, a cocktail that's partly familiar and comforting, to accompany the other part, which is spicy and sparkly and unknown. The familiar helps the unfamiliar go down smoothly, like Mary Poppins's spoonful of sugar.

One of the biggest problems with writing historical fiction is not knowing how familiar your readers are with the historical event in question. This poses a quandary for the writer: how much do you assume? You don't want to bore your readers by including all sorts of facts they already know. At the same time, you don't want to assume too much knowledge and risk making the reader an outsider to an inside joke.

So it was with *The Hunger*. Americans are no longer taught the story of the Donner Party, and the few who do recognize the name are usually hazy on the details. For readers outside the USA, I imagine it must be even less familiar. These are the basic facts: two families set out from Springfield, Illinois on 15 April, 1846, heading to Independence, Missouri, the "jumping off" point for the trip west. The families—headed by George and Jacob Donner and James Reed, accompanied by a few family friends and other individuals—are the nucleus of what will be known as the Donner Party. They join up with a much larger party, the Russell Party, and travel with them until the split in the trail known as the "parting of the ways." The Donners and Reeds have heard of a new cut-off that promises to shave 300 miles off the trip. They have no way of knowing that the cut-off is little more than a notion in the mind of Lansford Hastings, or that Hastings is a bit of a charlatan, trying to lure settlers to California in order to wrestle the territory away from Mexico, to which California belongs.

The Donner Party decide to try their luck. They would not have made this choice if they knew there are over a thousand inhospitable miles ahead of desiccated salt lake, scrub prairie, and the nearly impenetrable forests of the Wasatch Mountains. Hacking thirty miles through the Wasatch takes eighteen days, time they can ill afford. They know the mountain passes will close off once the snow starts, and snow comes early at the higher elevations.

Which is how they come to find themselves stranded on the wrong side of a mountain pass on 1 November when the snow starts falling and refuses to stop. They try to make it up to the pass, but by 8 November, they are immobilized. Snow is piled over their heads, over the roofs of their makeshift cabins. They have almost no supplies. Only a few of the livestock survived the punishing trip. There will be no escape until the spring thaw, but no one knows when that will be.

There were ninety pioneers at Truckee Lake and Alder Creek when the snow started falling; only fifty will survive.

But the story is about more than what happened to those ninety people. The biggest challenge of telling the Donner Party's story—and the thing that ultimately made working on it so satisfying—is that, in many ways, the story of the pioneers is the story of America. The pioneer spirit is what most Americans think of when they think of their country. The Donner Party's story is one of immigrants, of people looking for a better life—but it's also the story of America's restless expansionist spirit, the willingness of those people to leave homes and kin, uproot themselves, load their possessions into a wagon, and head into the unknown.

Americans had been migrating to the west since the Louisiana Purchase in 1803, and by the time the Donner Party struck out in 1846, about 40 per cent of the population lived west of the Appalachian Mountains. But migration to California was not yet at the epic levels of the Gold Rush and the West was largely uncharted territory. At the time, most settlers who headed to California stayed with the Oregon Trail as it began to climb north-north-west and didn't break off from it until Fort Hall. But they were anxious to shorten the trip with a more efficient passage. A few wagon parties tried to find a viable cut-off prior to the Donners, including the Bidwell–Bartleson Party (1841) and the Stephens–Townsend–Murphy Party (1844), who were generally believed to have constructed the cabins at Truckee Lake in which the Donner Party ended up sheltering. But for the most part journeys through this territory had been made by mountain men or parties on horseback, not families weighed down with wagons.

At the time when the Donner Party took to the trail, the area south and west of the Great Salt Lake was still not well known. There may have been a handful of trails cutting through the deserts and mountain ranges, but there was no support system travelers could fall back on. Between Fort Hall (in present-day Idaho) and Sutter's Fort (in what is now California), there were few trading posts, farms or settlers to lend a helping hand or sell a sack of oats if you ran out of food along the way. Today, we can only marvel at their confidence, traveling under these conditions with babies and children, the elderly and the sick. They let nothing stop them; Sarah Keyes—James Reed's mother-in-law—was seventy years old and in poor health, and ended up being the wagon party's first casualty. Others traveled without wagon or oxen. Some had nothing more than a mule. A few even expected to make the two-thousand-mile journey completely on foot.

Americans made the perilous journey because they believed in 'Manifest Destiny', the idea that they were an exceptional people who were ordained by God to occupy the territory clear to the Pacific Ocean. They had held romantic notions about the unknown and unexplored western part of the country since colonial times. By settling the West, they felt they were fulfilling a long-promised destiny.

But Manifest Destiny is problematic: it's not as though this territory was unoccupied, free for the taking. That's the darker side of America's expansionist aspirations. Texas's war for independence emboldened some to think that California, too, could be prised away from Mexico. Some have said this was the real reason why Lansford Hastings zealously promoted his cut-off: to lure more American settlers to the Mexican-owned territory and, eventually, force America to defend the interests of its citizens. And the darkness doesn't stop there: trails cut through the middle of Indian Territory. You can't discuss the westward migration without looking at the devastating effect it had on the Native American tribes residing in the territory. And lastly, it's also about religious freedom. Mormons were starting to look west to build a community after violence had driven them out of Missouri and Illinois.

Dark stories indeed.

Ultimately, the Donner Party's story is meant to be a cautionary tale. There are reasons why nearly half the wagon party died, and we would be doing a disservice to the dead to ignore these. Not all of the reasons were within their control—the horrendous weather that winter, for instance—but many were. The group let themselves be divided by pettiness and class differences. They let themselves be fooled by businessmen who valued personal profit over human lives. They selected the wrong man to be their leader and refused to listen to the people among them who knew better. They paid for their hubris, yes, but you only need to look around to realize that things haven't changed that much today, 170 years later.

And this is the true lesson of the Donner Party.

ACKNOWLEDGMENTS

Readers familiar with the tragic story of the Donner Party will quickly realize that I've taken many liberties in shaping the material for fiction. Names, locations, and dates have remained but much else has been changed to fit the story. I even added a few completely fictional characters: Walton Gow, Edwin Bryant's mentor, did not exist in real life, although Davy Crockett did have his appendix removed while serving in the Tennessee legislature. Thomas, Elitha's ill-fated love, is based on John Baptiste Trudeau. I'd intended to use Trudeau but when the plot called for changes that would conflict with Trudeau's history, I decided to create a new character on whom we could make any demands required by the story. This is why Trudeau doesn't appear in the novel.

I have Tiffany Morris to thank for a thorough, culturally sensitive read of the manuscript and for providing extensive notes on problematic paradigms and tropes to avoid. It is always difficult to balance historical inclusion of the very real—and often very harmful—prevailing attitudes that existed at the time, in particular toward native peoples and their cultures, and at the same time not to in any way *perpetuate* or advocate for those views. The often problematic attitudes toward Native American groups demonstrated in some of the white settlers in the text do not reflect the feelings and thoughts of myself or the team.

Even a "reimagining" of a historical event, of course, requires a considerable amount of research. Much has been written about the Donner Party tragedy, which turns out to be both a blessing and a curse. A blessing, because you can usually find the answer to your question if you keep digging; a curse because there's no end to the amount of material to dig through. If you are looking to learn more about the true-life events, I recommend two books that I relied on most heavily: the superb *The Donner Party Chronicles: A Day-by-Day Account of a Doomed Wagon Train (1846–1847)* by Frank Mullen Jr. (Halcyon, Nevada Humanities Committee) and *Desperate Passage: The Donner Party's Perilous Journey West* by Ethan Rarick (Oxford University Press). Additionally, I was able to absorb some of the flavor of the period from *Covered Wagon Women: Diaries and Letters from the Western Trails, 1840–1849*, Kenneth L. Holmes, editor (University of Nebraska Press). I'd also like to thank the staff at the Donner Memorial State Park in Truckee, California, and the Fort Bridger State Historic Site in Wyoming for their hospitality during my visits.

This novel is truly a joint effort, the product of close collaboration with Glasstown Entertainment's Lauren Oliver and Lexa Hillyer. Thanks also to Glasstown editor Jessica Sit, whose input helped to make this novel what it is, as well as to Lynley Bird and Emily Berge for their careful reads.

Heartfelt thanks, too, to Sally Kim at G. P. Putnam's Sons, the most gracious and capable editor an author could hope for, and to my agent Richard Pine, Eliza Rothstein, and Glasstown's agent Stephen Barbara for their good counsel and patience. Lastly, thanks to Howard Sanders and Jason Richmond at the United Talent Agency for their work on bringing *The Hunger* closer to the big screen.

ABOUT THE AUTHOR

A graduate of the Master's writing program at Johns Hopkins University in Baltimore, Alma Katsu worked briefly in advertising and PR before moving into the intelligence world, working as a senior analyst for several US agencies, including the CIA and the American equivalent of GCHQ. She was also a regular contributor to the Huffington Post. Alma Katsu lives in the Washington, DC area.

To find out more, visit www.almakatsubooks.com